The Nomad

The Michael Moorcock Collection

The Michael Moorcock Collection is the definitive library of acclaimed author Michael Moorcock's SF & fantasy, including the entirety of his Eternal Champion work. It is prepared and edited by John Davey, the author's long-time bibliographer and editor, and will be published, over the course of two years, in the following print omnibus editions by Gollancz, and as individual eBooks by the SF Gateway (see http://www.sfgateway.com/authors/m/moorcock-michael/ for a complete list of available eBooks).

ELRIC

Elric of Melniboné and Other Stories

Elric: The Fortress of the Pearl

Elric: The Sailor on the Seas of Fate

Elric: The Sleeping Sorceress

Elric: The Revenge of the Rose

Elric: Stormbringer!

Elric: The Moonbeam Roads
   comprising –
   Daughter of Dreams
   Destiny's Brother
   Son of the Wolf

CORUM

Corum: The Prince in the Scarlet Robe
   comprising –
   The Knight of the Swords
   The Queen of the Swords
   The King of the Swords

Corum: The Prince with the Silver Hand
   comprising –
   The Bull and the Spear
   The Oak and the Ram
   The Sword and the Stallion

HAWKMOON

Hawkmoon: The History of the Runestaff
   comprising –
   The Jewel in the Skull
   The Mad God's Amulet
   The Sword of the Dawn
   The Runestaff

Hawkmoon: Count Brass
   comprising –
   Count Brass
   The Champion of Garathorm
   The Quest for Tanelorn

JERRY CORNELIUS

The Cornelius Quartet
   comprising –
   The Final Programme
   A Cure for Cancer
   The English Assassin
   The Condition of Muzak

Jerry Cornelius: His Lives and His Times (short-fiction collection)

A Cornelius Calendar
   comprising –
   The Adventures of Una Persson
     and Catherine Cornelius in
     the Twentieth Century
   The Entropy Tango
   The Great Rock 'n' Roll Swindle
   The Alchemist's Question
   Firing the Cathedral/Modem
     Times 2.0

Von Bek
   comprising –
   The War Hound and the World's
     Pain
   The City in the Autumn Stars

The Eternal Champion
   comprising –
   The Eternal Champion
   Phoenix in Obsidian
   The Dragon in the Sword

The Dancers at the
End of Time
   comprising –
   An Alien Heat
   The Hollow Lands
   The End of all Songs

Kane of Old Mars
   comprising –
   Warriors of Mars
   Blades of Mars
   Barbarians of Mars

Moorcock's Multiverse
   comprising –
   The Sundered Worlds
   The Winds of Limbo
   The Shores of Death

The Nomad of Time
   comprising –
   The Warlord of the Air
   The Land Leviathan
   The Steel Tsar

Travelling to Utopia
   comprising –
   The Wrecks of Time
   The Ice Schooner
   The Black Corridor

The War Amongst the Angels
   comprising –
   Blood: A Southern Fantasy
   Fabulous Harbours
   The War Amongst the Angels

Tales From the End of Time
   comprising –
   Legends from the End of Time
   Constant Fire
   Elric at the End of Time

Behold the Man

Gloriana; or, The Unfulfill'd Queen

SHORT FICTION
My Experiences in the Third World
War and Other Stories: The Best
Short Fiction of Michael Moorcock
Volume 1

The Brothel in Rosenstrasse and
Other Stories: The Best Short Fiction
of Michael Moorcock Volume 2

Breakfast in the Ruins and Other
Stories: The Best Short Fiction of
Michael Moorcock Volume 3

The Nomad of Time

A Scientific Romance

The Warlord of the Air
The Land Leviathan
The Steel Tsar

MICHAEL MOORCOCK

Edited by John Davey

The right of Michael Moorcock to be identified as the author
of this work has been asserted by him in accordance with the
Copyright, Designs and Patents Act 1988.

This edition published in Great Britain in 2014 by
Gollancz
An imprint of the Orion Publishing Group
Orion House, 5 Upper St Martin's Lane,
London WC2H 9EA

An Hachette UK Company

1 3 5 7 9 10 8 6 4 2

A CIP catalogue record for this book is
available from the British Library

ISBN 978 0 575 09269 3

Typeset by Jouve (UK), Milton Keynes

Printed and bound by CPI Group (UK) Ltd, Croydon, CR0 4YY

The Orion Publishing Group's policy is to use papers
that are natural, renewable and recyclable products and
made from wood grown in sustainable forests. The logging
and manufacturing processes are expected to conform to
the environmental regulations of the country of origin.

www.multiverse.org
www.sfgateway.com
www.gollancz.co.uk
www.orionbooks.co.uk

Introduction to
The Michael Moorcock Collection
John Clute

H E IS NOW over 70, enough time for most careers to start and end in, enough time to fit in an occasional half-decade or so of silence to mark off the big years. Silence happens. I don't think I know an author who doesn't fear silence like the plague; most of us, if we live long enough, can remember a bad blank year or so, or more. Not Michael Moorcock. Except for some worrying surgery on his toes in recent years, he seems not to have taken time off to breathe the air of peace and panic. There has been no time to spare. The nearly 60 years of his active career seems to have been too short to fit everything in: the teenage comics; the editing jobs; the pulp fiction; the reinvented heroic fantasies; the Eternal Champion; the deep Jerry Cornelius riffs; NEW WORLDS; the 1970s/1980s flow of stories and novels, dozens upon dozens of them in every category of modern fantastika; the tales of the dying Earth and the possessing of Jesus; the exercises in postmodernism that turned the world inside out before most of us had begun to guess we were living on the wrong side of things; the invention (more or less) of steampunk; the alternate histories; the *Mitteleuropean* tales of sexual terror; the deep-city London riffs: the turns and changes and returns and reconfigurations to which he has subjected his oeuvre over the years (he expects this new Collected Edition will fix these transformations in place for good); the late tales where he has been remodelling the intersecting worlds he created in the 1960s in terms of twenty-first-century physics: for starters. If you can't take the heat, I guess, stay out of the multiverse.

His life has been full and complicated, a life he has exposed and hidden (like many other prolific authors) throughout his work. In *Mother London* (1988), though, a nonfantastic novel published at what is now something like the midpoint of his career, it may be possible to find the key to all the other selves who made the 100 books. There are three protagonists in the tale, which is set from about 1940 to about 1988 in the suburbs and inner runnels of the vast metropolis of Charles Dickens and Robert Louis Stevenson. The oldest of these protagonists is Joseph Kiss, a flamboyant self-advertising fin-de-siècle figure of substantial girth and a fantasticating relationship to the world: he is Michael Moorcock, seen with genial bite as a kind of G.K. Chesterton without the wearying punch-line paradoxes. The youngest of the three is David Mummery, a haunted introspective half-insane denizen of a secret London of trials and runes and codes and magic: he too is Michael Moorcock, seen through a glass, darkly. And there is Mary Gasalee, a kind of holy-innocent and survivor, blessed with a luminous clarity of insight, so that in all her apparent ignorance of the onrushing secular world she is more deeply wise than other folk: she is also Michael Moorcock, Moorcock when young as viewed from the wry middle years of 1988. When we read the book, we are reading a book of instructions for the assembly of a London writer. The Moorcock we put together from this choice of portraits is amused and bemused at the vision of himself; he is a phenomenon of flamboyance and introspection, a poseur and a solitary, a dreamer and a doer, a multitude and a singleton. But only the three Moorcocks in this book, working together, could have written all the other books.

It all began – as it does for David Mummery in *Mother London* – in South London, in a subtopian stretch of villas called Mitcham, in 1939. In early childhood, he experienced the Blitz, and never forgot the extraordinariness of being a participant – however minute – in the great drama; all around him, as though the world were being dismantled nightly, darkness and blackout would descend, bombs fall, buildings and streets disappear; and in the morning, as though a new universe had taken over from the old one and the world had become portals, the sun would rise on glinting rubble, abandoned tricycles, men and women going about their daily tasks as though nothing had happened, strange shards of ruin poking into altered air. From a very early age, Michael Moorcock's security reposed in a sense that everything might change, in the blinking of an eye, and be *rejourneyed* the next day (or the next book). Though as a writer he has certainly elucidated the fears and alarums of life in Aftermath Britain, it does seem that his very early years were marked by the epiphanies of war, rather than the inflictions of despair and beclouding amnesia most adults necessarily experienced. After the war ended, his parents separated, and the young Moorcock began to attend a pretty wide variety of schools, several of which he seems to have been expelled from, and as soon as he could legally do so he began to work full time, up north in London's heart, which he only left when he moved to Texas (with intervals in Paris) in the early 1990s, from where (to jump briefly up the decades) he continues to cast a Martian eye: as with most exiles, Moorcock's intensest anatomies of his homeland date from after his cunning departure.

But back again to the beginning (just as though we were rimming a multiverse). Starting in the 1950s there was the comics and pulp work for Fleetway Publications; there was the first book (*Caribbean Crisis*, 1962) as by Desmond Reid, co-written with his early friend the artist James Cawthorn (1929–2008); there was marriage, with the writer Hilary Bailey (they divorced in 1978), three children, a heated existence in the Ladbroke Grove/Notting Hill Gate region of London he was later to populate with Jerry Cornelius and his vast family; there was the editing of NEW WORLDS, which began in 1964 and became the heartbeat of the British New Wave two years later as writers like Brian W. Aldiss and J.G. Ballard, reaching their early prime, made it into a tympanum, as young American writers like Thomas M. Disch, John T. Sladek, Norman Spinrad and Pamela Zoline found a home in London for material they could not publish in America, and new British writers like M. John Harrison and Charles Platt began their careers in its pages; but before that there was Elric. With *The Stealer of Souls* (1963) and

Stormbringer (1965), the multiverse began to flicker into view, and the Eternal Champion (whom Elric parodied and embodied) began properly to ransack the worlds in his fight against a greater Chaos than the great dance could sustain. There was also the first SF novel, *The Sundered Worlds* (1965), but in the 1960s SF was a difficult nut to demolish for Moorcock: he would bide his time.

We come to the heart of the matter. Jerry Cornelius, who first appears in *The Final Programme* (1968) – which assembles and co-ordinates material first published a few years earlier in NEW WORLDS – is a deliberate solarisation of the albino Elric, who was himself a mocking solarisation of Robert E. Howard's Conan, or rather of the mighty-thew-headed Conan created for profit by Howard epigones: Moorcock rarely mocks the true quill. Cornelius, who reaches his first and most telling apotheosis in the four novels comprising *The Cornelius Quartet*, remains his most distinctive and perhaps most original single creation: a wide boy, an agent, a *flaneur*, a bad musician, a shopper, a shapechanger, a trans, a spy in the house of London: a toxic palimpsest on whom and through whom the *zeitgeist* inscribes surreal conjugations of 'message'. Jerry Cornelius gives head to Elric.

The life continued apace. By 1970, with NEW WORLDS on its last legs, multiverse fantasies and experimental novels poured forth; Moorcock and Hilary Bailey began to live separately, though he moved, in fact, only around the corner, where he set up house with Jill Riches, who would become his second wife; there was a second home in Yorkshire, but London remained his central base. *The Condition of Muzak* (1977), which is the fourth Cornelius novel, and *Gloriana; or, The Unfulfill'd Queen* (1978), which transfigures the first Elizabeth into a kinked Astraea, marked perhaps the high point of his career as a writer of fiction whose font lay in genre or its mutations – marked perhaps the furthest bournes he could transgress while remaining within the perimeters of fantasy (though *within* those bournes vast stretches of territory remained and would, continually, be explored). During these years he sometimes wore a leather jacket constructed out of numerous patches of varicoloured material, and it sometimes seemed perfectly fitting that he bore the semblance, as his jacket flickered and fuzzed from across a room or road, of an illustrated man, a map, a thing of shreds and patches, a student fleshed from dreams. Like the stories he told, he seemed to be more than one thing. To use a term frequently applied (by me at least) to twenty-first-century fiction, he seemed equipoisal: which is to say that, through all his genre-hopping and genre-mixing and genre-transcending and genre-loyal returnings to old pitches, *he was never still*, because 'equipoise' is all about *making stories move*. As with his stories, he cannot be pinned down, because he is not in one place. In person and in his work, it has always been sink or swim: like a shark, or a dancer, or an equilibrist...

The marriage with Jill Riches came to an end. He married Linda Steele in 1983; they remain married. The Colonel Pyat books, *Byzantium Endures* (1981), *The Laughter of Carthage* (1984), *Jerusalem Commands* (1992) and *The Vengeance of Rome* (2006), dominated these years, along with *Mother London*. As these books, which are non-fantastic, are not included in the current *Michael Moorcock Collection*, it might be worth noting here that, in their insistence on the irreducible difficulty of gaining anything like true sight, they represent Moorcock's mature modernist take on what one might call the rag-and-bone shop of the world itself; and that the huge ornate postmodern edifice of his multiverse *loosens* us from that world, gives us room to breathe, to juggle our strategies for living – allows us ultimately to escape from prison (to use a phrase from a writer he does not respect, J.R.R. Tolkien, for whom the twentieth century was a prison train bound for hell). What Moorcock may best be remembered for in the end is the (perhaps unique) interplay between modernism and postmodernism in his work. (But a plethora of discordant understandings makes these terms hard to use; so enough of them.) In the end, one might just say that Moorcock's work as a whole represents an extraordinarily multifarious execution of the fantasist's main task: which is to *get us out of here*.

Recent decades saw a continuation of the multifarious, but with a more intensely applied methodology. The late volumes of the long Elric saga, and the Second Ether sequence of meta-fantasies – *Blood: A Southern Fantasy* (1995), *Fabulous Harbours* (1995) and *The War Amongst the Angels: An Autobiographical Story* (1996) – brood on the real world and the multiverse through the lens of Chaos Theory: the closer you get to the world, the less you describe it. *The Metatemporal Detective* (2007) – a narrative in the Steampunk mode Moorcock had previewed as long ago as *The Warlord of the Air* (1971) and *The Land Leviathan* (1974) – continues the process, sometimes dizzyingly: as though the reader inhabited the eye of a camera increasing its focus on a closely observed reality while its bogey simultaneously wheels it backwards from the desired rapport: an old Kurasawa trick here amplified into a tool of conspectus, fantasy eyed and (once again) rejourneyed, this time through the lens of SF.

We reach the second decade of the twenty-first century, time still to make things new, but also time to sort. There are dozens of titles in *The Michael Moorcock Collection* that have not been listed in this short space, much less trawled for tidbits. The various avatars of the Eternal Champion – Elric, Kane of Old Mars, Hawkmoon, Count Brass, Corum, Von Bek – differ vastly from one another. Hawkmoon is a bit of a berk; Corum is a steely solitary at the End of Time: the joys and doleurs of the interplays amongst them can only be experienced through immersion. And the Dancers at the End of Time books, and the Nomad of the Time Stream books, and the Karl Glogauer books, and all the others. They are here now, a 100 books that make up one book. They have been fixed for reading. It is time to enter the multiverse and see the world.

September 2012

Introduction to
The Michael Moorcock Collection

Michael Moorcock

B Y 1964, AFTER I had been editing NEW WORLDS for some months and had published several science fiction and fantasy novels, including *Stormbringer*, I realised that my run as a writer was over. About the only new ideas I'd come up with were miniature computers, the multiverse and black holes, all very crudely realised, in *The Sundered Worlds*. No doubt I would have to return to journalism, writing features and editing. 'My career,' I told my friend J.G. Ballard, 'is finished.' He sympathised and told me he only had a few SF stories left in him, then he, too, wasn't sure what he'd do.

In January 1965, living in Colville Terrace, Notting Hill, then an infamous slum, best known for its race riots, I sat down at the typewriter in our kitchen-cum-bathroom and began a locally based book, designed to be accompanied by music and graphics. *The Final Programme* featured a character based on a young man I'd seen around the area and whom I named after a local greengrocer, Jerry Cornelius, 'Messiah to the Age of Science'. Jerry was as much a technique as a character. Not the 'spy' some critics described him as but an urban adventurer as interested in his psychic environment as the contemporary physical world. My influences were English and French absurdists, American noir novels. My inspiration was William Burroughs with whom I'd recently begun a correspondence. I also borrowed a few SF ideas, though I was adamant that I was not writing in any established genre. I felt I had at last found my own authentic voice.

I had already written a short novel, *The Golden Barge*, set in a nowhere, no-time world very much influenced by Peake and the surrealists, which I had not attempted to publish. An earlier auto-biographical novel, *The Hungry Dreamers*, set in Soho, was eaten by rats in a Ladbroke Grove basement. I remained unsatisfied with my style and my technique. *The Final Programme* took nine days to complete (by 20 January, 1965) with my baby daughters sometimes cradled with their bottles while I typed on. This, I should say, is my memory of events; my then wife scoffed at this story when I recounted it. Whatever the truth, the fact is I only believed I might be a serious writer after I had finished that novel, with all its flaws. But Jerry Cornelius, probably my most successful sustained attempt at unconventional fiction, was born then and ever since has remained a useful means of telling complex stories. Associated with the 60s and 70s, he has been equally at home in all the following decades. Through novels and novellas I developed a means of carrying several narratives and viewpoints on what appeared to be a very light (but tight) structure which dispensed with some of the earlier methods of fiction. In the sense that it took for granted the understanding that the novel is among other things an internal dialogue and I did not feel the need to repeat by now commonly understood modernist conventions, this fiction was post-modern.

Not all my fiction looked for new forms for the new century. Like many 'revolutionaries' I looked back as well as forward. As George Meredith looked to the eighteenth century for inspiration for his experiments with narrative, I looked to Meredith, popular Edwardian realists like Pett Ridge and Zangwill and the writers of the *fin de siècle* for methods and inspiration. An almost obsessive interest in the Fabians, several of whom believed in the possibility of benign imperialism, ultimately led to my Bastable books which examined our enduring British notion that an empire could be essentially a force for good. The first was *The Warlord of the Air*.

I also wrote my *Dancers at the End of Time* stories and novels under the influence of Edwardian humourists and absurdists like Jerome or Firbank. Together with more conventional generic books like *The Ice Schooner* or *The Black Corridor*, most of that work was done in the 1960s and 70s when I wrote the Eternal Champion supernatural adventure novels which helped support my own and others' experiments via NEW WORLDS, allowing me also to keep a family while writing books in which action and fantastic invention were paramount. Though I did them quickly, I didn't write them cynically. I have always believed, somewhat puritanically, in giving the audience good value for money. I enjoyed writing them, tried to avoid repetition, and through each new one was able to develop a few more ideas. They also continued to teach me how to express myself through image and metaphor. My Everyman became the Eternal Champion, his dreams and ambitions represented by the multiverse. He could be an ordinary person struggling with familiar problems in a contemporary setting or he could be a swordsman fighting monsters on a far-away world.

Long before I wrote *Gloriana* (in four parts reflecting the seasons) I had learned to think in images and symbols through reading John Bunyan's *Pilgrim's Progress*, Milton and others, understanding early on that the visual could be the most important part of a book and was often in itself a story as, for instance, a famous personality could also, through everything associated with their name, function as narrative. I wanted to find ways of carrying as many stories as possible in one. From the cinema I also learned how to use images as connecting themes. Images, colours, music, and even popular magazine headlines can all add coherence to an apparently random story, underpinning it and giving the reader a sense of internal logic and a satisfactory resolution, dispensing with certain familiar literary conventions.

When the story required it, I also began writing neo-realist fiction exploring the interface of character and environment, especially the city, especially London. In some books I condensed, manipulated and randomised time to achieve what I wanted, but in others the sense of 'real time' as we all generally perceive it was more suitable and could best be achieved by traditional nineteenth-century means. For the Pyat books I first looked back to the great German classic, Grimmelshausen's *Simplicissimus* and other early picaresques. I then examined the roots of a certain kind of moral fiction from Defoe through Thackeray and Meredith then to modern times where the picaresque (or rogue tale) can take the form of a road movie, for instance. While it's probably fair to say that Pyat and *Byzantium Endures* precipitated the end of my second marriage (echoed to a degree in *The Brothel in Rosenstrasse*), the late 70s and the 80s were exhilarating times for me, with *Mother London* being perhaps my own favourite novel of that period. I wanted to write something celebratory.

By the 90s I was again attempting to unite several kinds of fiction in one novel with my Second Ether trilogy. With Mandelbrot, Chaos Theory and String Theory I felt, as I said at the time, as if I were being offered a chart of my own brain. That chart made it easier for me to develop the notion of the multiverse as representing both the internal and the external, as a metaphor and as a means of structuring and rationalising an outrageously inventive and quasi-realistic narrative. The worlds of the multiverse move up and down scales or 'planes' explained in terms of mass, allowing entire universes to exist in the 'same' space. The result of developing this idea was the *War Amongst the Angels* sequence which added absurdist elements also functioning as a kind of mythology and folklore for a world beginning to understand itself in terms of new metaphysics and theoretical physics. As the cosmos becomes denser and almost infinite before our eyes, with black holes and dark matter affecting our own reality, we can explore them and observe them as our ancestors explored our planet and observed the heavens.

At the end of the 90s I'd returned to realism, sometimes with a dash of fantasy, with *King of the City* and the stories collected in *London Bone*. I also wrote a new Elric / Eternal Champion sequence, beginning with *Daughter of Dreams*, which brought the fantasy worlds of Hawkmoon, Bastable and Co. in line with my realistic and autobiographical stories, another attempt to unify all my fiction, and also offer a way in which disparate genres could be reunited, through notions developed from the multiverse and the Eternal Champion, as one giant novel. At the time I was finishing the Pyat sequence which attempted to look at the roots of the Nazi Holocaust in our European, Middle Eastern and American cultures and to ground my strange survival guilt while at the same time examining my own cultural roots in the light of an enduring anti-Semitism.

By the 2000s I was exploring various conventional ways of story-telling in the last parts of *The Metatemporal Detective* and through other homages, comics, parodies and games. I also looked back at my earliest influences. I had reached retirement age and felt like a rest. I wrote a 'prequel' to the Elric series as a graphic novel with Walter Simonson, *The Making of a Sorcerer*, and did a little online editing with FANTASTIC METROPOLIS.

By 2010 I had written a novel featuring Doctor Who, *The Coming of the Terraphiles*, with a nod to P.G. Wodehouse (a boyhood favourite), continued to write short stories and novellas and to work on the beginning of a new sequence combining pure fantasy and straight autobiography called *The Whispering Swarm* while still writing more Cornelius stories trying to unite all the various genres and sub-genres into which contemporary fiction has fallen.

Throughout my career critics have announced that I'm 'abandoning' fantasy and concentrating on literary fiction. The truth is, however, that all my life, since I became a professional writer and editor at the age of 16, I've written in whatever mode suits a story best and where necessary created a new form if an old one didn't work for me. Certain ideas are best carried on a Jerry Cornelius story, others work better as realism and others as fantasy or science fiction. Some work best as a combination. I'm sure I'll write whatever I like and will continue to experiment with all the ways there are of telling stories and carrying as many themes as possible. Whether I write about a widow coping with loneliness in her cottage or a massive, universe-size sentient spaceship searching for her children, I'll no doubt die trying to tell them all. I hope you'll find at least some of them to your taste.

One thing a reader can be sure of about these new editions is that they would not have been possible without the tremendous and indispensable help of my old friend and bibliographer John Davey. John has ensured that these Gollancz editions are definitive. I am indebted to John for many things, including his work at

Moorcock's Miscellany, my website, but his work on this edition has been outstanding. As well as being an accomplished novelist in his own right John is an astonishingly good editor who has worked with Gollancz and myself to point out every error and flaw in all previous editions, some of them not corrected since their first publication, and has enabled me to correct or revise them. I couldn't have completed this project without him. Together, I think, Gollancz, John Davey and myself have produced what will be the best editions possible and I am very grateful to him, to Malcolm Edwards, Darren Nash and Marcus Gipps for all the considerable hard work they have done to make this edition what it is.

Michael Moorcock

An incident from:
THE WARLORD
OF THE AIR
A new novel by
MICHAEL MOORCOCK

J. CAWTHORN·71

Contents

The First Adventure

The Warlord of the Air

For Michael Cornelius Dempsey,
who died, as he had lived,
a captain of his own ship

'The War is ceaseless. The most we can hope for are occasional moments of tranquillity in the midst of the conflict.'

– *Lobkowitz*

Editor's Note

I NEVER MET my grandfather Michael Moorcock and knew very little of him until my grandmother's death last year when I was given a box of his papers by my father. 'These seem to be more in your line than mine,' he said. 'I didn't know we had another scribbler in the family.' Most of the papers were diaries, the beginnings of essays and short stories, some conventional Edwardian poetry – and a typewritten manuscript which, without further comment, we publish here, perhaps a little later than he would have hoped.

Michael Moorcock,
Ladbroke Grove,
London,
January 1971

Book One

*How an English Army Officer
Entered the World of the Future
and What He Saw There*

Chapter One
The Opium Eater of Rowe Island

I N T H E S P R I N G of 1903, on the advice of my physician, I had
occasion to visit that remote and beautiful fragment of land in
the middle of the Indian Ocean which I shall call Rowe Island. I
had been overworking and had contracted what the quacks now
like to term 'exhaustion' or even 'nervous debility'. In other words
I was completely whacked out and needed a rest a long way away
from anywhere. I had a small interest in the mining company
which is the sole industry of the island (unless you count religion!) and I knew that its climate was ideal, as was its location – one
of the healthiest places in the world and fifteen hundred miles from
any form of civilisation. So I purchased my ticket, packed my boxes,
bade farewell to my nearest and dearest, and boarded the liner which
would take me to Jakarta. From Jakarta, after a pleasant and unevent-
ful voyage, I took one of the company boats to Rowe Island. I had
managed the journey in less than a month.

Rowe Island has no business to be where it is. There is nothing
near it. There is nothing to indicate that it is there. You come
upon it suddenly, rising out of the water like the tip of some vast
underwater mountain (which, in fact, it is). It is a great wedge of
volcanic rock surrounded by a shimmering sea which resembles
burnished metal when it is still or boiling silver and molten steel
when it is testy. The rock is about twelve miles long by five miles
across and is thickly wooded in places, bare and severe in other
parts. Everything goes uphill until it reaches the top and then, on
the other side of the hill, the rock simply falls away, down and
down into the sea a thousand feet below.

Built around the harbour is a largish town which, as you approach
it, resembles nothing so much as a prosperous Devon fishing
village – until you see the Malay and Chinese buildings behind the

façades of the hotels and offices which line the quayside. There is room in the harbour for several good-sized steamers and a number of sailing vessels, principally native dhows and junks which are used for fishing. Further up the hill you can see the workings of the mines which employ the greatest part of the population, which is Malay and Chinese labourers and their wives and families. Prominent on the quayside are the warehouses and offices of the Welland Rock Phosphate Mining Company and the great white-and-gold façade of the Royal Harbour Hotel, of which the proprietor is one Minheer Olmeijer, a Dutchman from Surabaya. There are also an almost ungodly number of missions, Buddhist temples, Malay mosques and shrines of more mysterious origin. There are several less ornate hotels than Olmeijer's, there are general stores, sheds and buildings which serve the tiny railway which brings the ore down from the mountain and along the quayside. There are three hospitals, two of which are for natives only. I say 'natives' in the loose sense. There were no natives of any sort before the island was settled thirty years ago by the people who founded the Welland firm; all labour was brought from the Peninsula, mainly from Singapore. On a hill to the south of the harbour, standing rather aloof from the town and dominating it, is the residence of the Official Representative, Brigadier Bland, together with the barracks which house the small garrison of native police under the command of a very upright servant of the Empire, Lieutenant Begg. Over this spick-and-span collection of white-washed stucco flies a proud Union Jack, symbol of protection and justice to all who dwell on the island.

Unless you are fond of paying an endless succession of social calls on the other English people, most of whom can talk only of mining or of missions, there is not a great deal to do on Rowe Island. There is an amateur dramatic society which puts on a play at the Official Representative's residence every Christmas, there is a club of sorts where one may play billiards if invited by the oldest members (I was invited once but played rather badly). The local newspapers from Singapore, Sarawak or Sydney are almost always at least a fortnight old, when you can find them, *The Times* is a month to six weeks old and the illustrated weeklies and monthly journals from home can be anything up to six months behind by the time you see them. This sparsity of up-to-date news is, of course, a very good thing for a man recovering from exhaustion. It is hard to get hot under the collar about a war which has been over a month or two before you read about it or a stock market tremor which has resolved itself one way or the other by the previous week. You are forced to relax. After all, there is nothing you can do to alter the course of what has become history. But it is when you have begun to recover your energy, both mental and physical, that you begin to realise how bored you are – and within two months this realisation had struck me most forcibly. I began to nurse a rather evil hope that something would happen on Rowe Island – an explosion in the mine, an earthquake, or perhaps even a native uprising.

In this frame of mind I took to haunting the harbour, watching the ships loading and unloading, with long lines of coolies carrying sacks of corn and rice away from the quayside or guiding the trucks of phosphate up the gangplanks to dump them in the empty holds. I was surprised to see so many women doing work which in England few would have thought women *could* do! Some of these women were quite young and some were almost beautiful. The noise was deafening when a ship or several ships were in port. Naked brown and yellow bodies milled everywhere, like so much churning mud, sweating in the intense heat – a heat relieved only by the breezes off the sea.

It was on one such day that I found myself down by the harbour, having had my lunch at Olmeijer's hotel, where I was staying, watching a steamer ease her way towards the quay, blowing her whistle at the junks and dhows which teemed around her. Like so many of the ships which ply that part of the world, she was sturdy but unlovely to look upon. Her hull and superstructure were battered and needed painting and her crew, mainly laskars, seemed as if they would have been more at home on some Malay pirate ship. I saw the captain, an elderly Scot, cursing at them from his bridge and bellowing incoherently through a megaphone while a half-caste mate seemed to be performing some peculiar, private dance of his own amongst the seamen. The ship was the *Maria Carlson*, bringing provisions and, I hoped, some mail. She berthed at last and I began to push my way through the coolies towards her, hoping she had brought me some letters and the journals which I had begged my brother to send me from London.

The mooring ropes were secured, the anchor dropped and the gangplanks lowered and then the half-caste mate, his cap on the back of his head, his jacket open, came springing down, howling at the coolies who gathered there waving the scraps of paper they had received at the hiring office. As he howled he gathered up the papers and waved wildly at the ship, presumably issuing instructions. I hailed him with my cane.

'Any mail?' I called.

'Mail? Mail?' He offered me a look of hatred and contempt which I took for a negative reply to my question. Then he rushed back up the gangplank and disappeared. I waited, however, in the hope of seeing the captain and confirming with him that there was, indeed, no mail. Then I saw a white man appear at the top of the gangplank, pausing and staring blankly around him as if he had not expected to find land on the other side of the rail at all. Someone gave him a shove from behind and he staggered down the bouncing plank, fell at the bottom and picked himself up in time to catch the small seabag which the mate threw to him from the ship.

The man was dressed in a filthy linen suit, had no hat, no shirt. He was unshaven and there were native sandals on his feet. I had seen his type before. Some wretch whom the East had ruined, who had discovered a weakness within himself which he might never have found if he had stayed safely at home in England. As he straightened up, however, I was startled by an expression of intense misery in his eyes, a certain dignity of bearing which was not at all common in the type. He shouldered his bag and began to make his way towards the town.

'And don't try to get back aboard, mister, or the law will have you next time!' screamed the mate of the *Maria Carlson* after him.

The down-and-out hardly seemed to hear. He continued to plod along the quayside, jostled by the coolies, frantic for work.

The mate saw me and gesticulated impatiently. 'No mail! No mail!'

I decided to believe him, but called: 'Who is that chap? What's he done?'

'Stowaway,' was the curt reply.

I wondered why anyone should want to stowaway on a ship bound for Rowe Island and on impulse I turned and followed the man. For some reason I believed him to be no ordinary derelict and he had piqued my curiosity. Besides, my boredom was so great that I should have welcomed any relief from it. Also I was sure that there *was* something different about his eyes and his bearing and that, if I could encourage him to confide in me, he would have an interesting story to tell. Perhaps I felt sorry for him, too. Whatever the reason, I hastened to catch him up and address him.

'Don't be offended,' I said, 'but you look to me as if you could make some use of a square meal and maybe a drink.'

'Drink?'

He turned those strange, tormented eyes on me as if he had recognised me as the Devil himself. 'Drink?'

'You seem all up, old chap.' I could hardly bear to look into that face, so great was the agony I saw there. 'You'd better come with me.'

Unresistingly, he let me lead him down the harbour road until we reached Olmeijer's. The Indian servants in the lobby weren't happy about my bringing in such an obvious derelict, but I led him straight upstairs to my suite and ordered my houseboy to start a bath at once. In the meantime I sat my guest down in my best chair and asked him what he would like to drink.

He shrugged. 'Anything. Rum?'

I poured him a stiffish shot of rum and handed him the glass. He downed it in a couple of swallows and nodded his thanks. He sat placidly in the chair, his hands folded in his lap, staring at the table.

His accent, though distant and bemused, had been that of a cultivated man – a gentleman – and this aroused my curiosity even further.

'Where are you from?' I asked him. 'Singapore?'

'From?' He gave me an odd look and then frowned to himself. He muttered something which I could not catch and then the houseboy entered and told me that he had prepared the bath.

'The bath's ready,' I said. 'If you'd like to use it I'll be looking out one of my suits. We're about the same size.'

He rose like an automaton and followed the houseboy into the bathroom, but then he re-emerged almost at once. 'My bag,' he said.

I picked up the bag from the floor and handed it to him. He went back into the bathroom and closed the door.

The houseboy looked curiously at me. 'Is he some – some relative, sahib?'

I laughed. 'No, Ram Dass. He is just a man I found on the quay.'

Ram Dass smiled. 'Aha! It is the Christian charity.' He seemed satisfied. As a recent convert (the pride of one of the local missions) he was constantly translating all the mysterious actions of the English into good, simple Christian terms. 'He is a beggar, then? You are the Samaritan?'

'I'm not sure I'm as selfless as that,' I told him. 'Will you fetch one of my suits for the gentleman to put on after he has had his bath?'

Ram Dass nodded enthusiastically. 'And a shirt, and a tie, and socks, and shoes – everything?'

I was amused. 'Very well. Everything.'

My guest took a long time about his ablutions, but came out of the bathroom at last looking much more spruce than when he had gone in. Ram Dass had dressed him in my clothes and they fitted extraordinarily well, though a little loose, for I was considerably better fed than him. Ram Dass behind him brandished a razor as bright as his grin. 'I have shaved the gentleman, sahib!'

The man before me was a good-looking chap in his late

twenties, although there was something about the set of his features which occasionally made him look much older. He had golden wavy hair, a good jaw and a firm mouth. He had none of the usual signs of weakness which I had learned to recognise in the others of his kind I had seen. Some of the pain had gone out of his eyes, but had been replaced by an even more remote – even dreamy – expression. It was Ram Dass, sniffing significantly and holding up a long, carved pipe behind the man, who gave me the clue.

So that was it! My guest was an opium eater! He was addicted to a drug which some had called the Curse of the Orient, which contributed much to that familiar attitude of fatalism we equate with the East, which robbed men of their will to eat, to work, to indulge in any of the usual pleasures with which others beguile their hours – a drug which eventually kills them.

With an effort I managed to control any expression of horror or pity which I might feel and said instead:

'Well, old chap, what do you say to a late lunch?'

'If you wish it,' he said distantly.

'I should have thought you were hungry.'

'Hungry? No.'

'Well, at any rate, we'll get something brought up. Ram Dass? Could you arrange for some food? Perhaps a cold collation? And tell Minheer Olmeijer that I shall have a guest staying the night. We'll need sheets for the other bed and so on.'

Ram Dass went away and, uninvited, my guest crossed to the sideboard and helped himself to a large whisky. He hesitated for a moment before pouring in some soda. It was almost as if he were trying to remember how to prepare a drink.

'Where were you making for when you stowed away?' I asked. 'Surely not Rowe Island?'

He turned, sipping his drink and staring through the window at the sea beyond the harbour. 'This is Rowe Island?'

'Yes. The end of the world in many respects.'

'The what?' He looked at me suspiciously and I saw a hint of that torment in his eyes again.

'I was speaking figuratively. Not much to do on Rowe Island. Nowhere to go, really, except back where you came from. Where did you come from, by the way?'

He gestured vaguely. 'I see. Yes. Oh, Japan, I suppose.'

'Japan? You were in the foreign service there, perhaps?'

He looked at me intently as if he thought my words had some hidden meaning. Then he said: 'Before that, India. Yes, India before that. I was in the Army.'

'How –?' I was embarrassed. 'How did you come to be aboard the *Maria Carlson* – the ship which brought you here?'

He shrugged. 'I'm afraid I don't remember. Since I left – since I came back – it has been like a dream. Only the damned opium helps me forget. Those dreams are less horrifying.'

'You take opium?' I felt like a hypocrite, framing the question like that.

'As much as I can get hold of.'

'You seem to have been through some rather terrible experience,' I said, forgetting my manners completely.

He laughed then, more in self-mockery than at me. 'Yes. Yes. It turned me mad. That's what you'd think, anyway. What's the date, by the way?'

He was becoming more communicative as he downed his third drink.

'It's the twenty-ninth of May,' I told him.

'What year?'

'Why, 1903!'

'I knew that really. I knew it.' He spoke defensively now. '1903, of course. The beginning of a bright new century – perhaps even the last century of the world.'

From another man, I might have taken these disconnected ramblings to be merely the crazed utterances of the opium fiend, but from him they seemed oddly convincing. I decided it was time to introduce myself and did so.

He chose a peculiar way in which to respond to this introduction. He drew himself up and said: 'This is Captain Oswald Bastable,

18

late of the 53rd Lancers.' He smiled at this private joke and went and sat down in an armchair near the window.

A moment later, while I was still trying to recover myself, he turned his head and looked up at me in amusement. 'I'm sorry, but you see I'm in a mood not to try to disguise my madness. You're very kind.' He raised his glass in a salute. 'I thank you. I must try to remember my manners. I had some once. They were a fine set of manners. Couldn't be beaten, I dare say. But I could introduce myself in several ways. What if I said my name was Oswald Bastable – Airshipman.'

'You fly balloons?'

'I have flown *airships*, sir. Ships twelve hundred feet long which travel at speeds *in excess of one hundred miles an hour!* You see. I am mad.'

'Well, I would say you were inventive, if nothing else. Where did you fly the airships?'

'Oh, most parts of the world.'

'I must be completely out of touch. I knew I was receiving the news rather late, but I'm afraid I haven't heard of these ships. When did you make the flight?'

Bastable's opium-filled eyes stared at me so hard that I shuddered.

'Would you really care to hear?' he said in a cold, small voice.

My mouth felt dry and I wondered if he were about to become violent. I moved towards the bell rope. But he knew what was in my mind because he laughed again and shook his head. 'I won't attack you, sir. But you see now why I smoke opium, why I know myself to be mad. Who but a madman would claim to have flown through the skies faster than the fastest ocean liner? Who but a madman would claim to have done this in the year 1973 AD – nearly three quarters of a century in the future?'

'You believe that you have done this? And no-one will listen to you. Is that what makes you so bitter?'

'That? No! Why should it? It is the thought of my own folly which torments me. I should be dead – that would be just. But instead I am half-alive, hardly knowing one dream from another, one reality from another.'

I took his empty glass from his hand and filled it for him. 'Look here,' I said. 'If you will do something for me, I'll agree to listen to what you have to say. There's precious little else for me to do, anyway.'

'What do you want me to do?'

'I want you to eat some lunch and try to stay off the opium for a while – until you've seen a doctor, at least. Then I want you to agree that you'll put yourself in my care, perhaps even return with me to England when I go back. Will you do that?'

'Perhaps.' He shrugged. 'But this mood could pass, I warn you. I've never had the inclination to speak to anyone about – about the airships and everything. Yet, perhaps history is alterable…'

'I don't follow you.'

'If I told you what I know, what happened to me – what I saw – it might make a difference. If you agreed to write it down, publish it, if you could, when you got back.'

'When *we* got back.' I said firmly.

'Just as you like.' His expression altered, became grim, as if his decision had a significance I had not understood.

And so the lunch was brought up and he ate some of the cold chicken and the salad. The meal seemed to do him good, for he became more coherent.

'I'll try to begin at the beginning,' he said, 'and go through to the end – telling it as it happened.'

I had a large notebook and several pencils by me. In the early days of my career I had earned my living as a Parliamentary Reporter and my knowledge of shorthand stood me in good stead as Bastable began to speak.

He told me his story over the next three days, in which time we scarcely left that room, scarcely slept. Occasionally Bastable would revive himself by recourse to some pills he had – which he swore to me were not opium – but I needed no other stimulant than Bastable's story itself. The atmosphere in that hotel room became unreal as the tale unfolded. I began by thinking I listened to the fantastic ravings of a madman but I ended by believing without any doubt that I had heard the truth – or, at least, *a* truth. It is up to you to decide if what follows is fiction or not. I can only assure you that Bastable said it was not fiction and I believe, profoundly, that he was right.

Michael Moorcock,
Three Chimneys,
Mitcham, Surrey.
October 1904

Chapter Two
The Temple at Teku Benga

I DON'T KNOW if you've ever been in North-East India (began Bastable) but if you have you'll know what I mean when I say it's the meeting place of worlds both old and immeasurably ancient. Where India, Nepaul, Thibet and Bhutan come together, about two hundred miles north of Darjiling and about a hundred west of Mt Kinchunmaja, you'll find Kumbalari: a state which claims to be older than Time. It's what they call a 'theocracy' – priest-ridden in the extreme, full of dark superstitions and darker myths and legends, where all gods and demons are honoured, doubtless to be on the safe side. The people are cruel, ignorant, dirty and proud – they look down their noses at all other races. They resent the British presence so close to their territory and over the past couple of hundred years we've had a spot or two of trouble with them, but never anything much. They won't go far beyond their own borders, luckily, and their population is kept pretty low thanks to their own various barbaric practices. Sometimes, as on this occasion, a religious leader pops up who convinces them of the necessity of some kind of jihad against the British or British-protected peoples, tells them they're impervious to our bullets and so forth, and we have to go and teach them a lesson. They are not regarded very seriously by the army, which is doubtless why I was put in charge of the expedition which, in 1902, set off for the Himalayas and Kumbalari.

It was the first time I had commanded so many men and I felt my responsibility very seriously. I had a squadron of a hundred and fifty sowars of the impressive Punjabi Lancers and two hundred fierce, loyal little sepoys of the 9th Ghoorka Infantry. I was intensely proud of my army and felt that if it had had to it could have conquered the whole of Bengal. I was, of course, the only white officer, but I was perfectly willing to admit that the native officers were men of much greater experience than myself and whenever possible I relied on their advice.

My orders were to make a show of strength and, if I could, to avoid a scrap. We just wanted to give the beggars an idea of what they would come up against if we started to take them seriously. Their latest leader – an old fanatic by the name of Sharan Khang – was their King, Archbishop and C-in-C all rolled into one. Sharan Khang had already burned one of our frontier stations and killed a couple of detachments of Native Police. We weren't interested in vengeance, however, but in making sure it didn't go any further.

We had some reasonably good maps and a couple of fairly trustworthy guides – distant kinsmen of the Ghoorkas – and we reckoned it would take us little more than two or three days to get to Teku Benga, which was Sharan Khang's capital, high up in the mountains and reached by a series of narrow passes. Since we were on a diplomatic rather than a military mission, we showed great care in displaying a flag of truce as we crossed the borders into Kumbalari, whose bleak, snow-streaked mountains lowered down at us on all sides.

It was not long before we had our first glimpse of some Kumbalaris. They sat on shaggy ponies which were perched like goats on high mountain ledges: squat, yellow-skinned warriors all swathed in leather and sheepskin and painted iron, their slitted eyes gleaming with hatred and suspicion. If these were not the descendants of Attila the Hun, then they were the descendants of some even earlier warrior folk which had fought on these slopes and gorges a thousand or two thousand years before the Scourge of God had led his hordes East and West, to pillage three quarters of the known world. Like their ancestors, these were armed with bows, lances, sabres, but they also had a few carbines, probably of Russian origin.

Pretending to ignore these watching riders I led my soldiers up the valley. I had a moment's surprise when a few shots rang out from above and echoed on and on through the peaks, but the guides assured me that these were merely signals to announce our arrival in Kumbalari.

It was slow going over the rocky ground and at times we had to dismount and lead our horses. As we climbed higher and higher the air grew much colder and we were glad when evening came and we could make camp, light warming fires and check our maps to see how much further we had to go.

The respective commanders of the cavalry and the infantry were Risaldar Jenab Shah and Subadar J.K. Bisht, both of them veterans of many similar expeditions. But for all their experience they were inclined to be warier than usual of the Kumbalaris and Subadar Bisht advised me to put a double guard on the camp, which I did.

Subadar Bisht was worried by what he called 'the smell on the wind'. He knew something about the Kumbalaris and when he spoke of them I saw a glint of what, in anyone but a Ghoorka's eyes, I might have mistaken for fear. 'These are a cunning and treacherous people, sir,' he told me as we ate together in my tent, with Jenab Shah, a silent giant, beside us. 'They are the inheritors of an ancient evil – an evil which existed before the world was born. In our tongue Kumbalari is called the Kingdom of the Devil. Do not expect them to honour our white flag. They will respect it only while it suits them.'

'Fair enough,' I said. 'But they'll have respect for our numbers and our weapons, I dare say.'

'Perhaps.' Subadar Bisht looked dubious. 'Unless Sharan Khang has convinced them that they are protected by his magic. He is known to draw much power from nameless gods and to have devils at his command.'

'Modern guns,' I pointed out, 'usually prove superior to the most powerful devil, Subadar Bisht.'

The Ghoorka looked grave. 'Usually, Captain Bastable. And then there is their cunning. They might try to split up our column with various tricks – so they can attack us independently, with more chance of success.'

I accepted this. 'We'll certainly be on guard against that sort of tactic,' I agreed. 'But I do not think I fear their magic.'

Risaldar Jenab Shah spoke soberly in his deep, rumbling voice. 'It is not so much what *we* fear,' he said, 'but what *they* believe.' He smoothed his gleaming black beard. 'I agree with the subadar. We must understand that we are dealing with crazy men – reckless fanatics who will not count the cost of their own lives.'

'The Kumbalaris hate us very much,' added Subadar Bisht. 'They want to fight us. They have not attacked. This I find suspicious. Could it be, sir, that they are letting us enter a trap?'

'Possibly,' I replied. 'But there again, Subadar Bisht, they may simply be afraid of us – afraid of the powers of the British Raj which will send others to punish them most severely if anything should happen to us.'

'If they are certain that punishment will not come – if Sharan Khang has convinced them thus – it will not help us.' Jenab Shah smiled grimly. 'We shall be dead, Captain Bastable.'

'If we waited here,' Subadar Bisht suggested, 'and let them approach us so that we could hear their words and watch their faces, it would be easier for us to know what to do next.'

I agreed with his logic. 'Our supplies will last us an extra two days,' I said. 'We will camp here for two days. If they do not come within that time, we will continue on to Teku Benga.'

Both officers were satisfied. We finished our meal and retired to our respective tents.

And so we waited.

On the first day we saw a few riders round the bend in the pass and we made ready to receive them. But they merely watched us for a couple of hours before vanishing. Tension had begun to increase markedly in the camp by the next night.

On the second day one of our scouts rode in to report that over a hundred Kumbalaris had assembled at the far end of the pass and were riding towards us. We assumed a defensive position and continued to wait. When they appeared they were riding slowly and through my field glasses I saw several elaborate horsehair standards. Attached to one of these was a white flag. The stand-ard-bearers rode on both sides of a red-and-gold litter slung between two ponies. Remembering Subadar Bisht's words of cau-tion, I gave the order for our cavalry to mount. There is hardly any sight more impressive than a hundred and fifty Punjabi Lancers with their lances at the salute. Risaldar Jenab Shah was by my side. I offered him my glasses. He stared through them for some moments. When he lowered them he was frowning. 'Sharan Khang seems to be with them,' he said, 'riding in that litter. Perhaps this is a genuine parley party. But why so many?'

'It could be a show of strength,' I said. 'But he must have more than a hundred warriors.'

'It depends how many have died for religious purposes,' Jenab Shah said darkly. He turned in his saddle. 'Here is Subadar Bisht. What do you make of this, Bisht?'

The Ghoorka officer said: 'Sharan Khang would not ride at their head if they were about to charge. The Priest-Kings of Kum-balari do not fight with their warriors.' He spoke with some contempt. 'But I warn you, sir, this could be a trick.'

I nodded.

Both the Punjabi sowars and the Ghoorka sepoys were plainly eager to come to grips with the Kumbalaris. 'You had better remind your men that we are here to talk peace, if possible,' I said, 'not to fight.'

'They will not fight,' Jenab Shah said confidently, 'until they have orders to do so. Then they will *fight*.'

The mass of Kumbalari horsemen drew closer and paused a few hundred feet from our lines. The standard-bearers broke away and, escorting the litter, came up to where I sat my horse at the head of my men.

The red-and-gold litter was covered by curtains. I looked enquir-ingly at the impassive faces of the standard-bearers, but they said nothing. And then at last the curtain at the front was parted from within and I was suddenly confronting the High Priest himself. He wore elaborate robes of brocade stitched with dozens of tiny mirrors. On his head was a tall hat of painted leather inlaid with gold and ivory. And beneath the peak of the hat was his wizened old face. The face of a particularly malicious devil.

'Greetings, Sharan Khang,' I said. 'We are here at the command of the great King-Emperor of Britain. We come to ask why you attack his houses and kill his servants when he has offered no hostility to you.'

One of the guides began to interpret, but Sharan Khang waved his hand impatiently. 'Sharan Khang speaks English,' he said in a strange, high-pitched voice. 'As he speaks *all* tongues. For all tongues come from the tongue of the Kumbalari, the First, the Most Ancient.'

I must admit I felt a shiver run through me as he spoke. I could almost believe that he was the powerful sorcerer they claimed him to be.

'Such an ancient people must therefore also be wise.' I tried to stare back into those cruel, intelligent eyes. 'And a wise people would not anger the King-Emperor.'

'A wise people knows that it must protect itself against the wolf,' Sharan Khang said, a faint smile curving his lips. 'And the British wolf is a singularly rapacious beast, Captain Bastable. It has eaten well in the lands of the south and the west, has it not? Soon it will turn its eyes towards Kumbalari.'

'What you mistake for a wolf is really a lion,' I said, trying not to show I was impressed by the fact that he had known my name. 'A lion which brings peace, security, justice to those it chooses to protect. A lion which knows that Kumbalari does not need its protection.'

The conversation continued in these rather convoluted terms for some time before Sharan Khang grew visibly impatient and said suddenly:

'Why are so many soldiers come to our land?'

'Because you attacked our frontier station and killed our men,' I said.

'Because you put your "frontier station" inside our boundaries.' Sharan Khang made a strange gesture in the air. 'We are not a greedy people. We have no need to be. We do not hunger for land like the Westerners, for we know that land is not important when a man's soul is capable of ranging the universe. You may come to Teku Benga, where all gods preside, and there I will tell you what you may say to this upstart barbarian lion who dignifies himself with grandiose titles.'

'You are willing to discuss a treaty?'

'Yes – in Teku Benga, if you come with no more than six of your men.' He gestured, let the curtain fall, and the litter was turned round. The riders began to move back up the valley.

'It is a trick, sir,' Bisht remarked at once. 'He hopes that in separating you from us he will cut off our army's head and thus make it easier to attack us.'

'You could be right, Subadar Bisht, but you know very well that such a trick would not work. The Ghoorkas are not afraid to fight.' I looked back at the sepoys. 'Indeed, they seem more than ready to go into battle at this moment.'

'We care nothing for death, sir – the clean battle-death. But it is not the prospect of battle which disturbs me. In my bones I feel something worse may happen. I know the Kumbalaris. They are a deeply wicked people. I dare not think what may happen to you in Teku Benga, Captain Bastable.'

I laid an affectionate hand on my subadar's shoulder. 'I am honoured you should feel thus, Subadar Bisht. But it is my duty to go to Teku Benga. I have my orders. I must settle this matter peacefully if it is at all possible.'

'But if you do not return from Teku Benga within a day, sir, we shall advance towards the city. Then, if we are not given full evidence that you are alive and in good health, we shall attack Teku Benga.'

'There's nothing wrong with that plan,' I agreed.

And so, with Risaldar Jenab Shah and five of his sowars, I rode next morning for Teku Benga and saw at last the walled mountain city into which no stranger had been admitted for a thousand years. Of course I was suspicious of Sharan Khang. Of course I wondered why, after a thousand years, he was willing to let foreigners defile the holy city with their presence. But what could I do? If he said he was willing to discuss a treaty, then I had to believe him.

I was at a loss to imagine how such a city, rearing as it did out of the crags of the Himalayas, had been built. Its crazy spires and domes defied the very laws of gravity. Its crooked walls followed the line of the mountain slopes and many of the buildings looked as if they had been plucked up and perched delicately on slivers of rock which could scarcely support the weight of a man. Many of the roofs and walls were decorated with complicated carvings of infinitely delicate workmanship, set with jewels and precious metals, rare woods, jade and ivory. Finials curled in on themselves and curled again. Monstrous stone beasts glared down from a score of places on the walls. The whole city glittered in the cold light and it did, indeed, seem older than any architecture I had ever seen or read about. Yet, for all its richness and its age, Teku Benga struck me as being a rather seedy sort of place, as if it had known better days. Perhaps the Kumbalaris had not built it. Perhaps the race which had built it had mysteriously disappeared, as had happened elsewhere, and the Kumbalaris had merely occupied it.

'Ooof! The stench!' With his handkerchief, Risaldar Jenab Shah fastidiously wiped his nose. 'They must keep their goats and sheep in their temples and palaces.'

Teku Benga had the smell of a farmyard which had not been too cleanly kept and the smell grew stronger as we entered the main gate under the eyes of the glowering guards. Our horses trod irregularly paved streets caked with dung and other refuse. No women were present in those streets. All we saw were a few male children and a number of warriors lounging, with apparent unconcern, by their ponies. We kept going, up the steeply sloping central street, lined with nothing but temples, towards a large square in what I judged to be the middle of the city. The temples themselves were impressively ugly, in a style which a scholar might have called decadent oriental baroque. Every inch of the buildings was decorated with representations of gods and demons from virtually every mythology in the East. There were mixtures

of Hindu and Buddhist decoration, of Moslem and some Christian, of what I took to be Egyptian, Phoenician, Persian, even Greek, and some which were older still; but none of these combinations was at all pleasing to the eye. At least I now understood how it came to be called the Place Where All Gods Preside – though they presided, it seemed to me, in rather uneasy juxtaposition to each other.

'This is distinctly an unhealthy place,' said Jenab Shah. 'I will be glad to leave it. I should not like to die here, Captain Bastable. I would fear what would happen to my soul.'

'I know what you mean. Let us hope Sharan Khang keeps his word.'

'I am not sure I heard him give his word, sir,' said the risaldar significantly as we reached the square and reined in our horses. We had arrived outside a huge, ornate building, much larger than the others, but in the same sickening mixture of styles. Domes, minarets, spiralling steeples, lattice walls, pagodalike terraced roofs, carved pillars, serpent finials, fabulous monsters grinning or growling from every corner, tigers and elephants standing guard at every doorway. The building was predominantly coloured green and saffron, but there was red and blue and orange and gold and some of the roofs were overlaid with gold- or silver-leaf. It seemed the oldest temple of them all. Behind all this was the blue Hima-layan sky in which grey and white clouds boiled. It was a sight unlike anything I had ever previously experienced. It filled me with a sense of deep foreboding as if I were in the presence of something not built by human hands at all.

Slowly, out of all the many doorways, saffron-robed priests began to emerge and stand stock-still, watching us from the steps and gal-leries of the building which was Temple or Palace, or both, I could not decide.

These priests looked little different from the warriors we had seen earlier and they were certainly no cleaner. It occurred to me that if the Kumbalaris disdained land, then they disliked water even more. I remarked on this to Risaldar Jenab Shah, who flung back his great turbaned head and laughed heartily – an action which caused the priests to frown at us in hatred and disgust. These priests were not shaven-headed, like most priests who wore the saffron robe. These had long hair hanging down their faces in many greasy braids and some had moustaches or beards which were plaited in a similar fashion. They were a sinister, unsavoury lot. Not a few had belts or cummerbunds into which were stuck scabbarded swords.

We waited and they watched us. We returned their gaze, trying to appear much less concerned than we felt. Our horses moved uneasily under us and tossed their manes, snorting as if the stink of the city was too much, even for them.

Then at last, borne by four priests, the golden litter appeared from what must have been the main entrance of the temple. The curtains were parted and there sat Sharan Khang.

He was grinning.

'I am here, Sharan Khang,' I began, 'to listen to anything you wish to tell me concerning your raids on our frontier stations and to discuss the terms of a treaty which will let us live together in peace.'

Sharan Khang's grin did not falter, but I'm afraid my voice did a little as I stared into that wrinkled, evil face. I had never before felt convinced that I was in the presence of pure evil, but I did at that moment.

After a moment he spoke. 'I hear your words and must consider them. Meanwhile you will be guests here –' he gestured behind him – 'here at the Temple of the Future Buddha which is also my palace. The oldest of all these ancient buildings.'

A little nervously we dismounted. The four priests picked up Sharan Khang's litter and bore it back inside. We followed. The interior was heavy with incense and poorly lighted by sputtering bowls of flaming oil suspended from chains fixed to the ceiling. There were no representations of the Buddha here, however, and I supposed that this was because the 'Future Buddha' had not yet been born. We followed the litter through a system of corridors, so complicated as to seem like a maze, until we reached a smallish chamber in which food had been laid on a low table surrounded by cushions. Here the litter was lowered and the attendant priests retired, apparently leaving us alone with Sharan Khang. He gestured for us to seat ourselves on the cushions, which we did.

'You must eat and drink,' intoned Sharan Khang, 'and then we shall all feel more like talking.'

After washing our hands in the silver bowls of warm water and drying them on the silken towels, we reached, rather reluctantly, towards the food. Sharan Khang helped himself to the same dishes and began to eat heartily, which was something of a relief to us. When we tasted the food we were glad that it did not seem poisoned, for it was delicious.

I complimented the High Priest sincerely on his hospitality and he accepted this graciously enough. He was beginning to seem a much less sinister figure. In fact I was almost beginning to like him.

'It is unusual,' I said, 'to have a temple which is also a palace – and with such a strange name, too.'

'The High Priests of Kumbalari,' said Sharan Khang smiling, 'are also gods, so they must live in a temple. And since the Future Buddha is not yet here to take up residence, what better place than this temple?'

'They must have been waiting a long time for him to come. How old is this building?'

'Some parts of it are little more than fifteen hundred to two thousand years old. Other parts are perhaps three to five thousand years old. The earliest parts are much, much older than that.'

I did not believe him, of course, but accepted what he said as a typical oriental exaggeration. 'And have the Kumbalaris lived here all that time?' I asked politely.

'They have lived here a long, long time. Before that there were – other beings...'

A look almost of fear came into his eyes and he smiled quickly. 'Is the food to your taste?'

'It is very rich,' I said. I felt an emotion of fondness for him, as I might have felt as a child to a kindly uncle. I looked at the others. And that was when I became suspicious, for all had stupid, vacant grins on their faces. And I was feeling drowsy! I shook my head, trying to clear it. I got unsteadily to my feet. I shook Risaldar Jenab Shah's shoulder. 'Are you all right, risaldar?'

He looked up at me and laughed, then nodded sagely as if I had made some particularly wise pronouncement.

Now I understood why I had felt so well-disposed towards the cunning old High Priest.

'You have drugged us, Sharan Khang! Why? You think any concessions we make in this state will be honoured when we realise what has been done to us? Or do you plan to mesmerise us – make us give orders to our men which will lead them into a trap?'

Sharan Khang's eyes were hard. 'Sit down, captain. I have not drugged you. I ate the food you ate. Am I drugged?'

'Possibly...' I staggered and had to force my legs to support me. The room had begun to spin. 'If you are used to the drug and we are not. What is it? Opium?'

Sharan Khang laughed. 'Opium! Opium! Why should it be, Captain Bastable? If you are feeling sleepy it is only because you have eaten so much of the rich food of Kumbalari. You have been living on the simpler diet of a soldier. Why not sleep for a while and...?'

My mouth was dry and my eyes were watering. Sharan Khang,

murmuring softly, seemed to sway before me like a cobra about to strike. Cursing him I unbuttoned my holster and drew out my revolver.

Instantly a dozen of the priests appeared, their curved swords at the ready. I tried to aim at Sharan Khang.

'Come closer and he dies,' I said thickly.

I was not sure that they understood the words, but they gathered my meaning.

'Sharan Khang.' My own voice seemed to come from a great distance away. 'My men will march on Teku Benga tomorrow. If I do not appear before them, alive and well, they will attack your city and they will destroy it and all who live in it.'

Sharan Khang only smiled. 'Of course you will be alive and well, captain. Moreover you will see things in an improved perspective, I am sure.'

'My God! You'll not mesmerise me! I'm an English officer – not one of your ignorant followers!'

'Please rest, captain. In the morning...'

From the corner of my eye I caught a movement. Two more priests were rushing me from behind. I turned and fired. One went down. The other closed with me, trying to wrench the gun from my grasp. I fired it and blew a great hole in him. With a cry he released my wrist and fell writhing to the ground. Now the Punjabis were beside me, their own pistols drawn, doing their best to support each other, for all were as badly drugged as was I. Jenab Shah said with difficulty: 'We must try to reach fresh air, captain. It might help. And if we can get to our horses, we may escape...'

'You'll be fools to leave this room,' said Sharan Khang evenly. 'Even we do not know every part of the maze which is the Temple of the Future Buddha. Some say that sections of it do not even exist in our own time...'

'Be silent!' I ordered, covering him again with my pistol. 'I'll not listen further to your lies.'

We began to back away from Sharan Khang and his remaining priests, our revolvers at the ready as we looked around for the entrance through which we had come. But all entrances were alike. At last we chose one and staggered through it, finding our-selves in almost total blackness.

As we blundered about, seeking a door which would lead us outside, I wondered again at the reasons for Sharan Khang's drug-ging us. I shall never know what his exact plans were, however.

Suddenly one of our men gave a yell and fired into the dark-ness. At first I saw nothing but a blank wall. Then two or three priests came running at us from thin air, apparently unarmed – but impervious to the man's bullets.

'Stop firing!' I rasped, convinced that this was an optical illusion. 'Follow me!' I stumbled down a flight of steps, pushed through an awning, found myself in another chamber laid out with food – but not the same chamber in which we had eaten. I hesitated. Was I already in the grip of a drugged dream? I crossed the room, knocking over a small stool as I passed the table, and dashed back a series of silk curtains until I discovered an exit. With my men behind me I passed through the archway striking my shoulders painfully as I weaved from side to side of the corridor. Another flight of steps. Another chamber almost exactly like the first, laid out with food. Another exit and still another flight of steps lead-ing downward. A passage.

I don't know for how long this useless stumbling about went on, but it felt like an eternity. We were completely lost and our only consolation was that our enemies seemed to have given up their pursuit. We were deep in an unlit part of the Temple of the Future Buddha. There was no smell of incense here – only cold, stale air. Everything I touched was cold; carved from rock and studded with raw jewels and metal, every inch of the walls seemed covered in gargoyles. Sometimes my fingers would trace part of a carving and then recoil in horror at the vision which was conjured up.

The drug was still in us, but the strenuous exercise had dis-missed part of its effect. My head was beginning to clear when at last I paused, panting, and tried to review our position.

'I think we are in an unused part of the temple,' I said, 'and a long way below the level of the street, judging by all those steps we went down. I wonder why they haven't followed us. If we wait here for a little while and then try to make our way back undetected, we stand a chance of reaching our men and warning them of Sharan Khang's treachery. Any other ideas, risaldar?'

There was silence.

I peered into the darkness. 'Risaldar?'

No reply.

I reached into my pocket and took out a box of matches. I lit one.

All I saw were the horrid carvings – infinitely more disgusting than those in the upper parts of the building. They seemed both inhuman and unbelievably ancient. I could understand now why we had not been followed. I dropped the match with a gasp. Where were my men?

I risked calling out. 'Risaldar? Jenab Shah?'

Still silence.

I shuddered, beginning to believe in everything I had been told about Sharan Khang's power. I found myself stumbling forward, trying to run, falling on the stone and picking myself up, running again, insane with terror, until, completely exhausted, I fell to the deathly cold floor of the Temple of the Future Buddha.

I might have passed out for a short while, but the next thing I remember was a peculiar noise – unmistakeably the sound of distant, tinkling laughter. Sharan Khang? No.

I reached out, trying to touch the walls. I found only empty space on both sides of me. I had left the corridor, I supposed, and entered a chamber. I shivered. Again that peculiar, tinkling laughter.

And then I saw a tiny light ahead of me. I got up and began to move towards it, but it must have been a very long way away, for it grew no larger.

I stopped.

Then the light began to move towards *me*!

And as it came closer, the sound of the unearthly laughter grew louder until I was forced to holster my pistol and cover my ears. The light intensified. I squeezed my eyes shut in pain. The ground beneath my feet began to sway. An earthquake?

I risked opening my eyes for a moment and through the

blinding white light got an impression of more inhuman carvings, or strange, complicated things which might have been machines built by the ancient Hindu gods.

And then the floor seemed to give way beneath me and I was plunging downwards, was caught by a whirlwind and hurled upward, was tossed head over heels, dashed from side to side, hurled downward again, until my senses left me altogether, save for that sensation of bitter, bitter cold.

Then I felt nothing, not even the cold. I became convinced that I was dead, slain by a force which had lurked below the temple since the beginnings of Time and which even Sharan Khang, Master Sorcerer of Teku Benga, had been afraid to face.

Then I ceased to think at all.

Chapter Three
The Shadow from the Sky

CONSCIOUSNESS RETURNED FIRST as a series of vague impressions: armies, consisting of millions of men, marching against a background of grey and white trees; black flames burning; a young girl in a white dress, her body pierced by dozens of long arrows. There were many images of that sort and slowly they became stronger and the colours grew richer and richer. I became aware of my own body. It was colder than ice – colder even than it had been before I had passed out. And yet, oddly, I felt no discomfort. I felt nothing – I just *knew* that I was cold.

I tried to move the fingers on my right hand (I could still see nothing) and thought that perhaps the index finger rose a fraction.

The images in my head grew more horrific. Corpses filled my skull – brutally maimed corpses. Dying children stretched out their hands to me for help. Bestial soldiers in colourless uniforms raped women. And everywhere there was fire, black smoke, collapsing buildings. I had to escape those images and I made a great effort to move my arm.

At last the arm began to bend, but it was amazingly stiff. And as it bent pain flooded through me so that I cried out – a strange, grating noise. My eyes sprang open and at first I saw nothing but a milky haze. I moved my neck. Again the sickening pain. But the images were beginning to fade. I bent my leg and gasped. Suddenly fire seemed to fill me, melting the ice which had frozen my blood. I began to shake all over, but the pain diminished. And now I saw that I lay on my back staring up at the blue sky. I seemed to be at the bottom of a pit, for there were steep walls on every side.

After a very long time I was able to sit upright and inspect my surroundings. I *was* in a pit of sorts – but a man-made pit, for the shaft was of carved stone. The carvings were similar to those I had glimpsed fleetingly before I collapsed. In the daylight they did not look quite so daunting, but they were ugly things nonetheless.

I smiled at my fears. Plainly there had been an earthquake and it had shaken down the Temple of the Future Buddha. The other things I had seen had been caused by the action of the drug on my frightened brain. Somehow I had escaped the worst of the earthquake and was relatively unhurt. I doubted if Sharan Khang and his people had been so lucky, but I had best go warily until I knew for certain that they were not waiting for me up above. Probably poor Risaldar Jenab Shah and the sowars had been killed in the catacombs. But at least Nature had done the work I had been commissioned to do – the earthquake would have 'pacified' even Sharan Khang. Even if he were not dead, he would now be discredited, for those of his people still alive would see the earthquake as a sign from the gods.

I got to my feet, staring at my hands. They were caked with dust that was not only thick but which seemed to have been there for ages. And my clothes were in rags. As I slapped at the dust, bits of cloth fell away. I fingered my jacket. The fabric seemed to have *rotted*! I was momentarily disturbed, but then reasoned that they had been affected by the action of some peculiar gas which filled the deeper chambers of the temple – a gas which had perhaps combined with the drug to make me suffer those strange hallucinations.

When I felt in slightly better shape, I began, as cautiously as I could, to try to make my way up to the top of the pit, which was some thirty feet above my head. I was extremely weak and frightfully stiff and the rock was soft, often breaking away as I tested it for a foothold. But by using the gargoyles as steps, I slowly managed to clamber to the top of the pit, haul myself over the edge and peer cautiously around me.

There was no sign of Sharan Khang or his men. Indeed, there was no sign of life at all. Everywhere I looked I saw ruins. Not a single building in Teku Benga had escaped the earthquake. Many of the temples seemed to have disappeared altogether.

I stood up and began to walk over the cracked remains of the pavements.

And then I stopped suddenly and, for the first time since I had awakened, I realised that there was something I could not rationalise.

There were no corpses – which might have been expected if the earthquake had occurred the previous night, as I thought. But perhaps the people had managed to escape the city. I could accept that.

What brought me up short was not that the pavements were cracked – *but that weeds grew in profusion between the cracks!*

And now that I looked, there were creepers, tiny mountain flowers, patches of heather growing everywhere on the ruins. These ruins were *old*. It had been years since anyone had occupied them!

I licked my lips and tried to pull myself together. Perhaps I was not in Teku Benga at all? Perhaps I had been carried from Sharan Khang's city and left to die among the ruins of another city?

But this was plainly Teku Benga. I recognised the ruins of several buildings. And there was hardly another city *like* Teku Benga, even in the mysterious Himalayas.

Besides, I recognised the surrounding mountains, the distant pass which led up to what had been the city wall. And it was obvious that I stood in the ruins of the central square in which the Temple of the Future Buddha had been erected.

Again I experienced a dreadful shiver of fear. Again I glanced down at my dust-caked body, at my rotting clothes, at the weeds beneath my split boots, at all the evidence – evidence which mocked my sanity – evidence to show that not hours but *years* had passed since I had sought to escape the trap which Sharan Khang had set for me!

Could I still be dreaming? I asked myself. But if this were a dream, it was unlike anything I had ever dreamed before. And one can always tell a dream from reality, no matter how sharp and coherent a dream it is. (That is what I felt then, but now I wonder, I wonder...)

I seated myself on a slab of broken masonry and tried to think. How was it possible that I could still be alive? At least two years must have passed since the earthquake – if earthquake it were – and while my clothes had been subjected to the normal processes of Time, my flesh was unaffected. Could the gas I suspected as having caused the rot have actually preserved me? It was the only explanation – and a wild enough one, at that. It would take a clever scientist to investigate the matter. I wasn't up to it. Now my job was to get back to civilisation, contact my regiment and find out what had been going on since I had lost consciousness.

As I clambered over the ruins I tried to force the astounding thoughts from my brain and concentrate on my immediate problem. But it was difficult and I still could not rid myself entirely of the idea that I had gone quite mad.

Eventually I reached the crumbling walls and hauled my aching body over them. Reaching the top I looked down the other side, seeking the road which had been there. But it was gone. In its place was a yawning chasm, as if the rock had cracked wide open and the part of the mountain on which the city had stood had moved at least a hundred feet away from the rest. There was absolutely no way of crossing to the other side. I began to laugh – a harsh, exhausted cackle – and then was seized by a series of dry, racking sobs. Somehow Fate had spared my life, only to present me with the prospect of a lingering death as I slowly starved on this lifeless mountain.

Wearily, I lay down my head and must have slept a natural sleep for an hour or two, for when I awoke the sun was lower in the sky. It was about three o'clock in the afternoon.

I dragged myself to my feet, turned and began to move back through the ruins. I would try to get to the other side of the city and see if there were any other means of climbing down the mountain.

All around me were the snow-capped flanks of the Himalayas: impassive, uncaring. And above me was the pale blue sky in which not even a hawk flew. It was almost as if I were the last creature alive in the world.

I stopped myself from continuing this line of thought, for I knew that madness would be the result if I did begin to reason in that way.

When I did eventually reach the far side of the city hopelessness once again consumed me, for on all the remaining quarters there were sheer cliffs going down several hundred feet at least. That was doubtless the reason for locating the city here in the first place. There was only one approach – or had been – and it meant that Teku Benga was safe from anything but a frontal attack. I shrugged in despair and began to wonder which of the plants might be edible. Not that I was hungry at that moment. I smiled bitterly. Why should I be, if I had remained alive for at least two years? The joke made me laugh. It was a crazy laugh. I stopped myself. The sun was beginning to set and the air had grown cold. At length I crawled into a shelter formed by two slabs of masonry and fell once more into a deep, dreamless sleep.

It was dawn when I next awoke. I felt a new confidence and I had devised a plan of sorts. My leather belt and shoulder strap had been unaffected by time and though slightly cracked were still strong. I would search the ruins until I found more leather. Somewhere there must still be store chests, even the remains of the Kumbalari warriors who had died in the earthquake. I would devote what remained of my energy to discovering enough leather out of which I might plait a rope. With a rope I could try to get down the mountain. And if I died in the attempt, well, it would be no worse than the alternative means of dying which were presented to me.

I spent the next several hours clambering in and out of the ruins, discovering first a skeleton still dressed in the furs, iron and leather of a Kumbalari soldier. Around his waist was wound quite a good length of leather cord. I tested it and it was still strong. My spirits lifting, I continued to search.

I was crouching in the ruins of one of the temples, trying to drag out another skeleton, when I heard the sound. At first I thought it was a noise made by the bones scraping on the rock, but it was too soft. Then I wondered if I were not, after all, alone in the ruins. Could I be hearing the purr of a tiger? No – though that was more like the sound. I stopped tugging at the skeleton and cocked my head, trying to listen harder. A drum, perhaps? A drumbeat echoing through the mountains? It could be fifty miles away, however. I crawled back through the gap and as I did so a shadow began to spread across the rubble before me. A huge, black shadow which might have been that of an enormous bird, save that it was long, regular in shape and curved.

Again I doubted my own sanity and in some trepidation I forced myself to look upward.

I gasped in astonishment. This was no bird, but a gigantic, cigar-shaped balloon! And yet it was like no balloon I had ever seen, for its envelope seemed rigid – constructed of some silvery metal – and attached to this envelope (not swinging from it by ropes) was a gondola almost the length of the balloon itself.

What astonished me even more was the slogan, inscribed in huge lettering on the hull:

ROYAL INDIAN AIR SERVICE

From its stern projected four triangular 'wings' which resembled nothing so much as the flukes of a whale. And painted on each of these in shining red, white and blue was a large Union Jack.

For a moment I could only stare at the flying monster in incredulous wonderment. And then I began to leap about the ruins, waving and yelling for all I was worth!

Chapter Four

An Amateur Archaeologist

I MUST HAVE seemed a pretty strange sight myself, with my filthy body clad in rotting clothes, dancing and roaring like a madman among the ruins of that ancient city, just as if I were some castaway of old who had at last caught sight of the schooner which could save him. But it did not look as if this schooner of the air had seen me. Imperturbably it sailed on, heading towards the distant northern mountains, its four great engines thumping out their smooth, regular beat, turning the massive, whirling screws which apparently propelled the vessel.

It passed over the ruins and seemed to be continuing on its course, as unaware of me as it might have been of a fly settling on its side.

The engines stopped. I waited tensely. What would the balloon do next? It was still moving forward, carried on by its own momentum.

When the engines started again their sound was more high-pitched. I sank down in despair. Possibly the flyers (assuming there *were* men in the monster) had thought they had seen something but then decided it was not worth stopping to investigate. A tremor ran through the great silver bulk and then, very slowly, it began to drift backwards – back to where I sat panting and anxious. The screws had been put into reverse, rather as the screws on a steamer are reversed.

Again I leapt up, my face splitting into a huge grin. I was to be saved – even if it were by the strangest flying machine ever invented.

Soon the great bulk – the size of a small steamer itself – was over my head, blotting out the sky. Half-crazy with joy, I continued to wave. I heard distant shouts from above but could not distinguish the words. A siren started to blow, but I took this to be a greeting, like a ship's whistle.

Then, suddenly, something dropped from the ship. I was struck savagely in the face and smashed backwards against the rock. I gasped for breath, unable to understand the reason for the attack or, for that matter, what missile had been used.

Blinking, I sat up and peered around me. For yards in all directions the ruins glistened wetly – and there were several huge puddles now in evidence. I was soaked through. Was this some rather bad joke at my expense – their way of telling me that I needed a bath? It seemed unlikely. Shakily, I got up, half-expecting the airship to send down another mass of water.

But then I realised that the vessel was sinking rapidly towards the ruins, looming low in the sky, still sounding its siren. It was lucky for me it had not carried sand as ballast – for ballast was what that water had been! Much lightened, the balloon was able to come to my assistance with less risk to itself.

Soon it was little more than twenty feet above me. I stared hard at the slogan on its side, at the Union Jacks on its tail-fins. There was no question of its reality. I had once seen an airship flown by Mr Santos-Dumont, but it had been a crude affair compared with this giant. There had been a great deal of progress in the last couple of years, I decided.

Now a circular hatch was opened in the bottom of the metal gondola and amused British faces peered over the lip.

'Sorry about the bath, old son,' called one in familiar Cockney tones, 'but we did try to warn you. Understand English?'

'I *am* English!' I croaked.

'Blimey! Hang on a minute.' The face disappeared.

'All right,' said the face, reappearing. 'Stand clear there.'

I stepped back nervously, expecting another drenching, but this time a rope ladder snaked down from the hatch. I ran forward and grabbed it in relief but as soon as my hand clasped the first rung I heard a yell from overhead:

'Not yet! Not yet! Oh, Murphy, the idiot! The –'

I missed the rest of the oath for I was being dragged over the rocks until I managed to let go of the rung and fall flat on my face. The flying machine had yawed round a fraction in the sky – a fraction being a good few feet – and laid me low for a second time! I got up and did not attempt to grab the rope ladder again.

'We'll come down,' shouted the face. 'Stay where you are.'

Soon two smartly dressed men clambered from the hatch and began to descend the ladder. They were dressed in white uniforms very similar to those worn by sailors in the tropics, though their jackets and trousers were edged with broad bands of light blue and I did not recognise the insignia on their sleeves. I admired the casual skill and speed with which they climbed down the swaying ladder, paying out a rope which led upwards into the ship. When they were a few rungs above me they tossed me the rope.

'Easy now, old son,' called the man who had originally addressed me. 'Tie this round you – under your arms – and we'll take you up! Understand?'

'I understand.' Swiftly I obeyed his instructions.

'Are you secure?' called the man.

I nodded and took a good grip on the rope.

The sky 'sailor' signalled to an unseen shipmate. 'Haul away, Bert!'

I heard the whine of a motor and then I was being dragged upwards. At first I began to spin wildly round and round and felt appallingly sick and dizzy until one of the men on the ladder leaned out and caught my leg, steadying my ascent.

After what must have been a minute but which seemed like an hour I was tugged over the side of the hatch and found myself in a circular chamber about twelve feet in diameter and about eight feet high. The chamber was made entirely of metal and rather resembled a gun-turret in a modern ironclad.

The small engine-driven winch which had been the means of bringing me up was now switched off by another uniformed man, doubtless 'Bert'. The other two clambered aboard, gathered in the rope ladder in an expert way, and shut the hatch with a clang, bolting it tight.

There was one other man in the chamber, standing near an

oval-shaped door. He, too, was dressed in 'whites', but wore a solar topee and had major's pips on the epaulettes of his shirt. He was a smallish man with a sharp, vulpine face, a neat little black moustache which he was smoothing with the end of his swagger stick as he peered at me, poker-faced.

After a pause, while his large, dark eyes took in my appearance from head to toe, he said: 'Welcome aboard. English are you?'

I finished removing the rope from under my arms and saluted. 'Yes, sir. Captain Oswald Bastable, sir.'

'Army, eh? Bit odd, eh? I'm Major Powell, Royal Indian Air Police – as you've probably noticed, what? This is the patrol ship *Pericles*.' He scratched his long nose with the edge of his stick. 'Amazin' – amazin'. Well, we'll talk later. Sick Bay for you first, I'd say, what?'

He opened the oval door and stood aside while the two men helped me through.

I now found myself in a long passageway, blank on one side but with large portholes on the other. Through the portholes I could see the ruins of Teku Benga slowly falling away below us. At the end of the passage was another door and, beyond the door, a corner into a shorter passage on both sides of which were ranged more doors bearing various signs. One of the signs was SICK BAY.

There were eight beds inside, none of which was occupied. There were all the facilities of a modern hospital, including several gadgets at whose use I could not begin to guess. I was allowed to undress behind a screen and take a long bath in the tub I found there. Feeling much better, I got into the pair of pyjamas (also white and sky-blue) provided and made my way to the bed which had been prepared up at the far end of the room.

I was in something of a trance, I must admit. It was difficult to remember that I was in a room which at this moment was probably floating several hundred feet or more above the mountains of the Himalayas. Occasionally there was a slight motion from side to side or the odd bump, such as one might feel on a train, and, in fact, it did rather feel as if I were on a train – a rather luxurious first-class express, perhaps.

After a few minutes the ship's doctor entered the room and had a few words with the orderly who was folding up the screens. The doctor was a youngish man with a great round head and a shock of red hair. When he spoke it was in a soft Scottish accent.

'Captain Bastable is it?'

'That's right, doctor. I'm all right, I think. In my body, at any rate.'

'Your body? What d'you think's wrong with your head?'

'Frankly, sir, I think I'm probably dreaming.'

'That's what *we* thought when you were first spotted. How on earth did you manage to get into those ruins? I thought it was impossible.' As he spoke he checked my pulse, looked at my eyes and did the usual things doctors do to you when they can't find anything specifically wrong.

'I'm not sure you'd believe me, doctor, if I told you I rode up on horseback,' I said.

He gave a peculiar laugh and stuck a thermometer into my mouth. 'No, I don't think I would! Rode up! Ha!'

'Well,' I said cautiously, after he had removed the thermometer. 'I did ride up there.'

'Aye.' Plainly he didn't believe me. 'Possibly you think you did. And the horse jumped that chasm, did it?'

'There wasn't a chasm there when I went there.'

'No chasm –?' He laughed aloud. 'My stars! No chasm! There's always been a chasm there – for a damned long time, at any rate. That's why we were flying over the ruins. The only way to reach them is by airship. Major Powell's a bit of an amateur archaeologist. He's got permission to reconnoitre this area with a view to exploring Teku Benga some time. He knows more about the lost civilisations of the Himalayas than anyone. He's a scholar, our Major Powell.'

'I'd hardly count Kumbalari as a *lost* civilisation,' I said. 'Not in the strict sense. That earthquake could only have happened a couple of years ago, surely. That's when I went there.'

'Two years ago? You've been in that God-forsaken place for two years? You poor fellow. But you're remarkably fit on it, I'll say that.' He frowned suddenly. 'Earthquake? I haven't heard of an earthquake in Teku Benga. Mind you…'

'There hasn't been an earthquake in Teku Benga in living memory.' It was the sharp, precise voice of Major Powell, who had come in as we talked. He looked at me with a certain wary curiosity. 'And I very much doubt that anyone could live there for two years. There's nothing to eat, for one thing. On the other hand, there's no other explanation as to how you got there – unless a private expedition I haven't heard about *flew* there two years ago.'

It was my turn to smile. 'Hardly likely, sir. No ship of this kind existed two years ago. In fact, it's remarkable how…'

'I think you had better check him up here, Jim,' said Major Powell tapping his head with his stick. 'The poor chap's lost all sense of time – or something. What was the date when you left for Teku Benga, Captain Bastable?'

'June twenty-fifth, sir.'

'Um. And what year?'

'Why, 1902, sir.'

The doctor and the major stared at each other in some concern.

'That's when the earthquake happened, all right,' Major Powell said quietly. '1902. Almost everyone killed. And there *were* some English soldiers there… Oh, by God! This is ridiculous!' He returned his attention to me. 'You are in a serious condition, young man. I wouldn't call it amnesia – but some sort of false memory. Mind playing you tricks, um? Maybe you've read a lot of history, eh, like me? Perhaps you're an amateur archaeologist, too? Well, I expect we can soon cure you and learn what really happened.'

'What's so odd about my story, major?'

'Well, for one thing, old chap, you're a bit too well-preserved to have gone up to Teku Benga in 1902. That was over seventy years ago. This is July the fifteenth. The year, I'm afraid, is 1973; AD, of course. Does that ring a bell?'

I shook my head. 'Sorry, major. But I'll agree with you on one thing. I'm obviously completely insane.'

'Let's hope it's not permanent,' smiled the doctor. 'Probably been reading a bit too much H.G. Wells, eh?'

Chapter Five
My First Sight of Utopia

EVIDENTLY OUT OF a mistaken sense of kindness, both the doctor and Major Powell left me alone. I had received a hypodermic injection containing some kind of drug which made me drowsy, but I could not sleep. I had become totally convinced now that some peculiar force in the catacombs of the Temple of the Future Buddha had propelled me through Time. I *knew* that it was true. I *knew* that I was not mad. Indeed, if I were mad, then there would be little point in fighting such a detailed and consistent delusion – I might just as well accept it. But now I wanted more information about the world into which I had been plunged. I wanted to discuss the possibilities with the doctor and the major. I wanted to know if there were any evidence of such a thing having happened before – any unexplained reports of men who claimed to have come from another age. At this thought I became depressed. Doubtless there *were* other accounts. And doubtless, too, those men had been considered mad and committed to lunatic asylums, or charlatans and committed to prison. If I were to remain free to see more of this world of the Future, to discover, if I could, a means of returning to my own time, then it would not do for me to make too strong a claim for the truth. It would be better for me to affect amnesia. That they would understand better. And if they could invent an explanation as to how I came to be in the ruins of Teku Benga seventy years after the last man had been able to set foot there, then good luck to them!

Feeling much happier about the whole thing, having made my decision, I settled back in the pillows and fell into a doze.

'The ship's about to land, sir.'

It was the voice of the orderly which wakened me from my

trance. I struggled up in the bed, but he put a restraining hand on me. 'Don't worry, sir. Just lie back and enjoy the ride. We're transferring you to the hospital as soon as we're safely moored. Just wanted to let you know.'

'Thanks,' I said weakly.

'You must have been through it, sir,' said the orderly sympathetically. 'Mountain climbing is a tricky business in that sort of country.'

'Who told you I'd been mountain climbing?'

He was confused. 'Well, nobody, sir. We just thought... Well, it was the obvious explanation.'

'The obvious explanation? Yes, why not? Thank you again, orderly.'

He frowned as he turned away. 'Don't mention it, sir.'

A little while later they began to remove the bolts which had fixed the bed to the deck. I had hardly been aware – save for a slight sinking sensation and a few tremors – that the ship had landed. I was wheeled along the corridors until we reached what I guessed to be the middle of the ship. Here huge folding doors had been lowered to form steps to the ground and a ramp had been laid over the steps to make it possible to wheel my bed down.

We emerged into clear, warm air and the bed bumped a trifle as it was wheeled over flattened grass to what was plainly a hospital van, for it had large red crosses painted on its white sides. The van was motorised, by the look of it. There were no horses in evidence. Glancing around me I received my second shock of pure astonishment at the sight which now met my gaze. Dotted about a vast field were a number of towers, smaller than, but strongly resembling, the Eiffel Tower in Paris. About half of these towers were in use – great pyramids of steel girders to which were moored the best part of a dozen airships, most of which were considerably larger than the giant in which I had been brought! It was obvious that not all the flying monsters were military vessels. Some were commercial, having the names of their lines painted on their sides and decorated rather more elaborately than, for instance, the *Pericles*.

The doctor came up alongside as my bed bumped across the grass. 'How are you feeling?'

'Better, thanks. Where are we?'

'Don't you recognise it? It's Katmandu. Our headquarters are here.'

Katmandu! The last time I had seen the city it had been very distinctly an Eastern capital with architecture in the age-old style of these parts. But now in the distance, beyond the great mooring towers, I could see tall white buildings rising up and up, storey upon storey, so that it seemed they almost touched the clouds. Certainly there were Nepaulese buildings, too, but these were completely dwarfed by the soaring white piles. I noticed something else before I was lifted into the motor van – a long ribbon of steel, raised on a series of grey pillars, which stretched away from the city and disappeared over the horizon.

'And what is that?' I asked the doctor.

He looked puzzled. 'What? The monorail? Why, just a monorail, of course.'

'You mean a train runs along that single track?'

'Exactly.' He paused as he got into the van with me and the doors closed with a soft hiss of air. 'You know, Bastable, your surprise is damned convincing. I wish I knew what was really wrong with you.'

I decided to propose my lie. 'Could it be amnesia, doctor?' There was a soft bump as the van began to move. But I did not hear the familiar clatter of an internal-combustion engine. 'What's powering this thing?'

'What did you expect? It's steam, of course. This is an ordinary Stanley flash-fired steamer van.'

'Not a petrol engine?'

'I should hope not! Primitive things. The steam motor is infinitely more efficient. You must know all this, Bastable. I'm not saying you're deliberately trying to deceive me, but...'

'I think you'd better assume that I've forgotten everything but my name, doctor. All the rest is probably a delusion I went through. Something brought on by exposure and despair at ever being rescued. You'll probably find I'm the survivor of a mountain-climbing expedition which disappeared some time ago.'

'Yes.' He spoke in some relief. 'I thought it might be mountain climbing. You can't remember going up? What the names of the others were – things like that?'

'Afraid not.'

'Well,' he said, satisfied, 'we're beginning to make a start, at any rate.'

Eventually the van stopped and I was wheeled out again, this time onto a raised loading platform plainly designed for the purpose, through a pair of doors (which opened apparently without human agency) and into a clean, bright corridor until I reached a room which was equally clean and bright – and featureless.

'Here we are,' said the doctor.

'And here is?'

'The Churchill Hospital – named after the late Viceroy, Lord Winston. Did a lot for India, did Churchill.'

'Is that the Churchill who wrote the books? The war reports? The chap who charged with the 21st Lancers at Omdurman in '98?'

'I think so. That was early on in his career. You certainly know your history!'

'Well, he must have settled down a lot,' I smiled, 'to have become the Viceroy of India!'

The doctor offered me another strange look. 'Aye, well, Captain Bastable. You'll only be in Katmandu a day or two – until the hospital train leaves for Calcutta. I think you need a specialist in – amnesia. The nearest is at Calcutta.'

I held my tongue. I was about to wonder, aloud, if Calcutta had changed as much as Katmandu.

'And it's peaceful, these days,' I said, 'around here, is it?'

'Peaceful? I should hope so. Oh, there's the odd bit of trouble from extreme nationalist groups from time to time, but nothing serious. There haven't been any *wars* for, what, a hundred years.'

'My amnesia *is* bad,' I said, smiling.

He stood awkwardly at my bedside. 'Aye – well... Ah!' He exclaimed in relief. 'Here's your nurse. Cheerio, Bastable. Keep your spirits up. I'll just –' He took the nurse by her elbow and steered her outside, closing the door.

I would not be a man, with a man's instincts, if I did not admit I had been both surprised and delighted at the appearance of my nurse. It had only been a glimpse, but it showed me just how much things had changed since 1902. The nurse's uniform had been starched white and blue, with a stiff cap on her neatly pinned auburn hair. A fairly ordinary nurse's uniform, save for one thing: her skirt was at least *twelve inches* clear of the floor and revealed the prettiest pair of calves, the neatest set of ankles I had ever seen off the stage of The Empire, Leicester Square! It certainly gave the nurse greater freedom of movement and was, essentially, practical. I wondered if all women were dressed in this practical and attractive way. If so, I could see unexpected pleasures arising from my unwitting trip into the Future!

I think I alarmed my nurse when she returned, for I was both embarrassed and fascinated by her appearance. It was hard to see her as an ordinary, decent – indeed, rather prim – young woman when she was, in the terms of my own day, dressed like a ballet girl! I think I must have been blushing rather noticeably, for the first thing she did was to take my pulse.

A little while later, Major Powell came in and drew up the steel-framed chair beside the bed. 'Well, how are you feeling now, old chap?'

'Much better,' I said. 'I think I must have amnesia.' (I had repeated this line so frequently it was almost as if I were trying to convince myself!)

'So the doc was saying. More like it. And you remember something about a mountain-climbing expedition, do you?'

'I think I do remember going up the mountain,' I said truthfully.

'Splendid! It won't take long for your memory to come back. Mind you, I'm damned interested in what you were saying. It would have been good luck for me if you really had come from 1902, what?'

I smiled weakly. 'Why is that, major?'

'Would have helped my researches. I'm particularly interested in Teku Benga. It's an enigma, you know, architecturally and historically speaking. It has no right to be there, by all logic. And the aerial photographs we've got of it show a mixture of architectural styles which suggests that it was for a time a meeting place for all the world's cultures. Hard to credit, I know.'

'I agree with you, though,' I said. 'And I also believe that there are some cultures represented there which existed before any sort of recorded history. They are very, very old buildings, indeed.'

'There are a few legends, of course. Remarkably few, really. Most of the Kumbalari priests were killed in the 1902 earthquake and the rest of the people are pretty ignorant. After the earthquake, they stopped talking about Teku Benga altogether and most of the oral tradition had died out by the time trained scientists went up there. I suppose that's what you were after, eh? Looking for a clue. A damned dangerous expedition. Not one I'd like to risk, even by airship. Weather conditions change so quickly. The best-equipped expedition could get stranded.' He frowned. 'It's still funny I never read about it. I thought I'd read everything on the subject. I've got our records people onto you, by the way. Trying to find out what regiment you belonged to, that sort of thing. You'll soon know who you are. Then, if you've relatives at home, we'll send you back to them.'

'That's kind of you,' I said.

'Least we could do. Are you an archaeologist, by the by? Do you remember?'

'I suppose I am in a way,' I admitted. 'I seem to know a lot about the past and nothing at all about the – present.'

He laughed briefly. 'Think I understand you. Same here, really. Always digging about in the past. In many ways it was a damned sight better than today, eh?'

'I could answer that if I could remember anything about today.' I laughed in turn.

'Yes, of course.' His face became serious. 'You mean you know everything that happened up until the year 1902 – well before you were born – and remember nothing since. It's certainly the funniest case of amnesia I've ever heard of. You must have been a pretty good scholar, if your "memory" is that detailed. Is there anything I can do to help trigger your memory in some way?'

'You could give me a brief outline of history since 1902.' I thought I had been very clever in leading into this.

He shrugged. 'Nothing much has happened really. Seventy years of glorious peace, all in all. Damned dull.'

'No wars at all?'

'Nothing you'd call wars, no. I suppose the last scrap was the Boer War.'

'A war in South Africa, eh?'

'Yes – in 1910. Boers made a bid for independence. Had some justice to it, I gather. But we calmed them down, fought them for six months then made a lot of concessions. It was a pretty bloody war while is lasted, from all I've read.' He took a cigarette case from his jacket pocket. 'Mind if I smoke?'

'Not at all.'

'Care for one?'

'Thanks.' I accepted.

He grinned crookedly as he lit my cigarette with something which resembled a tinder box but which hissed – a sort of portable gas-jet, I gathered. I tried not to goggle at it as I leaned forward to receive the light. 'I feel like a prep-school master,' he said, putting the portable gas-jet away. 'Telling you all this, I mean. Still, if it helps…'

'It really does,' I assured him. 'What about the other Great Powers – France, Italy, Russia, Germany…'

'… and Japan,' he said, almost disapprovingly.

'What sort of trouble have they had with their colonies?'

'Not much. They deserve trouble, some of them, mind you. The way the Russians and the Japanese administer their Chinese territories.' He cleared his throat. 'I can't say I like their methods. Still, they can be a pretty unruly lot, the Chinese.' He drew deeply on his cigarette. 'The Americans can be a bit soft – particularly in their Indo-Chinese colonies – but I'd rather see it that way than the other.'

'The Americans have colonies?'

He laughed at this. 'Seem strange, does it? Cuba, Panama, Hawaii, the Philippines, Viet Nam, Korea, Taiwan – oh, yes, they've a fair-sized Empire all right. Not that they call it that, of course. The Greater American Commonwealth. They've had a rather strained relationship with France and Russia, but luckily England's got her fill of responsibilities. Let them get on with it, say I. Our Empire – and the Pax Britannica – will outlast them all, in my opinion.'

'There were some people,' I said cautiously, 'in 1902 or there-abouts, who foresaw the British Empire crumbling...'

Major Powell laughed heartily. 'Crumbling, eh? You mean pessimists like Rudyard Kipling, Lloyd George, people like that? I'm afraid Kipling's rather been discredited these days. His heart was in the right place, of course, but it seems to me he lost faith at the last minute. If he hadn't been killed in the Boer War, he might have changed his mind, I suppose. No, I think it's fair to say that the old Empire's brought a stability to the world it has never known before. It's maintained the balance of power pretty successfully – and it hasn't done that badly for the natives, after all.'

'Katmandu has certainly changed a great deal – since 1902...'

He gave me another of his odd, wary looks. 'Ah,' he said. 'You know, Bastable, if I didn't know better I could almost believe you had been on that damned mountain for seventy years. It's pretty strange, listening to a chap as young as you talking about the past in that way.'

'I'm sorry,' I said.

'Don't apologise. Not your fault. You'll be a joy for the brain-doctors to get their teeth into, I must say!'

I smiled. 'You don't make it sound very attractive for me.' I gestured towards the window. 'Would you mind raising the blind?'

He tapped a little box which lay on the bedside table. The box had three switches mounted on it. 'Press this one,' he said. I did as he suggested and was amazed to see the blind wind itself slowly up, revealing a view of the white towers of Katmandu and, beyond them, a section of the airship park.

'Those ships are magnificent,' I said.

'Why, yes,' he said. 'I suppose they are. Take 'em a bit for granted, you know. But the airship has done a lot for India. For the Empire, come to that – for the whole world, if you like. Faster communications. Swifter trade exchanges. Greater mobility of troops.'

'What surprises me,' I said, 'is how they can stay up. I mean, those gasbags seem made of metal.'

'Metal!' he laughed heartily. 'I wish I could think you were having a joke with me, Bastable. Metal! The hulls are made of boron-fibre. It's stronger than steel and infinitely lighter. The gas is helium. There's some metal in the gondola sections, but mainly it's plastic.'

'"Plastic" – plastic what?' I asked curiously.

'Um – plastic material – it's made of chemicals – Good God, you must have heard of plastic, man. I suppose it's sort of rubber, but it can be made to harden at different strengths, in different forms, different degrees of pliability...'

I gave up trying to understand Major Powell. I was never much of a scientist at the best of times. I accepted the mystery of this 'plastic' as I had accepted, while a schoolboy, the mysteries of electrical lighting. Still, it was a comfort to me, in the face of all these new wonders, that some things had not changed a great deal. Indeed, they had improved.

The carping critics of imperialism in my own day would have been silenced pretty sharply if they had heard what I had just heard – and seen the evidence of prosperity and stability which I could now see from my window. I warmed with pride at that moment, and thanked Providence, for this vision of Utopia. Over the past seventy years the White Man had shouldered his burden jolly well, it seemed to me.

Major Powell stood up and went to the window, echoing my own thoughts as he stared out, his hands clasped over his swagger stick behind his back. 'How those Victorians would have loved to see all this,' he murmured. 'All their ideals and dreams realised so fully. But there's still work for us to do.' He turned and looked hard at me, his face half in shadow. 'And a proper study of the lessons of the past, Bastable, helps us with that work.'

'I'm sure you're right.'

He nodded. 'I know I am.' He came to attention and saluted me with his swagger stick. 'Well, old chap, I must be off. Duty calls.'

He began to walk towards the door.

Then something happened. A dull *thump* which seemed to shake the whole building. In the distance I heard sirens sounding, bells ringing.

Major Powell's face was suddenly grim and white and his dark eyes blazed with anger.

'What is it, major?'

'Bomb.'

'Here?'

'Anarchists. Madmen. European troublemakers, almost certainly. Not the Indians at all. Germans – Russians – Jews, they've all got a vested interest in the disruption of order.'

He ran from the room. Duty was indeed calling him now.

The sudden change from tranquillity to violence had taken my breath away. I lay back in the bed trying to see what was happening outside. I saw an army motor race across the airpark. I heard the sound of another far-off explosion. Who on earth could be insane enough to plot the destruction of such a Utopia as this?

Chapter Six
A Man Without a Purpose

T HERE WAS LITTLE point in speculating about the causes of the explosions, any more than there was in brooding about how I had managed to fall through Time to 1973. The events which followed the bomb incidents in Katmandu moved rapidly for me as I was shifted about the world, a bit like a rare museum specimen. The next morning I was bundled aboard the 'monorail' train for Calcutta. The train was shaped rather like an airship itself – though this was truly of steel, all gleaming with brasswork and new paint – and it pulled fifty carriages behind it at a terrifying speed touching almost a hundred miles an hour on some straight sections of its raised track. The motive power for this incredible machine was, I learned, electricity. Making a few short stops, we had reached Calcutta within the day! My impression of Calcutta was of a vast city – much larger in area than the Calcutta we know – with gleaming towers of concrete, glass and steel dwarfing anything I had earlier marvelled at in Katmandu. In Calcutta General Hospital I was tested by a score of experts, all of whom pronounced themselves baffled, and it was decided to ship me, post-haste, to England by the first available airship. The thought of sailing such a huge distance through the sky filled me with some perturbation – I still could not get used to accepting that a material lighter than steel could yet be stronger than steel and it was also difficult to conceive of Man's ability to fly six thousand miles without once landing.

The authorities preferred me in England for a number of reasons, but one of them was, of course, that they had been unable to trace a Captain Oswald Bastable as missing from any British regiment in the last decade. They had, however, checked the records of my own regiment back to 1902 and discovered, naturally, that a Captain Bastable *had* been killed at Teku Benga. I was not, now, just a puzzle for the doctors but a problem for army intelligence, who were curious to know how the 'Mystery Man' (as they called me) could have assumed the identity of someone who had been dead for seventy years. I think they suspected that I might be some sort of foreign spy, but their notions were as vague as mine on that score, I later learned.

And so I took passage on the great liner of the clouds, the AS (for Air Ship) *Light of Dresden*, a commercial vessel owned jointly by the German firm of Krupp Luftschiffahrt AG and the British firm of Vickers Imperial Airways. As far as registration was concerned, the *Light of Dresden* was completely British and bore the appropriate insignia on her tail-fins, but the captain was a German as were at least half the crew. The Germans, it had emerged, had been the first to develop airship flight on any sort of scale and for some time the now defunct Zeppelin Company had led the world in airship development, until Britain and America, working together, had invented the boron-fibre hull and a method of raising and lowering the ships in the air without recourse to ballast, as such. The *Light of Dresden* was equipped with this device, which involved both heating and cooling the helium gas at great speed and intensity. The massive liner also had the latest example of an electrically powered mechanical calculating machine which the people of 1973 called a 'computer' and which was capable of correcting the ship's trim automatically, without recourse to human involvement. The nature of the engine I could never quite determine. It was a single huge gas turbine engine which powered a gigantic single screw – or more properly 'propeller' – at the back of the ship. This screw was housed within the span of the great tail-fins. There were subsidiary oil-driven engines which helped adjust the ship's trim, could swivel through 360 degrees, and were variably pitched and reversible, able to push the ship upward or downward.

But I have not really described the most immediately impressive feature of this mighty ship of the air and that was that she was well over a thousand feet long and three hundred feet high (much of this bulk being, of course, her great gas-container). She had three decks, one beneath the other, arranged with the first-class deck at the bottom and the third-class deck at the top. This single great gondola was, in fact, indivisible with the 'hull' (as the gasbag was called). At the front, in the ship's tapering nose, was the control bridge where, for all the delicate machinery 'thinking' for the ship, there were more than a dozen officers on duty at any one time.

The *Light of Dresden* needed three mooring masts to keep her safely near the ground and, when I first glimpsed her at the Calcutta Airpark (which was, in fact, about ten miles from the city) I gasped, for she made all the other ships – and there were some largish ones moored nearby – look like minnows surrounding a whale. I had already heard that she could carry four hundred passengers and fifty tons of cargo without trouble. When I saw her, I believed it.

I went aboard the airship via a lift which bore me and several other passengers up through the metal cage which was the mooring mast and set us off level with a covered catwalk leading into the passage below the ship's bridge. I was travelling first class with my 'guide', a Lieutenant Jagger, into whose keeping I had been put until we reached London. The amenities on the ship were astonishingly luxurious and put to shame anything to be found on the finest ocean liners of our own time. I began to relax somewhat as I looked around me. And when, later, the *Light of Dresden* let go her moorings and began to sweep with magnificent dignity into the sky, I felt almost safer than I had felt on land.

The journey from Calcutta to London took, with short stops at Karachi and Aden, seventy-two hours! Three days in which we had sailed over India, Africa and Europe, over three great oceans, through most kinds of weather. I had seen cities laid out before me. I had seen deserts, mountains, forests, all speeding past below. I had seen clouds which resembled organic objects. I had been *above* the clouds when it had rained, drifting tranquilly in a blue, sunny sky while the people below were drenched! I had eaten luncheon at a table as steady as a table at the Ritz (and laid with a meal almost as good as one would receive there) while we crossed the Arabian Sea and I had enjoyed my dinner while flying high above the burning sands of the Sahara Desert!

By the time we got to London, I had become quite blasé about flying. It was certainly the most comfortable form of travel I had ever experienced – and also the most civilised.

I was, I will admit, beginning to count myself the luckiest man in the history of the world. I had been taken from the grip of a deadly earthquake in 1902 and placed in the lap of luxury in 1973 – a world which appeared to have solved most of its problems. Was not that the best kind – the most unbelievable kind – of good fortune? I thought so then, I must admit. I was yet to meet Korzeniowski and the others...

I apologise for the digression. I must try to tell my story as it happened, give you an idea of my feelings at the time things were happening, not what I felt about everything later.

At sunset of our third day, we crossed the Channel and I had the experience of seeing the white cliffs of Dover far below me. Shortly after that we circled over the indescribably immense airpark at Croydon in Surrey and began our mooring manoeuvres. Croydon was the main airpark for London because, naturally, a big airpark can hardly be placed in the middle of Piccadilly. The Croydon Airpark was, I discovered later, the largest in the world and had a circumference of nearly twelve miles. The airpark was crowded, needless to say, with scores of airships both large and small, commercial and military, old and new. Those of us who had journeyed all the way from India had no need to pass the Customs inspection and we went through the reception buildings and took our places on the special monorail train for London. Once again I was dazed by all that was going on and was grateful for the steady, solid presence of Lieutenant Michael Jagger, who steered me to my seat and took his place beside me.

Lieutenant Jagger had purchased a newspaper at Croydon and he offered it to me. I accepted gratefully. The size of the paper and the type were unfamiliar, as were some of the abbreviations, but I gathered the gist of most that was printed. It was the first newspaper I had seen since arriving in 1973. I had ten minutes to scan it before we reached London. In that time I learned of a new treaty which had been signed by all the Great Powers, guaranteeing a fixed scale of tariffs on many goods (how those Free Traders would have hated this!) and the recognition of various general laws, applying to all countries and their citizens. It would no longer be possible in the future, the newspaper told me, for a criminal to commit a crime in Taiwan and escape across the sea to, for instance, Japanese Manchuria or even British Canton. The law, it appeared, had been agreed on unanimously by all the Great Powers, and had been inspired by the increasing incidence of lawlessness created by groups of Nihilists, Anarchists or Socialists who, the paper informed me, were bent only upon destruction for its own sake. There were other news reports, some of which I could barely understand and others of a slight nature. But I read over the reference to nihilists for it had some relation to what I had experienced on my first day in the hospital at Katmandu. As the paper suggested, these acts of violence seemed totally without logical point in a world which was steadily marching towards peace, order and justice for all. What could these madmen want? Some, of course, were native nationalists who demanded dominion status rather before they were ready for it. But the others – what did they demand? How is it possible to improve Utopia? I thought wonderingly.

And then we had arrived at Victoria Station which, in its main features, was little changed from the Victoria Station I had known in 1902.

As we disembarked from the monorail train and walked towards the exit I saw that, though it was night, the city was alive with light!

Electrical illuminations of all imaginable colours and combinations of colours blossomed from every slender tower and massive dome. Brightly lit ramps bore motor traffic around these towers on many levels, winding up and down as if supported on the very air itself.

In this London there were no ugly billboards, no illuminated advertisements, no tasteless slogans and, as we climbed into the steam-brougham and began to move along one of the ramps, I realised that there were no seedy slums of the sort found in many parts of the London I had known in 1902. Poverty had been banished! Disease had been exiled! Misery must surely be unknown!

I hope I have managed to convey some of the elation I experienced when first encountering the London of 1973. There is no question of its beauty, its cleanliness, its marvellously ordered civic amenities. There is no question that the people were well fed, cheerful, expensively dressed and, all in all, very much satisfied with their lot. During the next day or so I was taken around London by a Doctor Peters who hoped that some familiar sight might awaken my brain from its sleep. I went through with this charade because there was precious little else I could do. Eventually, I knew, they would give up. I would then be free to choose a profession – perhaps rejoin the army, since I was used to army life. But until that time I was a man without a purpose and I might just as well do what others wanted me to do. Everywhere I went I was amazed at the change which had taken place in that once dirty, fogbound city. Fog was a thing of the past and the air was clean and sharp. Trees and shrubs and flowers grew wherever there was a space to plant them. Butterflies and birds flew about in great profusion. Fountains played in pretty squares and sometimes we would come upon a brass band entertaining the public, or a conjuror, or a Punch and Judy show, or some nigger minstrels. Not all the old buildings had gone. As fresh and clean as if they had just been built I saw Tower Bridge and the Tower of London itself, St Paul's, the Houses of Parliament and Buckingham Palace (where a new King Edward – King Edward VIII, now quite an old man – had his residence). The British people were, as always, accepting the best of the new and conserving the best of the old.

I began to see my visit to 1973 as a wonderful holiday. A holiday which, if I were lucky, might go on for ever.

Book Two

More Strange Events – A Revelation – and Several Disasters!

Chapter One
A Question of Employment

O VER THE NEXT six months I must admit that I led a life of ease. I continued to feign amnesia and, naturally enough, nothing the doctors could do would bring back my 'memory'. Sometimes it even seemed to me that the world of 1902 had been nothing more than an extremely detailed dream. At first this worried me, but eventually it no longer came to matter to me in which period of time I 'belonged'.

I was regarded as something of a phenomenon and, for a short time, was a celebrity. Newspaper articles were written about my mysterious appearance in the Himalayan mountains and the speculation, particularly in the farthing press, grew wilder and wilder. Some of those articles were so fanciful that they even touched on the truth! I was interviewed for the kinematograph (whose coloured pictures could now talk as well as move), for the Marconiphone – now a version of the telephone which, from central stations, broadcast news reports, plays and popular music to almost every home where receiving equipment was installed. These receivers were amplified so that they no longer had to be lifted to the ear, but could be heard from another room if desired. I attended a reception at which the Liberal Prime Minister, Sir George Brown, was present (the Liberals had been in office for over thirty years and the Conservatives were very much a party in decline) and learned that socialist agitation in the late nineteenth and early twentieth centuries had actually had a good effect on saner political parties, like the Liberals, and had, in fact, given a certain amount of impetus to many of the social improvements I had witnessed. Only recently had the serpent of socialism – almost incredibly – begun to rear its head again in political life. Not that the creed had any support from the British people. As usual a few fanatics and neurotic intellectuals used it as a means of rationalising their own insane dreams.

During this first six months I was taken by monorail, or airship, or steamer or electrical carriage to all parts of Britain and, of course, little was recognisable. All major cities were modelled on similar lines to London and there was constant and rapid movement between these great 'conurbations' as they were called. Where Trade had encouraged improvements in travel and communications, these benefits had now been extended to everyone for their convenience and their pleasure.

The population had risen considerably, but the working man was as well-to-do as many middle-class people of 1902 and he had only to work a thirty-hour week to keep himself in virtual luxury. And there was no problem of finding a well-appointed house to live in or a job of work to do, for the excess population of the nation was more than willing to expand beyond the British Isles. Every year thousands left to go out to all corners of the Empire: to Africa, to India, to the protectorates in China or the dominions of Australia, New Zealand and Canada. All over the world the British were settling and administering – and so civilising – even the most inaccessible areas, thanks to the invention of the airship.

At home, rural England was unspoiled and as lovely as it had ever been. No steam locomotives cast palls of smoke over trees and plants, and advertisement hoardings had long since been abolished, as had all the uglier features of English life at the beginnings of the twentieth century. Electrically driven bicycles were available to those of the most modest income and it meant that town people could enjoy the pleasures of the countryside whenever they desired. Prices were low and wages were high (some skilled workmen getting as much as £5 per week) and if one had a few extra sovereigns to spare, then an air trip to France or Germany was often in order. By a little diligent saving, the man in the street could even afford passage by airship to visit relatives in the more distant lands of the Empire. And as for the seamier side of life, well, there was hardly any at all, for the social and moral evils which had created them had been abolished. The Suffragettes of my own day would have been happy to hear that women over thirty now had the vote and there was talk of extending the franchise to women of twenty-one. The length of girls' frocks, incidentally, was if anything shorter in London than the first I had seen in Katmandu. After some months I managed to work up courage to invite one or two pretty girls to the theatre or to a concert. Usually these were the daughters of the doctors or army officers with whom I spent my leisure time and, by our standards, the girls were rather 'forward', accepting very much an equal position in society and as outspoken as any man. After my initial surprise I found this most refreshing – as I found the plays I saw, which had many rather daring Shavian qualities (though politics, thankfully, was missing from them).

Eventually my notoriety faded and I began to feel uneasy about my long 'holiday' in the Future. I refused offers from publishers to write my memoirs (rather difficult if I really were suffering from amnesia!) and began to consider the various forms of honest employment open to me. Since my career had originally been in the army, I decided that I would prefer to continue, if possible, to serve my country in this way. However, I also entertained the notion that I should like to fly in airships and after making a few enquiries discovered that, without a great deal of training in the various functions of airship flying and navigation, I could obtain a position in the recently formed Special Air Police. There would be various exams and I should have to train for a minimum of six months, but I was confident that I could get through all that without too much trouble. It would not take me long to learn service discipline, for instance!

The new branch of the service, the Special Air Police, had been drawn from the army, primarily, but there were also volunteers from the navy and the air service. It had been formed to protect civil aircraft against acts of piracy in the air, against potential saboteurs (there had been threats from fanatics but so far no serious damage done) and to protect passengers who might be bothered either by thieves aboard or criminals, for instance, on the run.

And so I applied and was accepted. I was taken to the Air Service Training School at Cardington and taught some of the mysteries of the wireless telephone used to communicate within the ship and also with the ground, when necessary. I learned how an airship was flown and what the various technical terms meant. I was given a little practical experience in flying – this was really the only exciting part of my training – and taught the mysteries of meteorology and so forth. Although an air policeman was an army officer rather than a flyer, therefore not expected to fly a vessel, it was considered necessary to know what to do, in case of emergencies. Thus, by the end of my first year in the future (a strange sort of contradiction that, in a way) I was commissioned as a Lieutenant in His Majesty's Special Air Police and assigned to the AS *Loch Ness*.

For all she invited the name, the *Loch Ness* was no monster, but a trim little airship of not much more eighty tons, with a useful lift of about sixty tons, and she handled beautifully. I was lucky to be assigned to her, though the captain pooh-poohed the necessity of having me aboard and at first was a bit cool towards me. The bigger an airship, the more docile she normally is, but the little *Loch Ness* was quick-witted, good-natured and reliable. She was never a long hauler. I think the longest run we ever went on was to Gibraltar and the *Loch Ness* was not really equipped for that, being what was called a 'soft-covered' ship (her hull was fabric not 'plastic'), and she didn't have an automatic temperature control, so it was the very devil keeping her gas from expanding in the sort of heat you got in the Med. She taught me a lot about airships. It was a bit of a wrench to leave her, for you become attached to an airship rather as a navy man becomes attached to an ordinary ship. But I had only been assigned to her in order to gain some practical experience and I gather I did pretty well because the Macaphee house (who owned the *Loch Ness*) asked for my CO to put me on board the pride of their line, the recently built *Loch Etive*.

The *Loch Etive* was similar to the first commercial ship on which I'd flown, the *Light of Dresden*. But now that I was familiar with the details of airships, I could fully appreciate her marvels. She was a thousand feet long, with eight diesel engines mounted four a side, with reversible propellers. Her helium capacity was twelve million cubic feet, contained in twenty-four separate bags inside the hull. Her frame was 'duralloy' and she could carry a maximum of four hundred passengers and fifty tons of cargo. She could cruise easily at 100 miles an hour and her top speed was 150 mph in good weather. All her works were housed inside the hull, with the exception of the engine casings and propellers. The inspection catwalks on the top and sides of the hull were covered in and for emergencies we had parachutes, inflatable boats, life jackets and a couple of non-rigid balloons. For the entertainment of the passengers there were kinemas, ballrooms, phonographs, deck sports and party games, restaurants – all anyone might desire concentrated in a space of a quarter of a mile floating two or three thousand feet above the surface of the Earth!

We were doing the round-the-world cruise on what was called the All Red Route (i.e. the colour on the map of the countries in question) but with a trip over the USA thrown in for good measure. We went from Britain via Canada and the USA down to British Ecuador and across to Australia, Hong Kong, Calcutta, Aden, Cairo and back to London. My job was to keep a lookout for suspicious customers, check for weapons, bombs, that sort of thing, and – the least pleasant bit – deal with passenger complaints ranging from petty thefts and card-sharping to suspected sabotage attempts. It was a job which, on the whole, left me plenty of time to enjoy the flights and there were rarely any serious emergencies. We had an interesting selection of passengers from all nations and of all colours and creeds – Indian princes, African tribal leaders, British diplomats, American congressmen, high-ranking soldiers, and once we carried the ageing president of the Chinese Republic (which was scarcely more, I'm sorry to say, than a collection of provinces under the control of various warlords). I was particularly impressed by the education and sophistication of the native leaders, particularly the Africans, many of whom might have been mistaken for English gentlemen, save for the colour of their skins.

The man who had overall responsibility for every detail of the running of the *Loch Etive* and for every soul aboard her was old Captain Quelch, who had been flying airships almost from the start, when it had been altogether a much more perilous business. He had, I learned, been one of the last to command a 'flying bomb', as they called the ships which had been filled with explosive gases, like hydrogen, before the *Elephant* disaster of 1936, when all hydrogen-filled ships had, by international agreement, been grounded and broken up. I gathered that he was not altogether happy about commanding a passenger liner, particularly one as modern as the *Loch Etive*, but on the other hand he hated the idea of retiring. The air, he said, was his natural environment and he was damned if he was going to spend more of his life than he had to in some blasted birdcage in Balham. I got the impression that he would die if he was forced to give up flying. He was one of the most decent men I had ever met and I developed an enormous affection for him, spending much time in his company during the long periods aboard when there was nothing much to do. 'They don't need a blasted captain on that gadget-run bridge,' he would say, a trifle bitterly. 'They could command it by telephone from London if they wanted to.'

I suppose it was my strong affection for Captain Quelch which led to the first disaster of my new life. A disaster which was to lead to others, of increasing consequence, until the final one... But again I'm running ahead of my story.

It all began with a freakish change in the weather after we had left San Francisco, bound for British Ecuador, Tahiti, Tonga and points west. You could blame it on the elements, I suppose, or on me – but I'm rather inclined to blame an offensive little Californian 'scout-leader' called 'Reagan'. Certainly, if Reagan had not come aboard the *Loch Etive* I should not have found myself at the centre of subsequent events – events which were to alter the destinies of a good many people and perhaps even the whole world.

Chapter Two
A Man with a Big Stick

W E WERE MOORED at Berkeley Airpark, taking on cargo and passengers. Because of a delay in finding mast-space, we were a bit behind schedule and hurrying to make up the time as fast as we could. I was keeping an eye on both cargo and passengers, watching the great crates being winched into the bowels of the ship through her loading hatches underneath the lower deck. The liner was secured by about fifty thick steel cables, keeping her perfectly steady at her mast. In the bright sunlight, she cast a wide shadow across the field. I couldn't help feeling proud of her as I looked up. Her hull was silver-blue and the round Union Jack shields shone on her huge tailplanes. Her particulars were emblazoned on her main hull: RMA 801 (her registration number) *Loch Etive*, London. Macaphee Lines, Edinburgh.

All about me were moored ships of American Imperial Airways, the Versailles Line, Royal Austro-Prussian Aerial Navigation Company, Imperial Russian Airship Company, Air Japan, Royal Italian Air Lines and many smaller lines, but the *Loch Etive*, it seemed to me, was the finest. She was certainly one of the most famous aerial passenger liners.

Some distance away from the airpark buildings I made out a green electric omnibus, bouncing over the turf towards our mast. These would be the last of our passengers. Rather late, I thought. I had been warned that the *William Randolph Hearst*, of American Imperial, had developed engine trouble and that, since we flew basically the same route, some of her passengers were being transferred to our ship. Probably these were they. We were almost ready to go. I watched the last item of cargo being winched aboard, saw the loading doors shut in the ship's belly, and with a sense of relief went back towards the mast.

Although there was a lift moving up and down in the central column of the mooring mast, this was for the use of passengers and officers. The ground crew were using the spiral staircase which wound round the lift shaft. I watched them hurrying up to take their positions. The fuel lighters had long since been towed away.

At the entrance to the lift shaft I stood beside the embarkation officers who stood on both sides of the doors, checking boarding cards and tickets. There was nothing suspicious about the well-to-do Americans who were coming aboard, though they seemed a trifle annoyed at discovering they were to fly on a different ship.

I smiled a little as I saw the man at the end of the queue. He was about fifty and dressed rather ridiculously in khaki shorts, knee stockings and green badge-festooned shirt. He carried a polished pole with a little flag on it and on his head was a wide-brimmed brown hat. His comical appearance was heightened by the look of stern self-importance on his red, lumpy face. His knees shone as redly as his nose and I wondered if he were, perhaps, a kinematograph or music-hall comedian who had not had time to change. Behind him were a score of similarly clad boys of about twelve years old, with knapsacks on their backs and poles in their hands, all looking as deadly serious as the man.

'Why on earth is he dressed like that?' I asked the nearest officer.

'It's the American version of the Baden-Powell Youth Brigade,' said the man. 'Weren't you ever in the Brigade?'

I shook my head. 'And what are these?'

'The Roosevelt Scouts,' my informant told me. 'The Young Roughriders, I believe they're called.'

'Their leader doesn't look too young.' The man had now turned his back on me, presenting a bulging posterior on which the khaki cloth threatened to burst.

'A lot of these people stay in the scouts,' said the officer. 'They never grow up. You know the type. Enjoy ordering the kids around.'

'I'm glad I'm not in charge of that gang,' I said feelingly, casting my eye over the pimply faces which glowered nervously now from beneath the brims of their hats. They had plainly not been on an airship before.

Then I noticed something which made me realise I was forgetting my duties. Around the scout-leader's rather portly middle was strapped a leather belt and on the belt was attached a large pistol holster. When he came up to the officer inspecting tickets I waited until he was finished and then saluted politely.

'I'm sorry, sir, but I'm afraid all weapons must be given into the care of the purser until you disembark. If you wouldn't mind handing me your revolver...'

The man gestured angrily with his pole and tried to push past me.

'Come on, boys!'

'I'm sorry, sir, I can't allow you to go aboard until –'

'It is my right to wear a gun if I choose. What sort of tomfool...?'

'International airshipping regulations, sir. If you'll allow me to take the gun I'll get a receipt for it and you can claim it –' I glanced at his tickets – 'when you reach Sydney, Mr Reagan.'

'Captain Reagan,' he snapped. 'Roughriders.'

'Captain Reagan. Unless you give me your pistol, we can't allow you to join the flight.'

'I wouldn't have this trouble on an American ship. Wait until –'

'International regulations apply to American ships as well as British, sir. We shall have to leave without you.' I glanced significantly at my watch.

'Snotty-nosed upstart!' Purple with rage he snarled something else under his breath, then fumbled with his buckle and slid the holster off his belt. He hesitated, then handed it to me. I snapped it open and looked at the gun.

'I know,' he said. 'It's an air pistol. But it's very powerful.'

'The regulations still apply, sir. Are – um – any more of your chaps armed in this way?'

'Of course not. I was in the Roughriders. The real Roughriders. One of the last to be disbanded. Come on, men.' He pointed forward with his pole and marched into the lift, the earnest troop behind him all glaring at me in outrage at my having caused their leader to lose dignity. There was room in the lift for me, but I decided to use the stairs. I wasn't sure I could keep a straight face for very much longer.

Once aboard I gave the gun to the purser and received a receipt in exchange. I gave the receipt to the first steward I encountered and told him to take it to Captain Reagan's cabin. Then I went up to the bridge. We were about to let go. This was when it was worth being on the bridge and I never tired of the experience. One by one the anchor cables were released and I felt the ship surge a little as if impatient to be freed completely and get back aloft. The motors began to murmur and in the side-mirrors I could see the propellers slowly turning. The captain looked forward and then below and checked his periscopes to make sure our stern was clear. He gave the instructions and the catwalk was drawn away from the mast, back into the hull. Now all that held the ship were the couplings attaching her to the mast.

Captain Quelch spoke into the telephone. 'Stand by to slip.'

'Ready to slip, sir,' replied the Mast Controller's voice from the receiver.

'Slip.'

There was a slight jerk as the couplings fell free. The *Loch Etive* began to turn, her nose still nestling in the cone.

'All engines half-speed astern.' By his tone, Captain Quelch was relieved to be on his way. He stroked his white walrus moustache rather as a satisfied cat might stroke its whiskers. The diesels began to roar as we pulled out of the cone. Our bow rose.

'Half-speed ahead,' said the captain. 'Two degrees to port, steering coxswain.'

'Aye, aye, sir. Two degrees to port.'

'Take us up to five hundred feet, height coxswain, and hold steady.'

'Five hundred feet, sir.' The height cox turned the large wheel at which he was positioned. All around us on the spacious bridge instruments were whirring and clicking and we were presented with a display of readings which would have thoroughly confused an old-time ship's captain.

The vast airpark fell away below us and we turned towards the sparkling ocean of San Francisco Bay. We saw the hulls of the land-bound ships dwindling in size. The *Loch Etive* was behaving as beautifully as usual, almost flying herself.

Now we were over the ocean.

'Five degrees to port, steering coxswain,' said Captain Quelch, leaning over the computer console.

'Five degrees to port, sir.'

We began to turn so that from our starboard portholes we could see the skyscrapers of San Francisco – painted in a thousand dazzling colours.

'Take her up to two thousand feet, height coxswain.'

'Two thousand feet, sir.'

Up we went, passing through a few wisps of cloud, into the vast sea of blue which was the sky.

'All engines full ahead.'

With a great roar of power, the mighty engines pushed the ship forward. She surged on at a steady hundred and twenty miles an hour, heading for South America, carrying 385 human souls and 48 tons of cargo as effortlessly as an eagle might carry a mouse.

By that evening, the story of my encounter with the scout-leader had spread throughout the crew. Fellow officers stopped me and asked how I was getting on with 'Roughrider Ronnie' as someone had nicknamed him, but I assured them that, unless he proved to be a dangerous saboteur, I was going to avoid him punctiliously for the rest of the voyage. However, it was to emerge that he did not share my wish.

My second encounter came that night when I was making my tour of duty through the ship, normally a long and rather boring business.

The fittings of the *Loch Etive* were described in the company's brochures as 'opulent' and, particularly in the first-class quarters, they were certainly lavish. Everywhere the 'plastic' was made to look exactly like marble, like oak, mahogany and teak, like steel or brass or gold. There were curtains of plush and silk drawn back from the wide observation ports running the length of the ship, there were deep carpets in blue and red and yellow, comfortable armchairs in the lounges or on the decks. The recreation decks, restaurants, smoking rooms, bars and bathrooms were all equipped with the latest elegant gadgets and blazed with electric lighting. It was this luxury which made the *Loch Etive* one of the most expensive aerial liners in the skies, but most passengers thought it worth paying for.

By the time I had reached the third-class section I was looking forward to turning in. Then, suddenly, from out of a subsidiary passage leading to the dining rooms, stormed the Captain of Roughriders himself. His face was scarlet. He was spluttering with rage and he grabbed me by the arm.

'I've a complaint!' he shouted.

I hadn't expected a compliment. I raised my eyebrows.

'About the restaurant,' he continued.

'That's something to take up with the stewards, sir,' I said in relief.

'I've already complained to the chief steward and he refused to do anything about it.' He eyed me narrowly. 'You are an officer, aren't you?'

I admitted it. 'However, my job is to look after the security of the ship.'

'What about the morals?'

I was frankly astonished. 'Morals, sir?' I stuttered.

'That's what I said, young man. I have a duty to my scouts. I hardly expected them to be subjected to the indignities, the display of loose behaviour... Come with me.'

Out of curiosity more than anything else, I allowed him to lead me into the dining room. Here a rather insipid jazz band was playing and a few couples were dancing. At the tables people were eating or talking and not a few were staring at the table where all twenty boy Roughriders were seated.

'There!' hissed Reagan. 'There! What do you say now?'

'I can't see anything, sir.'

'Nobody told me that I was coming aboard a flying Temple of Jezebel! Immoral women displaying themselves – look! Look!' I was bound to say that the girls were wearing rather scanty evening frocks, but nothing one would not see every night in London. 'And disgusting music – jungle music!' He pointed at the bored-looking band on the rostrum. 'And, worse than that.' He drew closer and hissed in my ear, 'There are, young man, *niggers* eating right next to us. What kind of a decent ship do you call this?'

At the nearest table to the scouts sat a party of Indian civil servants who had recently finished their exams in London and were on their way to Hong Kong. They were well-dressed and sat quietly talking among themselves.

'White boys being forced to eat elbow to elbow with niggers,' Reagan continued. 'We were transferred without our agreement to this ship, you know. On a decent American ship…'

The chief steward came up. He gave me a weary, apologetic look. I thought of a solution.

'Perhaps this passenger and his boys could eat in their cabins,' I suggested to the steward.

'That won't do!' There was a hard, mad gleam in Reagan's eye. 'I have to supervise them. Make sure they eat properly and keep themselves clean.'

I was ready to give up when the steward suggested, poker-faced, that screens might be placed around the table. They would not keep out the music, of course, but at least the captain and his lads would not be forced to see either the scantily dressed ladies or the Indian civil servants. Reagan accepted this compromise with poor grace and was about to return to his table when one of the boys came rushing up, his handkerchief over his mouth, his face very green indeed. Another boy followed. 'I think Dubrowski's being airsick, sir.'

I hurried off, leaving Reagan shouting wildly for a 'medic'.

For all that it is primarily a psychological illness, airsickness can be catching and I soon learned to my relief that Reagan and his entire troop had gone down with it. When, two days later, we reached

Quito in British Ecuador, I had heard nothing more of the scout-master, though I believe one of the ship's doctors had been kept pretty busy.

We made a quick stopover at Quito and took on a few passengers, some airmail and a couple of cages of live monkeys bound for a zoo in Australia.

By the time we headed out over the Pacific, Reagan was well known to crew and passengers alike and though there were some who supported him, he had become to most a figure of some considerable entertainment value.

Captain Quelch had not directly encountered Reagan and he was faintly amused by the reports he had heard concerning my own embarrassment. 'You must be more firm with him, Lieutenant Bastable. It is a particular knack, you know, controlling a difficult passenger.'

'This one's mad, skipper.' We were having a drink in the little bar above the control cabin which was especially for the officers. 'You ought to see his eyes,' I said.

Quelch smiled sympathetically, but it was obvious he put much of my trouble down to my own inexperience and the fact that I was essentially a groundman.

Our crossing of that wide stretch of ocean between South America and the first of the South Sea islands was as peaceful as usual and we flew through blue and sunny skies.

By the time we sighted Puka Puka, however, we were receiving telephoned messages about a freak storm blowing up in the Papeete region. Heavy electrical interference soon cut these messages off, but at this stage we had no trouble keeping the ship in trim. Stewards warned the passengers that it was likely to get a bit bumpy as we neared Tahiti, but we expected to reach the island on time. We took the ship up to 2,500 feet and hoped to avoid the worst of the winds. The engineers working in the diesel nacelles were ordered to keep the *Loch Etive* at full speed ahead when we hit the disturbance.

A few minutes later it became strangely dark and a peculiar, cold grey light streamed through our portholes. The electrics were switched on.

Next moment we had plunged into the storm and heard the thunder of hailstones beating against the huge hull. The sound was like a thousand machine guns going off at once and we could hardly hear one another speak. The temperature dropped dramatically and we shivered with cold until the ship's heating system responded to our need. As thunder and lightning crashed and flashed around us the *Loch Etive* shook a little but her engines roared defiantly back and we plunged on into the swirling black cloud. There was no danger of lightning striking our fully insulated hull. Occasionally the clouds would part to show us the sea boiling about below.

'Glad I'm not down there,' said Captain Quelch with a grin. 'Makes you grateful the airship was invented.'

Soft music began to sound from the telephone receivers on the bridge. The skipper told his second officer to switch it off. 'Never could understand the theory behind that.'

My stomach turned over as the ship fell a few feet and then recovered. I began to feel little tendrils of fear creep into my mind. It was the first time I had felt nervous aboard an airship since Major Powell had picked me up at Teku Benga. That seemed centuries ago now.

'Very dirty weather, indeed,' murmured the captain. 'Worst I've ever known at this time of year.' He buttoned up his jacket. 'How's our height, height cox?'

'Holding steady, sir.'

The door to the bridge opened and the third officer came in. He was furious.

'What's up?' I said.

'Damn it!' he swore. 'I've just had a tangle with your chap, Bastable. Bloody fellow Reagan! Screaming about life rafts and parachutes. He's berserk. Never known a passenger like it. Says we're going down. I've had the most awful shouting match with him. He wanted to see you, sir.' The third officer addressed the captain.

I smiled at Quelch, who grinned wryly back. 'What did you tell him, number three?'

'I think I calmed him down in the end, sir.' The third officer frowned. 'It was all I could do to stop myself punching him on the jaw.'

'Better not do that, number three.' The captain took out his pipe and began to light it. 'Not very good for the company if he sues us, eh? And we've a special responsibility, too – courtesy to American Imperial, that sort of thing.'

The third officer turned to me. 'I suppose he's told you he's got powerful political connections in America. That he'll have you drummed out of the service.'

I laughed. 'No, I haven't had that one yet.'

Then the hail hit us even harder and the wind howled in fury as if at our insolence in remaining airborne. The ship dropped horribly and then readjusted. She shuddered the length of her hull. It was black as night outside. Lightning spat at us on all sides. With some idea of reassuring the passengers and, since there was nothing practical I could do on the bridge, I went towards the door.

And at that moment it burst open and in rushed Reagan, the picture of terrified anger, his white-faced scouts behind him. Reagan gesticulated wildly with his pole as he advanced towards Captain Quelch. 'I've a duty to these boys. Their parents entrusted me with their lives! I demand that life rafts and parachutes be issued to us at once!'

'Please return to your cabin, sir,' said Quelch firmly. 'The ship is perfectly safe. It is much better, however, if passengers are not wandering about – particularly on the bridge. If you are nervous, one of the ship's doctors will give you a sedative.'

Reagan screamed something incoherent in reply. Captain Quelch put his pipe in his mouth and turned his back.

'Please leave my bridge, sir.'

I stepped forward. 'I think you'd better –'

But Reagan had put his beefy hand on Captain Quelch's shoulder. 'Now just look here, captain. I've a right...'

The skipper turned, speaking very coldly. 'I wonder if one of you gentlemen would mind escorting this passenger back to his cabin?'

The third officer and I took hold of Reagan and dragged him back. He made surprisingly little resistance. He was trembling all over. We took him out of the bridge and into the passage, where I called for a couple of ratings to take over from me, for I was furious at the way Reagan had treated Quelch and did not trust myself to deal calmly with the man.

When I got back to the bridge Quelch was sucking on his pipe as if nothing had happened. 'Damned hysterical fool,' he said to no-one in particular. 'Hope this storm blows over soon.'

Chapter Three
Disaster – and Disgrace!

W HEN AT LAST we reached Tahiti and began to drop through
the clouds in the hope of mooring, it became evident that
a full-scale typhoon had hit the island. The ship shuddered and
swerved about in the sky and it was all we could do to keep her in
reasonable trim.

Below whole groves of palms had been bent to the ground by
the wind and a number of buildings had been severely damaged.
Only the three mooring masts in the airpark stood upright and to
these there were already two ships anchored. A whole web of
extra cables had been used to secure them.

After sizing up the situation the skipper ordered the steering
cox to keep circling over the airpark and then left the bridge. 'Back
in a moment,' he said.

The third officer winked at me. 'Gone for a shot of rum, I
shouldn't wonder. Can't blame him, what with the storm *and* that
Reagan chap.'

The big ship continued to circle at full speed against the howling force of a storm which showed no sign of abating. Every so
often I looked down at the airpark and saw that the savage winds
still swept it.

A quarter of an hour passed and still the captain did not reappear
on the bridge. 'It's not like him to be gone so long,' I said.

The third officer tried to get through to the captain's cabin by
telephone but there was no reply. 'Expect he's on his way back,'
he said.

Another five minutes passed and then the third officer told a
rating to go and look in the captain's cabin to make sure he was all
right.

A couple of moments later the rating came running back, a look of terrible consternation on his face. 'It's the captain, sir. Up in the parachute lockers – hurt, sir. There's a doctor coming.'

'Parachute lockers? What's he doing up there?' Since it was impossible for any of the other airship officers to leave the bridge, I followed the rating down the narrow passage and up the short companion ladder leading to the officers' quarters. We passed the captain's cabin and reached another short ladder to the catwalk between the lockers where the life-saving equipment was stored. The light was dim here, but I could make out the captain lying at the foot of the ladder, his face twisted in pain. I knelt beside him.

'Fell down the damned ladder.' The captain spoke with difficulty. 'Broken my leg, I think.' The ship shook as another great gust of wind hit her. 'Blasted Reagan feller – found him trying to open the parachute lockers. Went up to make him come down. He pushed me – ah!'

'Where's Reagan now, sir?'

'Ran off. Scared, I suppose.'

The doctor arrived and inspected the leg. 'A fracture, I'm afraid. You'll be grounded for quite a while, captain.'

I saw the look in the captain's eyes when he heard the doctor's words. It was a look of pure fear. If he was grounded now it would mean he was grounded for ever. He was already well past retirement age. Scout-leader Reagan had successfully ended Quelch's flying days – and therefore ended his life. If I had been close to Reagan at that moment, I think I would have killed him!

Eventually the storm blew itself out and within half an hour we were manoeuvring into the waiting cone on the airpark mast. The sky was completely clear and the sun was shining and Tahiti looked as beautiful as ever. Apart from a bit of damage to some buildings and a few broken trees, you might never have known that the typhoon had been there.

Later, I watched the medical orderlies pick up the captain's stretcher and carry it down to the nose. I saw the lift bear Captain Quelch down to the ground to where the ambulance awaited.

I was miserable. And I was sure I would never see the skipper again. God, how I hated Reagan for what he had done! I have never hated anyone so much in my life. Quelch had been one of the few people in this world of the future to whom I could properly relate – perhaps because Quelch was an old man and therefore more of my world than of his own – and now he was gone. I felt damned lonely, I can tell you. I decided to keep a special watch on 'Captain' Reagan now.

Tonga came and went and we were soon heading for Sydney, making a speed of just under 120 mph against a headwind which was scarcely more than a gentle breeze compared with the typhoon we had recently experienced.

For the whole time since arriving in Tahiti, Reagan and his scouts only left their cabins to eat their meals behind their foolish screens.

At least he seemed cowed by his own stupidity and he knew he had got off lightly regarding the affair of the parachute lockers. When, once, we met in a corridor, he lowered his eyes and did not speak to me as we passed each other.

But then came the incident which was to lead to the real disasters of the coming months.

On the last night before we were due to reach Sydney, a call came through to the bridge from the third-class dining room. Trouble of some kind. It was my duty to go there and sort it out.

Reluctantly, I left the bridge and made my way to the dining hall. In the corner near the galley door there was confusion. White-coated stewards, ratings in midnight blue, men in evening dress and girls in short frocks, were all scuffling about, dragging at a man dressed in the all-too-familiar khaki shorts and green shirt of a Young Roughrider. Around the edges of this mêlée stood a number of frightened boy scouts. I glimpsed Reagan's face then. He was clutching his pole in his hands and striking out at those who tried to hold him. His eyes were staring, his face was purple and he resembled some ludicrous tableau of Custer at the Victory of Little Bighorn. He was screaming incoherently and I caught only a single, distasteful word:

'Niggers! Niggers! Niggers!'

To one side, some of the Indian civil servants were talking to the young officer who had summoned me.

'What's all this about, Muir?' I asked.

Muir shook his head. 'As far as I can tell, this gentleman,' he indicated the civil servant, 'asked if he could borrow the salt from Mr Reagan's table. Mr Reagan hit him, sir, then started on this gentleman's friends...'

I saw now that there was a livid mark on the Indian's forehead.

I pulled myself together as best I could and called out: 'All right, everybody. Let him go. Could you please stand back? Stand back, please.'

Gratefully, the passengers and crew members moved away from Reagan, who stood panting and glaring and plainly out of his mind. With a sudden movement he leapt onto a nearby table, hunched with his stick at the ready.

I tried to speak civilly, remembering that it was my duty to protect both the good name of the shipping company, to protect the name of my own service and to give Mr Reagan no opportunity to sue anyone or use his political connections to harm anyone. It was hard to remember all this, particularly when I hated the man so much. I did my best to feel sorry for him, to humour him. 'It's over now, Captain Reagan. If you will apologise to the gentleman you struck –'

'Apologise? To that scum!' With a snarl, Reagan aimed a blow at me with his pole. I grabbed it and dragged him off the table. If I had struck him then, in order to calm him down, I might have been forgiven. But it was as if his own madness was infectious.

Reagan put his snarling face up against mine and growled: 'Give me my stick, you damned nigger-loving British sissy!'

It was too much for me.

I don't actually remember striking the first blow. I remember punching and punching and being pulled back. I remember seeing his blood flowing from his cut face. I remember shrieking something about what he had done to the skipper. I remember his pole clutched in my hands rising and falling and then I was being pulled back by several ratings and everything became suddenly, terrifyingly calm and Reagan lay on the floor, bruised and bloody and completely insensible, perhaps dead.

I turned, dazed, and saw the shocked faces of the scouts, the passengers, the crew.

I saw the second officer, now in command, come running up. I saw him look down at Reagan's body and say, 'Is he dead?'

'He should be,' said someone. 'But he isn't.'

The second officer came up to me and there was pity in his face. 'You poor devil, Bastable,' he said. 'You shouldn't have done it, old man. You're in trouble now, I'm afraid.'

Of course, I was suspended from duty as soon as I got to Sydney and reported to the local S.A.P. headquarters. Nobody was unsympathetic, especially when they had heard the full story from the other officers of the *Loch Etive*. But Reagan had already given *his* story to the evening papers. The worst was happening. AMERICAN TOURIST ATTACKED BY POLICE OFFICER, said the *Sydney Herald*, and most of the reports were of the sensational kind and most of them were on the front page. The company and the name of the ship were mentioned; His Majesty's most recently formed service, the Special Air Police, were mentioned ('Is this what we may expect from those commissioned to protect us?' asked one paper). Passengers had been interviewed and a non-committal statement from the company's Sydney office was quoted. I had said nothing to the Press, of course, and some of the newspapers had taken this as an admission that I had set upon Reagan without provocation and tried to kill him. Then I received a cable from my CO in London. RETURN AT ONCE.

Depression filled my mind and set there, hard and cold, and I could think nothing but black thoughts on the journey back to London in the aerial man-o'-war *Relentless*. There was no possible excuse, as far as the army was concerned, for my behaviour. I knew I would be court-martialled and almost certainly cashiered. It was not a pleasant prospect.

When I arrived in London I was taken immediately to the S.A.P. headquarters near the small military airpark at Limehouse.

I was confined to barracks, pending a decision from my CO and the War Office as to what to do with me.

As it emerged, Reagan was persuaded to drop his charges against everyone and was further persuaded to admit that he had seriously provoked me, but I had still behaved badly and a court-martial was still in order.

Several days after hearing about Reagan's decision, I was summoned to the CO's office and asked to sit down. Major-General Nye was a decent type and very much of the old school. He understood what had happened but put his position bluntly:

'Look here, Bastable, I know what you've been through. First the amnesia and now this – well, this fit of yours, if you like. Fit of rage, what? I know. But you see we can't be sure you won't have another. I mean – well, the old brainbox and all that – a trifle shaky, um?'

I smiled wryly at him, I remember. 'You think I'm mad, sir?'

'No, no, no, of course not. Nervy, say. Anyway, the long and the short of it is this, Bastable: I want your resignation.'

He coughed with embarrassment and offered me a cigar without looking at me. I refused.

Then I stood up and saluted. 'I understand perfectly, sir, and I appreciate why you want to do it this way. It's decent of you, sir. Of course, you shall have my resignation from the service. Morning all right, sir?'

'Fine. Take your time. Sorry to lose you. Good luck, Bastable. I gather you needn't worry about Macaphees taking any action. Captain Quelch spoke up for you with the owners. So did the rest of the officers, I gather.'

'Thank you for letting me know, sir.'

'Not at all. Cheerio, Bastable.' He got up and shook my hand. 'Oh, by the way, your brother wants to see you. I got a message. He'll meet you at the Royal Aeronautical Club this evening.'

'My brother, sir?'

'Didn't you know you had one?'

I did have a brother. In fact I had three. But I had left them behind in 1902.

Feeling as if I had gone completely mad I left the CO's office, went back to my quarters, composed my letter of resignation, packed my few things into a bag, changed into civilian clothes and took an electric hansom to Piccadilly and the Royal Aeronautical Club.

Why should someone claim to be my brother? There was probably a simple explanation. A mistake, of course, but I could not be sure.

Chapter Four

A Bohemian 'Brother'

A s I sat back in the smoothly moving cab, I stared out of the windows and tried to collect my thoughts. Since the incident with Reagan I had been stunned and only now that I had left my barracks behind me was I beginning to realise the implications of my action. I also realised that I had got off rather lightly, all things considered. Yet my efforts to become accepted by the society of 1974 had, it now appeared, been completely wasted. I was much more of an outsider than when I had first arrived. I had disgraced my uniform and put myself beyond the pale.

What was more, the euphoric dream had begun to turn into a crazy nightmare. I took out my watch. It was only three o'clock in the afternoon. Not evening by anyone's standards. I was uncertain as to what kind of reception I might have at the R.A.C. I was, of course, a member, but it was quite possible they would wish me to resign, as I had resigned from the S.A.P. I couldn't blame anyone for wishing this. After all, I was likely to embarrass the other members. I would leave my visit until the last possible moment. I tapped on the roof and told the cabbie to stop at the nearest pedestrian ingress, then I got out of the cab, paid my fare and began to wander listlessly around the arcades beneath the graceful columns supporting the traffic levels. I stared at the profusion of exotic goods displayed in the shop windows; goods brought from all corners of the Empire, reminding me of places I might never see again. Searching for escape I went into a kinema and watched a musical comedy set in the sixteenth century and featuring an American actor called Humphrey Bogart playing Sir Francis Drake and a Swedish actress (Bogart's wife, I believe) called Greta Garbo as Queen Elizabeth. Oddly, it is one of the clearest impressions I have of that day.

At about seven o'clock I turned up at the club and slipped unnoticed into the pleasant gloom of the bar, decorated with dozens of airship mementoes. There were a few chaps chatting at tables but luckily nobody recognised me. I ordered a whisky and soda, and drank it down rather quickly. I had had several more by the time someone touched me on the arm and I turned suddenly, fully expecting to be asked to leave.

Instead I was confronted by the cheerful grin on the face of a young man dressed in what I had learned was the fashion amongst the wilder undergraduates at Oxford. His black hair was worn rather long and brushed back without a parting. He wore what was virtually a frock coat, with velvet lapels, a crimson cravat, a brocade waistcoat and trousers cut tightly to the knee and then allowed to flare at the bottoms. We should have recognised it in 1902 as being very similar to the dress affected by the so-called aesthetes. It was deliberately Bohemian and dandified and I regarded people who wore this 'uniform' with some suspicion. They were not my sort at all. Where I had escaped notice, this young man had the disapproving gaze of all. I was acutely embarrassed.

He seemed unaware of the reaction he had created in the club. He took my limp hand and shook it warmly. 'You're brother Oswald, aren't you?'

'I'm Oswald Bastable,' I agreed. 'But I don't think I'm the one you want. I have no brother.'

He put his head on one side and smiled. 'How d'you know, eh? I mean, you're suffering from amnesia, aren't you?'

'Well, yes...' It was perfectly true that I could hardly claim to have lost my memory and then deny that I had a brother. I had placed myself in an ironic situation. 'Why didn't you come forward earlier?' I countered. 'When there was all that stuff about me in the newspapers?'

He rubbed his jaw and eyed me sardonically. 'I was abroad at the time,' he said. 'In China, actually. Bit cut off there.'

'Look here,' I said impatiently, 'you know damn' well you're not my brother. I don't know what you want, but I'd rather you left me alone.'

He grinned again. 'You're quite right. I'm not your brother. The name's Dempsey actually – Cornelius Dempsey. I thought I'd say I was your brother in order to pique your curiosity and make sure you met me. Still –' he gave me that sardonic look again – 'it's funny you should be suffering from total amnesia and yet know that you haven't got a brother. Do you want to stay and chat here or go and have a drink somewhere else?'

'I'm not sure I want to do either, Mr Dempsey. After all, you haven't explained why you chose to deceive me in this way. It would have been a cruel trick, if I had believed you.'

'I suppose so,' he said casually. 'On the other hand you might have a good reason for *claiming* amnesia. Maybe you've something to hide? Is that why you didn't reveal your real identity to the authorities?'

'What I have to hide is my own affair. And I can assure you, Mr Dempsey, that Oswald Bastable is the only name I have ever owned. Now – I'd be grateful if you would leave me alone. I have plenty of other problems to consider.'

'But that's why I'm here, Bastable, old chap. To help you solve those problems. I'm sorry if I've offended you. I really did come to help. Give me half an hour.' He glanced around him. 'There's a place round the corner where we can have a drink.'

I sighed. 'Very well.' I had nothing to lose, after all. I wondered for a moment if this dandified young man, so cool and self-possessed, actually knew what had really happened to me. But I dismissed the idea.

We left the R.A.C. and turned into the Burlington Arcade, which was one of the few places which had not changed much since 1902, and stepped into Jermyn Street. At last Cornelius Dempsey stopped at a plain door and rapped several times with the brass knocker until someone answered. An old woman peered out at us, recognised Dempsey, and admitted us to a dark hallway. From somewhere below came the sound of voices and laughter and, by the smell, I judged the place to be a drinking club of some kind. We went down some stairs and entered a poorly lit room in which were set out a number of plain tables. At the tables sat young men and women dressed in the same Bohemian fashion as Dempsey. One or two of them greeted him as we made our way among the tables and sat down in a niche. A waiter came up at once and Dempsey ordered a bottle of red Vin Ordinaire. I felt extremely uncomfortable, but not as badly as I had felt at my own club. This was my first glimpse of a side of London life I had hardly realised existed. When the wine came I drank down a large glass. If I were to be an outcast, I thought bitterly, then I had best get used to this kind of place.

Dempsey watched me drink, a look of secret amusement on his face. 'Never been to a cellar club before, eh?'

'No.' I poured myself another drink from the bottle.

'You can relax here. The atmosphere's pretty free and easy. Wine all right?'

'Fine.' I sat back in my chair and tried to appear confident. 'Now what's all this about, Mr Dempsey?'

'You're out of work at the moment, I take it?'

'That's an understatement. I'm probably unemployable.'

'Well, that's just it. I happen to know there's a job going if you want one. On an airship. I've already talked to the master and he's willing to take you on. He knows your story.'

I became suspicious. 'What sort of a job, Mr Dempsey? No decent skipper would...'

'This skipper is one of the most decent men ever to command a ship.' He dropped his bantering manner and spoke seriously. 'I admire him tremendously and I know you'd like him. He's straight as a die.'

'Then why –?'

'His ship is a bit of a crate. Not one of your big liners or anything like that. It's old-fashioned and slow and carries cargo mainly. Cargo that other people aren't interested in. Small jobs. Sometimes dangerous jobs. You know the kind of ship.'

'I've seen them.' I sipped my wine. The chance was the only sort I might expect and I was incredibly lucky to get it. It was logical that small 'tramp' airships should be short of trained airshipmen when the rewards for working for the big ships were so much greater. And yet, at that moment, I hardly cared. I was still full of bitterness at my own foolishness. 'But are you sure the captain knows the whole story? I was chucked out of the army for good reason, you know.'

'I know the reason,' said Dempsey earnestly. 'And I approve of it.'

'Approve? Why?'

'Just say I don't like Reagan's type. And I admire what you did for those Indians he attacked. It proves you're a decent type with your heart in the right place.'

I'm not sure I appreciated such praise from that young man. I shrugged. 'Defending the Indians was only incidental,' I told him. 'I hated Reagan, because of what he did to my skipper.'

Dempsey smiled. 'Put it how you like, Bastable. Anyway, the job's going. Want it?'

I finished my second glass of wine and frowned. 'I'm not sure…'

Dempsey poured me another glass. 'I'm not trying to persuade you to do something you don't want to – but I might point out that few people will want to employ you as anything more than a deckhand – for a while, at least.'

'I'm aware of that.'

Dempsey lit a long cheroot. 'Perhaps you have friends who've offered you a ground job?'

'Friends? No. I've no friends.' It was true. Captain Quelch had been the nearest thing I had had to a friend.

'And you've experience of airships. You could handle one if you had to?'

'I suppose so. I passed an exam equivalent to a second officer's. I'm probably a bit weak on the practical side.'

'You'll soon learn that, though.'

'How do you happen to know the captain of an air freighter?' I asked. 'Aren't you a student?'

Dempsey lowered his eyes. 'You mean an undergraduate? Well, I was. But that's another story altogether. I've followed your career, you know, since you were found on that mountain-top. You captured my imagination, you might say.'

I laughed then, without much humour. 'Well, I suppose it's generous of you to try to help me. When can I see this captain of yours?'

'Tonight?' Dempsey grinned eagerly. 'We could go down to Croydon in my car. What do you say?'

I shrugged. 'Why not?'

Chapter Five
Captain Korzeniowski

D EMPSEY DROVE DOWN to Croydon at some speed but I was forced to admire the way he controlled the old-fashioned Morgan steamer. We reached Croydon in half an hour.

The town of Croydon is an airpark town. It owes its existence to the airpark and everywhere you look there are reminders of the fact. Many of the hotels are named after famous airships and the streets are crowded with flyers of every nationality. It is a brash, noisy town compared with most and must be quite similar to some of the old sea-ports of my own age (perhaps I should use the future tense for all this and say 'will be' and so on, but I find it hard to do, for all these events took place, of course, in my personal past).

Dempsey drove us into the forecourt of a small hotel in one of the Croydon backstreets. The hotel was called the Airman's Rest and had evidently been a coaching inn in earlier days. It was, needless to say, in the old part of the town and contrasted rather markedly with the bright stone-and-glass towers which dominated most of Croydon.

Dempsey took me through the main parlour full of flyers of the senior generation who plainly preferred the atmosphere of the Airman's Rest to that of the more salubrious hotels. We went up a flight of wooden stairs and along a passage until we came to a door at the end. Dempsey knocked.

'Captain? Are you receiving visitors, sir?'

I was surprised at the genuine tone of respect with which the young man addressed the unseen captain.

'Enter.' The voice was harsh and guttural. A foreign voice.

We walked into a comfortable bed-sitting room. A fire blazed in the grate, providing the only illumination. In a deep leather armchair sat a man of about sixty. He had an iron-grey beard cut in the Imperial style and hair to match. His eyes were blue-grey and their gaze was steady, penetrating, totally trustworthy. He had a great beak of a nose and a strong mouth. When he stood up he was relatively short but powerfully built. His handshake was dry and firm as Dempsey introduced us.

'Captain Korzeniowski, this is Lieutenant Bastable.'

'How do you do, lieutenant.' The accent was thick but the words were clear. 'Delighted to meet you.'

'How do you do, sir. I think you'd better refer to me as plain "mister". I resigned from the S.A.P. today. I'm a civilian now.'

Korzeniowski smiled and turned towards a heavy oak sideboard. 'Would you care for a drink – *Mister* Bastable?'

'Thank you, sir. A whisky?'

'Good. And you, young Dempsey?'

'A glass of that Chablis I see, if you please, captain.'

'Good.'

Korzeniowski was dressed in a heavy white roll-neck pullover. His trousers were the midnight blue of a civil flying officer. Over a chair near the desk, against the far wall I saw his jacket with its captain's rings, and on top of that his rather battered cap.

'I put the proposal to Mr Bastable, sir,' said Dempsey as he accepted his glass. 'And that's why we're here.'

Korzeniowski fingered his lips and looked thoughtfully at me. 'Doubtless,' he murmured. 'Doubtless.' After giving us our drinks he went back to the sideboard and poured himself a modest whisky, filling the glass up with soda. 'You know I need a second officer pretty badly. I could do with a man with rather more experience of flying, but I can't get anyone in England and I don't want the type of man I'd be likely to find out of England. I've read about you. You're hot-tempered, eh?'

I shook my head. Suddenly it seemed to me that I wanted very much to serve with Captain Korzeniowski for I had taken an instant liking to the man. 'Not normally, sir. These were – well, special circumstances, sir.'

'That's what I gathered. I had a fine second officer until recently.

Chap named Marlowe. Got into some trouble in Macao.' The captain frowned and took a cheroot case from his desk. He offered me one of the hard, black sticks of tobacco and I accepted. Dempsey refused with a grin. As he spoke, Captain Korzeniowski kept his eyes on me and I felt he was reading my soul. He spoke rather ponderously and all his actions were slow, calculated. 'You were found in the Himalayas. Lost your memory. Trained for the air police. Got into a fight with a passenger on the *Loch Etive*. Lost your temper. Hurt him badly. Passenger was a bore, eh?'

'Yes, sir.' The cheeroot was surprisingly mild and sweet-smelling.

'Objected to eating with some Indians, I gather?'

'Among other things, sir.'

'Good.' Korzeniowski gave me another of his sharp, penetrating glances.

'Reagan was responsible, sir, for our skipper's breaking his leg. It meant that the old man would be grounded for good. The skipper couldn't bear that idea, sir.'

Korzeniowski nodded. 'Know how he feels. Captain Quelch. Used to know him. Fine airshipman. So your crime was an excess of loyalty, mm? That *can* be a pretty serious crime in some circumstances, eh?'

His words seemed to have an extra significance I couldn't quite divine. 'I suppose so, sir.'

'Good.'

Dempsey said, 'I think, sir, that temperamentally at any rate he's one of us.'

Korzeniowski raised his hand to silence the young man. The captain was staring into the fire, deep in consideration of something. A few moments later he turned round and said, 'I am a Pole, Mr Bastable. A naturalised Briton, but a Pole by birth. If I went back to my homeland, I would be shot. Do you know why?'

'No, sir.'

The captain smiled and spread his hands. 'Because I am a Pole. That is why.'

'You are an exile, sir? The Russians…?'

'Exactly. The Russians. Poland is part of their Empire. I felt that this was wrong, that nations should be free to decide their own destinies. I said so – many years ago. I was heard to say so. And I was exiled. That was when I joined the British Merchant Air Service. Because I was a Polish patriot.' He shrugged. I wondered why he was telling me this, but I felt there must be a point to it, so I listened respectfully. Finally he looked up at me. 'So you see, Mr Bastable, we are both outcasts, in our way. Not because we wish it, but because we have no choice.'

'I see, sir.' I was still puzzled, but said no more.

'I own my ship,' said Korzeniowski. 'She isn't much to look at, but she's a good little craft. Will you join her, Mr Bastable?'

'I would like to, sir. I'm very grateful…'

'You've no need to be grateful, Mr Bastable. I need a second officer and you need a position. The pay isn't very high. Five pounds a month, all found.'

'Thank you, sir.'

'Good.'

I still wondered what connection there could possibly be between the young Bohemian and the old airship skipper. They seemed to know each other quite well.

'I think you'll be able to find accommodation for the night in this hotel, if it suits you,' Captain Korzeniowski continued. 'Join the ship tomorrow. Eight o'clock be all right?'

'Fine, sir.'

'Good.'

I picked up my bag and looked expectantly at Dempsey. The young man glanced at the captain, grinned at me and patted me on the arm. 'Get yourself settled in here. I'll join you later. One or two things to discuss with the captain.' Still in something of a daze I said goodbye to my new skipper and left the room. As I closed the door I heard Dempsey say, 'Now, about the passengers, sir…'

Next morning I took an omnibus to the airpark.

There were dozens of airships moored there, coming and going like monstrous bees around a monstrous hive. In the autumn sunshine the hulls of the vessels shone like silver or gold or alabaster. Before he had left the previous night Dempsey had given me the name of the ship I was to join. She was called *The Rover* (a rather romantic name, I thought) and the airpark authorities had told me she was moored to Number 14 mast. In the cold light of day I was beginning to wonder if I had not accepted the position rather hastily but it was too late for second thoughts. I could always leave the ship later if I found that I wasn't up to what was expected of me.

When I got to Number 14 mast I found that she had been shifted to make room for a big Russian freighter with a combustible cargo which had to be taken off in a hurry. Nobody seemed to know where *The Rover* was now moored.

Eventually, after half an hour of fruitless wandering about, I was told to go to Number 38 mast, right on the other side of the park. I trudged beneath the huge hulls of liners and cargo ships, dodging between the shivering mooring cables, circumnavigating the steel girders of the masts, until at last I saw Number 38 and my new craft.

She was battered and she needed painting, but she was as brightly clean as the finest liner. She had a hard hull, obviously converted from a soft, fabric cover of the old type. She was swaying a little at her mast and seemed, by the way she moved in her cables, very heavily loaded. Her four big, old-fashioned engines were housed in outside nacelles which had to be reached by means of partly covered catwalks, and her inspection walks were completely open to the elements. I felt like someone who had been transferred from the *Oceanic* to take up a position on a tramp steamer. For all that I came from a period of time before any airship had seemed a practical means of travel, my interest in *The Rover* was almost one of historical curiosity as I looked her over. She was certainly weather-beaten. The silvering on her hull was beginning to flake and the lettering of her number (806), name and registration (London) had peeled off in places. Since it was illegal to have even a partially obliterated registration, there were a couple of airshipmen hanging in a pulley platform suspended from the topside catwalk, touching up the transfers with black creosote. She was even older than my first ship, the *Loch Ness*, and much more primitive, with a slightly piratical look about her. I doubted she boasted such things as computers, temperature regulators or anything but the most unsophisticated form of wireless telephone, and her speed could not have been much over 80 mph.

I had a moment of trepidation as I stood there, watching her turn sluggishly in her cables and then, reluctantly, swing back to her original position. She was about six hundred feet long and not an inch of her looked as if it should have been passed as airworthy. I began to climb the mast, hoping that my lateness had not held the ship up.

I got to the top of the mast and entered the cone. From cone to ship there was a narrow gangplank with rope sides. It bent as I set foot on it and began to cross. No special covered gangways for *The Rover*, no reinforced plastic walls so that passengers needn't see the ground a hundred feet below. A peculiar feeling of satisfaction crept over me. After my initial shock, I was beginning to like the idea of flying in this battered old tramp of the skylanes. She had a certain style and there was nothing fancy about her fixtures. She had something of the aura of the early pioneer ships which Captain Quelch had often reminisced about.

As I reached the circular embarkation platform I was greeted by an airshipman in a dirty pullover. He jerked his thumb towards a short aluminium companionway which wound up from the centre of the platform. 'You the new number two, sir? Captain's expecting you on the bridge.'

I thanked him and climbed the steps to emerge on the bridge. It was deserted but for the short, stocky man in the well-pressed but threadbare uniform of a Merchant Air Service captain. He turned, his blue-grey eyes as steady and as contemplative as ever, one of his black cheroots in his mouth, his grey Imperial jutting as he stepped towards me and shook my hand.

'Glad to have you aboard, Mr Bastable.'

'Thank you, sir. Glad to be aboard. I'm sorry I'm late, but...'

'I know, they shifted us to make way for that damned Russian freighter. You haven't delayed us. We're still giving our registration particulars a lick of paint and our passengers haven't arrived yet.' He pointed to where a flight of six steps led to a door in the stern of the bridge. 'Your cabin's through there. You mess with Mr Barry this voyage, but you'll have your own quarters as soon as we drop the passengers. We don't often carry many – though we've deck passengers coming aboard at Saigon – and your cabin's the only one suitable. All right?'

'Thank you, sir.'

'Good.'

I hefted my bag.

'Cabin's on the right,' said Korzeniowski. 'Mine's directly ahead and the passengers' – what will be yours – is on the left. I think Barry's expecting you. See you in fifteen minutes. Hoping to cast off, then.'

I climbed the companionway and opened the connecting door to find myself in a short passage with the three doors leading off it. The walls were of plain grey colour, chipped and scored. I knocked on the door to my right.

'Enter.'

Inside a tall, thin man with a great shock of red hair was sitting in his underclothes on the unmade bottom bunk. He was pouring himself a generous measure of gin. As I entered he looked up and nodded sociably. 'Bastable? I'm Barry. Drink?' He extended the bottle then, as if remembering his manners, offered me the glass.

I smiled. 'Bit early for me. I'm on the top bunk, eh?'

'Afraid so. Not what you're used to, probably, after the *Loch Etive*.'

'It suits me.'

'You'll find a couple of uniforms in the locker, yonder. Marlowe was about your size, luckily. You can stow your other gear there, too. I heard about your fight. Good for you. This is a whole bloody ship of misfits. Not too strong on formal discipline, but we work hard and the skipper's one of the best.'

'I liked him,' I said. I began to put my gear in the locker and then took out a crumpled uniform. Barry was dragging on his trousers and a jersey.

'One of the best,' he repeated. He finished his drink and carefully put bottle and glass away. 'Well, I think I heard the passengers come aboard. We can leave at last. See you on the bridge when we let go.'

As he opened the door to leave I glimpsed the back of one of the passengers entering the opposite cabin. A woman. A woman in a dark, heavy travelling coat. It was odd that Captain Korzeniowski should take on passengers. He didn't seem the type to welcome groundmen. But then it was likely that The Rover was glad to make any extra profit she could. Ships like her ran on a very narrow margin.

A short while later I joined the captain and Mr Barry on the bridge. Height and steering coxswains where at their controls and the wireless-telephone operator was crouched in his cubbyhole in contact with the main traffic building, waiting to be told when we could let slip from our mast.

I looked through the wrap-round window of the bridge at all the fine ships. Our little freighter seemed so out of place here that I would be very glad to get away.

Captain Korzeniowski picked up a speaking tube. 'Captain to all engines. Make ready.'

A second later I heard the grumble of the diesels as their engineers began to warm them up.

The order came through from ground control. We could leave.

The captain took his position in the bow and peered down so that he could see the main mooring chains and the gangway. Barry went to the annunciator and stood by with the tube in his hand. The bosun stood halfway down the companionway to the embarkation platform, his body bisected by the deck of the bridge.

'Gangway withdrawn,' said the captain. 'Close and seal embarkation doors, bosun.'

The bosun relayed this order to an unseen man below. There were noises, thumps, shouts. Then the bosun's head appeared on the companionway again. 'All ready to slip, sir.'

'Let slip.' The captain straightened his back and drove both hands into the pockets of his jacket, his cheroot clamped between his teeth.

'Let slip below,' said Barry into the tube.

There was a jerk as we were released by the mast.

'All cables free.'

'All cables free, below,' said Barry.

The mooring cables snapped away and we were released into the air.

'Engines full astern.'

Barry adjusted a switch. 'All engines full astern.' He was speaking now to the engineers crouched in their outside nacelles, nursing their diesels.

The ship shuddered and bucked slightly as the engines backed her away from the mast.

'Two hundred and fifty feet, height coxswain,' said the captain, still peering through the bow observation port.

'Two hundred and fifty, sir.' The coxswain spun his great metal wheel.

Slowly we crawled into the sky, our bow tilting upward slightly as the elevator coxswain operated his controls, adjusting the tailplanes.

And for the first time I had a sense of loss. I felt I was leaving behind everything I had come to understand about this world of the 1970s, embarking on what for me would be a fresh voyage of discovery. I felt a bit like one of the ancient Elizabethan navigators who had set off to look for the other side of the planet.

Croydon Airpark dropped behind us and we cruised over the fields of Kent towards the coast, gradually rising to a height of a thousand feet, moving at something under fifty miles an hour. The ship responded surprisingly well and I began to realise that there was more to *The Rover* than I had thought. I was learning not to judge an airship by her appearance. Primitive though her controls where, she flew smoothly and steadily and was almost stately in her progress through the sky. Barry, whom I had taken for a drunkard at the end of an unsavoury career, proved an efficient officer and I was to discover he drank heavily only when he was not in the air. I hoped that my stiff manner did not make my fellow officers think me a bit of a prig.

During the first day and night of our journey the passengers failed to emerge from their cabin. This did not strike me as particularly eccentric. They could be suffering from airsickness or perhaps they had no desire to go anywhere. After all, there were no promenade decks or kinemas on *The Rover*. If one wished to walk the length of the ship and see anything but the cargo stacked in semi-darkness, one had to go out onto the outside catwalks and cling to the rails for fear of being blown overboard.

I performed my duties with enthusiasm, if awkwardly at first, anxious to show Captain Korzeniowski that I was keen. I think both the skipper, Barry and the crew understood this and I soon found I was beginning to relax.

By the time we were over the bright blue waters of the Mediterranean and heading for Jerusalem, our first port of call, I had started to get the feel of *The Rover*. She had to be treated gently and with what I can only describe as 'grace'. Handled in this way, she would do almost anything you asked of her. This may seem sentimental and foolish, but there was a sense of affection on that ship – a sense of humanity which extended to crew and craft alike.

But still I didn't see the passengers. They took their meals in their cabin and not in the little mess next to the galley where officers and ratings ate. It began to seem that they were shy of being seen, save by Captain Korzeniowski or Mr Barry, both of whom visited them occasionally.

We had no-one on board who was specifically a navigator or meteorological officer. These duties were shared between the skipper, Barry and myself. The night before we arrived at Jerusalem, I had taken the dog-watch and was checking our course against our charts and instruments when the telephone operator wandered in and started up a conversation. At length he said:

'What do you make of our passengers, Bastable?'

I shrugged. 'I don't make anything of them, Steeton. I've only had a glimpse of one of them. A woman.'

'I think they're refugees,' Steeton said. 'The old man says they're getting off at Brunei.'

'Really. Not the safest spot in the world. Haven't they had bandit trouble there?'

'Terrorists of some kind. Well-organised, I gather. I heard the Germans and Japanese are backing them. Want some of our colonies, I shouldn't wonder.'

'There are agreements. They wouldn't dare.'

Steeton laughed. 'You are a bit green, you know, Bastable. There's trouble brewing all over the East. Nationalism, old man. India, China, South-East Asia. People are getting worried.'

Steeton was a pessimist who relished such prospects. I took everything he said with a pinch of salt.

'I shouldn't be surprised if our passengers aren't countrymen of the old man. Polish exiles. Or even Russian anarchists, eh?'

I laughed aloud. 'Come off it, Steeton. The skipper would have nothing to do with that sort of thing.'

Steeton shook his head in mock reproof. 'Oh dear, oh dear, Bastable. You *are* green. Sorry to have interrupted.' He sauntered out of the bridge. I smiled and dismissed his bantering. He was plainly trying to agitate me. The sort of joke which is often played on 'new boys' on board any ship. Still, the passengers did seem anxious to keep themselves to themselves.

Next morning we moored at Jerusalem and I changed into my whites before seeing to the cargo, which was mainly boxes of farming machinery being delivered to the Palestinian Jewish immigrants. It was hot and dry and there was some confusion over two boxes which they had been expecting and which hadn't arrived.

Since I hadn't joined the ship until the cargo had all been taken on, I sent someone to find the captain. While I waited I bought an English-language newspaper from the boy who was selling them around the airpark. I glanced at it casually. The only real news concerned a bomb explosion at the house of Sir George Brown a few days earlier. Luckily Sir George had been away and a servant had been the sole person slightly hurt. But the papers were understandably upset by the outrage. The words *Freedom for the Colonies* had been scrawled on the wall of the house. The whole thing was plainly the work of fanatics and I wondered what kind of madmen could consider such means worthwhile. There were six or eight photographs of people suspected of being connected with the murder attempt, among them the notorious Count Rudolf von Bek, who had long since been chased out of his Saxon homeland and had, until the bombing, been thought to be in hiding in Italy. Why a nobleman should turn against his own kind and all the ideals of his upbringing, nobody could understand.

Eventually the captain arrived and began to sort out the confusion. I folded the newspaper in my back pocket and continued with my duties.

The ways of Fate are strange indeed. It is hard to understand their workings – and I should know, for I have had enough experience of them, one way or another. What happened next is a fair example.

One of the cargo handlers had left a baling hook in a packing case and, as I moved into the hold, I caught my shirt against it, ripping it right across the back. It wasn't serious and I carried on with my job until the captain noticed what had happened.

'You'll get your back sunburned, if you're not careful,' he said. 'You'd better go and change, Mr Bastable.'

'If you think so, sir.' I let one of our riggers keep an eye on the cargo, went through the main passage between the holds and climbed the companionway up to the bridge and from there to my cabin. It was stinking hot in the little passage and all the doors of the cabins were open. For the first time, I got a clear look at the passengers as I passed. I couldn't stop and gape at them, though it took a considerable effort of will not to do so. I went into my own cabin and closed the door.

I was shaking as I sat down on the lower bunk and slowly removed the folded newspaper from my pocket. I had seen a man and a woman in the passenger cabin. The woman I had not recognised, but the face of the man was all too familiar. I opened the newspaper and looked again at the photographs of the anarchists wanted in connection with the attempt on Sir George Brown's life. My brain seething with a hundred different thoughts, I looked hard at one of the photographs. There was no doubt about it. The tall, handsome man I had seen in the cabin was Count Rudolf von Bek, the notorious anarchist and assassin!

Tears came into my eyes as the implications of this revelation dawned on me.

The kindly old airship skipper who had impressed me so much as a man of character and integrity, into whose hands I had so willingly put my fate, was himself at very least a socialist sympathiser!

I was overwhelmed by a profound sense of betrayal. How could I have misjudged someone so badly?

I should, of course, contact the authorities and warn them at once. But how could I leave the ship without arousing suspicion? Doubtless all the officers and every member of the crew were of the same desperate persuasion as their captain. It was unlikely that I would reach the police in Jerusalem alive. And yet it was my duty to try.

Time must have passed rapidly while I carried on this debate with myself for, suddenly, I felt the ship lurch and I realised that we had already let slip from the mooring mast.

I was aloft, helpless now to do anything, in a ship full of dangerous and fanatical men who would certainly stop at nothing to silence me if they realised I suspected them.

With a groan I buried my head in my hands.

What a fool I had been to trust Dempsey – evidently, now, one of the same gang! I put it down to the fact that I had been badly disorientated after giving in my resignation.

The door opened suddenly and I jumped nervously. It was Barry. He was smiling. I looked at him in horror. How could he disguise his true nature so well?

'What's the matter, old chap?' he asked blandly. 'Touch of the sun? The old man sent me to see if you were all right.'

'Who –?' I spoke with great effort. 'The – the passengers – why are they aboard?' I wanted to hear him give me an answer which would prove his and Captain Korzeniowski's innocence.

He looked at me in surprise for a moment and then said, 'What – them across the passage? Why, they're just old friends of the skipper's. He's doing them a favour.'

'A favour?'

'That's right. Look here, you'd better lie down for a bit. You should have worn a hat, you know. Would you like a drop of something strong to pull you round?' He moved towards his locker.

How could he act so casually? I could only suppose that a life led so long beyond the bounds of the Law created an attitude of indifference both to the suffering caused to others and the corruption in one's own soul.

What chance had I against such men as Barry?

Book Three

The Other Side of the Coin — The Tables Turned — Enter the Warlord of the Air — and Exit the Temporal Excursionist...

Chapter One
General O.T. Shaw

A s I LAY there in the cabin thinking back over the events of the past few days, I realised how Cornelius Dempsey, and later his compatriots in crime, had come to believe I was one of them. Seen from their perspective, my attack on Reagan had been an attack on the kind of authority he represented. Several hints had been dropped and, in misinterpreting them, I had allowed myself to be sucked into this appalling situation.

'We are both outcasts, in our way,' Captain Korzeniowski had said. Only now was I aware of the significance of those words! He thought me as desperate a character as himself! A socialist! An anarchist, even!

But then it began to dawn on me that I was in the perfect position to win back my honour – for every disgrace to be forgotten – to ensure that I was reinstated in the service I loved.

For they did not suspect me. They thought me one of themselves, still. If I could somehow seize control of the ship and force it to turn back to a British airpark, I could then deliver the lot of them to the police. I should become a hero (not that I wanted honours for their own sake) and almost certainly I would be asked to rejoin my regiment. And then in my mind's eye I saw Captain Korzeniowski's face, his steady eyes, and I felt a dreadful pang. Was I to deliver this man into captivity? A man who had befriended me? A man who seemed so decent on the surface?

I hardened my heart. That was why he had managed to remain at liberty for so long – because he *seemed* so decent. He was a devil. Doubtless he had deceived many others in his long career of anarchy and crime, fooling them as he had fooled me.

I stood up, moving stiffly as if under the power of a mesmerist. I walked to Barry's locker, where I knew he kept a large service revolver. I opened the locker. I took out the revolver and made sure that it was loaded. I tucked it into my belt and put on my jacket so that the gun was hidden.

Then I sat down again and tried to make a plan.

Our next port of call was Kandahar in Afghanistan. Although nominally allied to Britain, Afghanistan was notoriously fickle in her loyalties. In Kandahar there were Russians, Germans, Turks and Frenchmen, all conspiring to win that mountainous state to their side, all playing what Mr Kipling calls the Great Game of politics and intrigue. Even if I was able to leave the ship, there was no certainty that I should find a sympathetic ear in Kandahar. What then? Force the ship to turn back to Jerusalem? There were difficulties there, too. No, I must wait until we had let slip from Kandahar airpark and were on our way to the third port of call – Lahore, in British India.

So, until Kandahar was behind us, I must continue to try to act normally. Reluctantly, I replaced Barry's revolver in his locker. I drew a deep breath, tried to relax my features, and went up onto the bridge.

How I managed to deceive my new 'friends' I shall never know. I carried out my normal duties over the next few days and was as efficient as ever. Only in conversation with Korzeniowski, Barry or the others did I have difficulty. I simply could not bring myself to speak casually with them. They thought that I was still suffering some slight effects from the sun and were sympathetic. If I had not discovered them for what they were, I should have believed that their concern was genuine. Perhaps it was genuine – but they thought they were concerned for the well-being of one of their own.

Kandahar was reached – a walled city of bleak stone buildings which had not changed since my own day – and then we had left it. The tension within me increased. Again I availed myself of Barry's revolver. I checked the charts assiduously, waiting for the moment when we had crossed the border and arrived in India (which was now, of course, completely under British rule). Within a day we should be in Lahore. Feigning sickness once more,

I remained in my cabin and in my mind sketched out the final details of my plan.

I had ensured that none of the crew members nor the officers carried weapons. My plan depended on this fact.

The hours ticked by. We were due to moor at Lahore at noon. At eleven o'clock I left my cabin and went onto the bridge.

Captain Korzeniowski was standing with his back to the door, staring down through wisps of cloud at the brown, sun-beaten plains drifting past below us. Barry was at the compass, working out the best path of approach to Lahore airpark. The telephone operator was bent over his apparatus. Height and steering coxes were studying their controls. Nobody saw me as I entered silently and drew the revolver from my belt, holding it behind my back.

'Everything clear for Lahore?' I said.

Barry looked up, frowning. 'Hello, Bastable. Feeling better?'

'Absolutely top-hole,' I said. There was a funny note to my voice which even I heard.

Barry's frown darkened. 'Splendid,' he said. 'If you feel like resting a bit longer, there's three quarters of an hour at least before we moor...'

'I'm fine. I just wanted to make sure we do get to Lahore.'

Korzeniowski turned, smiling. 'Why shouldn't we? Have you seen something in your teacup?'

'Not my teacup... I'm afraid you've been under a misapprehension about me, captain.'

'Have I?' He raised his eyebrows and continued to puff on his pipe. His coolness maddened me. I revealed the gun in my hand. I cocked the hammer.

'Yes,' he said, without changing his tone or his expression. 'I think you may be right. More than a touch of the sun, mm?'

'Nothing to do with the sun, captain. I trusted you – trusted you all. I suppose it isn't your fault – after all, you thought I was one of you. "Temperamentally, at least", to quote your friend Dempsey. But I'm not. I made the mistake of thinking you decent men – and you made the mistake of thinking me a villain like yourselves. Ironic, isn't it?'

117

'Very.' Still Korzeniowski's demeanour did not alter. But Barry was looking startled, glancing first at my face and then at the captain's, as if he thought we had both gone mad.

'You know what I'm talking about, of course,' I said to Korzeniowski.

'I must admit I'm not sure, Bastable. If you want my frank opinion, I think you're having a fit of some kind. I hope you don't intend to hurt anyone.'

'I'm extremely rational,' I said. 'I have discovered what you and your crew are, captain. I mean to take this ship to Lahore – the military section of the airpark – and there deliver it and you up to the authorities.'

'For smuggling, perhaps?'

'No, captain – for treason. You pointed out to me that you were a British subject. For harbouring wanted criminals – your two passengers. Von Bek and the girl. You see, I know who they are. And I know what you are – anarchist sympathisers, at best. At worst, well…'

'I see that I did misjudge you, my boy.' Korzeniowski removed the pipe from his mouth. 'I did not want you to find out about our passengers because I wanted you to share no part of the burden – in case we were caught. My sympathies do, in fact, lie with people like Count von Bek and Mrs Persson – she is the count's lady friend. They are what I think of as moderate radicals. You think they had something to do with the bombings?'

'The newspapers do. The police do.'

'That is because they will brand everyone with the same iron,' Korzeniowski said. 'As you doubtless do.'

'You can't talk your way out of this, captain.' My hand had begun to shake and for a moment I felt a weakening of my resolve. 'I know you for the hypocrite you are.'

Korzeniowski shrugged. 'This is silly. But I agree – it is also ironic. I thought you, well, neutral, at least.'

'Whatever else I am, captain, I am a patriot,' I said.

'I think that I am that, too,' he smiled. 'I believe most strongly in the British ideal of justice. But I should like to see that ideal spread a little further than the shores of one small island. I should like to see it put into practice the world over. I admire what Britain stands for in many ways. But I do not admire what she has done to her colonies, for I have had some experience of what it is to live under foreign rule, Bastable.'

'Russia's conquest of Poland is scarcely the same as Britain's administration of India,' I said.

'I see no great difference, Bastable.' He sighed. 'But you must do what you think right. You have the gun. And the man with the gun is always right, eh?'

I refused to be drawn into this trap. A typical Slav, he had proved to be a superb logic-splitter.

Barry broke in, his Irish brogue seemingly thicker than before. 'Conquest – administration – or, in the American's terms, the loan of "advisors" – it's all the same, Bastable, me boy. And it has the same vice at its root – the vice of greed. I've yet to see a colony that is better off than the nation which colonised it. Poland – Ireland – Siam...'

'Like most fanatics,' I pointed out coolly, 'you share at least one characteristic with children – you want everything *now*. All improvements take time. You cannot make the world perfect over-night. Things are considerably better for more people today than they were in my – in the early years of this century, for instance.'

'In some ways,' Korzeniowski said. 'But the old evils remain. And will continue until those who have the most power are made to understand that they *are* promoting evil.'

'And you would make them understand by exploding bombs, murdering ordinary men and women, agitating ignorant natives to take part in risings in which they are bound to come off worst? That is not my idea of people who oppose evil.'

'Nor is it mine, in those terms,' said Korzeniowski.

'Von Bek has never let off a bomb in his life!' said Barry.

'He has given his blessing to those who do. It is the same thing,' I countered.

I heard a small sound behind me and tried to back away to see what caused it. But then I felt something press forcefully into my ribs. A hand appeared and covered the cylinder of my revolver and a quiet, slightly amused voice said:

'I suppose you are right, Herr Bastable. When all is said and done, we are what we are. Our temperaments are such that we support one side or the other. And, I'm afraid, your side is not doing too well today.'

Before I could think, he had taken the gun from my hand and I turned to confront the cynically smiling face of the arch-anarchist himself. Behind him stood a pretty girl dressed in a long, black travelling coat. Her short, dark hair framed her heart-shaped, serious little face and she stared at me curiously with steady, grey eyes which reminded me immediately of Korzeniowski's.

'This is my daughter, Una Persson,' said the captain from over my shoulder. 'You know Count von Bek already, of course.'

Once again I had failed to fulfil an ambition in this world of the future. I became convinced that I was doomed never to succeed in anything I set out to do. Was it simply because I was a man existing in a period of history not his own? Or, faced with similar situations in my own time, would I have bungled my opportunities as I had these?

This was the drift of my thoughts as I sat in my cabin, a prisoner, as the ship came and went from Lahore and began heading for its next destination, which was Calcutta. After Calcutta was Saigon where the 'deck passengers' were due to come aboard, and then Brunei, where von Bek and his beautiful woman friend were bound (doubtless to join the terrorists seeking to end British rule there). After Brunei we were due to pay a call at Canton, where we would put off the pilgrims who were our deck passengers (or more likely terrorist friends of Korzeniowski's!) and then start back, via Manila and Darwin. I wondered which of these ports I should visit before the anarchists decided what to do with me. Probably they were trying to decide that now. It should not be difficult to claim that I had been lost overboard at some convenient point.

Barry brought my food in, his own revolver once again in his possession. So distorted was his point of view that he seemed genuinely sorrowful that I had turned out to be a 'traitor'. Certainly he seemed more sympathetic than angry. I still found it hard to see Barry and Korzeniowski as villains and once I asked Barry if Una Persson, the captain's daughter, was in some way a hostage for the captain's good behaviour. Barry laughed at this and shook his head. 'No, me boy. She's her father's daughter, that's all there is to that!' But it was evidently the connection – why *The Rover* had been chosen as the vessel in which they had made their escape from Britain. It also proved to me that the captain's moral sensibilities must be stunted, to say the least, if he allowed his daughter to share a cabin with a man to whom she was evidently not married (where was Mr Persson? I wondered – doubtless another anarchist who *had* been apprehended). Plainly I did not have much chance of living more than a few hours longer.

I had one hope. Steeton, the telephone operator, had certainly not been in the know about von Bek's identity. Although he might have other reasons for choosing to serve aboard *The Rover*, he was not the committed socialist the others were. Perhaps I could bribe Steeton in some way? Or offer him help, if he needed it, if he would help me now. But how was I to contact Steeton? And if I did contact him, would he not fall under suspicion and be unable to get a telephone message out to a British airpark?

I stared through the tiny porthole of my cabin. When we had berthed at Lahore, von Bek had kept me at gunpoint so that I might not shout out or drop a message through. I could see nothing but grey clouds going on and on for miles. And all I could hear was the steady roar of *The Rover*'s cumbersome engines, bearing me, it seemed, closer and closer to my doom.

At Calcutta, von Bek once again joined me in my cabin, his revolver pointing at my breast. I glanced out at the sunshine, at a distant city I had known and loved in my own time but now could not recognise. How could these anarchists say that British rule was bad when it had done so much to modernise India? I put this to von Bek, who only laughed.

'Do you know how much a pair of good boots costs in England?'

'About ten shillings,' I said.

'And here?'

'Probably less.'

'About thirty shillings in Calcutta – if you are an Indian. About five shillings if you are a European. Europeans, you see, control the bootmaking trade. While they are able to buy from source, the Indian has to buy from a shop. Retail shops need to charge thirty shillings and this is what the average Indian earns in a month. Food costs more in Delhi than it does in Manchester, but the Indian workman earns a quarter of what the English workman earns. You know why this is?'

'No.' It seemed a pack of lies to me.

'Because Britain's prices and incomes are maintained artificially, at the expense of her colonies. All trade agreements favour her. She sets the price at which she buys. She controls the means of production so that the price remains stable, no matter how the market fluctuates. The Indian starves so that the Briton may feast. It is the same in all colonies and "possessions" and protectorates, no matter how it is dressed up.'

'But there are hospitals, welfare programmes, there is a dole system,' I said. 'The Indian does not starve.'

'True – he is kept alive. It is silly to let your pool of available labour die altogether, for you never know when you may next need it. Slaves represent wealth, do they not?'

I refused to rise to this sort of inflammatory stuff. I was not sure his economics were particularly sound, for one thing, and for another I was certain that he saw everything through the distorting glass of his own mind.

'All I know is that the average Indian is better off than he was in 1900,' I said. 'Better off than many English people were in those days.'

'You have seen only the cities. Do you know that Indians are only allowed to come to the cities if they have permission from the government? They must carry passes which say they have a job here. If they have no job, they are returned to the countryside where they live in villages where schools, hospitals and all the other advantages of British rule are few and far between. This sort of system applies throughout Africa and the East. It has been developed over the years and now even applies to some European colonies – Poland under the Russians, Bohemia under the Germans.'

'I know the system,' I said. 'It is not inhumane. It is merely a means of controlling the flow of labour, of stopping the cities from turning into the slums they once were. Everyone benefits.'

'It is a system of slavery,' said the aristocratic anarchist. 'It is unjust. It leads to further erosions of liberty. You support tyrants, my friend, when you support such a system.'

I smiled and shook my head. 'Ask the Indian man in the street how he feels. He will tell you he is satisfied, I am sure.'

'Because he knows no better. Because the British conspire to teach him just a little – enough to confuse his mind and let him swallow their propaganda, no more. It is strange that their educational spending remains the same, when certain other forms of "welfare" spending go up to meet the demand. Thus have you broken the spirit of those you have conquered. You are the ones who speak complacently of free enterprise, of a man standing on his own feet, of "bettering himself" by his own efforts – and then are horrified when those you colonise resent your patronage, your "system of controlling the flow of labour". Bah!'

'I might remind you,' I said, 'that, compared with seventy years ago, this world has a stability it has previously never known. There have been no major wars. There have been a hundred years of peace throughout most of the world. Is that an evil?'

'Yes – for your stability has been achieved at the expense of the pride of others. You have destroyed souls, not bodies, and in my opinion that is an evil of the worst kind.'

'Enough of this!' I cried impatiently. 'You're boring me, Count von Bek. You should feel satisfied that you have defeated my plans. I'll listen no longer. I regard myself as a decent man – a humane man – indeed, a liberal man – but your kind makes me want to – want to – well, I had better not say...' I controlled my temper.

'You see!' von Bek laughed. 'I am the voice of your conscience. That which you refuse to hear. And you are so determined not to hear it that you would wipe out anyone who tries to make you hear! You are so typical of all those "decent", "humane" and "liberal" men who hold two thirds of the world in slavery.' He gestured with his pistol. 'It is strange how all authoritarians automatically assume that the libertarian wishes to impose his own views on them when all he actually wants to do is to appeal to the authoritarian's better nature. But I suppose you authoritarians can only see things in your own terms.'

'You cannot confuse me with your arguments. At least give me the privilege of spending my last hours in silence.'

'As you wish.'

Until we let slip from the mooring mast, he said little, save to mutter something about the 'dignity of man' having come to mean nothing more than the 'arrogance of the conqueror'. But I shut my ears to his ravings. It was he who was arrogant, in seeking to foist his revolutionary notions onto me.

During the next part of the voyage I made desperate efforts to contact Steeton, saying that I was sick of my food being brought by Barry and I would enjoy seeing a face other than his.

Instead, they sent me the captain's daughter. Her grace and her beauty were such that I could scarcely scowl at her as I had at the others. I tried, once or twice, to find out from her what her father intended to do with me but she said he was still 'puzzling it over'. Would she help me? I asked directly. She seemed astonished at this and made no reply of any sort, but left the cabin in some haste.

At Saigon – I could tell it must be Saigon by the glitter of gilded temples in the distance – I heard the babble of the Indo-Chinese pilgrims taking their places in the space allotted for them amongst the bales of cargo. I did not envy them those hot, cramped quarters, but, of course, they were lucky – if they were genuine Buddhist pilgrims – to get an airship passage at all.

Once again – although Saigon was a 'free' port, under American patronage – I was guarded vigilantly by a Count Rudolf von Bek, who seemed less sure of himself than on the previous occasions we had met. He was definitely ill at ease and it occurred to me that the American authorities might have had some wind of *The Rover*'s mission and were asking awkward questions. We certainly left in what seemed to be a hurry and took the air scarcely three hours after we had moored and refuelled, the engines going full out.

Later that evening I heard from across the little passage the sounds of voices raised in argument. I recognised the voices as belonging to von Bek, the captain, Barry and Una Persson – and there seemed to be another voice, softer and very calm, which I did not recognise.

I heard a few words – 'Brunei' – 'Canton' – 'Japanese' – 'Shantung' – mainly names of places which I recognised, but I could not guess the nature of the argument.

A day passed and I was brought food only once – by Una Persson, who apologised that it was a cold meal. She looked strained and rather worried. I asked her if anything were wrong. It was politeness which made me ask. She gave me a baffled look and a brief, bewildering smile. 'I'm not sure,' was all she said before leaving and locking my door on the outside as usual.

It was at midnight, when we must have been well on our way to Brunei, that I heard the first shot. At first I thought it was a sound made by one of the engines, but I knew at once that I was wrong.

I got up, still dressed in my clothes, and stumbled to the door, pressing my ear against it and listening hard. Now I heard more shots – shouting – the sound of running feet. What on earth was happening? Had the villains fallen out amongst themselves? Or had we landed without my realising it and taken on a boarding party of British or American police?

I went to the porthole. We were still airborne, flying high over the China Sea, if my guess were right.

The sounds of fighting went on for at least another half an hour. Then there were no more shots, but voices raised in angry exchange. Then the voices died. I heard footfalls in the passage, I heard the key turn in the lock on my door.

Light burst in and half-blinded me.

I blinked at the tall figure which stood framed in the opening, a revolver in one hand, his other hand on the doorknob. He was dressed in flowing Asiatic robes but his handsome face was distinctly Eurasian – a mixture of Chinese and English if I were not mistaken.

'Good morning, Lieutenant Bastable,' he said in perfect Oxford English. 'I am General O.T. Shaw and this ship is now under my command. I believe you have some flying time. I should be very grateful if you would allow me to avail myself of that experience.'

My jaw dropped in stupefied astonishment.

I knew that name. Who did not? The man who addressed me was known far and wide as the fiercest of the bandit chieftains who plagued the Central Government of the Chinese Republic. This was Shuo Ho Ti – Warlord of Chihli!

Chapter Two
The Valley of the Morning

MY FIRST THOUGHT was that I had been lifted out of the frying pan into the fire. But then I realised that it was the habit of many Chinese warlords to hold their European prisoners to ransom. With luck, my government might pay for my release. I smiled to myself when I thought that Korzeniowski and company had innocently taken on board a gang of rascals even more villainous than themselves. Here was the best irony of them all.

General O.T. Shaw (or Shuo Ho Ti as he styled himself for the sake of his Chinese followers) had built himself an army of bandits, renegades and deserters so big that it controlled large areas of the provinces of Chihli, Shantung and Kiangsu, giving Shaw a stranglehold on the routes between Peking and Shanghai. He charged such an extortionate sum as a 'toll' on trains and motors which came through his territory that trade and communications between the two cities were now conducted almost wholly by airship – and not every airship was safe if it flew low enough to be shot at by Shaw's cannon. The Central Government was powerless against him and too fearful of seeking assistance from the foreigners who administered large parts of China which were not in the Republic. For the foreigners – Russians and Japanese for the most part – might make it their excuse to occupy that territory and refuse to leave. This was what gave Shaw – and warlords like him – his power.

I had been taken aback at meeting such a famous and romantic figure in the flesh. But now I managed to speak.

'Why – why should you want me to fly the ship?'

The tall Eurasian smoothed his straight, black hair and looked more like a devil than ever as he replied softly: 'I'm afraid Mr

Barry is dead. Captain Korzeniowski is wounded. You are the only person qualified to do the job.'

'Barry dead?' I should have been exultant, but instead I felt a sense of loss.

'My men reacted hastily when they saw he had a gun. They are frightened, you see, of being so high in the air. They feel that if they die the spirits of the upper regions – devils all – will capture their souls. They are ignorant, superstitious men, my followers.'

'And how badly is Captain Korzeniowski hurt?'

'A head wound. Not a serious one. But, naturally, he is very dizzy and not up to commanding the ship.'

'His daughter – and Count von Bek?'

'They are locked in their cabin, with the captain.'

'Steeton?'

'He was last seen on the outer catwalk. I believe he fell over-board during a fight with some of my men.'

'My God,' I muttered. 'My God.' I felt sick. 'This is piracy. Murder. I can hardly believe it.'

'It is all of those things, I regret to say,' said Shaw. I recognised the soft voice now, of course. I had heard it earlier when they had been arguing in the opposite cabin. 'But we do not wish to kill any more, now that we have control of the ship and can fly it to Shan-tung. None of this would have happened if your Count von Bek had not insisted we go to Brunei, even though I warned him that the British were aware he was aboard *The Rover* and would be waiting for him there.'

'How did you know that?'

'It is the duty of a leader to know everything he can and so bene-fit his people accordingly,' was the rather ambiguous reply.

'And what will you do for me if I agree to help you?' I asked.

'It is what we shall do to the others which might interest you more. We shall refrain from torturing them to death. This might not impress you, however, since they are enemies of yours. But they *are* –' he lifted his right eyebrow sardonically – 'fellow white men.'

'Whatever they are – and I've nothing but contempt for them – I wouldn't want them tortured by your ruffians.'

'If all goes well, nobody will be harmed.' Shaw uncocked his revolver and lowered it, but he did not put it back in the holster at his hip. 'I assure you that I do not enjoy killing and I give you my word that the lives of all aboard *The Rover* will be spared – *if* we reach the Valley of the Morning safely.'

'Where is this valley?'

'In Shantung. It is my headquarters. We will guide you when you reach Wuchang. It is expedient that we reach there quickly. Originally we meant to go to Canton and move overland from there, but someone had telephoned that we were aboard – Steeton, I suppose – and it became obvious we must go directly to our base, without pause. If Count von Bek had not objected to this plan, all trouble might have been averted.'

So Steeton had been on my side! In trying to save me and warn the authorities of all that was happening aboard *The Rover*, he had brought about this disaster and caused his own death.

It was horrible. Steeton had, in effect, died trying to save me. And now his killer was asking me to fly him to safety. But if I did not, others would die, too. Though some of them deserved death, they did not deserve to have it served to them in the manner which Shaw had hinted at. I sighed deeply and my shoulders sagged as I made my reply. All heroics seemed pointless now.

'I have your word that we shall not be harmed if I do as you wish?'

'You have my word.'

'Very well, General Shaw. I'll fly your damned airship.'

'That's very decent of you, old man,' said Shaw beaming and clapping me on the shoulder. He holstered his revolver.

When I arrived on the bridge my horror was increased by the sight of the blood spattered everywhere on the floor, the bulkheads, the instruments. At least one person had been shot at close range – probably poor Barry. The coxswains were at their positions. They looked pale and shocked. Beside each coxswain stood two Chinese bandits, their bodies criss-crossed with bandoliers of bullets, their belts bristling with knives and small arms. I had never in my life seen such a murderous gang as Shaw's followers. No attempt had been made to clean the mess, and charts and log-tables were scattered about the bridge, some of them soaked in blood.

'I can do nothing until all this is cleaned up,' I said bleakly. Shaw said something in Cantonese and, very reluctantly, two of the bandits left the bridge to return with buckets and mops. As they worked, I inspected the instruments to make sure they were still in working order. Apart from some dents caused by bullets, nothing was badly damaged except the telephone, which looked to me as if it had been scientifically destroyed, perhaps by Steeton himself before he had made a run for the outer catwalk.

At last the bandits finished. Shaw gestured towards the main controls. We were flying very low at not much more than three hundred feet – a dangerous height.

'Put her up to seven hundred and fifty feet, height coxswain,' I said grimly. Without a word, the coxswain did as he was ordered. The ship tilted steeply and Shaw's eyes narrowed, his hand going to his holster, but then we levelled out. I found the appropriate charts for China and studied them.

'I think I can get us to Wuchang,' I said. If necessary, we could always follow the railway line, but I doubted if Shaw was prepared to drop speed. He seemed anxious to get into his own territory by morning. 'But before I begin, I want to be certain that Captain Korzeniowski and the others are still alive.'

Shaw pursed his lips and gave me a hard look. Then he turned on his heel. 'Very well. Follow me.' Another order in Cantonese and a bandit fell into step behind me.

We reached the middle cabin and Shaw took a key from his belt, unlocking the door.

Three wretched faces stared up at us from the cabin. A crude bandage had been tied around Captain Korzeniowski's head. It was soaked in blood. His face was ashen and he looked much older than the last time I had seen him. He did not appear to recognise me. His daughter was cradling his head in her lap. Her hair was awry and she seemed to have been crying. She offered Shaw a glare of hatred and contempt. Von Bek saw us and looked away.

'Are you – all right?' I asked rather foolishly.

'We are not dead, Mr Bastable,' von Bek said bitterly, standing up and turning his back on us. 'Is that what you meant?'

'I am trying to save your lives,' I said, a little priggishly under the circumstances, but I wanted them to know that a chap of my sort was capable of generosity towards his enemies. 'I'm going to fly this ship to – General – Shaw's base. He says he'll not kill any of us if I do that.'

'His word's hardly to be trusted after what's happened tonight,' said von Bek. He gave a strange, harsh laugh. 'Odd that you should find our politics so disgusting when you can throw in your lot cheerfully with him!'

'He's scarcely a politician,' I pointed out. 'Besides, it wouldn't matter who he was. He holds all the cards – save the one I'm playing now.'

'Goodnight, Mr Bastable,' said Una Persson, stroking her father's head. 'I think you mean well. Thank you.'

Embarrassed I backed out of the cabin and returned to the bridge.

By morning we had reached Wuchang and Shaw was evidently much more relaxed than he had been during the night. He went so far as to offer me a pipe of opium, which I instantly refused. In those days opium seemed pretty disgusting stuff.

Wuchang was quite a large city, but we passed it before it was properly awake, flying over terraced roofs, pagodas, little blue-roofed houses, while Shaw got his bearings and pointed out the direction in which we should go.

There is nothing like a Chinese sunrise. A great watery globe appeared over the horizon and the whole land was turned to soft tones of pink, yellow and orange as we approached a line of sand-coloured hills. I felt that we offended such beauty with our battered, noisy airship full of so many cut-throats of various nationalities.

Then we were flying over the hills themselves and Shaw told us to slow our speed. He issued more rapid orders in Cantonese and one of his men left the bridge and made for the ladder which would lead him onto the outer catwalk on the top of the hull. Plainly the man was to make some sort of signal that we were friendly.

Then, suddenly, we were over a valley. It was a deep, wide valley through which a river wound. It was a green, lush valley which seemed to have no business in that rocky landscape. I saw herds of cattle grazing. I saw small farmhouses, rice fields, pigs and goats.

'Is this the valley?' I asked.

Shaw nodded. 'This is the Valley of the Morning. And look, Mr Bastable – there is my "camp"...'

He pointed ahead. I saw high, white buildings, separated by patches of greenery. I saw fountains splashing and nearby were the tiny figures of children at play. Over this modern township there flew a large, crimson flag – doubtless Shaw's battle flag. I was astonished to see such a settlement in these wilds and even more astonished to learn that it was Shaw's headquarters. It seemed so peaceful, so civilised!

Shaw was grinning at me, wholly amused by my surprise.

'Not bad for a barbarian warlord, eh? We built it all ourselves. It has every amenity – and some which even London cannot boast.'

I looked at Shaw through new eyes. Bandit, pirate, murderer he might be – but he must be something more than these to have built such a city in the Chinese wilderness.

'Haven't you read my publicity, Mr Bastable? Perhaps you haven't seen the *Shanghai Express* recently. They are calling me the Chinese Alexander! This is my Alexandria. This is Shawtown, Mr Bastable!' He was chuckling like a schoolboy, delighted at his own achievements. 'I built it.'

My first shock of amazement died away. 'Perhaps you did,' I murmured, 'but you built it from the flesh and bones of those you have murdered and painted it with the same crimson blood which stains your flag.'

'A rather rhetorical statement from you, Mr Bastable. As it happens, I am not normally much of a hand at murder. I'm a soldier, really. You appreciate the difference?'

'I appreciate the difference, but my experience has shown me that you are not anything more than a murderer, "General" Shaw.'

He laughed again. 'We'll see, we'll see. Now – look over there. Do you recognise her? There – on the other side of the city? There!'

I saw her at last, her huge bulk moving gently in the wind, her mooring ropes holding her close to the ground. And I recognised her, sure enough.

'My God!' I exclaimed. 'You've got the *Loch Etive*!'

'Yes,' he said eagerly, again like a schoolboy who has added a rather good new stamp to his collection. 'That's her name. She's to be my flagship. At this rate I'll soon have my own air fleet. What d'you think of that, Mr Bastable? Soon I'll control not only the ground, but the air as well. What a warlord I shall be! Something *of* a warlord, eh?'

I stared at his eager, glowing face and I could think of no reply. He was not mad. He was not naïve. He was not a fool. He was, in fact, one of the most intelligent men I had ever encountered. He baffled me absolutely.

He had thrown back his head and was laughing joyfully at his own cleverness – at his own wholly gargantuan act of cheek in stealing what was perhaps the finest and biggest aerial liner in the skies!

'Oh, my sainted aunt!' His half-Chinese features were still creased with mirth. 'What larks, Mr Bastable! What larks!'

Chapter Three
Chi'ng Che'eng Ta-Chia

T HERE WERE NO mooring masts on the flat space outside the city and so ropes had to be flung down to waiting men who manhandled the ship until the gondola touched the ground. Then cables and ropes were pegged into the earth, holding *The Rover* as, further away, the *Loch Etive* was held.

As we disembarked, under the suspicious gaze of Shaw's armed bandits, I expected to see coolies come hurrying up to strip the ship of its cargo, but the men who arrived were healthy, well-dressed fellows whom I first mistook for clerks or traders. Shaw had a word with them and they began to go aboard the airship, showing no subservience of the sort normally shown to bandit chieftains by their men. In fact the pirates who disembarked with their guns and knives and bandoliers, their ragged silks, sandals and beaded headbands, looked distinctly out of place here. Shortly after landing, they climbed into a large motor wagon and steamed away towards the far end of the valley. 'They go to join the rest of the army,' Shaw explained. 'Chi'ng Che'eng Ta-Chia is primarily a civilian settlement.'

I was helping Captain Korzeniowski, supporting one elbow while Una Persson supported the other. Von Bek strode moodily ahead of us as we moved towards the town. Korzeniowski was better today and his old intelligence had returned. Behind us streamed the crewmen of *The Rover*, looking about them in open amazement.

'What was the name you used?' I asked the 'General'.

'Chi'ng Che'eng Ta-Chia – it's hard to translate. The name of the city yonder.'

'I thought you called it Shawtown.'

He burst into laughter again, his great frame shaking, his hands on his hips. 'My joke, Mr Bastable! The place is called – well – Democratic Dawn City, perhaps? Dawn City Belonging to Us All? Something like that. Call it Dawn City, if you like. In the Valley of the Dawn. The first city of the New Age.'

'What New Age is that?'

'Shuo Ho Ti – his New Age. Do you want the translation of my Chinese name, Mr Bastable? It is "One Who Makes Peace" – The Peacemaker.'

'Now that isn't a bad joke at all,' I said grimly as we strode over the grass towards the first tall, elegant buildings of Dawn City. 'Considering that you've just murdered two English officers and stolen a British airship. How many people did you have to kill to get your hands on the *Loch Etive*?'

'Not many. You must meet my friend Ulianov – he will tell you that the ends justify the means.'

'And what exactly are your ends?' I grew impatient as Shaw flung an arm round my shoulders, his bland oriental face beaming.

'First – the Liberation of China. Driving out all foreigners – Russians, Japanese, British, Americans, French – all of them.'

'I doubt if you'll manage it,' I said. 'And even if you did, you'd probably starve. You need foreign money.'

'Not really. Not really. Foreigners – particularly the British with their opium trade – ruined our economy in the first place. It will be hard to build it up again alone, but we shall do it.'

I said nothing to this. His were evidently messianic dreams, not unlike those of old Sharan Khang – he believed himself much more powerful than he actually was. I almost felt sorry for him then. It would only take a fleet of His Majesty's aerial battleships to turn his whole dream into a nightmare. Now that he had committed acts of piracy against Great Britain he had become something more than a local problem to be dealt with by the Chinese authorities.

As if reading my thoughts, he said, 'The passengers and crew of the *Loch Etive* make useful hostages, Mr Bastable. I doubt if we'll be attacked by your battleships immediately, eh?'

'Perhaps you're right. What are your plans *after* you have liberated all China?'

'The world, of course.'

It was my turn to laugh. 'Oh, I see.'

He smiled a secret smile, then. 'Do you know who lives in Dawn City, Mr Bastable?'

'How could I? Members of your government-to-be?'

'Some of those, yes. But Dawn City is a town of outlaws. There are exiles here from every oppressed country in the world. It is an international settlement.'

'A town of criminals?'

'Some would call it that.' We were now strolling through wide streets flanked by willows and poplars, grassy lawns and bright beds of flowers. From the open window of one of the houses drifted the sound of a violin playing Mozart. Shaw paused and listened, the crew of *The Rover* coming to a straggling halt behind us. 'Beautiful, isn't it?'

'Very fine. A phonograph?'

'A man. Professor Hira. He's an Indian physicist. Because of his nationalist sympathies he was put in prison. My men helped him escape and now he is continuing his research in one of our laboratories. We have many laboratories – many new inventions. Tyrants hate original thinking. So the original thinkers are driven to Dawn City. We have scientists, philosophers, artists, journalists – even a few politicians.'

'And plenty of soldiers,' I said harshly.

'Yes, plenty of soldiers – lots of guns and stuff,' he said vaguely as if slightly put out by my interruption.

'And it will all be wasted,' said von Bek suddenly, turning to look back at us. 'Because you wish to control too much power, Shaw.'

Shaw waved a languid hand. 'I have been lucky in that, Rudy. I have the power. I must use it.'

'Against fellow comrades. I was expected in Brunei. A revolt was planned. Without me there to lead it, it would have collapsed. It must have collapsed by now.'

I stared at him. 'You know each other?'

'Very well,' von Bek said angrily. 'Too damn' well.'

'Then you, too, are a socialist?' I said to Shaw.

Shaw shrugged. 'I prefer the term communist, but names don't matter. That is von Bek's trouble – he cares about names. I told you, Rudy, that the British authorities were waiting to arrest you, that the Americans already knew there was something suspicious about *The Rover* when you reached Saigon. Your telephone operator must have been sending out secret messages to them. But you wouldn't listen – and Barry and the telephone man died because of your obstinacy!'

'You had no right to take over the ship!' shouted the Saxon count. 'No right at all.'

'If I had not, we should all be in some British jail by now – or dead.'

Korzeniowski said weakly, 'It's all over. Shaw has presented us with a fait accompli and there it is. But I wish you had better control over your men, Shaw... Poor Barry wouldn't have shot you, you know that.'

'*They* didn't know it. My army is a democratic army.'

'If you're not careful they'll destroy you,' Korzeniowski continued. 'They serve you only because they consider you the best bandit in China. If you try to discipline them, you'll find them cutting your throat.'

Shaw accepted this. He led the way up a concrete path towards a low pagoda-style building. 'I do not intend to rely on them much longer. As soon as my air fleet is ready...'

'Air fleet!' snorted von Bek. 'Two ships?'

'Soon I'll have more,' Shaw said confidently. 'Many more.'

We entered the cool gloom of a hallway. 'It is old-fashioned to rely on armies, Rudy,' Shaw continued. 'I rely on science. We have many projects nearing fruition – and if Project NFB is successful, then I think I'll disband the army altogether.'

'NFB?' Una Persson frowned. 'What's that?'

Shaw laughed. 'You are a physicist, Una – the last person I should tell anything to at this stage.'

A European in a neat, white suit appeared in the hallway. He smiled at us in welcome. He had grey hair, a wrinkled face.

'Ah, Comrade Spender. Could you accommodate these people here for a while?'

'A pleasure, Comrade Shaw.' The old man walked to a section of the blank wall and passed his hand across it. Instantly a series of rows of coloured lights appeared on the wall. Some of them were red, but most were blue. Comrade Spender studied the blue lights thoughtfully for a moment then turned back to us. 'We have the whole of Section Eight free. One moment, I'll prepare the rooms.' He touched a bank of blue lights and they changed to red. 'It is done. All operating now.'

'Thank you, Comrade Spender.'

I wondered what this peculiar ritual could mean.

Shaw led us down a corridor with wide windows which looked out onto a forecourt in which several fountains were playing. The fountains were in the latest styles of architecture – not all entirely to my taste. We came to a door with a large figure 8 stencilled on it. Shaw pressed his hand against the numeral and said: 'Open!' At once the door slid upwards, disappearing into the ceiling. 'You'll have to share rooms, I'm afraid,' said Shaw. 'Two of you in each room. There's everything you need and you can communicate any other wants by means of the telephones you'll find. Goodbye for now, gentlemen.' He turned and the door slid down behind him. I went up to it and put my palm against it.

'Open!' I said.

As I expected nothing happened. Somehow the door was keyed to recognise Shaw's hand and voice! This certainly was a city of scientific marvels.

After some discussion and a general pacing about and testing of the windows and doors we realised there was no easy means of escape.

'You'd better share a room with me, I suppose,' said von Bek, tapping me on the shoulder. 'Una and Captain Korzeniowski can go next door.' The crewmen were already entering their rooms, finding that the doors opened and shut on command.

'Very well,' I said distastefully.

We entered our room and found that there were two beds in it, a writing desk, wardrobes, chests of drawers, bookshelves filled with a wide variety of fiction and non-fiction, a telephone communicator and something with a milky-blue surface which was oval in shape and unidentifiable. Our windows looked out onto a sweet-scented rose garden, but the glass was unbreakable and the windows could only be opened wide enough to let in the air and the scent. Pale blue sleeping suits had been laid on the beds. Ignoring the suit, Rudolf von Bek flung himself on the bed fully clothed, turning his head and giving me a bleak smile.

'Well, Bastable, now that you've met a real, full-blooded revolutionary, I must look pretty pale in comparison, eh?'

I sat down on the edge of the bed and began to remove my boots which were pinching. 'You're as bad,' I said. 'All that makes Shaw different from you is his madness which is that much grander – and a thousand times more foolish! At least you confined your activities to what was possible. He dreams of the impossible.'

'That's what I like to think,' von Bek said seriously. 'But there again – he's built Dawn City up a lot since I was last here. And one would have thought it impossible to steal a liner the size of the *Loch Etive*. And there's no doubting that his scientific gadgets – this whole apartment building for instance – are in advance of anything which exists in the outside world.' He frowned. 'I wonder what Project NFB could be?'

'I don't care,' I said. 'My only wish is to get back to the civilisation I know – a sane world where people behave with a reasonable degree of decency!'

Von Bek smiled patronisingly. Then he sat up and stretched. 'By God, I'm hungry! I wonder if we get any food?'

'Food,' said a voice from nowhere. I watched, fascinated, as a face appeared in the milky-blue oval. It was a Chinese girl. She smiled and continued. 'What would you like to eat, gentlemen? Chinese food – or European?'

'Let's have some Chinese food, by all means,' said von Bek without consulting me. 'I'm very fond of it. What have you got?'

'We will send you a selection.' The girl's face vanished from the screen.

A few moments later, while we were still recovering from that experience, a section of the wall opened to reveal an alcove in which sat a tray piled high with all kinds of Chinese delicacies. Eagerly von Bek sprang up, seized the tray and placed it on our table.

Forgetting for an instant everything but the mouth-watering smell of the food, I began to eat, wondering, not for the first time, if this were not perhaps some fantastically detailed dream induced by Sharan Khang's drugs.

Chapter Four
Vladimir Ilyitch Ulianov

AFTER EATING I washed, dressed myself in the sleeping suit and climbed beneath the quilt covering the bed. The bed was the most comfortable I had ever slept in and soon I was fast asleep.

I must have slept through the rest of the day and the whole of the night, for I awoke the next morning feeling utterly splendid! I was able to look back on the events of the past few days with a philosophical acceptance I found surprising in myself. I still believed Korzeniowski, von Bek, Shaw and the rest totally misguided, but I could see that they were not inhuman monsters. They really believed they were working for the good of people they considered to be 'oppressed'.

I was feeling so rested I wondered if perhaps the food had been drugged but when I turned my head I saw that von Bek had evidently not slept as well. His eyes were red-rimmed and he was still in his outdoor clothes, his hands behind his head, staring moodily at the ceiling.

'You don't look too happy, Count von Bek,' I said, getting up and moving towards the washbasin.

'Why have any of us reason to be happy, Mr Bastable?' He uttered a sharp, bitter laugh. 'I am cooped up here at a time when I should be out in the world, doing my work. I've no relish for Shaw's theatrical revolutionary posturings. A revolutionist should be silent, unseen, cautious...'

'You're not exactly unknown to the world,' I pointed out, jumping a little as boiling hot water issued from the tap. 'Your picture is frequently in the newspapers. Your books are widely distributed, I understand.'

'That is not what I meant.' He glared at me and then shut his eyes as if to blot my presence from his mind.

I was faintly amused by the rivalries I had witnessed among the anarchists – or socialists or communards or whatever they chose to call themselves. Each seemed to have an individual dream of how the world should be ordered and resented all other versions of that dream. If they could only agree on certain essentials, I thought, they would be rather more effective.

I glanced out of the window as I dried my face. Not that Shaw had entirely failed. In the rose garden I saw children of various ages and a variety of nationalities playing together, laughing joyfully as they ran about in the morning sunshine. And along the paths strolled men and women, chatting easily to each other and smiling frequently. Some were evidently married and not a few were members of the coloured races married to members of the white race. This did not shock me as it should have done. It all seemed natural to me. I remembered what Shaw had said the city was called – Democratic Dawn City – the City of Equality. But was such equality possible in the outside world? Was not Shaw's dream city artificially conceived? I expressed this thought to von Bek, who had opened his eyes again, and added: 'It *does* look tranquil – but isn't this place built on piracy and murder, just as you said London was built on injustice?'

He shrugged. 'I don't much care to discuss Shaw's ambitions.' Then he paused for a while. 'But to be fair I think you could say that Dawn City is a beginning – it is conceived in terms of the future. London is an ending – the final conception of a dead ideology.'

'What do you mean?'

'Europe has used up its dream. It has no future. The future lies here, in China, which has a new dream, a new future. It lies in Africa, India – throughout the Middle East and the Far East – perhaps in South America, too. Europe is dying. I, for one, regret it. But before she dies, she offers certain notions of what is possible to the countries she has dishonoured...'

'You are saying we are decadent?'

'If you like. It is not what I said.'

I could not completely follow his argument so I let it drop.

I found my clothes, newly cleaned and pressed, at the end of my bed, and put them on.

A little later there was a tap at the door and an old, old man walked in. His hair was pure white and he had a long, white goatee beard after the Chinese fashion. He was dressed in simple cotton clothes and leaned on a stick. He looked as if he had lived a hundred years and seen a great deal of the world. When he spoke it was in a cracked, high-pitched voice with a thick accent I identified as Russian.

'Good morning, young man. Good morning, von Bek.'

Von Bek straightened up on the bed, his gloom forgotten, his face brightening.

'Uncle Vladimir! How are you?'

'I'm well, but feeling my age a little these days.'

Von Bek introduced us as the old man sat down in one of the easy chairs. 'Mr Bastable, this is Vladimir Ilyitch Ulianov. He was a revolutionist before any of us were born!'

I did not correct him on that point but shook hands with the old Russian.

Von Bek laughed. 'Mr Bastable is a confirmed capitalist, uncle. He disapproves of us all – calls us anarchists and murderers!'

Ulianov chuckled without rancour. 'It is always amusing to hear the mass-murderer accusing the man he seeks to destroy. I'll not forget the thousand accusations made against me in Russia in the twenties, before I had to leave. Kerensky was President then.'

'He died last year, uncle. They have elected a new President now. Prince Shevadnasy is leader of the Duma.'

'And doubtless licks the spittle of the Romanovs as his predecessor did. Duma! A travesty of democracy. I was a fool even to let myself be elected to it. That is not the way to challenge injustice. The Tsar still rules Russia – even if it is nowadays through his so-called parliament.'

'True, Vladimir Ilyitch,' murmured von Bek, and I got the impression he was humouring the man a little. There was no doubting his admiration of this ancient revolutionist – but now he was tolerating him as one would a man who had done great things in his day but had now turned a trifle senile.

'Ah, if only I had had the opportunity,' Ulianov went on, 'I would have shown Kerensky what democracy really meant. We should have chained the Tsar's power – perhaps even kicked him out altogether. Yes – yes – it might have been possible, if all the people had risen up and opposed him. There must have been one moment in history when that could have happened, and I missed it. Perhaps I was sleeping, perhaps I was exiled in Germany at the time, perhaps I was –' he smiled fondly – 'making love! Ha! But one day Russia *will* be free, eh, Rudolf? We shall make honest workers of the Romanovs and send Kerensky and his "parliament" to Siberia, just as they sent me there, eh? The revolution must come soon.'

'Soon, uncle.'

'Let the people starve a little longer. Let them be made to work a little harder. Let them know disease and fear and death a little better – then they will rise up. A tide of humanity which will sweep over the corrupt princes and merchants and drown them in their own blood!'

'As you say, uncle.'

'Oh! If only I had had my chance. If I could have controlled the Duma – but that weasel Kerensky tricked me, discredited me, chased me from my own homeland, my Russia.'

'You will return some day.'

Ulianov winked cunningly at von Bek. 'I have returned once or twice already. I have distributed a few pamphlets. I have visited my rich politician friend Bronstein and given him a fright in case the Okharna should discover me at his house and think him a revolutionist too. He *was* once, of course, but he chose to modify his views and keep his place in the Duma. Jews! They are all the same.'

Von Bek was disapproving of this sudden outburst. 'There are Jews and Jews, uncle.'

'True. But Bronstein – ah, what is the use – he is ninety-seven years old. Soon he will be dead and I will be dead.'

'But your writings, Vladimir Ilyitch, will always live. They will inspire each new generation of revolutionists – all those who learn to hate injustice.'

Ulianov nodded. 'Yes,' he said. 'Let us hope so. But you will not remember...' And now he launched on a new series of repetitive anecdotes while von Bek disguised his impatience and listened politely, even when the old man querulously attacked him, for a moment, as not following the True Way of the Revolution.

In the meantime I uttered the magic word 'Food' and the Chinese woman appeared in the milky-blue oval again. I asked for breakfast for three and it was duly delivered. Von Bek and I ate heartily, but Ulianov was loath to waste time eating. He continued to drone on as we enjoyed our breakfast. Ulianov reminded me somewhat of the old Holy Men, the lamas I had occasionally come across in my former life as an officer in the Indian Army. Often his conversation seemed as abstract as did theirs. And yet, as I had respected those lamas, I respected Ulianov – for his age, for his faith, for the way in which he would repeat the articles of his creed over and over again. He seemed a kindly, harmless old man – very different from my earlier image of a confirmed revolutionist.

The door opened as he launched into the phrase he had used earlier – 'Let the people starve a little longer. Let them be made to work a little harder. Let them know disease and fear and death a little better – then they will rise up! A tide...' It was Shaw who stood in the doorway. He was dressed in a white linen suit and there was a panama hat on his head. He was smoking a cigar. 'A tide of humanity which will sweep away injustice, eh, Vladimir Ilyitch?' He smiled. 'But I disagree with you, as ever.'

The old Russian looked up and wagged his finger. 'You should not argue with one as old as me, Shuo Ho Ti. That is not the Chinese way. You should respect my words.' He smiled back.

'What do you think, Mr Bastable?' Shaw asked banteringly. 'Does despair breed revolution?'

'I know nothing of revolutions,' I replied. 'Though I might be

induced to agree with you that a few reforms might be in order –
in Russia, for instance.'

Ulianov laughed. 'A few reforms! Ho! That is what Kerensky
wanted. But the reforms went by the board when it proved expedient to forget about them. It is always the same with "reforms".
The *system* must die!'

'It is hope, Mr Bastable, not despair, which breeds revolution,'
said Shaw. 'Give the people hope – show them what might be possible, what they can look forward to – then they might try to
achieve something. Despair breeds only more despair – people
lose heart and die in themselves. That is where Comrade Ulianov
and those who follow him make a mistake. They think that people
will rise up when their discomfort becomes unbearable. But that
is not true. When their discomfort becomes totally unbearable –
they *give up*. Offer them some extra comfort – and being human
they will ask for more – and more – and more! Then comes revolution. Thus we of Dawn City work to distribute extra wealth
among the coolies of China. We work to set an example in China
which will encourage the oppressed peoples of the whole world.'

Ulianov shook his head. 'Bah! Bronstein had some such idea –
but look what became of him!'

'Bronstein? Ah – your old enemy.'

'He was once my friend,' said Ulianov, suddenly sad. He got up
with a sigh. 'Still, we are all comrades here, even if we differ about
methods.' He gave me a long, hard look. 'Do not think we are divided because we argue, Mr Bastable.'

I had thought exactly that.

'We are human beings, you see,' Ulianov continued. 'We have
fantastic dreams – but what the human mind can conceive, it can
make reality. For good or ill. For good or ill.'

'Perhaps for good *and* ill,' I said.

'What do you mean?'

'Every coin has two sides. Every dream of perfection contains
a nightmare of imperfection.'

Ulianov smiled slowly. 'That is perhaps why we should not aim for absolutes, eh? Is it absolutes which destroy themselves as surely as they destroy us?'

'Absolutes – and abstractions,' I said. 'There are little acts of justice as well as large ones, Vladimir Ilyitch Ulianov.'

'You think that we revolutionists forsake our humanity to follow fantasies of Utopia?'

'Perhaps not you…'

'You have voiced the eternal problem of the dedicated follower of any faith, Mr Bastable. There is never a resolution.'

'Judging by my own experience,' I said, 'there is never a resolution to any problem concerning human affairs. I suppose you can call *that* philosophy "British pragmatism". Take it as it comes…'

'The British certainly took it,' said von Bek, and laughed. 'There is a particular joy, I am sure you will agree, in looking for alternatives and seeing whether those alternatives will work and if they are better.'

'There must be a better alternative to this world,' said Ulianov feelingly. 'There must be!'

Shaw had come to take us on a tour of his city. The four of us – Captain Korzeniowski, now fully recovered and with not even a scar to show for his head wound, Una Persson, Count von Bek and myself – followed Shaw from the apartment house and down a wide, sunlit street.

Dawn City continued to be an education for me, who had always seen revolutionists in terms of simple-minded nihilists, blowing up buildings, murdering people, with no idea of what they might want to build on the ruins of the world they were destroying. And here was their dream made reality.

But wasn't it a slightly spurious reality? I wondered. Could it actually be extended throughout the world?

When I had first been hurled into the world of the 1970s I had thought I found Utopia. And now I was discovering that it was only a Utopia for some. Shaw wanted a Utopia which would exist for all.

I remembered the blood I had seen spread across the bridge of

The Rover. Barry's blood. It was hard to reconcile that image with the one before us now.

Shaw took us to see schools, communal restaurants, workshops, laboratories, theatres, studios, all full of happy, relaxed people of a hundred different nationalities, races and creeds. I was impressed.

'This is what the whole of the East – and Africa – might have been like by now if it had not been for the European's greed,' Shaw told me. 'By now we would be economically stronger than Europe. That would be a true balance of power. Then you would see what justice was all about!'

'But it is a European ideal that you follow,' I pointed out. 'If we had not brought it…'

'We should have found it. People learn by example, Mr Bastable. They do not have to have ideas forced upon them.'

We had entered a darkened hall. Before us was a large kinema screen. Shaw bade us be seated and then the screen flickered into life.

I watched in horrified fascination as I saw pictures of Chinese men and women being decapitated in their scores.

'The village of Shihnan in Japanese Manchuria,' said Shaw in a hard flat voice. 'The villagers failed to produce their annual quota of rice and are being punished. This happened last year.'

I saw Japanese soldiers laughing as their long swords rose and fell.

I was stunned. 'But that is Japan…' was all I could say.

A new series of pictures. Coolies working on a railway line. Uniformed men were using whips to force them to work harder. The uniforms were Russian.

'Everyone knows the Russians are cruel in their treatment of subject peoples…'

Shaw made no comment.

A rabble of Asiatics – many of them women and children – armed with farm implements were rushing towards a stone wall. The people were all in rags and half-starved. Gunfire broke out from behind the wall and the people fell down, twisted, bleeding, shrieking in agony. I could hardly bear to look. The gunfire continued until all the people were dead.

Men in brown uniforms with wide-brimmed hats appeared from behind the wall and moved amongst the corpses, checking that none lived.

'Americans!'

'To be fair,' General Shaw said tonelessly, 'they were acting at the request of the Siam government. That scene took place a few miles from Bangkok. American troops are helping the government to keep order. There have been a number of minor rebellions in some parts of Siam recently.'

The next scene was an Indian township. Concrete huts were arranged in neat rows for as far as the eye could see.

'It's deserted,' I said.

'Wait.'

The camera took us along the desolate streets until we were outside the township. Here were soldiers in British red. They were wielding spades, heaping bodies into trenches filled with lime.

'Cholera?'

'There was cholera – typhoid – malaria – smallpox – but that was not why the whole village died. Look.'

The camera moved in closer and I saw that there were many bullet wounds in the bodies.

'They marched on Delhi without passes to enter the city limits,' said Shaw. 'They refused to halt when ordered to do so. They were all shot down.'

'But it could not have been an official decision,' I said. 'An officer panicked. It sometimes happens.'

'Were the Russians, the Japanese, the Americans panicking?'

'No.'

'This is how your kind of power is used when others threaten it,' said Shaw. I looked at his eyes. There were tears in them.

I knew something of what he was feeling. There were tears in my eyes, too.

I tried to tell myself that the films were counterfeit – played by actors to impress people like me. But I knew that they were not counterfeit.

I left the kinema. I was shaking. I felt sick. And I was still weeping.

We walked in silence through the tranquil City of the Dawn, none of us able to speak after what we had witnessed. We came to the edge of the settlement and looked out over the makeshift air-park. There were men there now, working on the girders for what was evidently to be a good-sized mooring mast. We saw *The Rover* still pegged to the ground in her spiderweb of cables, but the bigger ship had gone.

'Where is the *Loch Etive*?' It was Korzeniowski who spoke.

Shaw looked up absently and then, as if remembering a duty, smiled. 'Oh, she is on her way back. I hope her second mission will be as successful as her first.'

'Missions?' said von Bek. 'What missions?'

'Her first was to shoot down the Imperial Japanese Airship *Kanazawa*. We have armed her with some experimental guns. They are excellent. No recoil at all. Always the problem with big guns aboard an airship, eh?'

'True,' said Korzeniowski. He took out his pipe and began to light it. 'True.'

'And her second mission was to bomb a section of the Trans-Siberian railroad and steal the cargo of a certain Moscow-bound train. I recently heard that the cargo was stolen. If it is what I hope, we shall be able to speed up Project NFB.'

'Just was *is* this mysterious project?' Una Persson asked.

General O.T. Shaw gestured towards a large building like a factory which stood on the far side of the airpark. 'Over there. A very expensive project, I don't mind saying. But I can't tell you any more, I'm afraid. I hardly understand it myself. Most of our German and Hungarian exiles are working on it. There are one or two Americans, too, and an Englishman – all political refugees. But brilliant and original scientists. Dawn City benefits by the tyranny imposed on curiosity in the West.'

I could not believe that he had not considered the consequences of these actions. 'You have now earned the wrath of three great Powers,' I said. 'You stole a British airship to destroy a Japanese man-o'-war and a Russian railway. They are bound to get together. Dawn City will be lucky if it lasts a day!'

'We still have the hostages from the *Loch Etive*,' Shaw murmured serenely.

'Will that knowledge stop the Japanese or the Russians from bombing you to bits?'

'It offers a serious diplomatic problem. The three nations must argue it over for a while. In the meantime we are finishing off our defences.'

'Even you can't defend yourself against the combined aerial fleets of Britain, Japan and Russia!' I said.

'We shall have to see,' said Shaw. 'Now, Mr Bastable, what did you think of my magic lantern show?'

'You convinced me that a closer watch should be kept on how the natives are treated,' I said.

'And that is all?'

'There *are* other ways of stopping injustice,' I said, 'than revolution and bloody war.'

'Not if the cancer is to be burned out completely,' said Korzeniowski. 'I realise that now.'

'Aha,' said Shaw, looking towards the hills. 'Here comes the *Fei-chi*...'

'The what?'

'The flying machine.'

'I can't see it,' said Korzeniowski.

I, too, could see no sign of the *Loch Etive*, though I heard a drone like that of a mosquito.

'Look,' said Shaw, grinning, 'there!'

A speck appeared on the horizon and the droning became a shrill whine.

'There!' He giggled in excitement. 'I don't mean an airship – I mean the *Fei-chi* – the little hornet – here she comes!'

Instinctively I ducked as something whizzed over my head. I looked up. I had an impression of several windmill sails spinning at fantastic speed, of long, birdlike wings, and then it was disappearing in the distance, still voicing the same angry whine.

'My God!' said Korzeniowski, removing the pipe from his mouth and registering his amazement for the first time since I had met him. 'It's a heavier-than-air flying machine. I was sure – I was always told – such a thing was impossible.'

Shaw grinned, almost breaking into a dance in his delight. 'And I have fifty of them, captain! Fifty little hornets with very bad stings. Now you see why I feel up to defending Dawn City against anything the Great Powers send!'

'They seem a bit fragile to me,' I said.

'They are a bit,' Shaw admitted, 'but they can travel at speeds of nearly five hundred miles an hour. And that is their strength. Who would have time to train a gun on one of those before a *Feichi* was able to burst the hull of a flying ironclad with its special explosive bullets?'

'Who – how did you come by this invention?' von Bek wanted to know.

'Oh, one of my American outlaws had the idea,' Shaw returned airily. 'And some of my French engineers made it practicable. We built and flew the first machine in less than a week. Within a month we had developed it into what you have just seen.'

'I admire the man who would go up in one of those,' said von Bek. 'Aren't they crushed by such speeds?'

'They have to wear special padded clothing, certainly. And, of course, their reactions must be as fast as their machines if they are to control them properly.'

Korzeniowski shook his head. 'Well,' he said, 'I think I'll stick to airships. They're altogether more credible than those contraptions. I've seen it – but I still can't believe in heavier-than-air machines.'

Shaw looked almost cunningly at me. 'Well, Mr Bastable? Are you still convinced I am mad?'

I continued to stare into the sky where the *Fei-chi* had disappeared. 'You are not mad in the way I first thought,' I admitted. A sense of terrible foreboding seized me. I wished with all my heart that I was back in my own time where heavier-than-air flying machines and wireless telephones and coloured, talking kinemas which came to life in one's room were the fantasies of children and lunatics. I thought of Mr H.G. Wells and I turned, looking towards the buildings which housed Project NFB. 'I suppose you haven't invented a Time Machine, by any chance?'

The warlord grinned. 'Not yet, Mr Bastable. But we are thinking about it. Why do you ask?'

I shook my head and did not reply.

Von Bek clapped me on the back. 'You want to know where all this leads, don't you? You want to travel into the future and see General Shaw's Utopia!' He had been quite won over to Shaw's side now.

I shrugged. 'I think I've had my fill of Utopias,' I murmured.

Chapter Five
The Coming of the Air Fleets

THROUGHOUT THE DAYS which followed I made no attempt to escape Dawn City. The whole idea would have been pointless anyway. General O.T. Shaw's men controlled all roads and guarded both the airships and the sheds where the new *Fei-chi* 'hornets' were stored. Sometimes I would watch as the *Fei-chi* were tested by their tall, Chinese pilots – healthy, confident young men completely dedicated to Shaw's cause, able to accept the heavier-than-air machines as I could not.

Early on I assured myself that the *Loch Etive* hostages were safe and well and I chatted with one or two fellows I had known on board her, learning that Captain Quelch had indeed died not long after being sent home to that little house in Balham where he had lodged during his leaves. Another acquaintance had died, too. In an out-of-date newspaper I read that Cornelius Dempsey had been shot in a street battle with armed policemen. Dempsey had been part of a gang of anarchists trapped in a house in East London. So far his body had not been found, but several witnesses confirmed that he had been dead when his friends carried him away. I felt sadness overwhelming me and adding to that mood of bitterness and depression which had come while I watched those terrible kinema films.

More recent newspapers brought in by Shaw's men were full of reports of Shuo Ho Ti's daring raids, his acts of piracy and murder. One or two of the papers saw him as 'the first modern bandit' and it was they, I think, who had dubbed him 'Warlord of the Air'. Certainly, while England strove to halt Russian and Japanese military airships from taking instant vengeance and the Chinese Central Government vainly attempted to stop any aerial warships entering their territory, Shaw pulled off a series of amazing raids, descending from the sky on trains, motor convoys, ships and military and scientific establishments to get what he needed. What he did not need he distributed to the Chinese population – his repainted 'flagship', now no longer the *Loch Etive* but the *Shan-tien* (Lightning) and flying his familiar crimson flags, appearing in the skies over an impoverished village or town and showering money, goods and food – as well as pamphlets telling the people to join Shuo Ho Ti, the Peacemaker, in the freeing of China from foreign oppression. Thousands came to swell the ranks of his army at the far end of the Valley of the Morning. And Shaw added more ships to his fleet, bringing merchant vessels to land at gunpoint, releasing crews and passengers, flying the captured craft back to Dawn City and there refitting them with his new cannon. The only problem was a shortage among his own followers of men trained to fly the craft. Inexperienced commanders had put their ships into danger more than once and two had been lost through incompetence. A couple of times Shaw proposed that I should become his ally and help fly a ship of my choice, but I refused, for the only reason I would board an airship would be to escape and I did not wish to indulge in piracy just so that I might find a chance of gaining my freedom.

Nonetheless there were conversations with the warlord in which he described his past to me as he continued to try to win me over.

His was an interesting story. He had been the son of an English missionary and his Chinese wife who had worked in a remote Shantung village for years until they came to the attention of the old warlord – 'a *traditional* bandit' Shaw called him – of their part of the world. The warlord, Lao-Shu, had killed Shaw's father and taken his mother as a concubine. He had been brought up as one of Lao-Shu's many children and eventually ran away to Peking, where his father's brother taught. He had been sent to school in England where he had been very unhappy and learned to hate what he considered the English superiority towards other races, classes and creeds. Later he went to Oxford, where he did well and began to 'realise', as he put it, that imperialism was a disease which robbed the majority of the world's population of its dignity and the right to order its own affairs. These were English conceptions, he was the first to admit, but what he resented was that they were reserved for the English alone. 'The conqueror always assumes that his moral superiority – rather than his ferocious greed – is what has allowed him to triumph.' Leaving Oxford, he had entered the army and done well, learning all he could of English military matters, then getting transferred to the Crown Colony of Hong Kong to serve in the police – for, of course, he spoke fluent Mandarin and Cantonese. He had soon deserted the police, taking with him his whole detachment of native soldiers, two steam carts and a considerable amount of artillery. Then he had gone back to Shantung, where the warlord still ruled, and –

'There I killed my father's murderer and took his place,' he said baldly.

His mother had died in the meantime. With his connections with revolutionists throughout the world he had conceived the idea of Dawn City. He would take from Europe what, in its pride, it rejected – its brilliant scientists, engineers, politicians and writers who were too clever to be tolerated by their own governments – and he would use it to the benefit of his China.

'It is part of what Europe owes us,' he pointed out. 'And soon we shall be able to claim the rest of the debt. Do you know how they first began the ruin of China, Mr Bastable? It was the English, mainly, but also the Americans. They grew opium in India – vast fields of it – and secretly shipped it into China, where, officially, it was banned. This created such inflation (for those who smuggled it in were paid in Chinese silver) that the whole economy was ruined. When the Chinese government objected to this, the foreigners sent in armies to teach the Chinese a lesson for their arrogance in complaining. Those armies found a country in economic ruin and huge sections of the population smoking opium. Naturally, the only thing which could have brought this about was an innate decadence, a moral inferiority...' Shaw laughed. 'The opium clippers were specially designed for the China trade, to run swiftly from India with their cargoes, and often they carried Bibles as well as opium, for the missionaries would insist that if they, who could speak pidgin Chinese, were to translate for the smugglers, they must be allowed to distribute Bibles as well. After that, there was no looking back. And Europeans think Chinese hatred of them unreasonable!'

Shaw would become serious at times like these and would say to me: 'Foreign devils? You think "devils" is a strong enough word, Mr Bastable?'

Now his ambitions extended to the taking back of the whole of China:

'And soon the great grey factories of Shanghai will be ours. The laboratories and schools and museums of Peking will be ours. The trading and manufacturing centres of Canton will be ours. The rich rice fields – all will be ours!' His eyes gleamed. 'China will be united. The foreigners will be driven out and all will be equal. We shall set an example to the world.'

'If you are successful,' I said quietly, 'let the world also see that you are human. People are impressed by kindness as well as by factories and military strength.'

Shaw gave me a peculiar stare.

There were now some fifteen airships tied up to the mooring masts on the field beyond Dawn City and there were nearly a hundred *Fei-chi* in the hangars. The whole valley was defended with artillery and infantry and could withstand an attack from any quarter when it came; and we knew it would come.

We? I don't know how I had come to identify myself with bandits and revolutionists – and yet there was no mistaking the fact that I had. I refused to join them, but I hoped that they might win. Win against the ships of my own nation which would come against them and which, doubtless, would be destroyed by them. How I had changed in the past couple of weeks! I could contemplate, without horror, the bloody deaths of British servicemen. Comrades.

But I had to face the fact that the people of Dawn City were my comrades now – even though I would not commit myself to their cause. I did not want Dawn City and all it represented to be destroyed. I wanted General O.T. Shaw – the Warlord of the Air – to drive the foreigners from his nation and make it strong again.

I waited in trepidation for the 'enemy' – my countrymen – to come.

I was lying in my bed asleep when the news came through on the *tien-ying* ('electric shadow') machine. The milky-blue oval became General Shaw's face. He looked grim and he looked excited.

'They are on their way, Mr Bastable. I thought you might like to be awake for the show.'

'Who…?' I murmured blearily. 'What…?'

'The air fleets – American, British, Russian, Japanese and some French, I believe – they are coming to the Valley of the Morning – coming to punish John Chinaman…'

I saw his head move and he spoke more rapidly.

'I must go now. Shall we see you at the ringside – the main headquarters buildings?'

'I'll be there.' As the picture faded I sprang out of bed and washed and dressed then hurried through the quiet streets of Dawn City until I reached the circular tower which was the city's chief administrative building. There was, of course, furious activity. A wireless-telephone message had been received from the British flagship *Victoria Imperatrix* saying that if the *Loch Etive* hostages were freed Shaw might send out with them his people's women and children, who would not be harmed. Shaw replied bluntly. The hostages were already being taken to the far end of the valley, where they would be released. The people of Dawn City would fight together and, if necessary, die together. The *Victoria Imperatrix* offered the information that there were a hundred airships on their way to Dawn City and that therefore Dawn City could not possibly hope to last more than an hour against such a fleet. Shaw replied that he felt Dawn City might last a little longer and he looked forward to the arrival of the battle-fleet. In the meantime, he said, he had recently received the interesting news that two Japanese flying gunboats had devastated a village which had received help from Shaw. The British, doubtless, would be making similar reprisals? At this, HMAS *Victoria Imperatrix* cut off communication with Dawn City. Shaw smiled bleakly.

He saw me standing in the room. 'Hello, Bastable. By God! The Japanese have got a lot to answer for where China's concerned. I'd like to… What's this?' An assistant handed him a sheet of paper. 'Good. Good. Project NFB is proceeding apace.'

'Where is Captain Korzeniowski?' I saw Count Rudolf and Una Persson on the other side of the room talking to one of Shaw's cotton-clad 'majors', but I could not see Mrs Persson's father.

'Korzeniowski is back in command of *The Rover*,' said Shaw, pointing towards the airpark plainly visible from this tower. I saw tiny figures running back and forth as their ships prepared to take the air. So far there was no sign of the *Fei-chi* flying machines. 'And look,' added Shaw, 'here comes the battle-fleet.'

I thought at first that I saw a massive bank of black cloud moving over the horizon of the hills and blotting out the pale sunshine. With the cloud came a great thrumming sound, like many deep-voiced gongs being beaten rapidly in unison. The sound grew louder as the cloud began to fill the whole sky, casting a dark and ominous shadow over the Valley of the Morning.

It was the allied air fleet of five nations.

Each ship was a thousand feet long. Each had a hull as strong as steel. Each bristled with artillery and great grenades which could be dropped upon their enemies. Each ship moved implacably through the sky, keeping pace with its mighty fellows. Each was dedicated to exacting fierce vengeance upon the upstarts who had sought to question the power of those it served. A shoal of monstrous flying sharks, confident that they controlled the skies and, from the skies, the land.

Ships of Japan, with the Imperial crimson sun emblazoned on their white and gleaming hulls.

Ships of Russia, with great black double-headed eagles glaring from hulls of deepest scarlet, claws spread as if to strike.

Ships of France, on which the tricolour flag spread on backgrounds of blue was a piece of blatant hypocrisy; a sham of republicanism and an affront to the ideals of the French Revolution.

Ships of America, bearing the Stars and Stripes, no longer the banner of Liberty.

Ships of Britain.

Ships with cannon and bombs and crews who, in their pride, thought it was to be a simple matter to raze Dawn City and what it stood for.

Shark-ships, rapacious and cruel and arrogant, their booming engines like triumphant anticipatory laughter.

Could we withstand them, even for an instant? I doubted it.

Now our ground defences had opened up. Shells sped into the sky and exploded around the ships of the mighty air fleet, but on they came, through the smoke and flame, careless and haughty, closer and closer to Dawn City itself. And now our tiny fleet began to rise from the airpark to meet the invaders – fifteen modified merchantmen against a hundred specially designed men-o'-war. They had the advantage of the recoilless guns and could 'stand' in the air and shoot much longer and more accurately than the larger vessels, but there were few weak points on those flying ironclads and most of the explosive shells at worst only blackened the paint of the hulls or cracked the windows in the gondolas.

There was a bellow and fire sprouted from the leading British airship, HMAS *Edwardus Rex*, as its guns answered ours. I saw the hull of one of our ships crumple and the whole vessel plunge towards the rocky ground of the foothills, little figures leaping overboard in the hope of somehow escaping the worst of the impact. Black smoke curled everywhere over the scene. There came an explosion and a blaze of flame as the ship struck the ground and its engines blew up, the fuel oil igniting instantly.

Shaw was staring grimly through the window, controlling the formation of his ships through a wireless telephone. How hard it had been to make an impact on the enemy fleet – and how easily they had destroyed our ship!

Boom! Boom!

Again the great guns roared. Again an adapted merchantman buckled in the air and sank to the earth.

Only now did I wish that I had accepted a commission on one of the ships. Only now did I feel the urge to join the fight, to retaliate, as much as anything, out of a spirit of fair play.

Boom!

It was *The Rover*, spiralling down with two engines on fire and its hull buckling in half as the helium rushed into the atmosphere. I watched tensely as it fell, praying there would be enough gas left in the hull to let the ship come down relatively lightly. But that was a hundred tons of metal and plastic and guns and men falling through the sky. I closed my eyes and winced as I thought I felt the tremor of its impact with the ground.

I was in no doubt of Korzeniowski's fate.

But then, as if inspired by the old captain's heroic death, the *Shan-tien* (the *Loch Etive*) offered a broadside to the Japanese flagship, the *Yokomoto*, and must have struck right through to her ammunition store for she exploded in a thousand fiery fragments and there was scarcely a recognisable scrap of her left when the explosion had died.

Now we saw two more ships go down – an American and a French – and we cheered. We all cheered save for Una Persson who was looking bleakly out at the spot where *The Rover* had disappeared. Von Bek was in animated conversation with the major and did not seem to notice his mistress's grief. I went over to her and touched her shoulder.

'Perhaps he is only wounded,' I said.

She smiled at me through her tears and shook her head. 'He is dead,' she said. 'He died bravely, didn't he?'

'As he lived,' I said.

She seemed puzzled. 'I thought you hated him.'

'I thought I did. But I loved him.'

She pulled herself together at this and nodded, putting out a slender hand and letting the tips of the fingers rest for a moment on my sleeve. 'Thank you, Mr Bastable. I hope my father has not died for nothing.'

'We are giving a good account of ourselves,' I said.

But I saw that we had at most five ships left from the original fifteen and there were still nearly ninety allied battleships in the sky.

Shaw looked up, listening carefully. 'Infantry and motorised cavalry attacking the valley on all sides,' he said. 'Our men are standing firm.' He listened a little longer. 'I don't think we've much to fear from that quarter at the moment.'

The invading ships had not yet reached Dawn City. They had been forced to defend themselves against our first aerial attack and, now that our gunners were getting their range from the ground, one or two more were hit.

'Time to send up the *Fei-chi*, I think.' Shaw telephoned the order. 'The Great Powers think they have won! Now we shall show them our real strength!' He telephoned the soldiers defending the building housing Project NFB and reminded them that on no account should a ship be allowed to attack the place. The mysterious project was evidently of paramount importance in his strategy.

I could not see the hangars where the 'hornets' were stored

and my first glimpse of the winged and whirling little flying machines was when they climbed through the black smoke and began to spray the hulls of the flying ironclads with explosive bullets, attacking from above and diving down on their opponents who, doubtless, were still hardly aware of what was happening.

The *Victoria Imperatrix* went down. The *Theodore Roosevelt* went down. The *Alexandre Nevsky* went down. The *Tashiyawa* went down. The *Emperor Napoleon* and the *Pyat* went down. One after another they fell from the air, circling slowly or breaking up rapidly, but falling; without a doubt they were falling. And it did not seem that a single delicate *Fei-chi*, flown by only two men – an aviator and a gunner – had been hit. The guns of the foreign ships were simply not designed to hit such tiny targets. They roared and belched their huge shells in all directions, but they were baffled, like clumsy sea-cows attacked by sharp-toothed piranha fish, they simply did not know how to defend themselves. The Valley of the Morning was littered with their wreckage. A thousand fires burned in the hills, showing where the proud aerial ironclads had met their end. Half the allied fleet had been destroyed and five of our airships (including the *Shantien*) were now coming in to moor, leaving the fighting to the *Fei-chi*. Evidently the shock of facing the tiny heavier-than-air machines was too much for the attackers. They had seen their finest ships blown from the skies in a matter of minutes. Slowly the cumbersome men-o'-war turned and began to retreat. Not a single bomb had fallen on Dawn City.

Chapter Six

Another Meeting with the Amateur Archaeologist

WE HAD, AT some cost, won the first engagement, but there were many more still to come before we should know if we had driven the Great Powers away for good. We learned that their land invasion had also met with failure and that the allied forces had withdrawn. We exulted.

During the next few days we waited and recouped our strength and it was during this period that I, at last, offered my services to the Warlord of the Air, who accepted without comment of any kind and put me in command of my old ship, now the *Shan-tien*.

It was confirmed that Captain Korzeniowski and his entire crew had been killed when *The Rover* was shot down.

Then the attack began afresh and I prepared to go aboard my ship, but Shaw asked me to remain in the headquarters tower for it had become swiftly evident that the ships of the Great Powers had adopted a more cautious strategy. They came as far as the hills on the horizon and hovered there while they tried to shell the sheds where our *Fei-chi* were stored. I noticed, once again, that Shaw seemed more anxious for the safety of the Project NFB building than for the flying-machine sheds, but neither was badly hit, as it turned out.

I felt an appalling sense of outrage, however, when some of the shells exploded in Dawn City, damaging the pretty houses, breaking windows, blasting trees and flower beds, and I waited impatiently for orders to go to my ship. But Shaw remained cool and he let the enemy expend his fire-power for nearly an hour before he ordered the *Fei-chi* into the sky.

'But what about me?' I said, aggrieved. 'Aren't you going to let me have a crack at them? I've several deaths to avenge, you know – not least Korzeniowski's.'

'We all have much to avenge, Captain Bastable.' (As was his practice he had conferred a rank on me). 'And it is not quite the time, I'm afraid, to let you take yours. The *Shan-tien* is to fly the most important assignment of them all. But not yet – not yet…'

That was all I could get from him then.

Once again our heavier-than-air machines drove the flying ironclads beyond the hills and destroyed seven in the process. But this time we had casualties, for the airships had equipped themselves with fast-firing machine guns which could be mounted on the tops of the hulls in hastily manufactured armoured turrets where they could, while they lasted, give good retaliatory fire. The delicate two-man machines were easily destroyed once hit and we lost six during that second engagement.

The attack continued for nearly two weeks with constant reinforcements being brought up by the enemy, but with our own reserves slowly dwindling. I don't think even Shaw had expected the Great Powers to show such absolute resolve to destroy him. It was as if they felt their grip on all their territories would weaken if they were beaten by the warlord. We heard encouraging news, however. All over China peasants and workers and students were turning on their oppressors. The entire nation was in the grip of revolution. Shaw's hope was that trouble would break out in so many areas at once that the allied forces would be spread too thinly to be effective.

As it was, Dawn City had forced the Powers to concentrate much of their strength in one area and successful revolts had taken place in Shanghai (now in the control of a revolutionary committee) and Peking (where the occupying Japanese had been bloodily put to death) as well as other cities and parts of provinces.

From Dawn City Shaw heard the news of his revolution's spreading and his spirits rose, even as our supplies shrank.

Yet still we managed to hold the combined strength of the Great Powers at bay and Shaw took an even keener interest in the progress of that secret project of his.

One morning I was walking from my sleeping quarters to the central tower when I heard a commotion ahead of me and broke into a run. I found a crowd of people staring out at the airpark and pointing into the sky.

In astonishment I saw that a single airship was drifting in, its engines dead. There was no mistaking the Union Jack emblazoned on its tail planes. Hurriedly I ran towards the headquarters tower, certain that they must have seen the mysterious ship by now.

As I reached the door of the tower there came an enormous explosion which made the whole place shudder. I entered the lift and was borne swiftly up to the top of the building.

The little British airship – not nearly so large as the men-o'-war we had learned to expect – was bombing the *Fei-chi* sheds! It had waited for a favourable wind and then drifted in at night, unseen and unheard, with the object of destroying our flying machines.

Already every gun we had was opening up on the airship, which was very low in the sky. Luckily its bombs had not yet struck the sheds themselves, though several smoking craters showed that it had only just missed. This was no heavily armoured ship and its hull soon burst, the ship plummeting down stern first and bouncing right across the airpark, narrowly missing our tethered 'fleet' before coming to a stop. Immediately I and a number of others left the tower and climbed into a motor car. We raced out of Dawn City and across the airpark to where the ship was already being surrounded by Shaw's colourfully dressed bandit-soldiers. As I thought, few of the crew had been badly hurt. For the first time on that shattered hull I saw the name of the ship and I received a shock of recognition. I had almost forgotten it. It was the first airship I had ever seen. Evidently the British had called upon their Indian air fleet to give assistance. The survey ship I saw broken on the ground, quite close to the Project NFB building, was none other than the *Pericles* – the ship which had saved my life.

It gave me an odd turn to see that ship again, I don't mind admitting. I realised that the Great Powers must be using every ship they could spare in their efforts to destroy Dawn City.

And then I saw Major Enoch Powell himself come staggering from the wreckage, a wild look in his dark eyes. His face was smeared with oil and his uniform was torn. One arm was limp at his side, but he still clutched his baton as he supervised his men's escape from the ship. He recognised me right away.

His voice was high and strained. 'Hello, Bastable. In league with our Coloured Brethren now, are you? Well, well – wasn't much good saving your life, was it?'

'Good morning, major,' I said. 'Let me compliment you on your bravery.'

'Stupidity. Still, it was worth a try. You can't win, you know – for all your bloody little air boats. We'll get you in the end.'

'It's costing you rather a lot, though,' I pointed out.

Powell glared around suspiciously at Shaw's soldiers. 'What are they going to do? Torture us to death? Send our bodies back as a warning to others?'

'You'll be well treated,' I told him. I fell into step with him as he and his men were disarmed and escorted back towards Dawn City. 'I'm sorry about the *Pericles*.'

'So am I.' He was almost crying – whether with fury or with sorrow, I could not tell. 'So that's what you were – a bloody nihilist. That's why you claimed to have amnesia. And to think I believed you were one of us.'

'I was one of you,' I said quietly. 'Maybe I still am. I don't know.'

'This is a bad show, Bastable. All China in revolt. Parts of India have caught the fever now, not to mention what's going on in South-East Asia. Poor benighted natives think they've got a chance. They haven't, of course.'

'I think they have – now,' I said. 'The days of imperialism are ending – at least, as we understand it.'

'If they are ending – it's to plunge us all back into the Dark Ages. The Great Powers have ensured the peace of the world for a hundred years – and now it's all over. It'll take a decade to get back to normal, if we ever do.'

'It will never be "normal" again,' I said. 'That peace, major, was bought at too dear a price.'

He grunted. 'They've certainly converted you. But they'll never convert me. You'd rather have war in Europe, would you?'

'A war in Europe should have happened a long time ago. A war between the Great Powers would have destroyed their grip on their subject peoples. Don't you see that?'

'I don't see anything of the kind. I feel like someone witnessing the last days of the Roman Empire. Damn!' He winced as he struck his arm against a shed.

'I'll get that arm attended to as soon as we reach the city,' I said.

'Don't want your charity,' said Powell. 'Bloody Chinks and niggers running the world – that's a laugh.'

I left him then and I did not see him again.

If I had been in two minds about my loyalties before, I was no longer. Powell's parting sneer of contempt had succeeded in my deciding to choose Shaw's side once and for all. The mask of kindly patronage had dropped away to show the hatred and the fear beneath.

*

When I got back to the central tower Shaw was waiting for me. He looked resolute.

'That sneak attack determined something,' he said. 'Project NFB is complete. I think it will be successful, though there is no time – or method – to test it. We shall do what that ship did. We'll leave tonight.'

'I think you had better explain a little more clearly,' I smiled. 'What are we to do?'

'The Great Powers are using the big airship yards at Hiroshima as their main base. That is where they go for repairs and spares. It is the only relatively nearby place where they can be serviced properly. Also it is where many of the big flying ironclads are built. If we destroy that base – we have considerably greater flexibility of manoeuvre, Captain Bastable.'

'I agree,' I said. 'But we haven't enough airships to do it, General Shaw. We have very few bombs. The *Fei-chi* cannot fly that distance. Also there is every likelihood that we shall be sighted and shot down when we leave the Valley of the Morning or at any point beyond it. How can we possibly do it?'

'Project NFB is ready. Is there a chance of taking the *Shan-tien* out tonight and getting past the allied ships?'

'We've as good a chance as that ship had in reaching here,' I said. 'If the wind's right.'

'Then be ready to leave, Captain Bastable, at sunset.'

I shrugged. It was suicide. But I would do it.

Chapter Seven
Project NFB

BY SUNSET WE were all aboard. During the day there had been a few desultory attacks by the enemy airships, but no serious damage had been done.

'They are waiting for reinforcements,' Shaw told me. 'And those reinforcements, according to my information, are due to come from Hiroshima, starting out tomorrow morning.'

'It's going to be a long flight for us,' I said. 'We'll not be back by morning, even if we're successful.'

'Then we'll go to Peking. It is in the hands of fellow revolutionists now.'

'True.'

Ulianov, von Bek and Una Persson had come aboard with General Shaw. 'I want them to see it so that they will believe it,' he told me. Also on board were a number of scientists who had supervised the loading of a fairly large object into our lower hold. These were serious-looking Hungarians, Germans and Americans and they said nothing to me. But they had an Australian with them and I asked him what was going on.

He grinned. 'Going *up*, you mean. Ha ha! Somebody ought to tell you, but it's not my job. Good luck, sport.'

And he left with the rest of his fellow scientists.

General Shaw put an arm round my shoulders. 'Don't worry, Bastable. You'll know before we get there.'

'It must be a bomb,' I said. 'A particularly powerful bomb? Nitro-glycerin? A fire bomb?'

'Wait.'

We all stood on the bridge of the *Loch Etive* watching the sun go down. The ship – I should call her the *Shan-tien* – was not

171

the luxury liner I had known. She had been stripped of every non-essential fitting and through her portholes jutted the snouts of General O.T. Shaw's recoilless guns. What had been promenade decks were now artillery platforms. Where passengers had danced, ammunition was stored. If we were discovered, we should give a good account of ourselves. I thought back to that stupid incident with 'Roughrider Ronnie' Reagan. But for him, I should not today be in command of this ship, flying a foolhardy assignment whose nature I could not even guess at. It seemed that more time had passed since my encounter with Reagan than had passed since I had been flung from my own time into the future.

Ulianov came up beside me as I stood at my controls and began to prepare to let slip from the mast.

'Brooding, young man?'

I looked into his old, kindly eyes. 'I was wondering what made a decent English army officer turn into a desperate revolutionist overnight,' I smiled.

'It happens to many like that,' he said. 'I have seen them. But you have to show them so *much* injustice first... Nobody wants to believe that the world is cruel – or that one's own kind are cruel. Not to know cruelty is to remain innocent, eh? And we should all like to remain innocent. A revolutionist is a man who, perhaps, fails to keep his innocence but so desperately wants it back that he seeks to create a world where all shall be innocent in that way.'

'But can such a world ever exist, Vladimir Ilyitch?' I sighed. 'You're describing the Garden of Eden, you know. A familiar dream – but a reality? I wonder...'

'There are an infinite number of possible societies. In an infinite universe, all may become real sooner or later. Yet it is always up to mankind to make real what it really wishes to be real. Man is a creature capable of building almost anything he pleases – or destroying anything he pleases. Sometimes, as old as I am, I am astonished by him!' He chuckled.

I smiled back, reflecting that he would really be astonished if he knew that, in effect, I was older than he!

It was soon dark and I drew a deep breath. Our only light came from the illuminated instrument panels. I intended to get the ship up to three thousand feet and remain at that height for as long as possible. The wind was blowing in roughly a north-easterly direction and would take us the way we needed to go if we were to leave the valley without recourse to our engines.

'Let slip,' I said.

Our mooring lines fell away and we began to rise. I heard the wind whistling about our hull. I saw the lights of Dawn City dropping down below us.

'Three thousand feet, height coxswain,' I said. 'Take it slowly. Forty-five degrees elevation. Turn her port-side on to the wind, steering cox.' I checked our compass. 'Keep her steady.'

Everyone was silent. Von Bek and Una Persson stood at the window, staring down. Shaw and Ulianov stood near me, peering at instruments which meant next to nothing to them. Shaw was dressed in a blue cotton suit and was puffing on a cigarette. On his head was tilted a coolie hat of woven reeds. There was a holstered revolver at his belt. After a while he began to pace back and forth across the bridge.

We were drifting slowly over the hills. Within minutes we should be upon the main enemy camp and in range of their artillery. If we were sighted they could swiftly send up several ships and there would be little doubt of the outcome. We should be blown from the sky, along with Project NFB. With Shaw dead, I doubted if Dawn City would have the will to carry on the fight much longer.

But at last the camp was behind us and we relaxed slightly.

'Can we start the engines yet?' Shaw asked.

I shook my head. 'Not yet. Another twenty minutes, perhaps. Maybe longer.'

'We must get to Hiroshima before it is light.'

'I understand.'

'With those yards destroyed they will have almost as much difficulty replenishing their ammunition as we have. It will make it more of an equal fight.'

'I agree,' I said. 'And now, General Shaw, can you tell me what you hope to use to accomplish that destruction?'

173

'It is in the lower hold,' he said. 'You saw the scientists bring it aboard.'

'But what is it, this Project NFB?'

'I'm told it's a powerful bomb. I know very little more – it is *extremely* scientific – but it has been a dream of some scientists to make it since, I suppose, the beginnings of the century. It has cost us a lot of money and several years of research just to build one – the one in the lower hold.'

'How do you know it will work?'

'I do not. But if it does work, it should, in a *single explosion*, devastate the best part of the airship yards. The scientists tell me that when it is detonated the explosion will be equal to several hundred tons of TNT.'

'Good God!'

'I was equally incredulous, but they convinced me – particularly when three years ago they almost destroyed their entire laboratory with a very minor experiment along these lines. It is something to do with the atomic structure of matter, I believe. They had the theory for the bomb for a long time, but it took years to make the thing workable.'

'Well, let's hope they're right,' I smiled. 'If we drop it and it turns out to have the explosive power of a firecracker we are going to look very foolish.'

'Agreed.'

'And if it is as powerful as you say, we had better keep high enough up – blasts rise as well as spread. We should be at least a thousand feet above ground level when it goes off.'

Shaw nodded absently.

Soon I was able to start the engines and the *Shan-tien*'s bridge trembled slightly as we surged through the night at 150 mph with the wind behind us! The roar of her engines going full out was music to my ears. I began to cheer up and checked our position. We had not much time to spare. By my calculations we should reach the Hiroshima airship yards about half an hour before the first intimation of dawn.

For a while we were all lost in our own thoughts, standing on the bridge and listening to the rapid note of the engines.

It was Shaw who broke the silence.

'If I die now,' he said suddenly, expressing a notion not far from the minds of any of us, 'I think that I have sown the seeds for a successful revolution throughout the world. The scientists at Dawn City will perfect Project NFB even if *this* bomb is not successful. More of the *Fei-chi* will be built and distributed amongst other revolutionists. I will give power to the people. Power to decide their own fate. I have already shown them that the Great Powers are not invincible, that they can be overthrown. You see, Uncle Vladimir, it *is* hope and not despair which breeds successful revolution!'

'Perhaps,' Ulianov admitted. 'Yet hope alone is not sufficient.'

'No – political power grows out of the erupting casing of a bomb like the bomb we are carrying. With such bombs at their disposal, the oppressed will be able to dictate any terms they choose to their oppressors.'

'If the bomb works,' Una Persson said. 'I am not sure it can. Nuclear fission, eh? All very well – but how do you achieve it? I fear you may have been deceived, Mr Shaw.'

'We'll see.'

I remember the feeling of anticipation as the dark coast of Japan was sighted against the gleam of the moonlit ocean and once again we cut out the engines and began to drift on the wind.

I readied the controls which would release the safety bolts on the loading doors (the main bolts had to be drawn by hand) and let the bomb fall onto the unsuspecting airship yards. I saw ribbons of myriad coloured lights. The city of Hiroshima. Beyond it lay the yards themselves – miles of sheds, of mooring masts and repair docks, an installation almost entirely given over to military airships, particularly at this time. If we could destroy only a part of it, we should succeed in delaying the assault on Dawn City.

I remember staring at Una Persson and wondering if she were still thinking of her father's death. And what was von Bek brooding about? He had begun by hating Shaw but now he was bound to admit that the Warlord of the Air was a genius and that he had achieved what many another revolutionist had hoped to achieve. Ulianov, for instance. It seemed that the old man hardly realised that his dream was coming true. He had waited so long. I suppose I sympathise with Ulianov more than most now. He had waited all his life for revolution, for the rise of the proletariat, and he was never to see it actually taking place. Perhaps it never did...

Shaw was leaning forward eagerly as we drifted high above the airship yards. He had one hand on the holster, a cigarette in his other hand. His yellow coolie hat was pushed back off his head and with his handsome Eurasian features he looked every bit a hero of popular romance.

The yards were ablaze with light as men worked on the battleships which were to be ready for the big invasion on Dawn City next day. I saw the black outlines of the hulls, saw the flare of acetylene torches.

'Are we there?' Once again the warlord who had changed history looked like an excited schoolboy. 'Are those the yards, Captain Bastable?'

'That's them,' I said.

'The poor men,' said Ulianov, shaking his white head. 'They are only workers, like the others.'

Von Bek jerked his thumb back towards the city. 'Their children will thank us when they grow up.'

I wondered. There would be many orphans and widows in Hiroshima tomorrow.

Una Persson looked nervously at me. It seems she had lost her doubts about the efficacy of the bomb. 'Mr Bastable, as I understand it a bomb of this type can, in theory, produce incalculable destruction. Parts of the city might be harmed.'

I smiled. 'The city's nearly two miles away, Mrs Persson.'

She nodded. 'I suppose you're right.' She stroked her neat, dark hair, looking down at the yards again.

''Take her down to a thousand feet, height cox,' I said. 'Easy as she goes.'

We could see individual people now. Men moved across the

concrete carrying tools, climbing the scaffolding around the huge ironclads.

'There are the main fitting yards.' Shaw pointed. 'Can we get the ship over there without power?'

'We'll be spotted soon. But I'll try. Five degrees, steering cox.'

'Five degrees, sir,' said the pale young man at the wheel. The ship creaked slightly as she turned.

'Be ready to take her up fast, height cox,' I warned.

'Aye, aye, sir.'

We were over the fitting yards. I picked up my speaking tube.

'Captain to lower hold. Are the main loading doors ready?'

'Ready sir.'

I pressed the lever which would release the safety bolts.

'Safety bolts gone, sir.'

'Stand by to release cargo.'

'Standing by, sir.'

I was using a procedure normally used to lighten the ship in an emergency.

The huge ship sank down and down through the night. I heard a sighing breeze sliding about her nose. A melancholy breeze.

'Gunners make ready to fire. Return fire if fired upon.' This was in case we were recognised and attacked. I was relying on the surprise of the big explosion to give us time to get away.

'All guns ready, sir.'

Shaw winked at me and chuckled.

'Stand by all engines,' I said. 'Full ahead as soon as you hear the bang.'

'Standing by, sir.'

'Ready cargo doors.'

'Ready, sir.'

'Let her go.'

'She's gone, sir.'

'Elevation sixty degrees,' I said. 'Up to three thousand, height cox. We've made it.'

The ship tilted and we gripped the handrails as the bridge sloped steeply.

Shaw and the others were peering down. I remember their faces so well. Von Bek pursing his lips and frowning. Una Persson apparently thinking of something else altogether. Ulianov smiling slightly to himself. Shaw turned to me. He grinned. 'She's just about to hit. The bomb...'

I remember his face full of joy as the blinding white light flooded up behind him, framing the four of them in black silhouette. There was a strange noise, like a single, loud heartbeat. There was darkness and I knew I was blind. I burned with unbearable heat. I remember wondering at the intensity of the explosion. It must have destroyed the whole city, perhaps the island. The enormity of what had happened dawned on me.

Oh my God, I remember thinking, *I wish the damned airship had never been invented.*

Chapter Eight
The Lost Man

'A ND THAT'S ABOUT it.' Bastable's voice was harsh and
cracked. He had been talking for the best part of three days.

I laid down my pencil and looked wearily back through the
pages and pages of shorthand notes which recorded his fantastic
story.

'You really believe you experienced all that!' I said. 'But how do
you explain getting back to our own time?'

'Well, I was picked up in the sea, apparently; I was unconscious, temporarily blinded and quite badly burned. The Japanese
fishermen who found me thought I was a seaman who'd been
caught in an engine-room accident. I was taken to Hiroshima and
put into the Sailors' Hospital there. I was quite astonished to be
told it *was* Hiroshima, I don't mind admitting, since I was convinced the place had been blown to smithereens. Of course, it was
some time before I realised I was back in 1902.'

'And what did you do then?' I helped myself to a drink and
offered him one, which he refused.

'Well, as soon as I came out of hospital I went to the British
Embassy, of course. They were decent. I claimed I had amnesia
again. I gave my name, rank and serial number and said that the
last thing I remembered was being pursued by Sharan Khang's
priests in the Temple of the Future Buddha. They telegraphed my
regiment and, naturally, they confirmed that the particulars I had
given were correct. I had my passage and train fare paid to Luc-
know, where my regiment was then stationed. Six months had
passed since the affair at Teku Benga.'

'And your commanding officer recognised you, of course.'

Bastable gave another of his short, bitter laughs. 'He said that I
had died at Teku Benga, that I could not have lived. He said that

179

although I resembled Bastable in some ways I was an imposter. I was older, for one thing, and my voice was different.'

'You reminded him of things only you could remember?'

'Yes. He congratulated me on my homework and told me that if I tried anything like that again he would have me arrested.'

'And you accepted that? What about your relatives? Didn't you try to get in touch with them?'

Bastable looked at me seriously. 'I was afraid to. You see this is not completely the world I remember. I'm sure it's my memory. Something caused by my passage to and fro in Time. But there are small details which seem wrong...' He cast about with a wild eye, like one who suddenly realises he is lost in a place he presumed familiar. 'Small details...'

'The opium, perhaps?' I murmured.

'Maybe.'

'And that's why you're afraid to go home. In case your relatives *don't* recognise you?'

'That's why. I think I will have that drink.' He crossed the room and poured himself a large glass of rum. He had exhausted his supply of drugs while talking to me. 'After being kicked out by my CO – I recognised *him*, by the way – I wandered up to Teku Benga. I got as far as the chasm and sure enough the whole place was in ruins. I had a horrifying feeling that if I *could* cross that chasm I'd find a corpse and it would be mine. So I didn't try. I had a few shillings and I bought some native clothes – begged my way across India, sometimes riding the trains, looking, at first, for some sort of confirmation of my own identity, somebody to tell me I really was alive. I talked to mystics I met and tried to get some sense out of them, but it was all no good. So I decided I'd try to forget my identity. I took to swallowing opium in any form I could get it. I went to China. To Shantung. I found the Valley of the Morning. I don't know what I expected it to be. It was as beautiful as ever. There was a little, poor village in it. The people were kind to me.'

'Then you came here?'

'After a few other places, yes.'

I didn't know what to make of the chap. I could not but believe every word of what he had said. The conviction in his voice was so strong.

'I think you'd better come back to London with me,' I said. 'See your relatives. They'll be bound to identify you.'

'Perhaps.' He sighed. 'But you know, I think I'm not *meant* to be here. That explosion – that awful explosion over Hiroshima – it – it spat me out of one time in which I didn't belong – into another...'

'Oh, nonsense.'

'No, it's true. This is 1903 – or *a* 1903 – but it – it isn't *my* 1903.'

I thought I understood what he meant, but I could hardly believe that such a thing could be remotely true. I could accept that a man had gone forward in Time and been returned to his own period – but I couldn't believe that there might be an *alternative* 1903.

Bastable took another drink. 'And pray to God that it wasn't *your* 1973,' he said. 'Science run wild – revolutions – bombs which can destroy whole cities!' He shuddered.

'But there were benefits,' I said hesitantly. 'And I'm not sure the natives you mention weren't, on the whole, well off.'

He shrugged. 'Different ages make the same people think in different terms. I did what I did. There's nothing else to be said. I probably shouldn't do it now. Besides, there *is* more freedom in this world of ours, old man. Believe me – there is!'

'It's disappearing every day,' I said. 'And not everyone's free, I admit that privilege exists...'

He raised a silencing hand. 'No discussions of that kind, for God's sake.'

'All right.'

'You might as well tear those notes up,' he said. 'Nobody will believe you. Why should they? Do you mind if I take a bit of a stroll – get some fresh air, while I think what to do?'

'Yes. Very well.'

I watched him walk tiredly out of the room and heard his feet on the stairs. What a strange young man he was.

I glanced through my notes. Giant airships – mono-railways – electric bicycles – wireless telephones – flying machines – all the marvels. They could not have been invented by the mind of one young man.

I lay down on my bed, still mulling the problem over, and I must have fallen asleep. I remember waking briefly once and wondering where Bastable was, then I slept till morning, assuming he was in the next room.

But when I got up Ram Dass told me that the bed had not been slept in. I went and enquired of Olmeijer if he knew where Bastable was, but the fat Dutchman had not seen him.

I asked everyone in the town if they had come across Bastable. Someone told me that they had seen a young man staggering down by the harbour late at night and assumed him drunk.

A ship had left that morning. Perhaps Bastable had got aboard. Perhaps he had thrown himself into the sea.

I heard no more of Bastable, though I advertised for news of him and spent more than a year making enquiries, but he had vanished. Perhaps he had actually been snatched through Time again – to the past or the future or even to the 1903 he thought he should belong in?

And that was that. I've had the whole manuscript typed up, put it into order, cut out repetitions and some unnecessary comments Bastable made while he spoke. I've clarified where I could. But essentially this is Bastable's account as he told it to me.

Note (1907): Since I saw Bastable, of course, the air has been conquered by the Wright brothers and the powered balloon is being developed apace. Radiotelephony has become an actuality and I heard recently that there are several inventors experimenting with monorail systems. Is it all coming true? If so, for my own selfish reasons, I look forward to a world made increasingly peaceful and convenient, for I shall be dead before the world sees the revolutionary holocaust Bastable described. And yet there are a few things which do not coincide with his description. The heavier-than-air flying machine is an actuality already. People in France and America are flying them and there is even some talk of flying across the Channel in one! But perhaps these aeroplanes will not last or are not capable of very great speeds or sustained flight.

I have tried to interest a number of publishers in Bastable's account, but all judge it too fantastical to be presented as fact and too gloomy to be presented as fiction. Writers like Mr Wells seem to have the corner in such books. Only this one is true. I'm sure it is true. I shall continue to try to get it published, for Bastable's sake.

Note (1909): Bleriot has flown the Channel in an aeroplane! Again I tried to interest a publisher in Bastable's story and, like several others, he asked me to alter it – 'put in more adventures, a love story, a few more marvels' is what he said. I cannot alter what Bastable told me and so I consign the manuscript to the drawer for perhaps another year.

Note (1910): Off to China soon. Might look for the Valley of the Morning to see what it is like and perhaps hope to find Bastable there. He seemed to like the place, and the villagers, he said, looked after him well. China *is* full of revolutionists these days, of course, but I expect I'll be safe enough. I may even be there when it becomes a republic! Certainly things are shaky and it's likely the Russians and Japanese will try to grab large chunks of the country.

If I do not return from China, I should be grateful if someone continues to try to get this published.

MCM

Editor's Note

THE ABOVE WAS the last note my grandfather made on the manuscript – or the last we have found, anyway. He did return from China, but doubtless he didn't find Bastable there or he would have mentioned it. I think he must have given up trying to get the book published after 1910.

My grandfather went to France in 1914 and was killed on the Somme in October 1916.

Michael Moorcock,
1971

The Second Adventure

The Land Leviathan

To the Memory of
Steve Biko, Malcolm X, and Mongezi Feza

Introduction

My GRANDFATHER, WHO died relatively young after he had volunteered for service in the Great War, became increasingly secretive and misanthropic in his last years so that the discovery of a small steel safe amongst his effects was unsurprising and aroused no curiosity whatsoever in his heirs who, finding that they could not unlock it (no key ever came to light), simply stored it away with his papers and forgot about it. The safe remained in the attic of our Yorkshire house for the best part of fifty years and doubtless would still be there if it had not been for my discovery of the manuscript which I published a couple of years ago under the title *The Warlord of the Air*. After the book was published I received many interesting letters from people asking me if it was merely a piece of fiction or if the story had come into my hands as I had described. I, of course, believed Bastable's story (and my grandfather's) completely, yet sometimes felt quite as frustrated as my grandfather had done when he had tried to get people to share *his* belief, and I couldn't help brooding occasionally on the mystery of the young man's disappearance after those long hours spent talking to my grandfather on Rowe Island in the early years of the century. As it turned out, I was soon to find myself in possession of, for me, the best possible proof of my grandfather's veracity, if not of Bastable's.

I spent this past summer in Yorkshire, where we have a house overlooking the moors of the West Riding, and, having little to do but go for long walks and enjoy the pleasures of rock climbing, I took to looking through the rest of my grandfather's things, coming at length upon the old steel safe jammed in a corner under the eaves of one of our innumerable attics. The safe was hidden behind the moulting remains of a stuffed timber wolf which had terrified me as a child, and perhaps that was the reason why I had not previously found it. As I pushed the beast aside, his dusty glass eyes seemed to glare at me with hurt dignity and he toppled slowly sideways and fell with a muffled crash into a heap of yellowing newspapers which another of my relatives, for reasons of his own, had once thought worth preserving. It was as if the wolf had been guarding the safe since the beginning of Time, and I had a slight feeling of invading hallowed ground, much as some booty-hunting Victorian archaeologist must have felt as he chipped his way into the tomb of a dead Egyptian king!

The safe was about eighteen inches deep and a couple of feet high, made of thick steel. The outside had grown a little rusty and the handle would not budge when I tried it. I hunted about the house for spare keys which might fit the lock, finding the best part of a score of keys, but none which would open the safe. By now my curiosity was fully whetted and I manhandled the safe downstairs and took it into my workshop where I tried to force it. All I succeeded in doing was to break two or three chisels and ruin the blades of my hacksaw, so eventually I had to telephone a specialist locksmith in Leeds and ask for expert help in opening the thing. I was pessimistically certain that the safe would contain only some out-of-date share certificates or nothing at all, but I knew I should not be able to rest until it *was* opened. The locksmith came, eventually, and it took him only a short while to get the safe undone.

I remember the rather sardonic look he offered me as the contents were displayed for the first time in almost sixty years. It was plain that he thought I had wasted my money, for there were no family treasures here, merely a pile of closely written foolscap sheets, beginning to show their age. The handwriting was not even my grandfather's and I experienced a distinct sinking sensation, for obviously I had hoped to find notes which would tell me more about Bastable and my grandfather's experiences after he had set off for China to seek the Valley of the Morning, where he had guessed Bastable to be.

As he left, the locksmith gave me what I guessed to be a pitying look and said that his firm would be sending the bill along later. I sighed, made myself a pot of coffee, and then sat down to leaf through the sheets.

Only then did I realise that I had found something even more revealing than anything I had hoped to discover (and, it emerged, even more mystifying!) – *for these notes were Bastable's own.* Here, written in his hand, was an account of his experiences after he had left my grandfather – there was even a brief note addressed to him from Bastable:

Moorcock. I hope this reaches you. Make of it what you will. I'm going to try my luck again. This time if I am not successful I doubt I shall have the courage to continue with my life (if it is mine). Yours – Bastable.

Attached to this were some sheets in my grandfather's flowing handwriting and these I reproduce in the body of the text, making it the first section.

This first section is self-explanatory. There is little I need to add at all. You may read the rest for yourself and make up your own mind as to its authenticity.

Michael Moorcock,
Ladbroke Grove,
London,
September 1973

Prologue
In Search of Oswald Bastable

IF I WERE ever to write a book of travel, no matter how queer the events it described, I am sure I would never have the same trouble placing it with a publisher as I had when I tried to get into print Oswald Bastable's strange tale of his visit to the future in the year 1973. People are not alarmed by the unusual so long as it is placed in an acceptable context. A book describing as fact the discovery of a race of four-legged, three-eyed men of abnormal intelligence and supernatural powers who live in Thibet would probably be taken by a large proportion of the public as absolutely credible. Similarly, if I had dressed up Bastable's story as fiction I am certain that critics would have praised me for my rich imagination and that a reasonably wide audience would have perused it in a couple of summer afternoons and thought it a jolly exciting read for the money, then promptly forgotten all about it.

Perhaps it is what I should have done, but, doubtless irrationally, I felt that I had a duty to Bastable to publish his account as it stood.

I could, were I trying to make money with my pen, write a whole book, full of sensational anecdotes, concerning my travels in China – a country divided by both internal and external pressures, where the only real law can be found in the territories leased to various foreign powers, and where a whole variety of revolutionists and prophets of peculiar political and religious sects squabble continuously for a larger share of that vast and ancient country; but my object is not to make money from Bastable's story. I merely think it is up to me to keep my word to him and do my best to put it before the public.

Now that I have returned home, with some relief, to England, I have become a little more optimistic about China's chances of saving herself from chaos and foreign exploitation. There has been the revolution resulting in the deposing of the last of the Manchus and the setting up of a republic under Sun Yat-sen, who seems to be a reasonable and moderate leader, a man who has learned a great deal from the political history of Europe and yet does not seem content just to ape the customs of the West. Possibly there is hope for China now. However, it is not my business here to speculate upon China's political future, but to record how I travelled to the Valley of the Morning, following Bastable's somewhat vague description of its location. I had gathered that it lay somewhere in Shantung province and to the north of Wuchang (which, itself, of course, is in Hupeh). My best plan was to go as directly as possible to Shantung and then make my way inland. I consulted all the atlases and gazetteers, spoke to friends who had been missionaries in that part of China, and got a fairly clear idea of where I might find the valley, if it existed at all.

Yet I was still reluctant to embark upon what was likely to be a long and exhausting expedition. For all that I had completely believed Bastable, I had no evidence at all to substantiate my theory that he had gone back to the Valley of the Morning, which, by 1973, would contain the Utopian city built by General Shaw, the Warlord of the Air, and called Chi'ng Che'eng Ta-Chia (or, in English, roughly Democratic Dawn City). Even if he had gone there – and found nothing – he could easily have disappeared into the vastness of the Asian continent and as easily have perished in one of the minor wars or uprisings which constantly ravaged those poor and strife-ridden lands.

Therefore I continued to lead my conventional life, putting the whole perplexing business of Captain Bastable as far into the back of my mind as possible, although I would patiently send his original manuscript to a fresh publisher every time it came back from the last. I also sent a couple of letters to *The Times* in the hope that my story of my meeting with Bastable would attract the attention of that or some other newspaper, but the letters were never published. Neither, it seemed, were any of the popular monthlies, like *The Strand*, interested, for all that their pages were full of wild and unlikely predictions of what the future was bound to hold for us. I even considered writing to Mr H.G. Wells, whose books *Anticipations* and *The Discovery of the Future* created such a stir a few years ago, but Mr Wells, whom I understood to be a full-blooded socialist, would probably have found Bastable's story too much out of sympathy with his views and would have ignored me as cheerfully as anyone else. I did draft a letter, but finally did not send it.

It was about this time that it was brought to my attention that I was beginning to earn a reputation as something of a crank. This was a reputation I felt I could ill afford and it meant that I was forced, at last, to come to a decision. I had been noticing, for several months, a slightly odd atmosphere at my London club. People I had known for years, albeit only acquaintances, seemed reluctant to pass the time of day with me, and others would sometimes direct looks at me which were downright cryptic. I was not particularly bothered by any of this, but the mystery, such as it was, was finally made clear to me by an old friend of mine who was, himself, a publisher, although he concentrated entirely on poetry and novels and so I had never had occasion to submit Bastable's manuscript to him. He knew of it, however, and had initially been able to give me the names of one or two publishers who might have been interested. Now, however, he approached me in the library of the club where, after lunch, I had gone to read for half an hour. He attracted my attention with a discreet cough.

'Hope you don't mind me interrupting, Moorcock.'

'Not at all.' I indicated a nearby chair. 'As a matter of fact I wanted a word with you, old boy. I'm still having trouble placing that manuscript I mentioned...'

He ignored my offer of a chair and remained standing.

'That's exactly what I wanted to talk to you about. I've been meaning to speak to you for a month or two now, but to tell you the truth I've had no idea how to approach you. This must sound like damned interference and I'd be more than grateful if you would take what I have to say in the spirit it's meant.'

He looked extraordinarily embarrassed, squirming like a school-boy. I even thought I detected the trace of a blush on his cheeks.

I laughed.

'You're making me extremely curious, old man. What is it?'

'You won't be angry – no – you've every reason to be angry. It's not that I believe –'

'Come on, out with it.' I put my book down and gave him a smile. 'We're old friends, you and I.'

'Well, Moorcock, it's *about* Bastable's manuscript. A lot of people – mainly in publishing, of course, but quite a few of them are members of the club – well, they think you've been duped by the chap who told you that story.'

'Duped?' I raised my eyebrows.

He looked miserably at the carpet. 'Or worse,' he murmured.

'I think you'd better tell me what they're saying.' I frowned. 'I'm sure you mean well and I assure you that I'll take anything you have to say in good part. I've known you too long to be offended.'

He was plainly relieved and came and sat down in the next chair. 'Well,' he began, 'most people think that you're the victim of a hoax. But a few are beginning to believe that you've turned a bit – a bit eccentric. Like those chaps who predict the end of the world all the time, or communicate with the astral plane, and so on. You know what I mean, I suppose.'

My answering smile must have seemed to him a bit grim. 'I know exactly what you mean. I had even considered it. It must seem a very rum go to someone who never met Bastable. Now you mention it, I'm not surprised if I'm the gossip of half London. Why shouldn't people think such things about me? I'd be tempted to think them myself about *you* if you came to me with a story like Bastable's. As it is, you've been extremely tolerant of me!'

His smile was weak as he tried to acknowledge my joke. I went on:

'So they think I'm a candidate for Colney Hatch, do they? Well, of course, I've absolutely no proof to the contrary. If only I could produce Bastable himself. Then people could make up their own minds about the business.'

'It *has* become something of an obsession,' suggested my friend gently. 'Perhaps it would be better to drop the whole thing?'

'You're right – it is an obsession. I happen to believe that Bastable was telling the truth.'

'That's as may be…'

'You mean I should stop my efforts to get the account into print.'

There was a hint of sorrow in his eyes. 'There isn't a publisher in London, old man, who would touch it now. They have *their* reputations to think of. Anyone who took it would be a laughing stock. That's why you've had so much trouble in placing it. Drop it, Moorcock, for your sake and everyone else's.'

'You could be right.' I sighed. 'Yet, if I could come up with some sort of proof, possibly then they would stop laughing.'

'How could you find the proof which would convince them?'

'I could go and look for Bastable in China and tell him the trouble he's caused me. I could hope that he would come back to London with me – talk to people himself. I could put the matter into his hands and let him deal with his own manuscript. What would you say to that?'

He shrugged and made a gesture with his right hand. 'I agree it would be better than nothing.'

'But your own opinion is that I should forget all about it. You think I should burn the manuscript and have done with it, once and for all?'

'That's my opinion, yes. For your own sake, Moorcock – and your family's. You're wasting so much of your time – not to mention your capital.'

'I know that you have my interests at heart,' I told him, 'but I made a promise to Bastable (although he never heard me make it) and I intend to keep it, if I can. However, I'm glad that you spoke to me. It took courage to do that and I appreciate that it was done with the best of intentions. I'll think the whole thing over, at any rate.'

'Yes,' he said eagerly, 'do think it over. No point in fighting a losing battle, eh? You took this very decently, Moorcock. I was afraid you'd chuck me out on my ear. You had every right to do so.'

Again I laughed. 'I'm not that much of a lunatic, as you can see. I haven't lost all my common sense. But doubtless anyone with common sense would listen to me and become convinced that I *was* a lunatic! Whether, however, *I* have enough common sense to put the whole obsession behind me is quite another matter!'

He got up. 'Let's stop talking about it. Can I buy you a drink?'

For the moment it was obviously politic to accept his offer so that he should not think I had, after all, taken offence. 'I'd be glad of one,' I said. 'I hope the other members aren't afraid that I'm about to run riot with a meat-axe or something!'

As we left the library he clapped me on the shoulder, speaking with some relief. 'I don't think so. Though there was some talk of chaining down the soda siphon a week or two ago.'

I only went back to the club once more during that period and it was noticeable how much better the atmosphere had become. I determined, there and then, to give up all immediate attempts to get Bastable's story published and I began to make concrete plans for a trip to China.

And so, one bright autumn morning, I arrived at the offices of the Peninsular & Oriental Steam Navigation Company and booked the earliest possible passage on a ship called the *Mother Gangá*, which, I gathered, was not the proudest ship of that particular line, but would be the first to call at Weihaiwei, a city lying on the coast of that part of Shantung leased to Britain in 1898. I thought it only sense to begin my journey in relatively friendly country where I could seek detailed advice and help before pressing on into the interior.

Mother Gangá took her time. She was an old ship and she had evidently come to the conclusion that nothing in the world was urgent enough to require her to hurry. She called at every possible port to unload one cargo and to load another, for she was not primarily a passenger ship at all. It was easy to see why she rid herself of some of her cargoes (which seemed completely worthless), but hard to understand why the traders in those small, obscure ports should be prepared to exchange something of relative value for them!

I was prepared for the slowness of the journey, however, and spent much of my time working out the details of my plans and poring over my original shorthand notes to see if Bastable had told me anything more which might offer a clue to his whereabouts. I found little, but by the time I disembarked I was fit (thanks to my habit of taking plenty of exercise every day on board) and rested and ready for the discomforts which must surely lie ahead of me.

The discomfort I had expected, but what I had not anticipated was the extraordinary beauty and variety of even this relatively insignificant part of China. It struck me as I went up on deck to supervise the unloading of my trunks and I believe I must have gasped.

A huge pale blue sky hung over a city which was predominantly white and red and gold – a collection of ancient Chinese pagodas and archways mixed with more recent European building. Even these later buildings had a certain magic to them in that light, for they had been built of local stone and much of the stone contained fragments of quartz which glittered when the sun struck them. The European buildings were prominent on the waterfront where many trading companies had built their offices and warehouses and the flags of a score of different Western nations fluttered on masts extended into the streets, while the names of the various companies were emblazoned in their native alphabets and often translated into the beautiful Chinese characters, in black, silver or scarlet.

Chinese officials in flowing robes moved with considerable difficulty through throngs of sweating, near-naked coolies, British and Chinese policemen, soldiers and white-suited Europeans, sailors from a dozen different countries – all mingled casually and with few outward signs of discomfort in what seemed to me, the newcomer, like some huge, dreamlike rugger scrum.

A young Chinese boy in a pigtail took me in charge as I left the ship and shepherded me through the throng, finding me a rickshaw and piling me and my luggage aboard until the wickerwork groaned. I put what I hoped was an adequate tip into his outstretched hand and he seemed delighted, for he grinned and bowed many times, uttering the words 'God bless, God bless' over and over again before he told the celestial between the rickshaw's shafts that I wanted to go to the Hotel Grasmere, recommended by P. & O. as about the best British hotel in Weihaiwei.

With a lurch the rickshaw set off, and it was with some astonishment that I realised a moment or two later that I was being pulled by a slip of a girl who could not have been much older than sixteen. She made good speed through the crowded, narrow streets of the city and had deposited me outside the Grasmere within twenty minutes.

Again my donation was received with near ecstasy, and it occurred to me that I was probably being overgenerous, that a little money would go a very long way for the average Chinese living in Shantung!

The hotel was better than I had expected, with excellent service and pretty modern facilities. The rooms were pleasant and comfortable overlooking an exotic Chinese garden full of small, delicate sculptures, huge, richly coloured blooms and foliage of a score of different shades of green so that the whole thing looked like a jungle fancifully painted by some symbolist aesthete. The scents of the flowers, particularly during the morning and the evening, were overpowering. Electric fans (drawing their energy from the hotel's own up-to-date generator) cooled the rooms, and there were screens at the windows to keep the largest of the insects at bay. I rather regretted I would only be staying a short time in the hotel.

The morning after my arrival, I paid a visit on the British Consul, a youngish chap connected, I gathered, to one of our best families. A little on the languid, foppish side, he gave the impression of being infinitely bored with China and all things Chinese, but his advice seemed sound and he put me in touch with a local man who made regular trading visits into the hinterland of the province and who agreed, for a sum of money, to escort me all the way to the Valley of the Morning.

This chap was a tall, slightly stooped Chinese of early middle age, who carried himself with the utmost dignity and, while wearing plain cotton garments of the simplest sort, managed to convey the feeling (in me, at least) that he had not always been a mere merchant. I could not help but be reminded of the aristocratic merchant-adventurers of earlier European times and, indeed, it was soon revealed to me that Mr Lu Kan-fon betrayed a singularly fine command of English and French, knew German and Spanish pretty well and could communicate adequately in Dutch. I also gathered that he had a good knowledge of Japanese. Moreover, he had read a great deal in all of these languages, and, English aside, had a far better familiarity with the literature of those countries than had I. He had been educated, he said, by a European missionary who had taught him much of what he now knew, but I found the explanation inadequate, though I was too polite, of course, to tax him on it. I suspected him of being either a dishonoured aristocrat (perhaps from Peking) or the younger son of an impoverished family. The court intrigues of the Manchus and their followers were notorious and it was quite probable that he had, at some time, played a game of politics in Peking which he had lost. However, it was none of my business if he wished to disguise his past or his origins, and I was relieved for my part to know that I would be travelling in the company of a cultured companion whose English was almost as fluent as my own (I had privately dreaded the difficulties of communicating with a guide in the wilds of China, for my knowledge of Mandarin and Cantonese has never been particularly good).

Mr Lu told me that his little caravan would not be leaving Wei-haiwei for several days, so, accordingly, I spent the rest of the week in the city and did not waste it (as I saw it!) but assiduously enquired of anyone named Bastable, or answering Bastable's description, who might have been there. I received no information of any obvious value, but at least felt content that I had not made the ironic mistake of going off to look for a man who could, by the laws of coincidence, be found living in the next room to mine in the hotel!

At the end of the week I took a rickshaw to Mr Lu's large and rambling emporium near the centre of the Old Town, bringing with me the bare necessities I would need on the long journey. The rest of the party had already assembled by the time I arrived. They awaited me in a spacious stableyard which reminded me somewhat of a medieval English innyard. Riding horses and pack animals were being loaded and harnessed, their hoofs churning the ground to mud. Chinese, dressed in stout travelling-garments of heavy cotton, wool and leather, shouted to one another as they worked, and I noted that there was not a man, save for Lu Kan-fon himself, who did not have a serviceable modern rifle over his shoulders and at least one bandolier of cartridges strapped about him.

Lu saw me and came over to instruct his servants in the distribution of my luggage on the pack horses, apologising for the confusion and the condition of the horse I was to ride (it was a perfectly good beast). I indicated the arms which his men bore.

'I see that you are expecting trouble, Mr Lu.'

He shrugged slightly. 'One has to expect trouble in these times, Mr Moorcock. Those guns, however, should ensure that we see little of it!'

I was relieved that the horsemen were to ride with us. Outside the city I might well have mistaken them for the very bandits we feared. I reflected that if we were to meet any bandits who looked half as fierce as our own men, I would be more than a little perturbed!

At last we set off, Mr Lu at the head of the caravan. Through the crowded, bustling streets we rode, moving very slowly, for there seemed to be no established right of way – one took one's chances. I was expecting that we would head for the gates of the Old City, but instead we turned towards the more modern sections of the city and eventually arrived at the railway station (which might have been transported stone by stone from London, save for the Chinese words decorating it) and I found that we were riding directly through an archway and on to one of the main platforms where a train was waiting.

Mr Lu plainly enjoyed my surprise, for he smiled quietly and said: 'This first lap will be by train – but in case the train should meet obstacles, we take our horses with us. You call it insurance?'

I smiled back. 'I suppose we do.'

Horses and riders went directly into waiting goods trucks. I learned from Mr Lu that our entourage would travel with their animals, while we walked a little further along the train to where a first-class compartment had been prepared for us (Mr Lu seemed to have considerable influence with the railway company and I gathered that he travelled this route fairly frequently).

We settled into a carriage which would have put most British carriages to shame and were immediately served with tea and light refreshments.

It was then that Mr Lu, taking mild and humorous pleasure in mystifying me slightly, revealed the destination of the train.

'With luck, we should get as far as Nanking,' he told me. 'Under ordinary circumstances the journey would not take us more than three days, but we must be prepared for some delays.'

'What would be the cause of such delays?' I sipped the delicious tea.

'Oh, there are many causes.' He shrugged. 'Bandits blow up the lines. Peasants use the sleepers and the sections of rail for their own purposes. Then again there is the general incompetence of the company employees – and that's probably the greatest problem of them all!'

This incompetence was demonstrated very quickly. Our train was due to leave at noon, but in fact did not leave the station until just after four. However, any impatience I might have felt was soon dissipated by the sights of the interior which greeted me after the city was behind us. Immense stretches of flat paddy fields, interrupted by the occasional low hill around which a village was invariably built, shimmered in the soft light of the Chinese sun. Here was revealed the real, immutable wealth of China – her rice. The value of silver might fluctuate; industries would fail or prosper at the whim of the rest of the world; cities and states could rise and fall; conquerors would come and go, but China's rice and China's hardy peasantry were eternal. That, at any rate, is how it seemed to me then. I had never seen farming of any kind of such a scale as this. For miles and miles in all directions the fields stretched, predominantly green or yellow, intersected with low earthen dykes and somewhat broader ribbons of silver which were the irrigation canals, and above all this was the wide, hazy blue sky in which hung a few wisps of pale, lonely cloud.

The train chugged on, and while the landscape changed hardly at all it did not become boring. There was always something to see – a little group of scantily dressed peasants in their wide-brimmed straw hats and their pigtails, waving cheerfully to the train (I always waved back!) – a sampan making its way slowly up a canal – an ancient bridge which looked like a perfect work of art to me and yet which was plainly just a bridge built for an ordinary road between one tiny township and another. Sometimes, too, I saw pagodas, small walled cities (some virtually in ruins) with those highly ornate many-tiered gates typical of Chinese architecture, houses decorated with red and green tiles, with ceramic statuary, with bronzework and with mirror glass which made some of them seem as if they burned with a strange silver fire. When the train came, as it frequently did, to a sudden jerking stop, I had plenty of opportunities to study these sights in detail. It was on the third day, when we had made something over half of our journey to Nanking, that I began to notice significant changes in the demeanour of the people in the towns and villages we passed. The peasants rarely waved to the trains and were inclined to look upon us with a certain amount of apprehension and even downright suspicion. Moreover, it soon became obvious that there were a great many people about who were not local to the areas. I saw several detachments of cavalry on the roads we passed, and once thought I saw an infantry division moving through the paddy fields. Elsewhere there was evidence of, at very least, some sort of martial law in operation – more than once I saw peasants being stopped, questioned and searched by men in uniforms of a variety of descriptions. There was no question in my mind that this part of China was being disputed over, probably by at least three factions, amongst them the central authority. I had heard tales of the petty warlords who had sprung up in the last few years, claiming all sorts of honours, titles and rights – each one claimed to represent the forces of law and order, none would admit to being little more than a rapacious bandit – and now it looked as if I was witnessing the truth of the tales for myself. The long journey to Nanking passed without incident, however, and we disembarked from the train with some relief.

Nanking is a great and splendid city (if a little dilapidated here and there) and deserves a fuller description than I have space for. It is the capital of Kiangsu Province and one of China's major cities (it has, on occasions, been the capital). It lies at the foot of an impressive range of mountains whose slopes are thickly wooded and richly cultivated with terraced fields, and it is built on the banks of the mighty Yangtze Kiang river. It is at once one of China's most ancient cities and one of the most modern – ideal for trade, surrounded by some of the most fertile agricultural land in the world, it has a number of flourishing industries. Its financiers are famous for their wealth and their power and Nanking cuisine is highly regarded. In contrast to most Chinese towns, Nanking's ramparts are irregular, spreading from the river, along the banks of Lake Xuan-wu, to the Hill of the Rain of Flowers. The naval shipyards and the market places are on the west of the city, between the ramparts and the river. Again one finds a strange mixture of the old Chinese architecture – impressive, complicated buildings embellished with intricate ceramicwork – and more modern buildings, some of them very dull, but some of them wonders of late Victorian Gothic which, fortunately, is beginning to disappear in Europe to be replaced by the more gracious architecture of those influenced by the Art Nouveau movements. There is much shipping on the river – sampans, junks and steamers used for every possible purpose – as ferryboats, trading vessels, military craft and so on. There is a racecourse, an immense number of gardens, some large and ornate, some small and simple. There are libraries, museums, schools and art galleries, the consulates of all the great European Powers, luxurious hotels, temples, palaces, wide avenues lined with trees. I regretted greatly that our stay there was not to be longer, and made the best use of my time while Lu conducted his business, seeing as much of interest in the city as possible. I also called the British Consulate to apprehend them of my movements, enquire after Bastable and collect some cash I had arranged to be cabled there.

The second stage of our journey was by steamer, and still the horses had not been used! I began to envy the beasts – they seemed to be the most underworked animals I had ever come across. Stables had been prepared for them in the hold of the big paddle-steamer and they seemed content to return to their cramped quarters while Lu and myself retired to the merchant's stateroom where lunch was immediately forthcoming. The steamer left on time and we were soon heading up the broad Yangtze Kiang on our way to Wuchang, which would be our next stopping-place. I was fretting somewhat, for the journey was extremely roundabout, yet I was assured by Mr Lu that this was the safest route and the one most likely to get me to my ultimate destination, for this part of China in particular was in a highly unstable political state. He had learned, in fact, that an army under General Zhang Xun was rumoured to be advancing on the city and that there might well be heavy fighting in the outskirts. I had noted the number of soldiers occupying the streets around the centre and could well believe that we had narrowly missed being mixed up in a war.

At any other time I would have been delighted to have remained there and witnessed the sport, but it was important to me that Bastable be located and I could not risk losing as competent a guide and travelling companion as Lu Kan-fon. I had heard something of General Zhang Xun and gathered that he was a rascal of the first water, that his men had created terrible havoc in other parts of the province, stealing anything they could lay hands on, burning villages, molesting women and so forth.

Soon Nanking and her problems had disappeared behind us

and it seemed that we were the only moving object in the whole wide world at times, for as the river broadened we saw fewer and fewer other vessels. The paddles of the steamer swept us along slowly but surely with a heartening and steady beat. Our smoke drifted low behind us, hanging over the water which was sometimes deep and blue, sometimes shallow and yellow. There were hills on both sides of us now and the variety of shades of green would have put even the lovely English landscape to shame. Indeed I was reminded of the English landscape the more I saw of China. The only difference was the scale. What would have been a view stretching for a mile or two in England became a scene stretching for scores of miles in China! Like England, too, there was a sense of most of the landscape having been nurtured and cultivated for all of Time, used but used lovingly and with respect for its natural appearance.

It was on the third day of our journey upriver that the first serious incident took place. I was leaning on the rail of the ship, looking towards the west bank (which was closest) and enjoying my first pipe of the day when I suddenly heard a sharp report and, looking in the direction from which the sound had seemed to come, noticed a white puff of smoke. Peering more carefully, I made out several riders armed with rifles. More reports followed and I heard something whizz through the rigging over my head. I realised that we were being shot at and hastily ran along the deck to the wheelhouse with the intention of warning the Dutch skipper of the boat.

Old Cornelius, the skipper, smiled at me as I told him what was happening.

'Best stay inside, den, *Minheer,*' he said, puffing phlegmatically on his own pipe, his huge red face running with sweat, for it was all but airless in the wheelhouse.

'Should we not pull further out into midstream?' I enquired. 'We are surely in some danger.'

'Oh, yes, in danger ve are, most certainly, but ve should be in much greater danger if ve vent further to midstream. De currents – dey are very strong, sir. Ve must just hope dat not'in' serious is hit, eh? Dey are alvays shootin' at us, dese days. Any powered vessel is suspected off bein' a military ship.'

'Who are they? Can we not report them to the nearest authorities?'

'Dey could easily *be* de aut'orities, *Minheer*.' Cornelius laughed and patted me on the shoulder. 'Do not vorry, eh?'

I took his advice. After all, there was little else I could do! And soon the danger was past.

Nothing of a similar nature happened to us in the course of the next couple of days. Once I saw a whole town on fire. Lurid red flames lit up the dusk and thick, heavy smoke drifted over the river to mingle with ours. I saw panic-stricken people trying to crowd into sampans, while others hailed us from the bank, trying to get us to help them, but the skipper would have none of it, claiming that it was suicide to stop and that we should be overrun. I saw his logic, but I felt a dreadful pang, for we sailed close enough to be able to see, with the aid of field glasses, the fear-racked faces of the women and children. Many women stood up to their waists in water, holding their infants to them and screaming at us to help. The following morning I saw several detachments of cavalry in the uniforms of the Central Government, riding hell for leather along the bank, while behind them rode either irregulars attached to them, or pursuers, it was hard to tell. In the afternoon I saw field artillery being drawn by six-horse teams over a tall bridge spanning a particularly narrow section of the Yangtze Kiang. It had obviously been involved in a fierce engagement, for the soldiers were weary, wounded and scorched, while the wheels and barrels of the guns were thick with mud and there were signs that the guns had been fired almost to destruction (I saw only one ammunition tender and guessed that the others, empty, had been abandoned). Framed against the redness of the setting sun, the detachment looked as if it had returned from Hell itself.

I was glad to reach Wuchang, but somewhat nervous concerning the next stage of our journey, which would be overland by horse, backtracking to an extent, along the river and then in the general direction of Shancheng – unless we could get a train as far as Kwang Shui. It was what we had originally hoped to do, but we had heard rumours that the line to Kwang Shui had been blown up by bandits.

Wuchang faces the point where the Han Ho river merges with the Yangtze Kiang. It is one of three large towns lying close to each other, and of them Wuchang is the loveliest. Hanyang and Hankow are beginning to take on a distinctly European character, giving themselves over increasingly to industry and shipbuilding. But there was no real rest in Wuchang. Martial law had been declared and a mood of intense gloom hung over the whole city. Moreover, it had begun to rain – a thin drizzle which somehow managed to soak through almost any clothing one wore and chilled one to the very bone. The various officials who appeared at the dock as we came in were over-zealous in checking our papers and sorting through our baggage, suspecting us, doubtless, of being revolutionists or bandits. The better hotels had been taken over almost entirely by high-ranking officers and we were forced at last to put up at a none-too-clean inn near the quays, and even here there were a good many soldiers to keep us awake with their drunken carousing into the night. I pitied any town they might be called upon to defend!

Mr Lu disappeared very early the next morning and returned while I was eating an unpalatable breakfast of rice and some kind of stew which had been served to me with genuine apologies on the part of our host. There was little else, he said. The soldiers had eaten everything – and no-one was paying him.

Mr Lu looked pleased with himself and soon took the opportunity to let me know that he had managed to secure passage for us on the next train leaving Wuchang. The train was chiefly a troop transport, but would take a certain number of boxcars. If I did not mind the discomfort of travelling with the men and horses, we could leave almost immediately.

I was glad to agree and we gathered up our luggage and went to meet the rest of our party on the far side of town where they had been camped, sleeping in the open, curled up against their steeds. They looked red-eyed and angry and were cursing at each other as they saddled up and prepared the baggage for the pack animals.

We made our way to the station in something of a hurry, for there was precious little time. Mr Lu said that a troop transport was more likely to leave on time – or even ahead of time if it was ready to go. The army could decide.

We got to the station and the train was still in – drawn by one of the largest locomotives I have ever seen. It belonged to no class I recognised, was painted a mixture of bright blue and orange, and was bellowing more fire and smoke than Siegfried's dragon.

We crowded into the boxcars, the doors were shut on us, and off we jerked, hanging on for dear life as the train gathered speed.

Later we were able to get one of the sliding doors partly open and look out. We were in high mountain country, winding our way steadily upwards through some of the loveliest country I have ever seen in my life. Old, old mountains, clothed in verdant trees, the very image of those Chinese paintings which seem so formalised until you have seen the original of what the artist described. And then you realise that it is Nature herself who is formalised in China, that the country has been populated so long that there is scarcely a blade of grass, growing in no matter what remote spot, which has not in some way received the influence of Man. And here, as in other parts of China, the wilderness is not made any less impressive by this imprint. If anything, it is made more impressive. Mr Lu shared my pleasure in the sight (though he took a somewhat condescending, proprietorial attitude towards me as I gasped and exclaimed and wondered).

'I expected to be delighted with China,' I told him. 'But I am more than delighted. I am overawed – and my faith in the beauties of Nature is restored for ever!'

Mr Lu said nothing, but a little later he took out his cigarette case and, offering me a fine Turkish, remarked that even Nature at her most apparently invulnerable was still in danger from the works of mankind.

I had been thinking of Bastable and his description of the bomb which had blown him back into his own time, and I must admit that I gave Mr Lu a hard look, wondering if perhaps he knew more of Bastable than he had said, but he added nothing to this remark and I decided to accept it for one of generalised philosophy.

Accepting the cigarette, I nodded. 'That's true. I sincerely hope this civil strife does not destroy too much of your country,' I said, leaning forward to give him a match. The train swayed as it took a bend and revealed to me a lush forest, full of the subtlest greens I had ever seen. 'For I have fallen in love with China.'

'Unfortunately,' said Mr Lu in a dry but good-humoured tone, 'you are not the only European to be so smitten. But must one always take steps to *possess* that which one loves, Mr Moorcock?'

I accepted his point. 'I do not approve of my government's Chinese policies,' I told him. 'But you will admit that there is more law and order in the territories controlled by Britain than in other parts of China. After all, the Chinese Question remains a vexed one…'

'There would be no Chinese Question, Mr Moorcock,' said Mr Lu with a ghost of a smile, 'without Europe and Japan. Who was it introduced massive importation of opium into our country? Who was responsible for the devaluation of our currency? These were not internally created problems.'

'Probably not. And yet…'

'And yet I could be wrong. Who is to tell?'

'The Manchus cannot be said to be incorruptible,' I told him, and I smiled a smile which echoed his.

His own smile became a broad grin and he sat back against the wall, waving the hand which held the cigarette, granting me, as it were, the match. I think the gesture was made graciously rather than from any real agreement with the point of view I had presented.

The train travelled steadily through the rest of the day and into the night. We slept as best we could on the shuddering floor of the wagon, ever in danger of a horse breaking free and trampling us. It was almost dawn when the train came to a sudden screaming halt, causing the horses to buck about in fear, stamping and snorting, causing our men to leap to their feet, hands on their rifles.

The noise of the stop gave way to a peculiar and uncanny silence. In the distance we heard a few voices shouting back along the train and cautiously we slid the doors right back, peering into the murk to try to see what was happening.

'At least there's no gunfire,' said Mr Lu calmly. 'We are not under direct attack. Perhaps it is nothing more than a blockage on the line.'

But it was plain he was not convinced by his own suggestion. Together we clambered from the wagon and began to walk up the line towards the locomotive.

The big engine was still ejaculating huge clouds of white steam and through this steam moved dark figures. From the windows of the carriages there poked scores of heads as sleepy soldiers shouted enquiries or exchanged speculations about the reasons for our stopping.

Mr Lu singled out one of the more competent-looking officers and addressed a few short questions to him. The man replied, shrugging frequently, making dismissive gestures, pointing towards the north and up at the jagged mountain peaks above our heads.

The sun made its first tentative appearance as Mr Lu rejoined me.

'The line has been blown up,' he said. 'We are lucky that the driver acted with alacrity in stopping the train. There is no chance of continuing. The train will have to go back to the nearest town. We have the choice of going with it and enjoying the dubious security of travelling with these soldiers, or we can continue our journey on horseback.'

I made up my mind immediately, for I was slowly becoming impatient with the delays and diversions we had so far experienced. 'I should like to continue,' I told Mr Lu. 'It is time those horses were exercised!'

This was evidently the answer he had hoped for. With a quick smile he turned and began to stride back to our section of the train, calling out to his men to ready the horses and to load them, saying to me in an English aside:

'Personally I think we stand a much better chance on our own. This is territory at present controlled by the warlord General Liu Fang. His main interest is in wiping out the troops which have been sent against him. I do not think he will bother an ordinary caravan, particularly if we have a European gentleman travelling with us. Liu Fang hopes, I gather, to recruit allies from Europe. A plan which is almost certainly doomed to failure, but it will be of help to us.'

Accordingly, we were soon on horseback, heading down the long slope away from the stranded train. By noon we were deep into unpopulated country, following the course of a river along the floor of a valley. The valley was narrow and thickly wooded and at length we were forced to dismount and lead our horses through the moss-covered rocks. It had begun to rain quite heavily and the ground was slippery, slowing our progress even more. Moreover, it had become hard to see more than a few yards ahead of us. Owing to my lack of sleep and the hypnotic effect of the rain falling on the foliage above my head, I continued almost in a trance, hardly aware of my own tiredness. We exchanged few words and emerged from the forest and remounted when it was quite late in the afternoon, with only a few hours of daylight left. The river began to rise and we still followed it, from one valley into another, until we came upon some reasonably level ground where we decided to make camp and consult our maps to see what progress we had so far made.

It was as I watched the men erecting the tent which Lu and I would share that I glanced up into the hills and thought I saw a figure move behind a rock some distance away. I remarked on this to Mr Lu. He accepted that I had probably seen someone, but he reassured me.

'It is not surprising. Probably only an observer – a scout sent to keep an eye on us and make sure that we are not a disguised military expedition. I doubt if we shall be bothered by him.'

I could not sleep well that night and I must admit that in my exhaustion I had begun to regret the impulse which had sent me on this adventure. I wondered if it would all end in some sordid massacre, if, by morning, my stripped corpse would lie amongst the remains of our camp. I would not be the first European foolish enough to embark upon such a journey and pay the ultimate price for his folly. When I did sleep, at last, my dreams were not pleasant. Indeed, they were the strangest and most terrifying dreams I have ever experienced. Yet, for some reason, I awoke from all this feeling completely refreshed and cleansed of my fears. I began to be optimistic about our chances of reaching the Valley of the Morning and ate the crude fare served us for breakfast with immense relish.

Mr Lu was moved to comment on my demeanour. 'We Chinese are famous for our stoicism,' he said, 'but we could learn something from your British variety!'

'It's not stoicism,' I said. 'Merely a mood. I can't explain it.'

'Perhaps you sense good luck. I hope so.' He indicated the rocky hills on both sides of us. 'A fairly large company of men has been moved up in the night. We are probably completely surrounded.'

'Do they mean to attack, I wonder?' I glanced about, but could see no sign of the soldiers.

'I would suppose that this manoeuvre is a precaution. They are probably still wondering if we are spies or part of a disguised army.'

I now noticed that our men were betraying a certain nervousness, fingering their rifles and bandoliers, glancing around them at the rocks and muttering amongst themselves in an agitated fashion. Lu Kan-fon was the only person who seemed unconcerned; speaking rapidly, he gave orders for our pack horses to be loaded and, at first reluctantly, his men moved to obey. It was only when the last bundle had been secured and we prepared to mount that the soldiers revealed themselves.

Unlike many of the government troops, these men wore uniforms which were distinctly Chinese – loose smocks and trousers of black, yellow, white and red. On the backs and fronts of the smocks were big circles on which had been printed Chinese characters, evidently giving the rank and regiment of the soldier. Some wore skull-caps, while others had wide-brimmed straw hats. All were clean-shaven and well-disciplined and all possessed modern carbines, apparently of German manufacture. While their guns were pointed at us, they were held at the hip rather than at the shoulder, denoting that no immediate harm was intended to us. Immediately, Mr Lu held up his hand and ordered his men not to touch their own weapons, whereupon there emerged from behind a large bush a mounted figure of such splendid appearance that I thought at first he must surely be arrayed for a festival.

He rode his shaggy pony slowly down the hillside towards us. He must have been well over six feet in height and with massive shoulders and chest. He was wearing a long brocade gown embroidered for about a foot round the bottom with waves of the sea and other Chinese devices. Over this was a long satin coat with an embroidered breastplate and a similar square of embroidery on the back, with the horseshoe cuffs, forced upon the Chinese by the Manchus when the present dynasty came to the throne, falling over his hands. High official boots, an amber necklace of very large beads reaching to his waist and aureole-shaped official cap with large red tassel, completed the costume. There was a large sword at his side, but no other visible arms, and he guided his pony with one hand while keeping the other on the hilt of the sword, somehow managing to retain an impressive dignity while the horse picked its way down to where we waited, virtually frozen in position.

His face was expressionless as he rode into our camp and brought his mount to a halt, looking us over through his slanting, jet-black eyes. Mr Lu and myself came in for a particularly close examination, and it was while the man was inspecting me that I decided to try to break the atmosphere and bowed slightly, saying in English:

'Good morning, sir. I am a British citizen on a private journey with these traders. I regret it if we have inadvertently entered territory which you would prefer to remain untravelled...'

My rather mealy-mouthed speech was interrupted by a grunt from the magnificent rider, who ignored me and addressed Mr Lu in flowing Mandarin.

'You know who I am? You know where you are? What is your excuse for being here?'

Mr Lu bowed low before speaking. 'I know who you are, honourable one, and I most humbly ask your forgiveness for giving you the trouble of needing to inspect our little caravan. But we were travelling by train until yesterday when the train met an obstacle and was forced to return to the nearest town. We decided to continue overland...'

'You were seen leaving the troop train. You are spies, are you not?'

'Not at all, mighty General Liu Fang. The troop train was the only available transport. We are merchants: we are on our way to trade in Shantung.'

'Who is the foreigner?'

'An Englishman. A writer who wishes to write a book about our country.'

At this quick-witted piece of invention the legendary General Liu Fang showed a flicker of interest. He also appeared slightly mollified, for he had no reason to suspect I was anything but a neutral party in his territory (as, of course, I was) and probably thought it might be in his interest to cultivate the good will of one of the foreigners whose aid he was rumoured to be seeking.

'Tell your men to disarm themselves,' he ordered, and Mr Lu relayed the order at once. Scowling, his men unslung their guns and dropped them to the ground.

'And where is your immediate destination?' said the general to me in halting French.

I replied in the same tongue. 'I have heard of a particularly beautiful valley in these parts. It is called the Valley of the Morning.' I saw no point in beating about the bush, particularly since

I might not have another opportunity to discover the exact where-abouts of my destination for some time.

General Liu Fang plainly recognised the name, but his reaction was strange. He frowned heavily and darted a deeply suspicious look at me. 'Who do you seek there?'

'No-one in particular,' said I. 'My interest in the place is purely, as it were, geographical.' I, in turn, noting his reaction, had become cautious of revealing anything more.

He seemed to relax, momentarily satisfied with my reply. 'I would advise you against visiting the valley,' he said. 'There are bandits in the area.'

I wondered to myself sardonically what he called himself, but of course let nothing of this show on my face as I said: 'I am grateful for the warning. Perhaps with the protection of your army...'

He gestured impatiently. 'I am fighting a war, *monsieur*. I can-not spare men to escort foreign journalists about the country.'

'I apologise,' I said, and bowed again.

There was still considerable tension in the situation and I noted that the soldiers had not relaxed but were still pointing their rifles at us. There must have been at least a hundred of them in well-protected positions on both sides of the valley. The general returned his attention to Mr Lu. 'What goods do you carry for trade?'

Mr Lu had folded his arms. He said impassively: 'Many kinds. Mainly articles of artistic interest. Statuettes, ceramics and the like.'

'They will be inspected,' said the general. 'Instruct your men to unload the goods.'

Again Mr Lu obeyed without demur. As his men began to unpack the bundles which they had so recently strapped onto the pack horses, he said to me in English: 'We might escape with our lives, but not, I fear, our possessions...'

'Silence!' said the general firmly. He rode forward to where Mr Lu's goods had been laid out, looked them over with the shrewd eye of a Chinese peasant woman inspecting fish in a market and then rode back to where we stood. 'They will be requisitioned,' he said, 'to help us win freedom from the Manchus.'

Fatalistically, Mr Lu bowed. 'A worthy cause,' he said dryly. 'The horses –?'

'The horses will also be requisitioned. They will be of particular use…'

It was at this point that he was interrupted by the sound of machine-gun fire and I thought at first that he had somehow given the signal for our slaughter. But the gunfire came from higher up the hillside and I saw at once that it was his men who were the target for the attack. My spirits lifted. Surely these must be government troops coming to our rescue!

My relief was short-lived. Almost at once General Liu Fang shouted an order to his men and, head well down over the neck of his horse, spurred rapidly for the cover of some nearby rocks.

It had begun to rain suddenly – a heavy, misty rain which acted like fog to obscure visibility – and I had no idea of what was happening, save that the general's troops were firing on us.

Mr Lu's men dived for their own weapons, but half of them were cut down before they could reach their rifles. Those who remained snatched up their guns and sought what cover they could. Mr Lu grabbed my arm and together we ran towards a depression in the ground where we might escape the worst of the concentrated fire from above. We flung ourselves down and buried our faces in the soft moss while the three-sided battle went on all around us. I remember noting that the machine guns kept up an incredibly efficient chattering and I wondered how any Chinese army could have acquired such artillery (for the Chinese are notorious for the poor quality of their arms and their inefficiency in maintaining those that they have).

Bullets thudded about us and I expected to be hit at any moment. I shouted over the noise of gunfire and the cries of the wounded. 'Who are they, Mr Lu?'

'I do not know, Mr Moorcock. All I do know is that whereas we might have escaped with our lives, we now stand a very good

chance of being killed. They doubtless consider it more important to destroy General Liu Fang than to save us!' He laughed. 'I
regret that I shall be forced to return your fee – I have not kept my
part of the bargain. Your chances of finding the Valley of the
Morning have become exceptionally slender. My protection has
proved inadequate!'

'I am forced to agree with you, Mr Lu,' said I, and would have
continued had I not recognised the distinctive sound of a bullet
striking flesh and bone. I lifted my head, thinking at first that I had
been hit, but it was Mr Lu. He must have died instantly, for he had
been shot not once but twice, almost simultaneously, in the head.

I had an immediate sense of grief, realising how much I had
enjoyed the sophisticated company of the Chinese, but the
sight of his ruined head sickened me and I was forced to avert my
eyes.

The death of Mr Lu seemed to be a signal for the fighting to
stop. Shortly afterwards the sound of gunfire ended and I lifted
my head cautiously to peer through the drifting rain. Death was
everywhere. Our own men lay amongst the scattered and broken
remains of the works of art they had carried for so long and so far.
A few had once again laid down their weapons and were raising
their hands high above their heads. General Liu Fang was nowhere
to be seen (I learned later he had kept riding, abandoning his men
to their fate), but the warlord's soldiers lay in postures of death
everywhere I looked. I rose, raising my own hands. There came a
few more isolated shots and I surmised that, in Chinese fashion,
the wounded were being finished off.

I must have waited for at least ten minutes before I got my first
sight of our 'rescuers'. They were all mounted, all wearing leather
caps of a distinctively Mongolian appearance and all carried light
rifles of a decidedly unfamiliar pattern. Their loose shirts were of
silk or cotton and some wore leather capes to protect themselves
against the worst of the rain, while others wore quilted jackets.
They were mainly good-looking Northern Chinese, tall and
somewhat arrogant in their bearing, and none had pigtails. Most
had armbands as their only insignia – a fanciful design consisting

of a circle from which radiated eight slender arrows. I knew at once that they could not, after all, be government troops, but were doubtless some rival bandit army either fighting for themselves or allied with the government troops against General Liu Fang.

And then their leader rode into sight from out of the misty rain. I knew it must be the leader from the way in which the other riders fell back. Also it was rare to see a handsome black Arab stallion in these parts and that was what the leader rode. Slender, a graceful rider, dressed in a long black leather topcoat with a narrow waist and a flaring skirt, a broad-brimmed leather hat hiding the face, a long Cossack-style sabre hanging from a belt of elaborately ornamented silk, the bandit chief rode towards me, lifted the brim of the hat away from the face and showed evident, and almost childish, amusement at my astonishment.

'Good morning, Mr Moorcock.'

Her voice was clear and well-modulated – the voice of an educated Englishwoman (though bearing perhaps the slightest trace of an accent). She was young, no older than thirty at very most, and she had a pale, soft complexion. Her eyes were grey-blue and her mouth was wide and full-lipped. She had an oval face which would have been merely pretty had it not been for the character in it. As it was, I thought her the most beautiful woman I had ever seen. Her slightly waving black hair was short, framing her face but barely touching her shoulders.

And all I could blurt out was: 'How do you know my name?'

She laughed. 'Our intelligence is rather better than General Liu Fang's. I am sorry so many of your men were killed – and I particularly regret the death of Mr Lu. Though he did not know that it was I who attacked, we were old friends and I had been looking forward to meeting him again.'

'You take his death rather casually,' I said.

'It was a casual death. I have not introduced myself. My name is Una Persson. For some months we have been harassed by General Liu and this is the first opportunity we have had to teach him a lesson. We were originally coming to find you and take you with us to the Valley of the Morning, but I could not afford to miss the chance of ambushing such a large number of the general's troops.'

'How did you know I sought the Valley of the Morning?'

'I have known for at least a month. You have made many enquiries.'

'Your name is familiar – where have I heard it…?' Slowly it dawned on me. 'Bastable mentioned you! The woman on the airship – the revolutionist. Una Persson!'

'I am an acquaintance of Captain Bastable.'

My heart leapt. 'Is he there? Is he in the Valley of the Morning as I suspected?'

'He has been there,' she agreed. 'And he has left something of himself behind.'

'But Bastable? What of him? I am anxious to speak to him. Where is he now?'

And then this mysterious woman made the most cryptic utterance she had made so far. She shrugged and gave a little, tired smile, pulling on her horse's reins so that the beast began to move away. 'Where indeed?' she said. 'It is not a question easily answered, Mr Moorcock, for we are all nomads of the time streams…'

I stood there, puzzled, chilled, miserable and too weary to question her further. She rode to where Mr Lu's goods lay scattered about and beneath the corpses of men and horses. She dismounted and stooped to inspect one shattered figurine, dipped her finger into the hollow which had been revealed and lifted the finger to her nose. She nodded to herself as if confirming something she had already known. Then she began to give orders to her men in rapid Cantonese dialect which I could scarcely follow at all. Carefully, they gathered up both the fragments and the few figurines which were still unbroken. It did not take a particularly subtle intelligence to put two and two together. Now I knew why Mr Lu had taken such an oddly circuitous route and why he had been eager to leave the troop train as soon as possible. Plainly, he was an opium smuggler. I found it hard to believe that such an apparently decent and well-educated man could indulge in so foul a trade, but the evidence was indisputable. For some reason I could not find it in my heart to loathe the dead man and I guessed that some sort of perverted idealism had led him to this means of making money. I also had an explanation of the general's interest in Mr Lu's goods – doubtless the bandit chief had guessed the truth, which was why he had been so eager to 'requisition' the articles.

The booty was collected quickly and Una Persson mounted her sleek stallion without another glance at me, riding off through the rain. One of her silent warriors brought me a horse and signalled for me to climb into the saddle. I did so with eagerness, for I had no intention of becoming separated from the beautiful bandit leader – she was my first real link with Bastable and there was every chance she would take me to him. I felt no danger from these rascals and had an inkling that Una Persson was, if not sympathetic, at least neutral with regard to me.

Thus, surrounded by her men, I followed behind her as we left that little vale of death and the remnants of Mr Lu's party and cantered along a narrow track which wound higher and higher into the mountains.

I was hardly aware of the details of that journey, so eaten up was I with curiosity. A thousand questions seethed in my skull – how could a woman who had been described by Bastable as being young in the year 1973 be here, apparently just as young, in the year 1910? Once again I experienced that almost fearful frisson which I had experienced when listening to Bastable's speculations on the paradoxes of Time.

And would Democratic Dawn City – Chi'ng Che'eng Ta-Chia – that secret Utopian revolutionary citadel be there when we arrived in the Valley of the Morning?

And why was Una Persson taking part in China's internecine politics? Why did these tall, silent men follow her?

I hoped that I would have at least some answers to these questions when we arrived in the Valley of the Morning, but, as it emerged, I was to be in several ways disappointed.

It was after dark by the time that we reached Una Persson's

camp and the rain had fallen ceaselessly, so that it was still difficult to make out details, but it was obvious that this was no City of the Future – merely the ruins of a small Chinese township with a few houses still inhabitable. For the most part, however, the soldiers and their women and children lived in makeshift shelters erected in the ruins, while others had set up tents or temporary huts similar to the Mongolian yurt. Cooking fires guttered here and there amongst the fallen masonry and half-burned timbers which spoke of some disaster having befallen the town fairly recently. Much of the ground had been churned to mud and was made even more treacherous by the arrival of our horses. As I dismounted, Una Persson rode up and pointed with a riding crop at one of the still-standing houses.

'You'll be my guest for supper, I hope, Mr Moorcock.'

'You are kind, madam,' I replied. 'But I fear I am not properly dressed to take supper with such a beautiful hostess...'

She grinned at the compliment. 'You are picking up Chinese habits of speech, I see. Your clothes were rescued. You'll find them in your room. San Chui here will show you where it is. You'll be able to wash there, too. Until later, then.' She saluted me with the crop and rode off to supervise the unloading of her spoils (which also consisted of most of the weapons which had a short while ago belonged to Mr Lu's and the general's men). I had an opportunity to see one of the machine guns I had initially only heard and was astonished that it was so light and yet so capable of dealing out death with extraordinary efficiency. This, too, was of a completely unfamiliar pattern. Indeed, it was the sort of weapon I might have expected to find in a city of the future!

San Chui, impassive as his comrades, bowed and led the way into the house, which was carpeted in luxurious style throughout but was otherwise of a somewhat spartan appearance. In a room near the top of the house I found my baggage and my spare suit already laid out on my sleeping-mat (there was no bed). Shortly afterwards another soldier, who had changed into a smock and trousers of blue linen, brought me a bowl of hot water and I was able to get the worst of the mud and dust off my person, find

a reasonably uncrumpled shirt, don the fresh suit and walk down
to supper safe in the conviction that I was able to make at least an
approximate appearance of civilised demeanour!

I was to dine alone, it seemed, with my hostess. She herself had
changed into a simple gown of midnight-blue silk, trimmed with
scarlet in the Chinese fashion. With her short hair and her oval
face she looked, in the light of the candles burning on the dining table, almost Chinese. She wore no ornament and there was
no trace of paint on her face, yet she looked even more beautiful
than the first time I had seen her. When I bowed it was instinctively, in homage to that beauty. The ground-floor room held the
minimum of furniture – a couple of chests against the walls and
a low Chinese table at which one sat cross-legged on cushions
to eat.

Without enquiry, she handed me a glass of Madeira and I
thanked her. Sipping the wine, I found it to be amongst the very
best of its kind and I complimented her on it.

She smiled. 'Don't praise my taste, Mr Moorcock. Praise that
of the French missionary who ordered it in Shanghai – and who is
still, I suppose, wondering what has become of it!'

I was surprised by her easy (even shameless) admission of her
banditry, but said nothing. Never having been a great supporter of
the established Church, I continued to sip the missionary's wine
with relish, however, and found myself relaxing for the first time
since I had left civilisation. Although I had so many questions to
ask her, I discovered myself to be virtually tongue-tied, not knowing where to begin and hoping that she would illuminate me
without my having to introduce the subject, say, of Bastable and
how she came to know him. The last I had heard of her she had
been aboard the airship which had, in the year 1973, dropped a
bomb of immense power upon the city of Hiroshima. For the
first time I began to doubt Bastable's story and wonder if, indeed,
he had been describing nothing but an opium dream which had
become confused with reality to the extent that he had introduced
actual people he had known into it.

We seated ourselves to eat and I decided to begin in a somewhat elliptical manner, enquiring, as I sampled the delicious soup (served, in Western fashion, before the main courses): 'Any news of your father, Captain Korzeniowski?'

It was her turn to frown in puzzlement, and then her brow cleared and she laughed. 'Aha! Of course – Bastable. Oh, Korzeniowski is fine, I think. Bastable spoke well of you – he seemed to trust you. Indeed, the reason that you are here at all is that he asked me to do a favour for him.'

'A favour?'

'More of that later. Let us enjoy our meal – this is a luxury for me, you know. Recently we have not had the leisure or the means to prepare elaborate meals.'

Once again she had politely – almost sweetly – blocked my questions. I decided to proceed on a new tack.

'This village has sustained a bombardment by the look of it,' I said. 'Have you been attacked?'

She answered vaguely. 'It was attacked, yes. By General Liu, I believe, before we arrived. But one gets used to ruins. This is better than some I have known.' Her eyes held a distant, moody look, as if she were remembering other times, other ruins. Then she shrugged and her expression changed. 'The world you know is a stable world, Mr Moorcock, is it not?'

'Comparatively,' I said. 'Though there are always threats, I suppose. I have sometimes wondered what social stability is. It is probably just a question of points of view and personal experience. My own outlook is a relatively cheerful one. If I were, say, a Jewish immigrant in London's East End, it would probably not be anything like as optimistic!'

She appreciated the remark and smiled. 'Well, at least you accept that there *are* other views of society. Perhaps that is why Bastable talked to you; why he liked you.'

'Liked me? It is not the impression I received. He disappeared, you know, after our meeting on Rowe Island – without any warning at all. I was concerned for him. He was under a great strain. That, I suppose, is the main reason why I am here. Have you seen him recently? Is he well?'

'I have seen him. He was well enough. But he is trapped – he is probably trapped for ever.' Her next phrase was addressed to herself, I thought. 'Trapped for ever in the shifting tides of Time.'

I waited for her to elaborate, but she did not. 'Bastable will tell you more of that,' she said.

'Then he *is* here?'

She shook her head and her hair swayed like the branches of a willow in the wind. She returned her attention to the meal and did not speak for a while as we ate.

Now I had the strange impression that I was not quite real to her, that she spoke to me as she might speak to her horse or a household pet or a familiar picture on her wall, as if she did not expect me to understand and spoke only to clarify her own thoughts. I felt a little uncomfortable, just as someone might feel who was an unwilling eavesdropper on an intimate conversation. Yet I was determined to receive at least some clarification from her.

'I gather that you intend to take me to Bastable – or that Bastable is due to return here?'

'Really? No, no. I am sorry if I have misled you. I have many things on my mind at present. China's problems alone... The historical implications... The possibility of so much going wrong... Whether we should be interfering at all... If we *are* interfering, or only think we are...' She lifted her head and her wonderful eyes stared deep into mine. 'Many concerns – responsibilities – and I am very tired, Mr Moorcock. It is going to be a long century.'

I was completely nonplussed and decided myself to finish the conversation. 'Perhaps we can talk in the morning,' I said, 'when we are both more rested.'

'Perhaps,' she agreed. 'You are going to bed?'

'If you do not think it impolite. The dinner was splendid.'

'Yes, it was good. The morning...'

I wondered if she, like Bastable, was also a slave to opium. There was a trancelike quality in her eyes now. She could hardly understand me.

'Until the morning, then,' I said.

'Until the morning.' She echoed my words almost mindlessly.

'Goodnight, Mrs Persson.'

'Goodnight.'

I made my way back upstairs, undressed, lay myself down on the sleeping-mat and, it seemed to me, was immediately dreaming those peculiar, frightening dreams of the previous night. Again, in the morning, I felt completely refreshed and purged. I got up, washed in cold water, dressed and went downstairs. The room was as I had left it – the remains of the previous night's dinner were still on the table. And I was suddenly seized with the conviction that everything had been abandoned hastily – that I had also been abandoned. I walked outside into a fine, pale morning. The rain had stopped and the air smelled fresh and clean. I looked for signs of activity and found nothing. The only life I could see in the village consisted of one horse, saddled and ready to ride. Soldiers, women and children had all disappeared. Now I wondered if, inadvertently, I had sampled some of Mr Lu's opium and had dreamed the whole thing! I went back into the house calling out:

'Mrs Persson! Mrs Persson!'

There were only echoes. Not one human being remained in the ruined village.

I went out again. In the distance the low green hills of the Valley of the Morning were soft, gentle and glowing after the rain which must have stopped in the night. A large, watery sun hung in the sky. Birds sang. The world seemed to be tranquil, the valley a haven of perfect peace. I saw not one gun, one item of the spoils which the bandits had brought back with them. The cooking fires were still warm, but had been extinguished. The mud was still thick and deep and there was evidence of many horses having left the village fairly recently.

Perhaps the bandits had received intelligence of a large-scale counter-attack from General Liu's forces. Perhaps they had left to attack some new objective of their own. I determined to remain in the village for as long as possible in the hope that they would return.

I made a desultory perambulation of the village. I explored

each of the remaining houses; I went for a walk along the main road out of the place. I walked back. There was no evidence for my first theory, that the village had been about to suffer an attack.

By lunchtime I was feeling pretty hungry and I returned to the house to pick at the cold remains of last night's supper. I helped myself to a glass of the missionary's excellent Madeira. I explored the anterooms of the ground floor and then went upstairs, determined, completely against my normal instincts, to investigate every room.

The bedroom next to mine still bore a faint smell of feminine perfume and was plainly Una Persson's. There was a mirror on the wall, a bottle of eau de Cologne beside the sleeping-mat, a few wisps of dark hair in an ivory hairbrush on the floor near the mirror. Otherwise, the room was furnished as barely as the others. I noticed a small inlaid table near a window leading onto a small balcony which overlooked the ruins of the village. There was a bulky package lying on the table, wrapped in oilskin, tied with cord.

As I passed it on my way to look out of the window I glanced at the package. And then I gave it very much of a second glance, for I had recognised my own name written in faded brown ink on yellow paper! Just the word 'Moorcock'. I did not know the handwriting, but I felt fully justified in tearing off the wrappings to reveal a great heap of closely written foolscap pages.

It was the manuscript which you, its rediscoverer (for I have no intention of making a fool of myself again), are about to read.

There was a note addressed to me from Bastable – brief and pointed – and the manuscript itself was in the same writing.

This must be, of course, what Una Persson had been referring to when she had told me that Bastable had left something of himself behind in the Valley of the Morning. I felt, too, that it was reasonable to surmise that she had meant to give the manuscript to me before she left (if she had actually known she was going to leave so suddenly).

I took the table, a stool and the manuscript onto the balcony, seating myself so that I was looking out over the mysteriously deserted village and the distant hills containing the valley I had sought for so long, and I settled down to read a story which was, if anything, stranger than the first Bastable had told me...

Book One

The World in Anarchy

Chapter One
The Return to Teku Benga

Aᴰᵀᴇʀ I ʟᴇꜰᴛ you that morning, Moorcock, I had no intention of departing Rowe Island so hastily. I genuinely intended to do no more than take a stroll and clear my head. But I was very tired, as you know, and inclined to act impulsively. As I walked along the quayside I saw that a steamer was leaving; I observed an opportunity to stow away, did so, was undiscovered, and eventually reached the mainland of India, whereupon I made my way inland, got to Teku Benga (still hoping to get back to what I was convinced was my 'real' time), discovered that the way across remained impassable and considered the possibility of chucking myself off the cliff and having done with the whole mystery. But I hadn't the courage for that, nor the heart to go back to your world, Moorcock – that world that was so subtly different from the one I had originally left.

I suppose I must have gone into a decline of some sort (perhaps the shock, perhaps the sudden cessation of supplies of opium to my system, I don't know). I remained near the abyss separating me from what might have been the fountainhead of that particular knowledge I sought. I stared for hours at the dimly seen ruins of that ancient and squalid mountain fortress and I believe I must have prayed to it, begging it to release me from the awful fate it (or Sharan Khang, its dead priest-king) had condemned me to.

For some time (do not ask me how long) I lived the life of a wild beast, eating the small vermin I was able to trap, almost relishing the slow erosion of my mind and my civilised instincts.

When the snows came I was forced to look for shelter and was driven slowly down the mountainside until I discovered a cave which provided more than adequate shelter. The cave bore evidence that it had until recently been the lair of some wild beast, for there were many bones – of goats, wild sheep, hill dogs and the like (as well as the remains of more than one human being) – but there was no sign that its previous occupant was still in evidence. The cave was long and narrow, stretching so far back and becoming so dark that I never explored its whole extent and was content to establish myself close to the mouth, building no fire, but wrapping myself in the inadequately cured skins of my prey as the winter grew steadily colder.

The previous resident of the cave had been a huge tiger. I found this out one morning when I heard a peculiar snuffling noise and woke up to see the entrance blocked by a massive striped head and the beginnings of a pair of monstrous feline shoulders. The tiger regarded this cave as his winter home and plainly would not think much of the idea of sharing it equably with me. I leapt up and began to retreat into the depths of the cave, since my exit was completely blocked, as the tiger, who must have grown fatter during his summer in the lowlands, squeezed his way slowly in.

That was how I discovered the cave to be in actuality a tunnel – and moreover a man-made tunnel. It grew as dark as the grave as I continued my retreat along it. I steadied myself with my hands against the walls and slowly began to understand that the rough rock had given way to smooth and that the projections were, in fact, cunning carvings of a familiar pattern. I became a bit flustered, then – a bit mad. I remember giggling, then stopping myself, realising that the tiger might still be behind me. I paused, feeling carefully on both sides of the narrow passage. I received a sickening sense of disgust as my groping fingers made out details of the carvings; my dizziness increased. And yet at the same time I was elated, knowing for certain that I had stumbled into one of Teku Benga's many secret corridors and that I might well have found my way back, at last, to that warren of passages which lay beneath the immeasurably ancient Temple of the Future Buddha! There was no question in my mind that, failing to find a way across the gorge, I had inadvertently discovered a way *under* it, for now the floor of the passage began to rise steeply and I was attacked by a coldness of a quality and intensity which was totally unlike the coldness of the natural winter. I had been terrified when I had first experienced it and I was terrified now, but my terror was mixed with hope. Strange little noises began to assail my ears, like the tinkling of temple bells, the whispering of a wind which carried half-formed words in an alien language. Once I had sought to escape all this, but now I ran towards it and I believe that I was weeping, calling out. And the floor of the passage seemed to sway as I ran on, the walls widened out so that I could no longer stretch my arms and touch them and at last, ahead of me, I saw a point of white light. It was the same I had seen before and I laughed. Even then I found my laughter harsh and mad, but I did not care. The light grew brighter and brighter until it was blinding me. Shapes moved behind the light; there were nameless, glowing colours; there were webs of some vibrating metallic substance and once more I was reminded of the legends of Hindu gods who had built machines to defy the laws of Space and Time.

And then I began to fall.

Head over heels I spun. It was as if I fell through the void which lies between the stars. Slowly all the little consciousness that remained had left me and I gave myself up to the ancient power which had seized me and made me its toy...

I'm sorry if all this seems fanciful, Moorcock. You know that I'm not a particularly imaginative sort of chap. I began my maturity as an ordinary soldier, doing his duty to his country and his Empire. I should like nothing more than to continue my life in that vein, but fate had ordained otherwise. I awoke in darkness, desperately hoping that my flight through Time had been reversed and that I should discover myself back in my own age. There was no way of knowing, of course, for I was still in darkness, still in the tunnel, but the sounds had gone and that particular sort of coldness had gone. I got up, feeling my body in the hope that I'd discover I was wearing my old uniform, but I was not – I was still dressed in rags. This did not unduly concern me and I turned to retrace myself, feeling that if I was in the age I hoped to have left, then I would give myself up to the tiger and get it all over with.

At last I got back to the cave and there was no tiger. Moreover – and this improved my spirits – there was no sign that *I* had occupied the cave. I walked out into the snow and stood looking up at a hard, blue sky, taking great gulps of the thin air and grinning like a schoolboy, sure that I was 'home'.

My journey out of the mountains was not a pleasant one and how I ever escaped severe frostbite I shall never know. I passed through several villages and was treated with wary respect, as a Holy Man might be treated, and got warmer clothes and food, but none of those I spoke to could understand English and I had no familiarity with their dialect. Thus it was nearly a month before I could begin to hope for confirmation of my belief that I had returned to my own time. A few landmarks began to turn up – a clump of trees, an oddly shaped rock, a small river – which I recognised and I knew I was close to the frontier station which Sharan Khang had attacked and thus been the cause of my first visit both to Teku Benga and, ultimately, the future.

The station came in sight a day or so later – merely a barracks surrounded by a few native brick huts and the whole enclosed by a serviceable wall. This was where our Native Police and their commanding officer had been killed and I admit that I prayed that I would find it as I had left it. There *were* signs of fighting and few signs of habitation and this cheered me up no end! I stumbled through the broken gateway of the little fort, hoping against hope that I would find the detachment of Punjabi Lancers and Ghoorkas I had left behind on my way to Kumbalari. Sure enough there were soldiers there. I shouted out in relief. I was weak from hunger and exhaustion and my voice must have sounded thinly through the warm spring air, but the soldiers sprang up, weapons at the ready, and it was only then that I realised they were white. Doubtless the Indian soldiers had been relieved by British.

Yet these men had recently been in a fight, that was clear. Had another band of Sharan Khang's men attacked the fort while I had been on my expedition into the old hill fox's territory?

I called out: 'Are you British?'

I received the stout reply: 'I certainly hope we are!'

And then I fell fainting on the dry dust of the compound.

Chapter Two

The Dream – and the Nightmare –
of the Chilean Wizard

NATURALLY ENOUGH, MY first words on regaining consciousness, lying on a truckle bed in what remained of the
barracks' dormitory, were:

'What's the year?'

'The *year*, sir?' The man who addressed me was a young,
bright-looking chap. He had a sergeant's stripes on his dusty scarlet tunic (it was a Royal Londonderry uniform, a regiment having
close connections with my own) and he held a tin cup of tea in
one hand while the other was behind my head, trying to help me
sit up.

'Please, sergeant, humour me, would you? What's the year?'

'It's 1904, sir.'

So I had been 'lost' for two years. That would explain a great
deal. I was relieved. Sipping the rather weak tea (I was later to discover it was almost their last) I introduced myself, giving my rank
and my own regiment, telling the sergeant that I was, as far as I
knew, the only survivor of a punitive expedition of a couple of
years earlier – that I had been captured, escaped, wandered around
for a bit and had only just managed to make it back. The sergeant
accepted the story without any of the signs of suspicion which I
had come to expect, but his next words alarmed me.

'So you would know nothing of the War, then, Captain
Bastable?'

'A war? Here, on the Frontier? The Russians…'

'At the moment, sir, this is one of the few places scarcely
touched by the war, though you are right in supposing that the
Russians are amongst our enemies. The war is worldwide. Myself

237

and less than a score of men are all that remains of the army which failed to defend Darjiling. The city and the best part of these territories are either under Russian control or the Russians have been, in turn, beaten by the Arabian Alliance. Personally I am hoping that the Russians are still in control. At least they let their prisoners live or, at worst, kill them swiftly. The last news we had was not good, however...'

'Are there no reinforcements coming from Britain?'

A look of pain filled the sergeant's eyes. 'There will be little enough coming from Blighty for some time, I shouldn't wonder, sir. Most of Europe is in a far worse plight than Asia, having sustained the greatest concentration of bombs. The war is over in Europe, Captain Bastable. Here, it continues – a sort of alternative battleground, you might call it, with precious little for anyone to win. The power situation is grim enough – there's probably not one British keel capable of lifting, even if it exists...'

Now his words had become completely meaningless to me. I was aware of only one terrifying fact and I had become filled with despair: this world of 1904 bore even less relation to my own world than the one from which I had sought to escape. I begged the sergeant to explain recent history to me as he might explain it to a child, using my old excuse of partial amnesia. The man accepted the excuse and kindly gave me a breakdown of this world's history since the latter quarter of the nineteenth century. It was radically different either from your world, Moorcock or from the world of the future I described to you.

It appears that, by the 1870s, in Chile of all places, there had emerged the genius who had, in a few short years, been responsible for altering the lot of the world's poor, of providing plenty where once there had been famine, comfort where they had been only grinding misery. His name was Manuel O'Bean, the son of an Irish engineer who had settled in Chile and the Chilean heiress Esmé Piatnitski (perhaps the wealthiest woman in South or Central America). O'Bean had shown signs of an enormous capacity to learn and to invent at an extraordinarily young age. His father, needless to say, had encouraged him and O'Bean had learned everything his father could pass on by the time he was eight years old. With the resources made available by his mother's wealth, O'Bean had nothing to thwart this flowering of his mechanical genius. By the time he was twelve he had invented a whole new range of mining equipment which, when applied to his family's holdings, increased their wealth a hundredfold. Not only did he have an enormous talent for planning and building new types of machine, he also had the ability to work out new power sources which were less wasteful and infinitely cheaper than the crude sources up to that time in use. He developed a method of converting and reconverting electricity so that it did not need to be carried through wires but could be transmitted by means of rays to almost anywhere in the world from any other point. His generators were small, efficient and required the minimum of power, and these in turn propelled most of the types of machinery he invented. Other engines, including sophisticated forms of steam turbine depending on fast-heating liquids other than water, were also developed. As well as the mining and farming equipment he developed in those early years, O'Bean (still less than fifteen years old) invented a collection of highly efficient war machines (he was still a boy and was fascinated, as boys are, with such things), including underwater boats, mobile cannons, airships (in collaboration with the great flying expert, the Frenchman La Perez) and self-propelled armoured carriages sometimes called 'land ironclads'. However, O'Bean soon abandoned this line of research as his social conscience developed. By the time he was eighteen he had sworn never to put his genius to warlike purposes again and instead concentrated on machines which would irrigate deserts, tame forests, and turn the whole world into an infinitely rich garden which would feed the hungry and thus extinguish what he believed to be the wellspring of most human strife.

By the beginnings of the new century, therefore, it seemed that Utopia had been achieved. There was not one person in the world who was not well-nourished and did not have the opportunity to receive a good education. Poverty had been abolished almost overnight.

Man *can* live by bread alone when all his energies are devoted to attaining that bread, but once his mind is clear, once he has ceased to labour through all his waking hours to find food, then he begins to think. If he has the opportunity to gather facts, if his mind is educated, then he begins to consider his position in the world and compare it with that of other men. Now it was possible for thousands to understand that the world's power was in the hands of a few – the landowners, the industrialists, the politicians and the ruling classes. All these people had welcomed O'Bean's scientific and technical advances – for they were able to lease his patents, to build their own machines, to make themselves richer as those they ruled became better off. But twenty-five years is enough time for a new generation to grow up – a generation which has never known dire poverty and which, unlike a previous generation, is no longer merely grateful that it has leisure time and more than enough to eat. That generation begins to want to control its own fate in myriad ways. In short, it seeks political power.

By 1900, in this world, civil strife had become a fact of life in almost every nation, large and small. In some countries, usually those which had been the most backward, revolutions succeeded, and, attended by a fanatical nationalism, new power groups were formed. The Great Powers found their colonial territories snatched from them – in Asia, in Africa, in the Americas – and since the sources of power were cheap and O'Bean's patents were distributed everywhere, since military power no longer depended so much on large, well-trained armies (or even navies), these older nations were wary of starting wars with the newer nations, preferring to try to retain their positions by means of complicated diplomacy, by building up 'spheres of influence'. But complicated diplomatic games played in the far corners of the world tend to have a habit of creating stronger tensions at home, so in Europe, in particular, but also in the United States and Japan, nationalism grew stronger and stronger and fierce battles of words began to take place between the Great Powers. Trade embargoes, crippling and unnecessarily unfair tariff restrictions were applied and returned. A madness began to fill the heads of those who ruled. They saw themselves threatened from within by their young people, who demanded what they saw as more social justice, and from without by their neighbouring countries. More and more resources were devoted to the building up of land, sea and air fleets, of large guns, of armies which could control dissident populations (and at the same time, hopefully, absorb them). In many countries enforced military service, after the Prussian model, became the norm – and this in turn brought an increasingly furious reaction from those who sought to reform their governments. Active, violent revolutionary methods began to be justified by those who had originally hoped to achieve their ends by means of oratory and the ballot box.

What O'Bean himself thought of this nobody knows, but it was likely that he did feel enormously guilty. One story has it that on the inevitable day when the Great Powers went to war he quietly committed suicide.

The war was at first contained only in Europe, and in the first weeks most of the major cities of the Continent and Britain were reduced to ash and rubble. A short-lived Central American Alliance lasted long enough to go to war with the United States and quickly achieved a similar end. Huge mobile war machines rolled across the wasted land; sinister aerial battleships cruised smoke-filled skies; while under the water lurked squadrons of subaquatic men-o'-war, often destroying one another without ever once rising to the surface where more conventional ironclads blasted rivals to bits with the horrifically powerful guns invented by a boy of thirteen years old.

'But most of the *real* fighting's over now,' said the sergeant, with a tinge of contempt. 'The fuel ran out for the generators and the engines. The war machines that were left just – well – stopped. It all went back to cavalry and infantry and that sort of stuff for a while, but there was hardly anyone knew *how* to fight like that – and precious few people left to do it. And not much ammunition,

I shouldn't wonder. We're down to about one cartridge each.' He tapped the weapon which hung at his belt. 'It'll be bayonets, if we ever do meet the enemy. The bally Indians'll be top dogs – those who've still got swords and lances and bows and arrows and that...'

'You don't think the war will stop? People must be shocked by what's happened – sickened by it all.'

The soldier shook his head, waxing philosophical. 'It's a madness, sir. We've all got it. It could go on until the last human being crawls away from the body of the chap he's just bashed to bits with a stone. That's what war is, sir – madness. You don't think about what you're doing. You forget, don't you – you just go on killing and killing.' He paused, almost embarrassed. 'Leastways, that's what I think.'

I conceded that he could well be right. Filled with unutterable gloom, obsessed by the irony of my escape from a relatively peaceful world into this one, I yet felt the need somehow to get back to England, to see for myself if the sergeant had told me the truth, or whether he had exaggerated, either from a misguided sense of drama, or from despair at his own position.

I told him that I should like to try to return to my own country, but he smiled pityingly at me, telling me that there wasn't the slightest chance. If I headed, say, for Darjiling, then I was bound to be captured by the Russians or the Arabians. Even if I managed to reach the coast, there were no ships in the harbours (if there were harbours!) or the aerodromes. My best plan, he suggested, was to fall in with them. They had done their duty and their position was hopeless. They planned to get up into the hills and make some sort of life for themselves there. The sergeant thought that, with the population killing itself off so rapidly, game would proliferate and we should be able to live by hunting – 'and live pretty well, too'. But I had had enough of the hills already. For better or worse, as soon as I had recovered my strength I would try to get to the coast.

A couple of days later I bid farewell to the sergeant and his men. They begged me not to be so foolhardy, that I was going to certain death.

'There was talk of plague, sir,' said the sergeant. 'Terrible diseases brought about by the collapse of the sanitary systems.'

I listened politely to all the warnings and then, politely, ignored them.

Perhaps I had had my share of bad luck, for good luck stayed with me for the rest of my journey across the Indian sub-continent. Darjiling had, indeed, fallen to the Arabians, but they had evacuated the shell of that city soon after occupying it. Their forces were stretched pretty thin and had been needed on the home front. There were still one or two divisions left, but they were busy looking for Russians, and when they discovered that I was English they took this to mean that I was a friend (towards the end, I gathered, there had been some attempt to make a pact between Britain and Arabia) and these chaps were under what turned out to be the utterly false impression that we were fighting on the same side. I fell in with them. They were heading for Calcutta – or where Calcutta had once stood – where there was some hope of getting a ship back to the Middle East. There was a ship, too – a, to them, old-fashioned steamer, using coal-burning engines – and although the name on its side was in Russian, it flew the crossed-scimitar flag of the Arabian Alliance. It was in a state of terrible disrepair and one took one's life in one's hands when going aboard, but there had been a chance in a million of finding any kind of ship and I was not in a mood to miss it. She had been an old cargo ship and there was very little room, as such, for passengers. Most of the men were crowded into the holds and made as comfortable as possible. As an officer and a 'guest' I got to share a cabin with four of the Arabians, three of whom were Palestinians and one of whom was an Egyptian. They all spoke perfect English and, while somewhat reserved, were decent enough company, going so far as to lend me a captain's uniform and most of the necessities of life which I had learned, in recent months, to do without.

The ship made slow progress through the Bay of Bengal and I relieved my boredom by telling my companions that I had been the prisoner of a Himalayan tribe for several years and thus getting them to fill in certain details of their world's history which the sergeant had been unable to give me.

There was some talk of a man whom they called the 'Black Attila', a leader who had emerged of late in Africa and whom they saw as a threat to themselves. Africa had not suffered as badly from the effects of the war as Europe and most of her nations – many only a few years old – had done their best to remain neutral. As a result they had flourishing crops, functioning harvesting machines and a reserve of military power with which to protect their wealth. The Black Attila had growing support in the Negro nations for a jihad against the whites (the Arabians were included in this category, as were Asiatics), but, at the last my informants had heard, was still consolidating local gains and had shown no sign of moving against what remained of the countries of the West. There were other rumours which said that he had already been killed, while some said he had invaded and conquered most of Europe.

The ship had no radio apparatus (another example of my good fortune, it emerged, for the Arabians had never reached the point of signing a pact with Britain!), and thus there was no means of confirming or denying these reports. We sailed down the coast of India, through the Gulf of Mannar, managed to take on coal at Agatti in the Laccadives, got into heavy weather in the Arabian Sea, lost three hands and most of our rigging, entered the Red Sea and were a few days away from the approach to the Suez Canal when, without any warning at all, the ship was struck by several powerful torpedoes and began to sink almost immediately.

It was the work of an undersea torpedo boat – one of the few still functioning – and it was not, it emerged, an act of war at all, but an act of cynical piracy.

However, the pirate had done his work too well. The ship sighed, coughed, and went to the bottom with most of her passengers and crew. I and about a dozen others were left clinging to what little wreckage there was.

The undersea boat lifted its prow from the water for a few seconds to observe its handiwork, saw that there was nothing to be gained by remaining, and left us to our fate. I suppose we should have been grateful that it did not use the guns mounted along its sides to finish us off. Ammunition had become scarce almost everywhere, it seemed.

Chapter Three
The Polish Privateer

I SHAN'T DESCRIBE in detail my experiences of the next twenty-four hours. Suffice to say that they were pretty grim as I watched my companions sink, one by one, beneath the waves and knew that ultimately I should be joining them. I suppose I have had a great deal of practice in the art of survival and somehow I managed to remain afloat, clinging to my pathetic bit of flotsam, until the late afternoon of the next day when the monster rose from the waves, steaming water pouring off its blue-black skin, its great crystalline eyes glaring at me, and a horrible, deep-throated roaring issuing from its belly. At first my exhausted mind *did* see it as a living creature but my second thoughts were that the undersea torpedo boat had returned to finish me off.

Slowly the disturbance in the water ceased and the growling subsided to a quiet purring and the sleek and slender craft came to rest on the surface. From hatches fore and aft sailors in sea-green uniforms sprang onto the deck and ran quickly to the rails. One of them flung a lifebuoy out over the side and with the last of my strength I swam towards it, seizing it and allowing myself to be hauled towards the ship. Hands dragged me aboard and a cup of rum was forced down my throat while blankets were thrown around me and I was carried bodily along the rocking deck and down into the forward hatch. This hatch was closed swiftly over us and as I was borne below I could feel the ship itself descending back below the waves. The whole thing had taken place in the space of a few minutes and I had the impression of urgency, as if much had been risked in coming to the surface at all. I surmised that this could not be the same ship (it seemed larger, for one thing) which had left me to my fate, that it must be another. It was certainly not a British ship, and I could make little of the language spoken by the seamen who carried me to a small, steel-walled cabin and stripped me of my sodden Arabian uniform before lowering me into the bunk and drawing warm blankets over me. It was probably a Slavonic language and I wondered if I had been made a prisoner of war by the Russians. I heard the ship's engines start up again, and there was a barely perceptible lurch as we began to go forward at what I guessed to be pretty high speed. Then, careless of what my fate might be, I fell into a heavy and, thankfully, dreamless sleep.

Upon awakening, I glanced automatically towards the porthole but, of course, could not tell whether it was night or day, let alone what the time was! All I saw was dark green swirling water rushing past, faintly illuminated by the lights from the ship as it coursed with sharklike speed through the deeps. For a while I stared in fascination at the sight, hoping to make out some details of my first glimpse of the mysterious underwater world, but we were doubtless moving too rapidly. As I stared, the door of the cabin opened and a seaman entered, bearing a large tin cup which proved to contain hot, black coffee. He spoke in a thick accent:

'The captain's compliments, sir. Would you care to join him in his cabin, at your leisure.'

I accepted the coffee, noting that my borrowed uniform had been washed, dried and pressed and that a fresh set of undergarments had been laid out on the small table fixed against the opposite wall to the bunk.

'Gladly,' I replied. 'Will there be someone to escort me there when I have completed my toilet and dressed?'

'I will wait outside for you, sir.' The sailor saluted and left the cabin, closing the door smartly behind him. There was no question that this was a superbly disciplined ship – the efficiency with which I had been rescued spoke of that – and I hoped that the discipline extended to the honouring of the ordinary conventions of war!

As quickly as I could I readied myself and soon presented myself outside the cabin door. The sailor set off along the narrow, tubular passage which was remarkable for possessing cork cat-walks positioned on sides and ceiling as well as floor, indicating that the ship was designed to function at any of the main positions of the quadrant. My surmise proved to be accurate (there were also 'decks' on the outside of the hull to match the catwalks, while the main control room was a perfect globe pivoting to match the angle of the ship – merely, it emerged, one of O'Bean's 'throw-away' ideas!) and the underwater craft was essentially much in advance of anything I had encountered in that other future of 1973.

The tubular passage led us to an intersection and we took the port-side direction, climbed a small companionway and found our-selves outside a plain, circular steel door upon which the seaman knocked, uttering a few words in his unfamiliar language. A single word answered him from the other side of the door and he pulled back a recessed catch to open it and admit me, saluting again before he left.

I found myself in an almost familiar version of any captain's quarters of a ship of my own world. There was plenty of well-polished mahogany and brass, a few green plants in baskets hanging from ceilings and walls, a neatly made single bunk, a small chart table on which were several maps and around the edges of which were clipped a variety of instruments. Framed prints of clipper ships and of old charts were fixed to the walls. The lighting glowed softly from the whole ceiling and had the quality of daylight (yet another of O'Bean's casual inventions). A smallish, dapper figure, with whiskers trimmed in the Imperial style, rose to greet me, adjusting his cap on his head and smiling almost shyly. He was a young man, probably not much older that myself, but he had the lines of experience upon his face and his eyes were the eyes of a much older man – steady and clear, yet betraying a certain cool irony. He stretched out a hand and I shook it, finding the grip firm and not ungentle. There was something naggingly familiar about him, but my mind refused to accept the truth until, in good, but gutturally accented, English, he intro-duced himself:

'Welcome aboard the *Lola Montez*, captain. My name is Korzeniowski and I am her master.'

I was too stunned to speak, for I was confronting a much younger version of my old mentor from the days I spent aboard *The Rover*. Then, Korzeniowski had been (or would be) a Polish airship captain. The implications of all this were frightening. Was there now a chance that I might meet a version of *myself* in this other world? I recovered my politeness. Plainly Korzeniowski knew nothing of me and I introduced myself, for better or worse, by my name and my real regiment, explaining quickly how I had come to be wearing my rather elaborate Arabian uniform. 'I hope Poland is not at war with the Arabian Alliance,' I added.

Captain Korzeniowski shrugged, turning towards a cabinet containing a number of bottles and glasses. 'What will you have, Captain Bastable?'

'Whisky with a splash of soda, if you please. You are very kind.'

Korzeniowski took out the whisky decanter, gesturing casually with it as he extracted a glass from the rack. 'Poland is not at war with anyone now. First Germany broke her, then Russia extinguished her, then Russia herself ceased to exist, as a nation at least. Poor Poland. Her struggles are over for all time. Perhaps something less ill-fated will emerge from the ruins.' He handed me a full glass, made as if to toss off his own, in the Polish manner, then restrained himself and sipped it almost primly, tugging at the lobe of his left ear, seeming to reprove himself for having been about to make a flamboyant gesture.

'But you and your crew are Polish,' I said. 'The ship is Polish.'

'We belong to no nation now, though Poland was the birthplace of most of us. The ship was once the finest in our navy. Now it is the last survivor of the fleet. We have become what you might call "privateers". It is how we survive during the apocalypse.' His eyes held a hint of sardonic pride. 'I think we are rather good at it – though the prey becomes scarce. We had our eye on your ship for a while, but it did not seem worth the waste of a torpedo. You might be glad to know that the ship which attacked you was called the *Mannanan* and that she belonged to the Irish navy.'

'*Irish?*' I was surprised. Home Rule, then, was a fact in this world.

'We could not stop to pick you up right away, but decided that you would have to take your chances. The *Mannanan* was a well-equipped ship and we were able to wound her and force her to the surface quite easily. She was a "fine prize", as the buccaneers would say!' He laughed. 'We were able to take stores aboard which will keep us going for three months. And spare parts.'

She had deserved whatever Captain Korzeniowski had done to her. Doubtless he had shown more mercy in his treatment of the *Mannanan* than she had shown to our poor, battered steamer. But I could not bring myself to voice these sentiments aloud and thus condone what had been, after all, a similar act of piracy on the part of the *Lola Montez*.

'Well, Captain Bastable,' said Korzeniowski, lighting a thick cheroot and signalling for me to help myself from his humidor, 'what do you want us to do with you? It's normally our habit to put survivors off at the nearest land and let them take their chances. But yours is something of a special case. We're making for the Outer Hebrides, where we have a station. Is there anywhere between here and there that we can put you off? Not that there is anywhere particularly habitable on land, these days.'

I told him how I planned to try to reach England and that if there was any chance of being put off on the South Coast I would more than welcome it. He raised his eyebrows at this.

'If you had said Scotland I might have understood – but the South Coast! Having been the agent of your escape from death, I am not sure I could justify to my conscience my becoming the instrument of your destruction! Have you not heard? Have you any idea of the hell which Southern England has become?'

'I gather that London sustained some very heavy bombing...'

Evidently Korzeniowski could not restrain a bleak smile at this. 'I have always appreciated British understatement,' he told me. 'What else have you gathered?'

'That there is a risk of catching disease – typhus, cholera, and so on.'

'And so on, yes. Do you know what *kind* of bombs the air fleets were dropping towards the end, Captain Bastable?'

'Pretty powerful ones, I should imagine.'

'Oh, extremely. But they were not explosive – they were bacteria. The bombs contained different varieties of plague, captain. They had a lot of scientific names, but they soon became known by their nicknames. Have you seen, for instance, the effects of the Devil's Mushroom?'

'I haven't heard of it.'

'It is called by that name after the fungus which begins to form on the surface of the flesh less than two hours after the germs have infected the victim. Scrape off the fungus and the flesh comes away with it. In two days you look like one of those rotten trees you might have seen in a forest sometimes, but happily by that time you are quite dead and you have no pain at all. Then there's Prussian Emma, which causes haemorrhaging from all orifices – *that* death is singularly painful, I'm told. And there's Eye Rot, Red Blotch, Brighton Blight. Quaint names, aren't they? As colourful as the manifestations of the diseases on the skin. Aside from the diseases, there are roving gangs of cut-throats warring on one another and killing any other human being they find (not always prettily). From time to time you might set foot on a gas bomb which is triggered as you step on it and blows a poison gas up into your face. If you escape those dangers, there are a dozen more. Believe me, Captain Bastable, the only clean life now – the only life for a man – is on the high seas (or under them). It is to the sea that many of us have returned, living out our lives by preying upon one another, admittedly. But it is an existence infinitely preferable to the terrors and degradations of the land. And one still has a certain amount of freedom, is still somewhat in control of one's own fate. Dry land is what the medieval painters imagined Hell to be. Give me the purgatory of the sea!'

'I am sure I would agree with you,' I told him, 'but I would still see it for myself.'

Korzeniowski shrugged. 'Very well. We'll put you off at Dover, if you like. But if you should change your mind, I could use a trained officer, albeit an army officer, aboard this vessel. You could serve with me.'

This was indeed a case of history repeating itself (or was it prefiguring itself?). Korzeniowski did not know it, but I had already served with him – and not in the army either, but in airships. It would be second nature for me to sail with him now. But I thanked him and told him that my mind was made up.

'Nonetheless,' he said, 'I'll leave the berth open to you for a bit. You never know.'

A few days later I was put ashore on a beach just below the familiar white cliffs of Dover and waved goodbye to the *Lola Montez* as she sank below the surface of the waves and was gone. Then I shouldered my knapsack of provisions, took a firm grip on the fast-firing carbine I had been given, and turned my steps inland, towards London.

Chapter Four
The King of East Grinstead

IF I HAD considered Korzeniowski's description of post-war England to be fanciful, I soon had cause to realise that he had probably restrained himself when painting a picture of the conditions to be found there. Plague was, indeed, widespread, and its victims were to be seen everywhere. But the worst of the plagues were over, largely because most of the population remaining had been killed off by them and those who survived were resistant to most of the strains – or had somehow recovered from them. Those who *had* recovered were sometimes missing a limb, or a nose, or an eye, while others had had parts of their faces or bodies eaten away altogether. I observed several bands of these poor, half-rotted creatures, in the ruins of Dover and Canterbury, as I made my way cautiously towards London.

The inhabitants of the Home Counties had descended from the heights of civilisation to the depths of barbarism in a few short years. The remains of the fine towns, the clean, broad highways, the monorail systems, the light, airy architecture of the world O'Bean had created, were still there to speak of the beauty that had come and gone so swiftly, but now bands of beast-men camped in them, tore them down to make crude weapons and primitive shelters, hunted each other to death among them. No woman was safe and, among certain of the 'tribes' roving the ruins, children were regarded as particularly excellent eating! Former bank managers, members of the stock exchange, respectable tradesmen, had come to regard vermin as delicacies and were prepared to tear a man's jugular from his throat with their teeth if it would gain them the possession of a dead cat. Few modern weapons were in evidence (the production of rifles and pistols had been on the decline since the invention of airships and subaquatic boats), but rudely made spears, bows and arrows, knives and pikes could be found in almost every hand. By day I lay hidden wherever there was good cover, watching the savages go by, and I travelled at night, risking ambush, since I regarded my chances as being better at night when most of the 'tribesmen' returned to their camps. The country had not only sustained the most horrifying mass aerial bombardment, but had also (in this area in particular) received huge punishment from long-range guns firing from across the Channel. Twice the Home Counties had been invaded by forces coming from sea and air, and these had ravaged what remained, taking the last of the food, blowing up those buildings which still stood, before being driven back by the vestiges of our army. At night the hills of Kent and Surrey sparkled with points of light indicating the locations of semi-nomadic camps where huge fires burned day and night. The fires were not merely there for cooking and heating, but to burn the regular supply of plague-created corpses.

And so my luck held until I reached the outskirts of East Grinstead, once a pretty little village which I had known well as a boy, but now a wasteland of blasted vegetation and torn masonry. As usual I inspected the place from cover, noting the presence of what seemed to be a crudely made stockade of tree trunks near the northernmost end of the village. From this armed men came and went regularly, and I was surprised to see that many of them carried rifles and shotguns and were dressed in rather more adequate rags than the people I had seen to date. The community itself seemed to be a larger one than the others, and better organised, settled in one place rather than roaming about a small area of countryside. I heard the distinctive sounds of cattle, sheep and goats and surmised that a few of these animals had survived and were being kept for safety inside the stockade. Here was 'civilisation' indeed! I considered the possibility of making my presence known and seeking aid from the inhabitants, who might be expected to behave in a somewhat less aggressive manner than the people I had observed up to now. But, warily, I continued to keep watch on the settlement and see what information I could gather before I revealed myself.

It was a couple of hours later that I had reason to congratulate myself on my caution. I had hidden in a small brick building which had somehow survived the bombing. It had been used, I think, as a woodstore and was barely large enough to admit me. A grille, designed for ventilation, was the means by which I could look out at the stockade without being seen. Three men, dressed in a miscellaneous selection of clothing which included a black bowler hat, a deerstalker and a panama, a woman's fur cape, golfing trousers, a leather shooting-coat, a tailcoat and an opera cloak, were escorting a prisoner back along the path to the gate. The prisoner was a young woman, tall and dressed in a long black military topcoat which had evidently been tailored for her. She had a black divided skirt and black riding boots and there was no question in my mind that she, like me, was some sort of interloper. They were treating her roughly, pushing her so that she fell over twice and struggled to her feet only with the greatest difficulty (her hands were tied behind her back). There was something familiar about her bearing, but it was only when she turned her head to speak to one of her captors (evidently speaking with the greatest contempt, for the man struck her in the mouth by way of reply) that I recognised her. It was Mrs Persson, the revolutionist whom I had first met on Captain Korzeniowski's airship, *The Rover*, and whom I understood to be Korzeniowski's daughter. That could not be true now, for this woman was approximately the same age as Korzeniowski. I had had enough of speculating about the mysteries and paradoxes of Time – they were beginning to become familiar to me and I was learning to accept them as one might accept the ordinary facts of human existence, without question. Now I merely saw Una Persson as a woman who was in danger and who must therefore be rescued. I had my carbine and several magazines of ammunition and I had the advantage that none of the inhabitants of the stockade was aware of my presence. I waited for nightfall and then crept out of my hiding place, thanking Providence that the full moon was hidden behind thick cloud.

I got to the stockade and saw that it was an extremely crude affair – no savage would have owned to its manufacture – and easily scaled, so long as the timber did not collapse under me. Slowly I climbed to the top and got my first sight of the interior.

It was a scene of the utmost barbarity. Una Persson hung spread-eagled and suspended on a kind of trellis in the centre of the compound. In front of her, cross-legged, sat what must have been the best part of the 'tribe' – many of them bearing the deformities marking them as recipients of various plague viruses. Behind the scaffold was a sort of dais made from a large oak refectory table, and on the table there had been placed a high-backed, ornately carved armchair of the sort which our Victorian ancestors regarded as the very epitome of 'Gothick' good taste. The velvet of the chair was much torn and stained and the woodwork had been covered with some sort of poorly applied gold lacquer. A number of fairly large fires blazed in a semicircle behind the dais and oily smoke drifted across the scene, while the red flames leapt about like so many devils and were reflected in the sweating faces of the gathered inhabitants of the stockade. This was what I saw before I dropped to the other side of the fence and crept into the shadow of one of the ramshackle shelters clustered nearby.

A sort of hideous crooning now issued from the throats of the onlookers, and they swayed slowly from side to side, their eyes fixed on Una Persson's half-naked body. Una Persson herself did not struggle, but remained perfectly still in her bonds, staring back at them with an expression of utter disgust and contempt. As I had admired it once before, again I admired her courage. Few of us, in her position, could have behaved so well.

Since she did not seem to be in any immediate danger, I waited to see what would next develop.

From a hut larger than the rest and set back behind the semicircle of fires, there now emerged a tall and corpulent figure dressed in full morning dress, with a fine grey silk hat at a jaunty angle on his head, his right thumb stuck in the pocket of his waist-coat, a diamond pin in his cravat, looking for all the world like some music-hall performer of my own time. Slowly, with an air of insouciance, he ascended the dais and seated himself with great self-importance in his gold chair while the crowd ceased its humming and swaying for a moment to greet him with a mon-strous shout whose words I could not catch.

His own voice was clear enough. It was reedy and yet brutal and, for all that it was the uneducated voice of a small shopkeeper, it carried authority.

'Loyal subjects of East Grinstead,' it began. 'The man – or woman – who pulls their weight is welcome here as you well know. But East Grinstead has never taken kindly to foreigners, scroung-ers, Jews and loafers, as is also well known. East Grinstead knows how to deal with 'em. We have our traditions. Now this here inter-loper, this spy, was caught hanging round near East Grinstead obviously up to no good – and also, I might add, armed to the teeth. Well, draw your own conclusions, my subjects. There is not much doubt in my – our – mind that she is by way of being a def-inite foreign aviator, probably come back to see how we are getting on here after all them bombs she dropped on us did their damage. She has found a flourishing community – bloody but unbowed and ready for anything. Given half a chance, I shouldn't be surprised if she was about to report back to her compatriots that East Grin-stead wasn't finished – not by a long shot finished – and we could have expected another lot of bombs. But,' and his voice dropped and became ruthless and sinister, plainly relishing Una's pain, 'she won't *be* going back. And we're going to teach her a lesson, aren't we, about what foreign aviators and spies can expect if they try it on over East Grinstead and Major John!'

He continued in this vein and I listened in horror. Could this man once have served behind a counter in an ordinary suburban shop? Perhaps he had served me with an ounce of liquorice or a packet of tea. And his 'subjects', who growled and giggled and trembled with bloodlust, were these once the decent, conservative folk of the Home Counties? Did it take so little time to strip them of all their apparent civilisation? If ever I returned to my own world I would look on these people in a new light.

King John of East Grinstead had risen from his chair and someone had handed him a brand. The firelight turned his grey, unshaven face into the mask of a devil as he raised the brand above his head, his eyes glowing and his lips drawn back in a bestial grin.

'*Now* we'll teach her!' he yelled. And his subjects rose up, arms extended, screaming to him to do what he was about to do.

The brand came down and began to extend towards Una Persson's head. She could not see what was happening, but it was obvious that she guessed. She struggled once in the ropes, then her lips came firmly together and she closed her eyes as the brand moved closer towards her.

Scarcely thinking, I raised my carbine to my shoulder, took aim, and shot Major John, the King of East Grinstead, squarely between the eyes. His face was almost comic in its astonishment and then the great bulk fell forward off the dais and lay in a heap before its stunned subjects.

I moved quickly then, thankful for my army training.

While those hideously ravaged faces looked at me with expressions of horror, I ran to the trellis and with a few quick strokes of my knife cut Una Persson free.

Then, quite deliberately, I shot down three of the nearest men. One of them had been armed and I signed to Una Persson to pick up the rifle, which she did as quickly as she could, though she was plainly suffering a good deal of pain.

'This place is surrounded by men,' I told them. 'All are crack shots. The first to threaten us with his weapon will die as swiftly as your leader. As you can see, we are merciless. If you remain within the stockade and allow us to go through the gate unhampered, no more of you will be harmed.'

A few of the people growled like animals, but were too nonplussed and alarmed to do anything more. I could not resist a parting speech as we got to the gate.

'I might tell you that I am British,' I said. 'As British as you are and from the same part of the world. And I am disgusted by what I see. This is no way for Britons to behave. Remember your old standards. Recall what they once meant to you. The fields remain and you have stock. Grow your food as you have always grown it. Breed the beasts. Build East Grinstead into a decent place again...'

Una Persson put a hand on my arm, whispering: 'There is not much time. They'll soon realise that you have no men. They are already beginning to look for them and not see them. Come, we'll make for my machine.'

We backed out of the gate and closed it behind us. Then, bent low, we began to run. I followed Una Persson and she plainly had a good idea of where she was going. We ran through a wood and across several overgrown fields, into another wood, and here we paused, listening for sounds of pursuit, but there was none.

Panting, Una Persson pushed on until the forest thinned. Then she bent over a bush and without any apparent effort seemed to pull the whole thing up by the roots, revealing the faint gleam of metal. She operated a control, there was a buzz and a hatch swung upwards.

'Get in,' she said, 'there's just about room for both of us.'

I obeyed. I found myself in a cramped chamber, surrounded by a variety of unfamiliar instruments. Una Persson closed the hatch over her head and began turning dials and flicking switches until the whole machine was shaking and whining. She peered through a contraption which looked to me rather like a stereoscopic viewer, then pulled a large lever right back. The whining sound increased its pitch and the machine began to move – heading downwards into the very bowels of the earth.

'What sort of machine is this?' I enquired in my amazement.

'Haven't you seen one before?' she said casually. 'It's an O'Bean Mark Five tunneller. It's about the only way to move these days without being spotted. It's slow. But it's sure.' She smiled, pausing in her inspection of the controls to offer me her hand. 'I haven't thanked you. I don't know who you are, sir, but I'm very grateful for what you did. My mission in this part of Britain is vital and now it has some chance of success.'

It had become extremely hot and I fancied that we were nearing the core of the planet!

'Not at all,' I replied. 'Glad to be of service. My name's Bastable. You're Mrs Persson, aren't you?'

'Una Persson,' she said. 'Were you sent to help me, then?'

'I happened to be passing, that was all.' I wished now that I hadn't admitted to knowing her name – the explanation could prove embarrassing. I made a wild guess, remembering something of what I had been told about her when I flew with *The Rover*. 'I recognised your photograph. You were an actress, weren't you?'

She smiled, wiping the perspiration from her face with a large, white handkerchief. 'Some would say that I still am.'

'What sort of depth are we at?' I asked, feeling quite faint now.

'Oh, no more than a hundred feet. The air system isn't working properly and I don't know enough about these metal moles to fix it. I don't think we're in any immediate danger, however.'

'How did you come to be in East Grinstead, Mrs Persson?'

She did not hear me above the shaking of the machine and the weird whining of its engine. She made some sort of adjustment to our course as she cupped her hand to her ear and made me repeat the question.

She shrugged. 'What I was looking for was nearby. There was some attempt to set up a secret centre of government towards the end. There were plans for an O'Bean machine which was never perfected. There is only one of its type – in Africa. The plans will clarify one or two problems which were troubling us.'

'In Africa! You have come from Africa?'

'Yes. Ah, here we are.' She pushed two levers forward and I felt the tunnelling machine begin to tilt, rising towards the surface. 'The ground must have been mainly clay. We've made good speed.'

She cut off the engines, took one last glance into the viewer, seemed satisfied, moved to the hatch, pressed a button. The hatch opened, letting in the refreshing night air.

'You'd better get out first,' she said.

I clambered thankfully from the machine, waiting for my vision to adjust itself. The ground all around me was flat and even. I could

just make out the silhouette of what at first appeared to be buildings arranged in a circle which enclosed us. There was something
decidedly familiar about the place. 'Where are we?' I asked her.

'I think it used to be called The Oval,' she told me as she joined
me on the grass. 'Hurry up, Mr Bastable. My air boat should be
just over here.'

It was a ridiculous emotion to feel at the time, I know, but I could
not help experiencing a tinge of genuine shock at our having dese-
crated one of the most famous cricket pitches in the world!

Chapter Five
The Start of a New Career

U NA PERSSON'S AIR boat was very different from the sort of aircraft I had become used to in the world of 1973. This was a flimsy affair consisting of an aluminium hull from which projected a sort of mast on which was mounted a large, three-bladed propeller. At the tail was a rudder, and on either side of the rudder were two small propellers. From the hull sprouted two broad, stubby fins which, like the small propellers, helped to stabilise and to steer the boat once it had taken to the air. We rose, swaying slightly, from the ground, while the boat's motor gave out a barely heard purring. It was only now that I sought to enquire of our destination. We were flying at about a height of one thousand feet over the remains of Inner London. There was not a landmark left standing. The entire city had been flattened by the invader's bombs. The legendary vengeance of Rome upon Carthage was as nothing compared to this. What had possessed one group of human beings to do such a thing to another? Was this, I wondered, how Hiroshima had looked after the *Shan-tien* had dropped her cargo of death? If so, I had much on my conscience. Or had I? I had begun to wonder if I moved from dream to dream. Was reality only what I made of it? Was there, after all, any such thing as 'history'?

'Where are we headed for, Mrs Persson?' I asked, as we left London behind.

'My first stop will have to be in Kerry, where I have a refuelling base.'

'Ireland.' I remembered the first subaquatic vessel I had seen. 'I had hoped...'

I realised, then, that I had already made up my mind to accept Korzeniowski's offer. I had seen enough of my homeland and what its inhabitants had become. Korzeniowski's statements about the sea being the only 'clean' place to be were beginning to make sense to me.

'Yes?' She turned. 'I would take you all the way with me, Mr Bastable. I owe you that, really. But I have scarcely enough power to get myself back and another passenger would make a crucial difference. Secondly you would probably have no taste for the kind of life I would take you to. I could drop you somewhere less dangerous than Southern England. It is the best I can offer.'

'I was thinking of making for Scotland,' I said. 'Would I stand a better chance of survival there?' I was reluctant to disclose my actual destination. Korzeniowski would not appreciate my revealing his secret station.

She frowned. 'The coast of Lancashire is about the best I can suggest. Somewhere beyond Liverpool. If you avoid the large cities, such as Glasgow, you should be all right. The Highlands themselves sustained very little bombing and I doubt if the plagues reached there.'

And so it was that I bid farewell to Una Persson on a wild stretch of saltings beside the coast of Morecambe Bay near a village called Silverdale. It was dawn and the scenery around me made a welcome change from that I had so recently left. The air was full of the cries of seabirds searching for their breakfast and a few sheep grazed on the salt flats, taking a wary interest in me as they cropped the rich grass. In the distance was the sea, wide, flat and gleaming in the light of the rising sun. It was a comforting picture of rural tranquillity and much more the England I had hoped to find when I had first landed at Dover. I waved goodbye to Mrs Persson, watching her air boat rise rapidly into the sky and then swing away over the ocean, heading towards Ireland, then I shouldered my carbine and tramped towards the village.

The village was quite a large one, consisting mainly of those fine, stone houses one finds in such parts, but it was completely deserted. Either the inhabitants had fled under the threat of some supposed invasion, or else they had died of the plague and been buried by survivors who, in turn, had prudently gone away from the source of the disease. But there were no signs of any sort of disaster. Hoping to find food, maps and the like, I searched several houses, finding them completely in order. Much of the furniture had been neatly draped with dust-covers and all perishable food had been removed, but I was able to discover a good quantity of canned meats and bottled fruit and vegetables which, while heavy to carry, would sustain me for some time. I was also fortunate enough to find several good-quality maps of Northern England and Scotland. After resting for a day in Silverdale and granting myself the luxury of sleeping in a soft bed, I set off in the general direction of the Lake District.

I soon discovered that life was continuing at a fairly normal pace in these parts. The farming is largely sheep, and while the people who remained were forced to live in what was comparative poverty, the war had hardly altered their familiar pattern of existence. Instead of being regarded with fear and suspicion, as I had been in the Home Counties, I was welcomed, given food, and asked for any news I might have about the fate of the South. I was happy to tell all I knew, and to warn these friendly Northerners to beware of the insanity which had swept the counties around London. I was told that similar conditions existed near Birmingham, Manchester, Liverpool and Leeds, and I was advised to skirt Carlisle, if I could, for while the survivors of that city had not descended to the level of barbarism I had experienced in East Grinstead, they were still highly suspicious of those who seemed better off than themselves and there had been minor outbreaks of a variant of the disease known as Devil's Mushroom, which had not improved their disposition towards those who were not local to the area.

Heeding such warnings, proceeding with caution, taking advantage of what hospitality I was offered, I slowly made my way north, while the autumn weather – perhaps the finest I had ever known – lasted. I was desperate to get to the Islands before winter set in and the mountains became impassable. The Grampians, those stately monarchs of the Western Highlands, were reached, and at length I found myself crossing the great Rannoch Moor, heading in the general direction of Fort William, which lay under the shadow of Ben Nevis. The mountains shone like red Celtic gold in the clear sunshine of the early winter; there is no sight like it in the whole world and it is impossible to think of the British Isles as being in any way small, as they are in comparison with most other land areas, when you see the Grampians stretching in all directions, inhabited by nothing save the tawny Highland cattle, grouse and pheasant, their wild rivers full of trout and salmon. I ate like a king during that part of my journey – venison became a staple – and I was tempted to forget about my plan for joining Korzeniowski in the Outer Hebrides and to make my life here, taking over some abandoned croft, tending sheep, and letting the rest of the world go to perdition in any way it chose. But I knew that the winters could be harsh and I heard rumours that the old clans were beginning to re-form and that they were riding out on cattle raids just as they had done in the days before the dreams of that drunken dandy Prince Charles Edward Stuart had brought the old Highland ways of life to a final and bitter end.

So I continued towards Skye, where I hoped I might find some sort of ferry still operating on the Kyle of Lochalsh. Sure enough, the inhabitants of Skye had not abandoned their crucial links with the mainland. Sailing boats plied a regular trade with the island and a haunch of venison bought me a passage on one of them just as the first snows of the winter started to drift from out of vast and steely skies.

My real difficulties then began! The people of Skye are not unfriendly. Indeed, I found them among the most agreeable folk in the world. But they are close-mouthed at the best of times, and my enquiries as to the possible whereabouts of an underwater vessel called the *Lola Montez* fell on deaf, if polite, ears. I could not gain an ounce of information. I was fed, given a considerable quantity of strong, mellow local whisky, invited to dances all over the island (I think I was regarded as an eligible bachelor by many of the mothers!) and allowed to help with any work which needed to be done. It was only when I offered to go out with the fishing boats (hoping thus to spot Korzeniowski's ship) that my help was refused. From Ardvasar in the south to Kilmaluag in the north the story was the same – no-one denied that underwater boats called, from time to time, at the Islands, and no-one admitted it either. A peculiar, distant expression would come over the faces of young and old, male or female, whenever I broached the subject. They would smile, they would nod, they would purse their lips and they would look vaguely into the middle distance, changing the subject as soon as possible. I began to believe that not only was there at least one fuelling station in the Outer Hebrides but that the islanders derived a good deal of their wealth, and therefore their security in troubled times, from the ship or ships which used such a station. It was not that they mistrusted me, but they saw no point in giving away information which could change their situation. At least, that is what I surmised.

Not that this made any great difference to me, it emerged. It was evident that an effort was made to help, that the fuelling station was contacted and that my description and name were registered there, for one night, just after the spectacular New Year celebrations for which the Island folk are justly famous, I sat in a comfortable chair before a roaring fire in an excellent public house serving the township of Uig, sipping good malt whisky and chatting on parochial subjects, when the door of the hostelry opened, the wind howled in, bearing a few flakes of snow with it, until the door was slammed back in its face, and there, swathed in a heavy leather sea-cloak, stood my old friend Captain Josef Korzeniowski, bowing his stiff, Polish bow, and clicking the heels of his boots smartly together as he saluted me, his intelligent eyes full of sardonic amusement.

He was evidently well known to the regular customers of the inn and was greeted with warmth by several of them. I learned later that it was the captain's policy to share at least half of his booty with the islanders, and in return he received their friendship and their loyalty. When he needed new crew members, he recruited them from Skye, Harris, Lewis, North and South Uist and the smaller islands, for many had been professional seamen and, as Korzeniowski informed me, were among the most loyal, courageous and resourceful in the world, taking naturally to the dangers and the romance of his piratical activities!

We talked for hours, that night. I told him of my adventures and confirmed all he had said of what I would find in the South. In turn, he described some of his recent engagements and brought me up to date with what he knew of events in the rest of the world. Things had, if anything, gone from bad to worse. The whole of Europe and Russia had reverted almost completely to barbarism. Things were scarcely any better in North America. Most of the nations which had remained neutral were internally divided and took no interest in international problems. In Africa the infamous Black Attila had swept through the entire Middle East and incorporated it into his so-called 'Empire', had crossed the Mediterranean and claimed large areas of Europe, had conquered the best part of Asia Minor.

'There is even a story that he has designs on Britain and the United States,' Korzeniowski informed me. 'The only potential threat to his dreams of conquest would be the Australasian–Japanese Federation, but they pursue a policy of strict isolationism, refusing to become involved in any affairs but their own. It saved them from the worst effects of the war and they have no reason to risk losing everything by taking part in what they see as a conflict between different tribes of barbarians. The Black Attila has so far offered the A.J.F. no direct threat. Until he does, they will not move to stop him. The African nations who have so far been reluctant to join him are too weak to oppose him directly and are hopeful that if they do not anger him he will continue to concentrate on conquering territory which is, after all, already lost to civilisation.'

'But it is in the nature of such conquerors to consolidate easy gains before turning their attention on more powerful prey, is it not?' I said.

Korzeniowski shrugged and lit a pipe. The rest of the customers had long since gone home, and we sat beside a dying fire, the remains of a bottle of whisky between us. 'Perhaps his impetus will dissipate itself eventually. It is what most people hope. So far he has brought some kind of order to the nations he has conquered – even a form of justice exists, crude though it is, for those with brown, black or yellow skins. The whites, I gather, receive a generally rawer deal. He has a consuming hatred for the Caucasian races, regarding them as the source of the world's evils – though I have heard that he has some white engineers in his employ. Presumably they are useful to him and would prefer to serve him rather than be subjected to some of the awful tortures he has devised for other whites. As a result, his resources grow. He has great fleets of land ironclads, airships, undersea dreadnoughts – and they are increasing all the time as he captures the remnants of the world's fighting machines.'

'But what interest could he have in conquering England?' I asked. 'There is nothing for him here.'

'Only the opportunities for revenge,' said the Polish sea captain quietly. He looked at his watch. 'It is high time I returned to my ship. Are you coming with me, Bastable?'

'That was my reason for being here,' I said. I had a heavy heart as I digested the implications of all Korzeniowski had told me, but I tried to joke, remarking: 'I used to dream of such things, as a boy. But now the dream is reality – I am about to serve under the Jolly Roger. Will it be necessary to sign my articles in blood?'

Korzeniowski clapped me on the shoulder. 'It will not even be required of you, my dear fellow, to toast the Devil in grog – unless, of course, you wish to!'

I got my few possessions from my room and followed my new commander out into the chilly night.

Chapter Six
'A Haven of Civilisation'

F OR WELL OVER a year I sailed with Captain Korzeniowski aboard the *Lola Montez*, taking part in activities which would have carried the death sentence in many countries of my own world, living the desperate, dangerous and not always humane life of a latter-day sea wolf. In my own mind, if not in the minds of my comrades, I had become a criminal, and while my conscience still sometimes troubled me, I am forced to admit that I grew to enjoy the life. We went for the big game of the seas, never taking on an unarmed ship, and, by the logic which had come to possess this cruel and ravaged world, usually doing battle with craft who had as much to answer for in the name of piracy as had we.

But as the year progressed, and we roamed the seas of the world (ever cautious not to offend either the ships of the Australasian–Japanese Federation or those sailing under the colours of the Black Attila), we found our prey becoming increasingly scarce. As sources of fuel ran out or parts needed replacing, even the few ships which had survived the war began to disappear. I felt something of the emotions that an American buffalo-hunter must have felt as he began to realise that he had slaughtered all the game. Sometimes a month or more would pass without our ever sighting a possible prize and we were forced to take a decision: either we must risk the wrath of the two main Powers and begin to attack their shipping, or we must go for smaller game. Both prospects were unpleasant. We should not last long against the Powers and none of us would enjoy the sordid business of taking on craft not of our size. The only alternative would be to join the navy of one of the smaller neutral nations. There was no doubt that we should be welcomed with relief into their service (for we had been a thorn in their side as pirates and they would rather have a ship of our tonnage working with them – most would prefer to forget any thoughts of revenge), but it would not be pleasant to accept their discipline after having had virtually the freedom of the high seas. For all that I had reservations, mine was the chief voice raised in support of this latter scheme, and slowly I won Korzeniowski over to the idea. He was an intelligent, far-sighted skipper, and could see that his days as a pirate were numbered. He confided to me that he had yet another consideration.

'I could always scupper the *Lola Montez* and retire,' he told me. 'I'd be welcome enough in the Islands. But I'm afraid of the boredom. I once entertained the notion of writing novels, you know. I always felt I had a book or two in me. But the notion isn't as attractive as it once was – for who would read me? Who, indeed, would publish me? And I can't say I'm optimistic about writing for posterity when posterity might not even exist! No, I think you're right, Bastable. Time for a new adventure. There are still a couple of largish navies in South America and Indo-China. There are even one or two in Africa. I had hoped that one of the Scandinavian countries would employ us, but yesterday's news has scotched that scheme.'

The previous day we had heard that the armies of the Black Attila had finally reached Northern Europe and overrun the last bastions of Western culture. The stories of what had been done to the Swedes, the Danes and the Norwegians chilled my blood. Now black chieftains rode through the streets of Stockholm in the carriages of the murdered Royal Family and the citizens of Oslo had been enslaved, piecemeal, to build the vast generators and chemical plants required to power the mobile war machines of the Black Horde. There had been no-one to enslave in Copenhagen, for the city had resisted a massive siege and now nothing remained of it but smoking rubble.

Brooding on this, Korzeniowski added a little later: 'The other argument against retiring to the Islands is, of course, the rumour that the Black Attila has plans to invade Britain. If he did so, sooner or later the Highlands and Islands would be threatened.'

'I can't bear to think of that,' I said. 'But if it did happen, I would be for carrying on some sort of guerrilla war against him. We'd go under, sooner or later, but we'd have done something...'

Korzeniowski smiled. 'I have no special loyalties to Britain, Bastable. What makes you think I'd agree to such a scheme?'

I was nonplussed. Then his smile broadened. 'But I would, of course. The Scots have been good to me. If I have any sort of homeland now I suppose it is in the Outer Hebrides. However, I have a hunch that the black conquest of Britain would only be a token affair. Cicero Hood has his eye on larger spoils.'

General Cicero Hood (or so he called himself) was the military genius now known as the Black Attila. We had heard that he was not a native of Africa, at all, but had been born in Arkansas, the son of a slave. It was logical to suspect that his next main objective would be the United States of America (though 'United' meant precious little these days), if his main motive for attacking the Western nations was revenge upon the White Race for the supposed ills it had done him and his people.

I commented on the massive egotism of the man. Even his namesake had somewhat nobler motives than simple vengeance in releasing his Huns upon the world.

'Certainly,' agreed Korzeniowski, 'but there is a messianic quality about Hood. He pursues the equivalent of a religious jihad against the enslavers of his people. We have had leaders like that in Poland. You would not understand such feelings, I suppose, being British, but I think I can. Moreover, whatever your opinion of his character (and we know little of that, really), you must admit that he is something of a genius. First he united a vast number of disparate tribes and countries, fired them with his ideals, and worked with amazing speed and skill to make those ideals reality.'

I said that I did not doubt his ability as a strategist or, indeed, his intelligence, but it seemed to me that he had perverted a great gift to a mean-spirited ambition.

Korzeniowski only added: 'But then, Mr Bastable, you are not a Negro.'

I hardly saw the point of this remark, but dropped the subject, since there was nothing more I had to say on it.

It was perhaps ironic, therefore, that a couple of months later, having sounded out possible 'employers', we sailed for Bantustan with the intention of joining that country's navy.

Bantustan had been better known in my own world as South Africa. It had been one of the first colonies to make a bid for independence during those pre-war years when O'Bean's inventions had released the world from poverty and ignorance. Under the leadership of a young politician of Indian parentage called Gandhi, it had succeeded in negotiating a peaceful withdrawal from the British Empire, almost without the Empire realising what had happened. Naturally, the great wealth of Bantustan – its diamonds and its gold alone – was not something which British, Dutch and American interests had wished to give up easily, yet Gandhi had managed to placate them by offering them large shareholdings in the mines without their having to invest any further capital. Since most of the companies had been public ones, shareholders' meetings had all voted for Gandhi's schemes. Then the war had come and there was no longer any need to pay dividends to the dead and the lost. Bantustan had prospered greatly during and after the war and was well on its way to becoming an important and powerful force in the post-war political game. By building up its military strength, by signing pacts with General Hood which ensured him of important supplies of food and minerals at bargain prices, President Gandhi had protected his neutrality. Bantustan was probably one of the safest and most stable small nations in the world, and since it required our experience and our ship, it was the obvious choice for us. Moreover, we were assured, we should find no racialistic nonsense there. Black, brown and white races lived together in harmony – a model to the rest of the world. My only reservations concerned the political system operating there. It was a republic based upon the theories of a German dreamer and arch-socialist called Karl Marx. This man, who in fact lived a large part of his life in a tolerant England, had made most radicals sound like the highest of High Tories, and personally I regarded his ideas as at best unrealistic and at worst morally and socially dangerous. I doubted if his main theories could have worked in any society and I expected to have quick proof of this as soon as we docked in Cape Town.

We arrived in Cape Town on 14 September, 1906, and were impressed not only by a serviceable fleet of surface and underwater ships, but also a large collection of shipyards working at full capacity. For the first time I was able to see what O'Bean's world must have been like before the war. A great, clean city of tall, beautiful buildings, its streets filled with gliding electric carriages, crisscrossed by public monorail lines, the skies above it full of individual air boats and large, stately airships, both commercial and military. Well-fed, well-dressed people of all colours strolled through wide, tree-lined arcades, and the London I had visited in some other 1973 seemed as far behind this Cape Town as my own London had seemed behind that London of the future.

Suddenly it did not seem to matter what political theories guided the ruling of Bantustan, for it was obvious that it scarcely mattered, so rich was the country and so contented were its people. We had no difficulty in communicating with our new colleagues, for although the official language was Bantu, everyone spoke English and many also spoke Afrikaans, which is essentially Dutch. Here there had been no South African war and as a result there had been little bitterness between the English and Dutch settlers, who had formed a peaceful alliance well before President Gandhi had risen to political power. Seeing what South Africa had become, I almost wept for the rest of the world. If only it had followed this example! I felt prepared to spend my life in the service of this country and give it my loyalty as I had once given Britain my loyalty.

President Gandhi personally welcomed us. He was a small gnomelike man, still quite young, with an infectious smile. In recent years he had devoted quite a lot of his energies to attracting what remained of the West's skilled and talented people to Bantustan. He dreamed of a sane and tranquil world in which all that was best in mankind might flourish. It was his regret that he needed to maintain a strong military position (and thus in his opinion waste resources) in order to guard against attack from outside, but he managed it gracefully enough and felt, he told us at the private dinner to which Korzeniowski and myself were invited, that there was some chance of setting an example to men like Cicero Hood.

'Perhaps he will begin to see how wasteful his schemes are, how his talents could be better put to improving the world and making it into a place where all races live in equality and peace together.'

I am not sure that, presented with these ideas in my own world, I could have agreed wholeheartedly with President Gandhi, but the proof of what he said lay all around us. O'Bean had thought that material prosperity was enough to abolish strife and fear, but Gandhi had shown that a clear understanding of the subtler needs of mankind was also necessary – that a moral example had to be made, that a moral life had to be led without compromise – that hypocrisy (albeit unconscious) among a nation's leaders led to cynicism and violence among the population. Without guile, without deceiving those he represented, President Gandhi had laid the foundations for lasting happiness in Bantustan.

'This is, indeed, a haven of civilisation you have here,' Captain Korzeniowski said approvingly, as we sat on a wide verandah overlooking the great city of Cape Town and smoked excellent local cigars, drinking a perfect home-produced port. 'But you are so rich, President Gandhi. Can you protect your country from those who would possess your wealth?'

And then the little Indian gave Korzeniowski and myself a shy, almost embarrassed look. He fingered his tie and stared at the rooftops of the nearby buildings, and he sounded a trifle sad. 'It is something I wished to speak of later,' he said. 'You are aware, I suppose, that Bantustan has never spilled blood on behalf of its ideals.'

'Indeed we are!' I said emphatically.

'It never shall,' he said. 'In no circumstances would I be responsible for the taking of a single life.'

'Only if you were attacked,' I said. 'Then you would have to defend your country. That would be different.'

But President Gandhi shook his head. 'You have just taken service in a navy, gentlemen, which exists for only one reason. It is effective only while it succeeds in dissuading those we fear from invading us. It is an expensive and impressive scarecrow. But it is, while I command it, as capable of doing harm as any scarecrow you will find erected by a farmer to frighten the birds away from his fields. If we are ever invaded, it will be your job to take as many people aboard as possible and evacuate them to some place of relative safety. This is a secret that we share. You must guard it well. All our officers have been entrusted with the same secret.'

The enormity of President Gandhi's risk in revealing this plan took my breath away. I said nothing.

Korzeniowski frowned and considered this news carefully before replying. 'You place a heavy burden on our shoulders, President.'

'I wish that I did not have to, Captain Korzeniowski.'

'It would only take one traitor…' He did not finish his sentence.

Gandhi nodded. 'Only one and we should be attacked and overwhelmed in a few hours. But I rely on something else, Captain Korzeniowski. People like General Hood cannot believe in pacifism. If a traitor did go to him and inform him of the truth, there is every chance that he would not believe it.' He grinned like a happy child. 'You know of the Japanese method of fighting called Jui-Jit-Sui? You use your opponent's own violence against him. Hopefully, that is what I do with General Hood. Violent men believe only in such concepts as "weakness" and "cowardice". They are so deeply cynical, so rooted in their own insane beliefs, that they cannot even begin to grasp the concept of "pacifism". Suppose you were a spy sent by General Hood to find out my plans. Suppose you left here now and went back to the Black Attila and said to him, "General, President Gandhi has a large, well-equipped army, an air fleet and a navy, but he does not intend to use them if you attack him." What would General Hood do? He would almost certainly laugh at you, and when you insisted that this was a fact he would probably have you locked up or executed as a fool who had ceased to be of use to him.' President Gandhi grinned again. 'There is less danger, gentlemen, in living according to a set of high moral principles than most politicians believe.'

And now our audience was over. President Gandhi wished us happiness in our new life and we left his quarters in a state of considerable confusion.

It was only when we got to our own ship and crossed the gangplank to go aboard, seeing the hundred or so similar craft all about us, that Korzeniowski snorted with laughter and shook his head slowly from side to side.

'Well, Bastable, what does it feel like to be part of the most expensive scarecrow the world has ever known?'

Chapter Seven

A Legend in the Flesh

A PEACEFUL YEAR passed in Bantustan – peaceful for us, that is. Reports continued to reach us of the ever-increasing conquests of the Black Attila. We learned that he had raised his flag over the ruins of London and left a token force there, but had met with no real resistance and seemed, as we had guessed, content (like the Romans before him) to claim the British Isles as part of his new Empire without, at this moment in time, making any particular claims upon the country.

Our friends in the Outer Hebrides would be safe for at least a while longer. Our most strenuous duties were to take part in occasional naval manoeuvres, or to escort cargo ships along the coasts of Africa. These ships were crewed entirely by Negroes and we rarely had sight of land. It was regarded as politic for whites not to reveal themselves, even though Hood knew they were not discriminated against in Bantustan.

We had a great deal of leisure and spent it exploring President Gandhi's magnificent country. Great game reserves had been made of the wild veldt and jungle, and silent air boats carried one over them so that one could observe all kinds of wildlife in its natural state without disturbing it. There was no hunting here, and lions, elephants, zebra, antelope, wildebeest, rhinoceri roamed the land unharmed by Man. I could not help, sometimes, making a comparison with the Garden of Eden, where Man and Beast had lived side by side in harmony. Elsewhere we found model farms and mines, worked entirely by automatic machinery, continuing to add to the wealth of the country and, ultimately, the dignity of its inhabitants. Processing plants – for food as well as minerals – lay close to the coast where the food in particular was being stockpiled. Bantustan had more than enough to serve her own needs and the surplus was being built up or sold at cost to the poorer nations. I had begun to wonder why so much food was being stored in warehouses when President Gandhi called a meeting of a number of his air- and sea-officers and told us of a plan he had had for some time.

'All over the world there are people reduced to the level of savage beasts,' he said. 'They are brutes, but it is no fault of their own. They are brutes because they are hungry and because they live in fear. Therefore, over the last few years I have been putting aside a certain percentage of our food and also medical supplies – serums which my chemists have developed to cope with the various plagues still lingering in Europe and parts of Asia. You all know the function of your fleets is chiefly to give Bantustan security, but it has seemed a shame to waste so much potential, and now I will tell you of my dream.'

He paused, giving us all that rather shy, winning smile for which he was famous. 'You do not have to share it. I am asking only for volunteers, for there is danger involved. I want to distribute that food and medicine where it is most needed. You, Mr Bastable, have seen and reported what has happened in Southern England. Would you not agree that these supplies would help to alleviate some of the worst aspects of the conditions there?'

I nodded. 'I think so, sir.'

'And you, Mr Caponi,' said the President, addressing the dashing and idealistic young Sicilian aviator who had made such a name for himself when he had almost single-handedly saved the survivors of Chicago from the raging fires which had swept that city, by dropping again and again into the inferno, risking almost certain death to rescue the few who remained alive. 'You have told me how your countrymen have turned to cannibalism and reverted to their old, feuding ways. You would see that changed, would you not?'

Caponi nodded eagerly, his eyes blazing. 'Give me the supplies, Mr President, and I will have my keels over Sicily by morning!'

Most of the other commanders echoed Captain Caponi's sentiments and President Gandhi was well pleased by their response.

'There are matters I must attend to before we embark on this scheme,' he said, 'but we can probably begin loading the food and medicine by the end of the month. In the meantime I had better warn you, gentlemen, that General Hood is soon to make a state visit to Bantustan.'

The news was received with consternation by most of us – and with undisguised disgust by some, including Caponi, who was never one to hide his feelings. He expressed what a good many of us – particularly the whites – refrained from saying:

'The man is a mass-murderer! A bloody-handed looter! A maniac! Many of us have had relatives done to death by his minions! Why, I have sworn that if I should ever have the opportunity, I should kill him – with my bare hands I should kill him!'

The little President glanced at the floor in some embarrassment. 'I hope you will not be so tempted, Captain Caponi, when General Hood is here as my guest...'

'Your guest!' Caponi clapped his hand to his forehead. 'Your *guest!*' He broke into a stream of Sicilian oaths which I, for one, was glad I did not understand – although the import of the language was clear enough.

President Gandhi let him continue for a while and then interrupted mildly: 'Would it not be better, *capitano*, to have this man as our guest – rather than as our conqueror? By meeting him, I hope to influence him – to beg him to stop the senseless warfare, this vendetta against the white race which can only lead to more violence, more terror, more grief...'

Caponi spread his hands, his somewhat pudgy features displaying an expression which was almost pitying. 'You think he will listen, Mr President? Such a man cannot be reasoned with! I know to my sorrow how destructive a vendetta can be – but the Black Attila is a madman – a wild beast – a ferocious and senseless killer – a torturer of women and children. Oh, sir, you are too unworldly...'

President Gandhi raised his eyebrows, biting his lip. He sighed. 'I hope I am not,' he said. 'I understand all the arguments and I know how you must feel. But I must obey my conscience. I must make an effort to reason with General Hood.'

Captain Caponi turned away. 'Very well – reason with him – and see what good it does. Can you reason with a whirlwind? Can you reason with a rogue rhino? Reason with him, President Gandhi – and pray for the safety of your country!' And with that he walked rapidly from the room.

One or two of the other officers mumbled words which echoed Caponi's. We all loved President Gandhi, but we all felt that he was misguided in his hopes.

Finally, he said: 'Well, gentlemen, I hope some of you will agree to be present at the banquet I intend to hold for General Hood. If your voices are added to mine, at least you will know, as I will know, that you have done your best...'

He dismissed us, then, and we all left with heavy hearts, speculating variously on what General Hood would be like to meet in the flesh and how we should react when – or if – we saw him.

Personally I had mixed feelings. It was not every day, after all, that one received the opportunity of dining with a legend, a world-conquering tyrant whom history would rank with Genghis Khan or Alexander the Great. I was determined to accept the President's invitation. Besides, I had to admit that I was beginning to get a little bored with my life in Bantustan. I was first and foremost a soldier, a man of action, trained in a certain way of life and not, by nature, contemplative or much of an intellectual. General Hood's visit would, if nothing else, relieve that boredom for a while!

A week later there was a Black Fleet hanging in the skies of Cape Town. Between twenty and thirty good-sized keels lay anchored to specially built masts. They swayed slightly in the warm wind from the west, each of them displaying the insignia of the Black Attila's so-called New Ashanti Empire: a black, rampant, snarling African lion in a scarlet circle. Hood *claimed* as an ancestor the famous Quacoo Duah, King of Ashanti in the 1860s, and it was initially on the Gold Coast that he had begun to build his army – starting with a handful of Ashanti and Fanti nationalists pledged to the overthrow of the first native government of Ashantiland (as it had been renamed after Independence). Although the Black

Horde consisted of members of all African peoples, as well as those from beyond Africa, it had somehow retained the name of Ashanti, just as the Roman Empire had kept its name even after it had few connections with Rome at all. Also the Ashanti people were well-respected throughout most of Africa, and since Hood claimed to be Quacoo Duah's direct descendant, it suited him to keep the name.

Many of those who had sworn to have nothing whatsoever to do with the whole affair were drawn reluctantly to the streets or their balconies, to watch the descent of Cicero Hood and his retinue from the flagship (diplomatically named the *Chaka*) which hung just above the main formation. For the first time we saw Hood's famous Lion Guard – huge, perfectly formed warriors with skin like polished ebony and proud, handsome features, drawn from all the tribes of Africa. On their heads were steel caps from which projected tall, nodding ostrich plumes dyed scarlet and orange. From their shoulders hung short cloaks made from the manes and skins of male lions. They wore short, sleeveless jackets of midnight blue, similar to the jackets worn by French Zouaves, trimmed with gold and silver braid, and tight cavalry-style britches to match. High boots of black, gleaming leather were on their feet and each man carried two weapons, symbolic of the Old and the New Africa – an up-to-date carbine on the back and a long-shafted, broad-bladed spear in the right hand. Standing in the open-air carriages, scarcely moving a muscle, their faces expressionless, they were undoubtedly amongst the most impressive soldiers in the world. Their carriages formed a perfect circle around that of General Cicero Hood himself – a carriage painted in splendid colours and flying the black-and-scarlet flag of the Black Attila's Empire. From where I stood on the roof of my apartment building (many of my colleagues were with me, including Korzeniowski) I could see that there were two figures in the carriage, but I was too far away to make out details of their features, though it seemed to me that one of the occupants was white!

Upon landing, Hood and his Guard transferred to open electrical broughams and began a long procession through the streets of Cape Town that was received with surprising enthusiasm from many of the citizens (admittedly most of them Negroes), but I could see little of this procession from my vantage point. I retired to the bar downstairs where a number of other officers were coming back from the street, where they had witnessed the scene. Not a few of the white and a number of the black officers had looks of grudging admiration on their faces, for there had been no doubt about the excellence of the stage-management involved in Hood's arrival. A man I knew slightly who had been a land-fleet commander in India before he had joined the army of Bantustan (his name, as I recall, was Laurence), ordered himself a stiff brandy and drained it in a single swallow before turning to me and saying in a tone of awe: 'I say, Bastable, the chap's got a bally white woman in tow. Rum go, eh? His distaste for us doesn't seem to extend to the female of the species, what?'

Another acquaintance called Horton, who had been an officer in the Sierra Leone navy before the nation was annexed by Hood, said dryly: 'To the victor the spoils, old man.' There was a look of amusement on his brown face, and he winked at me, enjoying Laurence's discomfort.

'Well, I mean to say...' began Laurence, realising his lack of tact. 'It's not that I feel...'

'It's just that you do.' Horton laughed and turned to order Laurence another drink. 'You think Hood's taken a white concubine as a sort of gesture. It could be that he finds her so attractive he doesn't care what colour she is. I've heard of Europeans falling in love with African women. Haven't you?'

Laurence's next point was undeniably a good one. 'But not Europeans with a deep loathing of Negroes, Horton. I mean, it rather shakes his case about us being awful fiends, doesn't it?'

Horton grinned. 'Maybe he prefers the devil he knows.'

'I must admit,' put in a lieutenant who had begun his career in the Russian navy, Nicolai, 'I wouldn't mind knowing her myself. What a beauty! I think she's the most ravishing creature I've ever seen. Good luck to Hood on that score, say I!'

The conversation continued on these lines for a while until

those of us who had accepted invitations to attend the banquet had to leave to get ready. Korzeniowski and I and a party of other 'underwater sailors' were going together. Dressed in the simple, white dress uniforms of the Bantustan navy, we left for the palace in a large carriage rather like an electrically powered char-à-banc, were met at the steps and escorted into the great hall which normally housed the elected representatives of the people of Bantustan. Long tables had been laid out and each place was adorned with gold and silver plate and cutlery. We were privileged (if that is the word) to sit at the President's table and would thus be afforded a good chance of observing the infamous General Hood at close range.

When we were all seated, President Gandhi, General Hood and the general's lady consort entered through a door in the back of the hall and moved to take their places at the table.

I believe that I had by this time learned enough self-control not to register my surprise upon recognising the woman whose hand was now placed on the arm of the despot who had become master of most of Africa and all of Europe. Our eyes met and she acknowledged me with a ghost of a smile before turning her head to say something to Hood. It was Una Persson! Now I knew why she had wished to return to Africa so speedily and why she had been reluctant to take me with her. Had she, even then, been keeping this association with the Black Attila?

General Hood was not what I expected. He was as tall as any member of his 'Lion Guard', but fairly slender, moving with what I can only describe as a sort of awkward grace. He wore perfectly cut conventional evening dress which was entirely without decoration. I had expected a fierce-eyed warlord, but this man was close to middle age, with the distinguished air of a high-ranking diplomat. His hair and beard were greying a little and his large, dark eyes held a mildness which could only be deceptive. I was reminded, against my will, of a sort of black Abraham Lincoln!

President Gandhi was beaming. It seemed he had had a conversation with General Hood which had proved satisfactory to him. The little Indian was dressed, as always, in a light cotton suit of what we used to term 'Bombay cut'. They took their places and we, who had been standing, resumed ours. The meal began in a rather grim silence, but slowly the atmosphere improved. General Hood chatted amiably to President Gandhi, to the President's aides, and to Una Persson. I heard a little of the conversation – enough to know that it was the usual sort of polite small-talk which goes on among politicians on occasions like this one. From what might have been a mistaken sense of tact, I tried not to look at Mrs Persson during the dinner and addressed myself primarily to the lady on my left who seemed to be obsessed with the notion of trying to breed back, in Africa, many of the species of birdlife which had been made all but extinct during the wars in Europe.

The meal was an excellent compromise between European and African dishes, and I think it is probably the best I have ever eaten, but we were on the sweet course before I was saved from the conversation of the amateur ornithologist on my left. Quite suddenly I heard the deep, mellow tones of General Hood speaking my name and I looked up in some embarrassment.

'You are Mr Bastable, then?'

I stuttered a reply to the effect that his information was correct. I was not even sure how one addressed a despotic conqueror who had on his hands the blood of hundreds of thousands of innocents.

'You have my gratitude, Mr Bastable.'

I was conscious of a decided lull in the conversation around me and I think I might have been blushing a little. I noticed that Mrs Persson was smiling broadly at me, as was President Gandhi, and I felt very foolish, for no particular reason.

'I have, sir?' was, I think, what I answered. It sounded insane to my ears and I tried to recover my equilibrium by reminding myself that this man, in spite of appearances, was the sworn enemy of my race. It was, however, difficult to maintain an attitude of disdain while at the same time behaving in a way which suited the social situation. I had accepted the invitation to dine at the palace and therefore had a duty to President Gandhi not to offend his guests.

General Hood laughed a deep, full-throated laugh. 'You saved the life of someone I hold very dear.' He patted Una Persson's hand. 'Surely you remember, Mr Bastable?'

I said that it had been nothing, that anyone would have done the same, and so on.

'You showed great courage, Mrs Persson tells me.'

I made no answer to this. Then General Hood added: 'Indeed, if it had not been for you, Mr Bastable, it is unlikely that I should have been able to continue with certain military ambitions I have been entertaining. White though your skin is, I think you have the heart of a black man.'

A calculated irony, surely! He had managed to implicate me in his crimes and I think relished my embarrassment. Next he added:

'If, at any time, you wish to leave the employment of Bantustan, the Ashanti Empire could make use of your services. After all, you have already proved your loyalty to our cause.'

I saw the eyes of all the whites in the hall staring at me. It was too much. Seized by anger, I blurted back: 'I regret, sir, that my loyalty is to the cause of peace and the rebuilding of a sane world. The cold-blooded murder of the women and children of my own race is not something to which I could easily lend myself!'

Now the silence in the hall was total, but General Hood soon broke the atmosphere by leaning back in his chair, smiling and shaking his head. 'Mr Bastable, I have no dislike of the white man. In his place, he performs a large number of useful functions. I employ white men in a good many capacities. Indeed, there are individuals who show all the qualities I would value in an African. Such individuals are given every opportunity to shine in the Ashanti Empire. You have a poor impression of me, I fear – whereas I have nothing but respect for you.' He raised his glass to toast me. 'Your health, Mr Bastable. I am sincere in my offer. President Gandhi and I have been discussing exchanging emissaries. I shall put in a strong plea to him that you be among those invited to New Kumasi. There you shall see for yourself if I am the tyrant you have heard about.'

I was far too angry by now to make any sort of reply. President

Gandhi tactfully drew General Hood into conversation and a little later Korzeniowski came up behind me and tapped me on the shoulder, leading me from the hall.

My emotions were, to put it mildly, mixed. I was torn between boiling anger, social embarrassment, loyalty to President Gandhi and his dream of peace, and my own responses to Hood himself. It was no surprise, now, that he had risen so swiftly to eminence in the world. Tyrant and murderer he might be, but it was undeniable that he had a magnetic personality, that he had the power to charm even those who hated him most. I had expected a swaggering barbarian and had encountered, instead, a sophisticated politician, an American (I learned later) who had been educated at Oxford and Heidelberg and whose academic career had been an outstanding one before he put down his books and picked up the sword. I was shaking and close to tears as Korzeniowski took me back to my quarters and devoted himself to calming me down. But it was hours before I finished my mindless ranting. I drank a good deal, too, and I think that it was a combination of alcohol and emotional exhaustion which finally shut me up. One moment I was raging at the insults of the Black Attila and the next moment I had fallen face forward to the floor.

Korzeniowski must have put me to bed. In the morning I woke up with the worst headache of my life, still in a filthy temper, but no longer capable of expressing it. It was a knocking at the door which had awakened me. My batman answered it and a short while later brought me my breakfast tray. On the tray was an envelope bearing the seal of the President himself. I pushed the tray aside and inspected the envelope, hardly daring to open it. Doubtless it contained some kind of reproof for my behaviour of the previous evening, but I was unrepentant.

I lay in bed, the envelope still in my hand, considering the answers I should have given Hood if I had had my wits about me.

I was determined not to be charmed by him, to judge him only by his actions, to remember how whole European cities had been destroyed by him and their populations enslaved. I regretted that I had mentioned none of this during our encounter. I have never believed in violent solutions to political problems, but I felt if there was one man who deserved to be assassinated it was Cicero Hood. The fact that he had received an excellent education only made him more of a villain in my eyes, for he had perverted that education in order to pursue his racial jihad. He might blandly deny his policies of genocide, but what he had done in the past few years spoke for itself. At that moment, I felt I could, like Caponi, cheerfully kill him with my bare hands.

It was Korzeniowski turning up that forced me to control myself. He stood at the end of my bed, looking down at me with a kind of sympathetic irony, asking me how I felt.

'Not too good,' I told him. I showed him the letter. 'I think I'm due for the sack. I'll be leaving Bantustan soon enough, I shouldn't wonder.'

'But you haven't opened the letter, old man.'

I handed it up to him. 'You open it. Tell me the worst.'

Korzeniowski went to my desk and took a paper-knife to slit the top of the envelope. He removed the contents – a single sheet of paper – and read it out in his precise, guttural English:

'Dear Mr Bastable. If you have the time today, I should be grateful if you would visit me in my office. About five would be convenient for me, if that would suit you. Yours sincerely, Gandhi.'

Korzeniowski handed me the letter. 'Typical of him,' he said admiringly. 'If you have time, Mr Bastable. He is giving you the option. I shouldn't have thought that meant a carpeting, old chap, would you?'

I read the letter for myself, frowning. 'Then what on earth does it mean?' I said.

Chapter Eight
A Decision in Cold Blood

NEEDLESS TO SAY, although I hemmed and hawed a lot, I eventually arrived, scrubbed and neat, at the presidential palace at five o'clock sharp and was immediately escorted into President Gandhi's office. The office was as plain and functional as all the rooms he used. He sat behind his desk looking, for him, decidedly stern, and I guessed that, after all, I was in for a wigging, that my resignation would be demanded. So I stood smartly to attention and prepared myself to take whatever the President was about to give me.

He got up, rubbing his balding head with the palm of his hand, his spectacles gleaming in the sun which flooded through the open window. 'Please sit down, captain.' It was rare for him to use a military title. I did as I was ordered.

'I have had a long talk with General Hood today,' Gandhi began. 'We have, as you know, been discussing ways of cementing good relations between Bantustan and the New Ashanti Empire. On most matters we have reached an amicable understanding, but there is one detail which concerns you. You know that I believe in free will, that it is not part of my beliefs to force a man to do something he does not wish to do. So I will put the situation to you and you must make up your own mind about it. General Hood was not joking last night when he offered you employment...'

'Not joking? I hoped so, sir. I do not wish to be employed as a mass-murderer...'

President Gandhi raised his hand. 'Of course not. But General Hood, it seems, has taken a liking to you. He admired the way in which you answered him back last night.'

'I thought it a poor performance. I meant to apologise, sir.'

'No, no. I understand your position completely. You showed

great self-control. Perhaps that was what Hood was doing – testing you. He is genuinely grateful for the part you played, apparently, in saving Mrs Persson's life in England – and, I could be completely wrong, but I have the feeling he wants to vindicate himself in your eyes. Perhaps he sees you as representative of – in his terms – the better sort of white man. Perhaps he is tired of killing and actually does want to begin building a safer and saner world – though his present military plans seem to contradict that. Whatever the reason, Bastable, he has insisted that you be part of the diplomatic mission sent to his capital at New Kumasi – indeed, he has made it a condition. You will be the only, um, white member of the mission. Unless you go, he refuses to continue with our negotiations.'

'Well, sir, if those are not the actions of a madman, a despot, I do not know what they are!' I replied.

'Certainly, they are not based on the kind of logic I recognise. General Hood is used to having his way – particularly when it comes to the fate of white men. I do not deny that. However, you know how important these talks are to me. I hope to influence the general – at least to temper his future policies towards those he conquers. Everything I have dreamed of is endangered – unless you consider that you can accept his terms. You must look to your own conscience, Mr Bastable. I do not want to influence you, I have already gone against my principles – I am aware that I am putting moral pressure on you. You must forget what I want and do only what you think is right.'

It was then that I reached what was perhaps the most cold-blooded decision of my life. If I accepted, then I should be in an excellent position to get close to Hood and, if necessary, put an end to his ambitions for good and all. I had contemplated assassination – now I was being given the opportunity to perform it. I decided that I *would* go to New Kumasi. I *would* observe the Black Attila's actions for myself. I would be Hood's jury and his judge. And if I decided that he was guilty – then I would take it upon myself to be his executioner!

Naturally, I said nothing of this to President Gandhi. Instead, I frowned, pretending to consider what he had said to me.

I think I was a little mad, then. It seems so to me now. The strain of finding myself in yet another version of history, of being in no way in control of my own destiny, was probably what influenced me to seek to alter events in this world. Still, I will not try to justify myself. The fact remains that I had decided to become, if necessary, a murderer! I will leave it to you, the reader, to decide on what sort of morality it is that justifies such a decision.

At last I looked up at President Gandhi and said:

'When would I have to leave, sir?'

Gandhi seemed relieved. 'Within two weeks. I must select the other members of the mission.'

'Have you any idea, sir, what part Mrs Persson has played in this?'

'No,' he admitted. 'No clear idea. It could be quite a large one, for all I know. She seems to have considerable influence with General Hood. She is an extremely enigmatic woman.'

I was bound to agree with him.

It was with great regret that I said goodbye to Captain Korzeniowski and the other friends I had made in Cape Town. All felt that I had been forced into this position and I wished that I might confide in them my secret decision, but of course it was impossible. To share a secret is to share a burden and I had no intention of placing any part of such a burden on the shoulders of anyone else.

President Gandhi was sending some of his best people to New Kumasi – ten men, three women and myself. The others were either of Asian or African origin or of mixed blood. As the only white I did not feel out of place in their company, for I had long since become used to the easy terms on which the races mingled in Bantustan. In his choice, President Gandhi had shown that he was a shrewd as well as an idealistic politician, for two of the members of the mission were military experts briefed to observe all they could of General Hood's war-making capacity and discover as much intelligence as possible in respect of his long-term military ambitions. All, with the possible exception of myself, believed heart and soul in Gandhi's ideals.

The day came when we were ferried up to the waiting aerial frigate. Its hull was a gleaming white and it hung in the deep, blue sky like some perfectly symmetrical cloud, with the plain, pale-green flag of Bantustan flying from its rigging.

Within moments of our going aboard, the ship dropped its anchor cables and began to head north-west towards the shining waters of St Helena Bay.

I looked back at the slender spires of Cape Town and wondered if I should ever see that city of my friends again. Then I put such thoughts from my head and gave myself up to polite conversation with my colleagues, all of whom were speculating on what they would find in New Kumasi and how we might expect to be treated if relations between New Ashanti and Bantustan became strained. None of us was used to dealing with despots who had absolute powers of life and death over their subjects.

Twenty-four hours passed as we crossed the greater part of western Africa and hung, at last, in the air over General Cicero Hood's capital.

It was very different from Cape Town. Those new buildings which had been erected were of a distinctly African character and not, I must admit, unpleasant to look upon. A preponderance of cylindrical shapes topped by conical roofs reminded one somewhat of the kind of huts found in a typical kraal in the old days – but these 'huts' were many storeys high and built of steel, glass, concrete and modern alloys. The city was unusual, too, in that it seemed to be walled in the medieval manner, and on the walls was evidence that New Kumasi had been designed as a fortress – large guns could be seen, as well as 'pillbox' emplacements. The grandiose, barbaric lion flag of the Ashanti Empire flew everywhere, and military airships cruised around the perimeters like guardian birds of prey. Here there were no monorails or moving pavements or any of the other public-transport amenities of Bantustan's cities, but it was a well-run metropolis, as far as one could see – very much under the control of the army. Indeed, half the people I saw, after we had landed, were in uniform – both men and women. There was no sign of poverty, but no sign, either, of the bountiful wealth of Cape Town. The majority of the population were Negro and the only whites I saw seemed to be doing fairly menial tasks (one or two of the porters at the aerodrome were European) but were not evidently ill-treated. There were very few private vehicles in the streets, but a good many public omnibuses of, for this world, a slightly old-fashioned sort, running off wire-borne electrical current. Other than these, there were chiefly military vehicles moving about. Huge land ironclads rolled up and down the thoroughfares, evidently taking precedence over other vehicles. These were of the globular pattern, mounted on a wheeled frame but able, at a pinch, to release themselves from the frame and roll under their own volition, their speed and course being checked by telescopic legs which could be extended from most points on the hull. I had heard of these machines, but had never seen one at close quarters. If released upon a town, or an enemy position, they were capable of flattening it in moments without firing a shot from their steam-powered gatlings and electrical cannon. I could imagine the terror one might feel when such a monster came rolling towards one!

In contrast, the Guard of Honour which greeted us and escorted us to General Hood's headquarters was mounted on tall, white stallions, and the carriages into which we climbed were much more familiar to me than the rest of my colleagues – for they were horse-drawn, rather like the landaus of my own world. The nodding plumes of the Lion Guard horsemen flanking us, the discipline with which they sat their mounts, reminded me graphically of that world which I so longed to return to but which, now, I was reconciled never to seeing again.

The Imperial Palace of New Ashanti recalled, in its impressive beauty, what I had seen of the famous Benin culture. Like so many of the other buildings, it was cylindrical and topped by a conical roof which stretched beyond the walls, umbrella-fashion, and was supported by carved pillars, forming a kind of cloister or arcade faced with ivory, gold, bronze and silver, affording shade for the many guards who surrounded it. Every modern material and

architectural skill had been used in the building of the palace, yet
it was undeniably African, showing hardly any evidence of European influence. I was to learn later that it had been Cicero Hood's
firm policy to encourage what he called 'the practical arts' in his
Empire, and to insist that their expression be distinctly African in
conception. As one who had seen many foreign cities of Asia ruined
by ugly European-style architecture, who regretted the passing of
ethnic and traditional designs in buildings, as well as many other
things, I welcomed this aspect of Hood's rule, if no other.

Having had some experience of the petty tyrants of India, I
fully expected the Black Attila to behave as they behaved and to
keep us waiting for hours in his anterooms before we were
granted an audience, but we were escorted rapidly through the
exquisitely decorated passages of the palace and into a wide, airy
hall lit from above by large windows, its walls covered with friezes
and bas-reliefs of traditional African design but showing the events
of the recent past in terms of the heroic struggles and triumphs of
the New Ashanti Empire. Hood himself was recognisable as featuring in several scenes, including the Conquest of Scandinavia,
and there were representations of land fleets, aerial battles, underwater skirmishes and the like, giving the panels a very strange
appearance – a mingling of ancient and almost barbaric emotions
with examples of the most modern technical achievements of
mankind.

At the opposite end of the hall from the great double doors
through which we entered stood a dais carpeted in zebra skin, and
upon the dais (I was reminded, for a moment, of the King of East
Grinstead) was placed a throne of carved ebony, its scarlet, quilted
back bearing the lion motif one saw everywhere in New Kumasi.

Dressed in a casual, white tropical suit, Cicero Hood stood
near his throne, looking out of a tall window. He turned when we
were announced, dismissing the guards with one hand while
keeping the other in his trouser pocket, crossing with a light step
to a table where there had been arranged a variety of drinks and
non-alcoholic beverages (Hood had doubtless been informed that
there were several in our party who did not drink). He served each

of us personally and then moved about the hall arranging chairs so that we might all be seated close together. No European king could have behaved with greater courtesy to guests he was determined to honour (and yet equally determined to impress, for he had made sure we saw all the outward signs of his power!).

He had taken the trouble to find out the names of each individual in our party and to know something of their interests and special responsibilities in Bantustan and he chatted easily with them, showing a good knowledge of most subjects and ready to admit ignorance where he had it. Again, I was surprised. These were by no means the swaggering ill-manners of a parvenu monarch. There had been kings and emperors in my own world who might have learned much of the art of noblesse oblige from the Black Attila.

He did not address me individually until he had talked for a while with the others, then he grinned at me and shook me warmly by the hand and I had the unmistakeable impression that the tyrant actually *liked* me – a feeling I could not reciprocate and could not equate with my knowledge of his much-publicised hatred of the white race. My own response was polite, self-controlled, but reserved.

'I am so glad, Mr Bastable, that you could agree to come,' he said.

'I was not aware, sir, that I had a great deal of choice,' I answered. 'President Gandhi seemed to be under the impression that you had insisted on my being part of the mission.'

'I expressed the hope that you might be able to join it, certainly. After all, I must show impartiality.' This was said with a smile which doubtless he hoped would disarm me. 'The token European, you know.'

Deliberately or not, he had made me feel self-conscious by referring to the colour of my skin. Even a joke had the effect of emphasising the difference we both felt, and it would not have mattered if the man who made it had been my best friend, I should still have had the same feelings, particularly since there were no other whites in the room.

Noting my discomfort, Cicero Hood patted me on the shoulder. 'I'm sorry, Mr Bastable. A remark in bad taste. But hard for the son of a slave to resist, I'm sure you'd agree.'

'It would seem to me, sir, that your own success would be sufficient to help you forget any stigma...'

'Stigma, Mr Bastable?' His voice hardened. 'I assure you that I do not feel it is a stigma. The stigma, surely, belongs to those who enslaved my people in the first place.'

It was a good point. 'Perhaps you are right, sir,' I mumbled. I was no match for Hood's intellectual swiftness.

Hood's manner instantly became condescending again. 'But you are right. I have mellowed in the last year or two, thanks, in some measure, to the good fortune I have had. I have only one goal left and then I shall be content. However, that goal is the most difficult I have set myself, and I have a feeling I shall meet strong resistance from a certain Power which has, up to now, remained neutral.'

'You mean the Australasian–Japanese Federation, sir?' This was Field Marshal Akari, the man we had elected as chief spokesman for our mission. A distinguished officer and one of President Gandhi's oldest friends and supporters, he was owed much by Bantustan and had frequently acted as the President's deputy in the past. 'Surely they would not risk everything they have built up over the last few years? They cannot feel threatened by Ashanti!'

'I am afraid that they do, field marshal,' said Hood in a tone of the utmost regret. 'It would seem that they regard the Pacific as their territory and they have had some news of my plans – I have made no secret of them – and feel that if my ships begin to sail "their" ocean it will only be a matter of time before I cast greedy eyes upon their islands.'

Mrs Nzinga, but lately Minister of Communications in Gandhi's government, said quietly: 'Then you intend to attack the United States? Is that what you mean, sir?'

Hood shrugged. 'Attack is not the word I would choose, Mrs Nzinga. My intention is to liberate the black peoples of the United States, to help them build a new and lasting civilisation there. I know that I am thought of as a senseless tyrant by many – embarked upon a crazy course of genocide – a war of attrition against the whites – but I think there is a method to my "madness". For too long the so-called "coloured" peoples of the world have been made to feel inferior by the Europeans. In many parts of Africa an awful, soul-destroying apathy existed until I began to show those I led that the whites had no special skills, no special intelligence, no special rights to rule. My speeches against the whites were calculated, just as my nationalism was calculated. I knew that there was little time, after the war, to make the gains I had to make. I had to use crude methods to build up my resources, my territory, the confidence of those I led. I happen to believe, rightly or wrongly, that it is time the black man had a chance to run the world. I think if he can rid himself of the sickness of European logic, he can make a lasting Utopia. I admire President Gandhi, Mrs Nzinga – though you might find that strange in a "bloody-handed tyrant". I have not left Bantustan unthreatened because I fear your military strength. I want Bantustan to continue to exist because it is a symbol to the rest of the world of an ideal state. But it is Bantustan's *good fortune*, not any special virtue, which has made it what it is. The rest of the world is not so fortunate and if President Gandhi tried to set up his state, say, in India he would find that it would not last for long! First the world must be united – and the way to unite it is to form large empires – and the way to form large empires, I regret, madam, is by war and bloodshed – by ferocious conquest.'

'But violence will be met by violence,' said Professor Hira, whose university programme had been such a success in Bantustan. A small, tubby man, his shiny face positively glowed with emotion. 'Those you conquer will, sooner or later, try to rise up against you. It is in the nature of things.'

'Risings of the sort you describe, professor,' said General Hood grimly, 'are only successful where the government is weak. Tyrannies can last for centuries – have lasted for centuries – if the administration remains firmly in control. If it cultivates in itself the Stoic virtues. If it is, in its own terms, just.

'My Empire has been compared with that of Rome. The Roman Empire did not fall – it withered away when it was no longer of any use. It left behind it a heritage of philosophy alone which has continued to influence us all.'

'But you see Western thinking as having brought us to the brink of world annihilation,' I put in.

'In some ways only. That is not the point, however. I described an example. I believe that African thinking will produce a saner, more lasting civilisation than that of the West.'

'You have no proof of this,' I said.

'No. But a theory must be tested to be *dis*proved, Mr Bastable. I intend to test the theory and to ensure that the test is thorough. The experiment will continue long after my death.'

There was nothing much I could reply to this without getting involved in abstractions. I subsided.

'You may see my ambitions in America as being motivated merely by revenge,' Cicero Hood continued, 'but I wish to build something in the country of my birth as strong as that which I am building here. The whites of the United States are decadent – perhaps they have always been decadent. A new enthusiasm, however, can be generated amongst the blacks. I intend to put power into their hands. I intend to liberate America. Have you not heard what is happening there now? Having no real enemy to fight any longer, the whites turn, as always, upon the minorities. They wiped out the Red Indians – now they plan to wipe out the Negroes. It is the spirit of Salem – the corrupting influence of Puritanism which in itself is a perversion of the Stoic ideal – infecting what remains of a nation which could have set an example to the world, just as Bantustan now sets an example. That spirit must be exorcised for good and all. When the whites are conquered they will not be enslaved, as we were enslaved. They will be given a place in the New Ashanti Empire; they will be given a chance to *earn* their way to full equality. I shall take their power from them – but I shall not take their dignity. The two have been confused for too long. But only a black man realises that – for he has had the *experience* during centuries of exploitation by the whites!'

It was a noble speech (even if I was sceptical of its logic), but

I could not resist, at last, making a remark which General Hood was bound to find telling.

'It is possible, General Hood,' I said, 'that you can convince us that your motives are idealistic, but you have told us yourself that the Australasian–Japanese Federation is not so convinced. There is every chance that they will be able to thwart your scheme. What then? You will have risked everything and achieved nothing. Why not concentrate on building Africa into a single great nation? Forget your hatred of the United States. Let it find its own solutions. The A.J.F. is probably as powerful as the Ashanti Empire…'

'Oh, probably more powerful now!' It was the clear, sweet voice of Una Persson that interrupted me. She had entered through a door behind Hood's throne. 'I have just received confirmation, General Hood, of what I suspected. O'Bean is in Tokyo. He has been there, it seems, since the outbreak of the war. He has been convinced that Ashanti represents a further threat to the world. He has been working on plans for a new fleet for nearly two years. Already a score of his ships have been built in the yards of Sydney and Melbourne and are ready to sail. Unless we mobilise immediately, there is every chance that we shall be defeated.'

General Hood's response was unexpected. He looked first at me, then at Una Persson, then he threw back his head and he laughed long and heartily.

'Then we mobilise,' he said. 'Oh, by all means – we mobilise. I am going home, Mrs Persson. I am going home!'

Book Two

The Battle for Washington

Chapter One

The Two Fleets Meet

Looking back, I suppose I should count myself fortunate in being, by a strange set of circumstances, witness to Hood's decision to risk everything he had gained by invading America, and to experience the invasion (and its aftermath) itself. Not many young officers are given such an opportunity.

My determination to take the law into my own hands if I judged Hood 'guilty' remained as strong, but I was already beginning to realise that the Black Attila was a far subtler individual than I had at first supposed. Moreover, I soon came to learn that his ferocity, his reputation for putting to death or enslaving whole cities, was something of a myth which he encouraged. It was useful to him if his enemies believed the myth, for it quite often resulted in all but bloodless conquests! The defenders would prefer to parley rather than fight, and would often ask for terms quite inferior to those Hood was prepared to grant! This meant that, when he proposed terms which were better than they had expected, he gained the reputation of munificence which was quite undeserved, but encouraged the conquered to work willingly for him – out of a sense of relief as much as any other consideration!

I saw little of Hood or Una Persson in the following week. They were far too involved in their plans for mobilisation. We of the diplomatic mission could only gather what information was available and relay it to Bantustan. We were allowed, in the first days, to communicate information of all kinds freely to our own country, but a little later a certain censorship was imposed as General Hood became nervous of news reaching Tokyo. I think he had heard that the A.J.F. fleet was making for the Atlantic. The largest part of the Ashanti fleet had been based in Europe, where it was most useful, and some ships had to be recalled, while others were ordered to assemble in Hamburg, Copenhagen, Gothenburg and other Northern European ports, preparatory to sailing for America.

I gathered that Hood was not merely relying on his vast land, air and sea fleets, but had another counter to play. From something Una Persson had said, I thought her trip to England had played a part in Hood's 'secret weapon' being developed, but I was to learn more of this later.

My next surprise came a day or two before Hood was due to sail. Una Persson visited me at the legation, where I was busy with some sort of meaningless paperwork. She apologised for disturbing me and said that General Hood would like to see me for a few moments during luncheon.

I went unwillingly. Privately I was sure that the powerful Australasian–Japanese Federation would put a stop to his dreams of conquest for ever and that I no longer had a part to play in the history of this world. I was looking forward to returning to Bantustan when the Ashanti Empire collapsed, as it was bound to do.

Hood had almost finished luncheon when I arrived at the palace. He was sitting at the head of a long table surrounded by his chief ministers and generals. There were charts spread among the remains of a simple meal and black faces were bent over them, conversing in low, urgent tones. All looked up as I arrived, and several frowned, making insulting remarks about their meal being spoiled by the sight of a white man. I had become quite used to this sort of thing from Hood's lieutenants (though, to be fair, not all were so ill-mannered) and was able to ignore the comments, saying: 'You sent for me, general?'

Hood seemed surprised to see me. He looked vaguely at me for a moment and then snapped his fingers as if remembering why he had sent for me. 'Ah, yes, Mr Bastable. Just to tell you to have a bag packed by tomorrow morning and to present yourself to the captain of the *Dingiswayo*. He is expecting you. I've exchanged communications with President Gandhi and he is agreeable to the scheme. You have been seconded to my staff. You're coming with us to America, Mr Bastable. Congratulations.'

There was nothing I could say. I tried to think of some retort, failed, and saluted. 'Very well, sir.' Whether there was some deeper motive involved, or whether this was just another example of Hood's quixotic and whimsical behaviour where my fate was concerned I did not know. It seems that by taking my initial decision I was now bound to follow it through all the way.

And that was how I came to be the only white officer to accompany the sea-borne Black Horde when it sailed out over the Atlantic bound for New York with the express intention of destroying for ever the power of the Caucasian race!

My life has been full of ironies since my first, ill-fated expedition to Teku Benga, but I think that that remains the greatest irony of them all.

Hood had thrown virtually everything he had into the invasion fleet. Surface and underwater vessels, airships of every description, came together at last just off the coast of Iceland – a fleet which filled the sky and occupied the ocean for as far as the eye could see. Aboard the ships were stored Hood's vast collection of land ironclads and in the centre of all these there rose a gigantic hull, specially built but utterly mysterious in its purpose, which could not progress under its own power but which had to be towed by thirty other battleships. I guessed that this must surely be Hood's secret weapon, but neither I nor any of the other officers aboard the *Dingiswayo* had any inkling of its nature!

And all the while news was coming through of the Australasian–Japanese fleet converging on our own.

Hood's hope was that we could run ahead of the A.J.F. fleet and get to the coast of North America before it caught up with us, but these new ships of O'Bean's were much faster than ours (their fire-power was a completely unknown factor) and I knew that we had no chance. There was a school of thought which said that we should disperse our own fleet, but Hood was against this, feeling that we had a better chance if we concentrated our forces. Also, as was evident, he was prepared to risk almost everything to protect the vast hull we towed (or, at least, the contents of the hull) and I had the impression that he might consider sacrificing everything else so long as that hull arrived eventually in New York.

There was scarcely a ship in the fleet which would not have dwarfed one of the ironclads of my own day. Equipped with long-snouted naval guns which could put a stream of incredibly powerful shells into the air in the time it took one of my world's ships to fire a single shot, capable of cruising at speeds reaching ninety knots, of manoeuvring with the speed and ease of the lightest cruiser, a couple of them could have given our good old British navy a pretty grim time. Hood had a hundred of these alone in his fleet, as well as over fifty underwater battleships and nearly seventy big aerial men-o'-war (which, in turn, were equipped with light fighting air boats capable of leaving the mother ship, striking rapidly at an enemy and returning to safety above the clouds). As well as this massive fighting strength, there were dozens of smaller vessels, many cargo ships, carrying land 'clads and infantry, gunboats and torpedo boats – virtually all the remaining fighting ships of the nations of the world which had taken part in the war.

If I had believed in the cause of the Ashanti Empire I am sure I would have felt a surge of pride when I looked upon the splendour of that fleet as it steamed away from Reykjavik in the early morning of 23 December, 1907 – a mass of black and scarlet upon the grey field of the wintry sea. Wisps of fog drifted from time to time across the scene and, standing on the quarter-deck of the *Dingiswayo*, listening to the sound of ships' horns bellowing in the distance, I was overwhelmed with a sense of awe. How, I wondered, could anything in the world resist such might? And if there was a God, how could He allow it to have been created in the first place?

It seemed to me, at that moment, that I had been torn from my own world to witness a vision of Armageddon – and, oddly enough, I felt privileged!

I think that it was then that the notion first occurred to me that perhaps I had been selected by Providence to be involved in a countless series of what might be called alternative versions of the Apocalypse – that I was doomed to witness the end of the world over and over again and doomed, too, to search for a world where Man had learned to control the impulses which led to such

suicidal conflicts, perhaps never to find it. I still do not quite understand my motives in recording my experiences, but it could be that
I hope that, if they are ever read, they will serve as a lesson to a
world which has so far managed to avert its own destruction.

But, as I have said before, I am neither introspective nor morbid
by nature, and my thoughts soon returned to the more immediate aspects of my situation.

It was about four p.m. on Christmas Day, 1907, that the Australasian–
Japanese fleet was sighted speeding rapidly from south-south-west
out of the twilight, firing as it came.

Night had fallen by the time we properly engaged and the
fighting was confused. The air was full of fire and noise. Above us
the air fleets were locked in terrible conflict, while on every side
huge guns poured forth destruction seemingly at random, and
when, at sudden moments, there came a lull, when there was a
second or two of silence and blackness, I experienced a cold and
impossible fear, certain that it was all over, that the world itself
had been destroyed and that the sun would never rise again.

By means of wireless telegraphy, Hood was able to direct the
battle from the *Chaka*, which was riding somewhere above the
clouds, and it became evident to me that he was building up a
defensive position around the contents of that huge and mysterious hull at the centre of our fleet. The *Dingiswayo*, also close to
the centre, was not therefore immediately engaged in battle, but
impatiently awaited orders to have a crack at the enemy, firing
occasionally, when so commanded, into the sky at one of the
Australasian–Japanese airships, which would return our shots
with bombs and concentrated cannon-fire, none of which happily
scored a direct hit and all of which failed to pierce our super-
strong steel armour.

At last we received an order to break formation and moved at
full speed to a position on the starboard flank of the main
Australasian–Japanese grouping, where our own ships were sustaining particularly heavy losses.

We seemed at first to be moving away from the main battle – away from the crimson and yellow flashes of the guns, the incessant booming, and into utter blackness. Then, suddenly, as if receiving warning of our presence, two battleships turned their searchlights on us. Powerful beams of white light struck us in the eyes and blinded us for the moment. I was still on the quarter-deck, with precious little to do, not being a regular officer of the ship. I heard the captain shouting from the bridge, saw our long guns begin to swing into position, felt the *Dingiswayo* roll as she turned at an acute angle, broadside to the enemy, giving me my first clear view of two long lines of battleships, some mere silhouettes in the darkness, and others speckled with reflected light from the gun-flashes to port. Then the air was full of the whine of shells, the chunky, throaty noise of those shells hitting the water ahead and astern of us, but never, thankfully, scoring on either our hull or superstructure. Then all our guns began to go off and the *Dingiswayo* shuddered from stem to stern so that I thought she might well shake herself to pieces. Our shells left the muzzles of the guns with a kind of high-pitched yell – almost an exultation – and the enemy ships were grouped so tightly together that we could not miss. The shells hit the battleships and exploded. Heavy smoke drifted back to us and we were all forced to don the special masks designed for the purpose of protecting our lungs in just such circumstances.

The air had been cold, the temperature well below zero, but now it began to heat up, becoming tropical, as far as we were concerned. We went about and sought the darkness again, knowing that we had been lucky and that we could not expect to take on a dozen or more battleships alone.

For a while the searchlights roamed across the sea, trying to pick us out, but we skulked just out of their range, using their own lights to try to get some idea of our best chance. A battleship had detached itself from the main formation and was rushing blindly towards us, apparently unaware of our presence in its path. It was a splendid opportunity for us. I heard the order given to release torpedoes but to hold off firing. There was a faint sound, like the striking of a bell, and the torpedoes sped silently towards their prey, darting from our tubes while the enemy ship remained unaware that she was under attack!

The torpedoes scored direct hits below the battleship's water-line. She was holed in five places and was sinking even before she realised it. I heard a confused shouting from her decks, and her searchlights came on, but already she was keeling over and the lights slowly rose into the sky like the fingers of a clutching, imploring hand. She went down without having fired a single shot. For a little while I saw her electrics gleaming below the surface, winking out slowly as she sank, and then the water was black again, dotted with a few bits of wreckage and a handful of wailing sailors.

There was no time to pick up survivors, even if we had wished to (and the Ashanti did not believe in showing much mercy to defeated enemies). We had been sighted again and two battleships were rushing towards us at speeds which would have seemed incredible on land and which were, to me, all but impossible on sea! We were capable of not much more than half their speed, but again we were successful in finding covering darkness.

It seemed to me that we had moved quite a long way off from the main conflict. At least a mile away now, the sea and the sky seemed to be one vast mass of flame, lighting a wide area and revealing wreck upon wreck. The entire sea was filled with broken remains – both of ordinary battleships and fallen airships – while beneath this mass of torn metal and blazing oil and wood could sometimes be seen the dark shapes of the underwater boats, like so many gigantic killer whales, seeking out fresh prey.

Once I had a glimpse of two subaquatic destroyers locked in conflict several fathoms below, searchlights piercing the gloom, guns flashing in what was to me an eery silence. Then one of the boats wheeled and dived deeper and the other followed it, still fir-ing. I saw something flicker down there and then suddenly the water above the scene gushed up like a monstrous geyser, flinging fragments of metal and corpses high into the air, and I knew it was all over for one of the vessels.

My attention went back to the two battleships whose search-lights had picked us up. Our decks were suddenly flooded with light and almost immediately the enemy guns began to go off. This time we were not so lucky. An explosive shell hit us some-where amidships and I was flung backwards by the force of the blast. A firefighting team ran past me, paying out a hose behind it, and I saw the fire flicker out in what must have been seconds. I pulled myself to my feet and climbed the companionway to the bridge, where the captain, peering through a pair of night-glasses, was rapping out orders through an electrical loud-hailer which amplified his clicking, harshly accented speech (it was an Ivory Coast dialect with which I was unfamiliar). Again the *Dingiswayo* went about, taking evasive action, all her port guns firing at once and scoring at least two hits on the vessel which had damaged us. We saw her lurch heavily over to one side and settle in the water, part of her hull glowing red-hot and a shower of sparks streaming into the air from a point near her afterbridge. We must have hit some vital part of her, for a moment later there came an awesome explo-sion which flung me backwards once again so that this time my spine struck the rail and winded me horribly. Oily black smoke was borne on the wind of the explosion and blinded us, and the *Dingiswayo* was buffeted as badly as if she had been seized sud-denly by a hurricane, but then the smoke cleared and we saw little of the other ship, just something which might have been her top-mast standing out for a second above the waterline and then this, too, disappeared.

Her sister ship now commenced a heavy cannonade and again we were hit, though not badly, and were able to fire back until the enemy evidently thought better of continuing the engagement, turned about and sped at its maximum rate of knots back into the darkness.

This cautious action on the part of the enemy skipper had a considerable effect on our own morale and a huge cheer went up from our decks while our forward gun fired one last, contemptu-ous shot at the stern of the retreating vessel.

It seemed to me (and I was later proved correct) that for all its superiority of speed and fire-power, the Australasian–Japanese navy had little stomach for fighting. They had had no direct experience of naval warfare, whereas the Ashanti had been fighting now for several years and were used to risking death almost daily. Faced with the terrible implications of actual battle, our enemy began to lose its nerve. This was the pattern, also, above and below the waves.

But by dawn we were still fighting. For miles in all directions battleship met battleship, steering through a veritable Sargasso Sea of wreckage (in many places it was virtually impossible to see the water at all), and the air continued to be filled with the booming of the guns, the whine of the shells and, less audible but far more chilling to my ears, the screams and the wails of the wounded, the drowning, the abandoned of both sides. Parts of the water were on fire, sending sooty smoke into the cold, grey sky, and now the cloud had come down so low that it was rare to catch sight of an aerial ironclad as it manoeuvred overhead, though we could hear the guns sounding like thunder and see occasional flashes of light, like lightning, every so often split those clouds. A couple of times I saw a blazing hull fall suddenly from out of the grey, boiling canopy above us.

We were soon engaged again, with a ship called the *Iwo Shima*, which had already seen some pretty fierce fighting by the look of her. Part of her bows, above the waterline, had been blown away and there was a great pile of miscellaneous junk in her starboard scuppers which had either been washed or blown there by whatever had damaged her bridge. But she was plucky and she still had a considerable amount of fire-power, as she proved. I think she felt that she was doomed anyway, and was determined to take the *Dingiswayo* to the bottom with her, for she showed no concern for her own safety, steaming directly at us, apparently with the intention of ramming us full on if her guns didn't sink us first.

In the distance there were a hundred ships of varying tonnage locked in similar struggles, but I saw no sign of the great hull we had been protecting, nor of the ships which had been assigned to tow her, and it seemed to me then that she had gone down.

The *Iwo Shima* did not waver in her course and we were forced to do what we could to avoid her, giving her everything we had left from our forward guns and, for the first time, using every machine gun that we had behind armour in the fighting tops. This manoeuvre brought us so close to the enemy that we almost touched and neither of us could use any of our big guns at such close range, nor risk using torpedoes. I got a good view of the Japanese seamen, their elaborate and somewhat unfunctional uniforms torn and dirty, their faces begrimed with blood, soot and sweat, watching us grimly as they sped past us, already beginning to turn in the hope of taking us in our stern. But we were turning, too, and a few minutes later the manoeuvre was all over. On our captain's orders, we released our starboard torpedoes the instant we were broadside of the *Iwo Shima*, at the same time pouring the last of our fire-power into her, every starboard gun firing at once. She was fast enough to escape most of what we sent, but her speed told against her, for her retaliatory fire went wide of us, scoring only one minor hit in our starboard bow. We had managed to upset most of the big guns in her battery, but she turned again, much slower now, for our torpedoes had damaged at least one of her screws. But now the sea had begun to rise, making it much more difficult to aim or, indeed, to see our enemy. Everywhere I looked there were walls of water containing all varieties of flotsam – metal, wood and flesh jostling together in some ghastly minuet – and then the sea would sink for a moment, revealing the *Iwo Shima*, and we would fire hastily until, momentarily, she disappeared again.

Our own damage was not slight. From somewhere below, our pumps were working full out to clear many of the compartments which were flooded. In several places the superstructure of the ship had fused into strange, jagged shapes, and corpses hung limply from damaged positions in the fighting tops, where medical staff had been unable to reach them. We had two big holes above the waterline and a smaller one below, amidships, and we had lost at least thirty men. In ordinary circumstances we might have retired with perfect honour, but all of us knew that this battle was crucial, and there was nothing for it but to fight on. We were closing on the *Iwo Shima* now, letting the sea carry us broadside on to the enemy ironclad, going about so that, with luck, we should be able to take her with our port battery which was in better condition and better equipped to deal with her.

We rose on the crest of a great wave and saw the *Iwo Shima* below us. She had taken in more water than her pumps could cope with and she was already beginning to list astern and to starboard. As the huge wave carried us down, we commenced firing.

The *Iwo Shima* went down without letting go another shot. The water foamed and hissed; and we saw her bows jutting stubbornly out of the green-grey ocean for a second or two and then she was gone. Immediately we went full astern, to avoid being dragged down by her undertow, and there came a massive, grumbling series of explosions from below, immediately followed by a roaring water spout which shot at least a hundred feet into the air and rained our decks with tiny pieces of shrapnel.

Again, cheering broke out all over the ship, but was swiftly stifled as a heavy black shape emerged from the clouds overhead. The *Iwo Shima* must have signalled to one of her sister airships for help just before she went down. We had hardly anything left with which to defend ourselves. Machine gunners in the fighting tops aimed their guns upwards, pouring round after round into the hull of the flying ironclad. I could hear a steady *ping ping* as our bullets struck metal, but they had about as much effect as a cloud of midges on a charging rhinoceros. It was our good fortune that this monster had evidently dropped all her bombs and spent her heavy artillery, for she answered us with a chatter of steam gatlings, raking our decks where our men were thickest and wreaking immediate havoc so that in one moment where there had been proud, cheering individuals, citizens of the Ashanti Empire, there was now a horrible mass of writhing, bloody flesh.

I could read the name emblazoned on the airship's dark hull – the RAA *Botany Bay* – and made out her insignia. This gave me a peculiar lurching sensation in the pit of my stomach, for she was flying the good old Union Jack inset with the crimson chrysanthemum of Imperial Japan! Half of me wanted to hail the ship as a friend, while the other half shared the emotions of my fellows aboard the *Dingiswayo* as they fought desperately and hopelessly back. Only our stern gun, a sort of latter-day Long Tom, was operational, and as the *Botany Bay* went past, we managed to get off three or four shots at her, holing her astern, just above her main propellers, but it was the best we could do. Apparently careless of the damage we had done to her, she made a graceful turn in the air and fell upon us again. This time I barely managed to get down behind the shield of one of our useless nine-inch guns before the bullets hailed across our decks.

When I next raised my head, I was fully expecting death, but saw instead the black-and-white markings of one of our own aerial cruisers, dropping down almost as if out of control, so swiftly did she move, clouds of grey smoke puffing from the length of her slender hull as she gave off a massive cannonade. Shell after shell struck the top of the *Botany Bay*'s armoured canopy, piercing it so that her buoyancy tanks were thoroughly holed. She turned first on one side and then on the other and it was a horrifying as well as an awe-inspiring sight to see such a huge beast rolling in the air almost directly above our heads! I have witnessed the death-agonies of more than one airship, but I have never seen anything quite like the death of the *Botany Bay*. She shuddered. She tried to right herself. She lost height and then shot into the air again, almost to the base of the clouds, then her nose dipped, her convulsions ceased and she smashed down into the sea, disappearing beneath the waves and bobbing up again on her side, steam hissing from her ports, to lie upon the face of the ocean like a dying whale. Few inside her could have survived that awful shaking and we made no attempt to discover if there were survivors. Our own flying cruiser dipped her tail to us by way of salute and climbed back into the clouds.

A few minutes later, as we moved among our wounded, trying to save those we could, news came over the wireless apparatus, telling us to rejoin the main fleet at a position which would put us only a few miles off the coast of Newfoundland. The Battle of the Atlantic was over, the enemy fleet having retired, but the Battle of America had not yet begun.

Chapter Two
The Land Leviathan

W HAT REMAINED OF our fleet regrouped the next morning. For all that we had defeated the Australasian–Japanese fleet, we had probably sustained greater losses. There were scarcely a dozen flying ironclads left, perhaps five underwater ships operational, and of the surface fleet half had been sunk, while most of the fifty or so surviving craft had all sustained damage, some of it crippling. The *Dingiswayo*, pumps still working full out, was perhaps in better condition than most of its sister craft, and the only ships to have received minimal damage were those which, under cover of the darkness, had towed the huge floating hull out of danger. I saw Hood's *Chaka* flying overhead, inspecting us as we rose and fell on a moderately heavy sea. A misty rain was falling, adding to the gloomy atmosphere permeating the whole fleet. Somehow the proud black-and-scarlet lion banners we flew did not look so splendid in the wintry, North Atlantic light as they had done under the blazing skies of Africa. Clad in heavy jerseys and sea-cloaks, our caps pulled well down to protect us from the worst of the drizzle, we stood on our decks, shivering, weary and pessimistic. Messages of approval began to come down from the *Chaka*, but could not break our mood. It was the first experience many of the Africans had had of real cold, the sort of cold which cuts into the marrow and threatens to freeze the blood, and liberal amounts of hot toddy seemed to have no effect at all against the weather.

I was standing on the bridge, discussing the conditions with the skipper, Captain Ombuto, who was dismayed to learn that temperatures seemed to me to be somewhat high for the time of year, when a message came through from the *Chaka* which directly concerned me. He read the message, raising his eyebrows and handing it to me. A decent sort, Captain Ombuto had shown me none of the prejudice I had experienced from some of his brother officers. He spoke English with a strong French accent (he had served for a while in the Arabian navy before the war). 'The top brass seems concerned for your safety, Bastable.'

The message was unsigned, save with the name of the flagship, and read: 'Urgent you give details of officers killed and wounded. How is Bastable? Report immediately.' The message was in English, although French was also used, pretty indiscriminately, as the lingua franca of Ashanti.

Captain Ombuto waited until he had a full list of his dead and wounded before relaying the details to the flagship, adding: 'Bastable unharmed' at the end of his reply. A little later there came a second message: 'Please relay my sympathy to those who lost so many comrades. You fought well and honourably. Send Bastable to flagship. Boat coming.' It was signed simply 'Hood'. Ombuto read the message aloud to me, shrugged and removed his cap, scratching his head. 'Until now Mrs Persson has been the only member of your race allowed aboard the flagship. You're going up in the world, Bastable.' He jerked his thumb in the air. 'Quite literally, eh!'

A short while later an air boat landed on the crippled deck of the *Dingiswayo* and I climbed into it, returning the smart salute of the shivering officer of the Lion Guard who commanded it. The poor man looked wretched and I reflected a little cynically that if Hood intended to drive through America into the Southern States, his men could not have a better incentive than the promise of warmer weather!

Twenty minutes later the air boat had entered the huge stern hatches of the *Chaka* and come to rest in the specially modified hangar adapted from the two lowest decks. An electric lift bore us upwards into the depths of the massive ship and soon I stood with my feet in the soft, scarlet plush of the control room carpet. The control room had windows all around it, but they did not look out from the ship but into its interior. From the windows could be seen the main battle-deck, the big guns jutting through their portholes, the bomb bays (mostly empty now) and the war-weary officers and men standing by their positions. General Hood had had, by the look of him, even less sleep than I, but Una Persson seemed extraordinarily fresh. It was she who greeted me first.

'Good morning, Mr Bastable. Congratulations on surviving the battle!'

General Hood said, half-proudly, 'It was probably the fiercest and biggest sea-battle in the history of the world. And we won it, Mr Bastable. What do you think of us now? Are we still nothing more than barbarians who pick upon the weak and innocent, the wounded and the defenceless?'

'Your men and your ships acquitted themselves with great bravery and considerable skill,' I admitted. 'And in this case I would say they had everything to be proud of – for the Australasian–Japanese fleet attacked us, without even bothering to parley.'

'Us?' Hood was quick to pick up the word. 'So you identify with our cause, after all.'

'I identified with my ship,' I said, 'for all that I had precious little to do aboard her. Still, I gather I am here as an observer, not a participant.'

'That is up to you, Mr Bastable,' retorted Hood, running his black hands through his greying hair. 'I have merely given you the opportunity to make your choice! We are about to have luncheon. Won't you join us?'

I made a stiff little bow. 'Thank you,' I said.

'Then, come.' He linked his arm in mine and ushered me from the control room into his private quarters, which were linked to the bridge by a short companionway leading directly into his cabin. Here lunch had already been laid out – an excellent selection of cold food which I could not resist. A fine hock was served and I accepted a glass readily.

'Conditions aboard airships seem rather better than those on ordinary ships,' I said. 'It's freezing down there, almost impossible to get warm unless you're actually in the boiler room. At least an old-fashioned ironclad, powered by coal, heated up in almost any temperatures!'

'Well, we'll be making landfall by tomorrow,' said Hood dismissively as he ate. 'However, if you would be more comfortable aboard the *Chaka* I would be glad to have you as my guest.'

I was about to reject his invitation when Una Persson, seated beside me and wearing a long, simple gown of brown velvet, put a hand on my arm. 'Please stay, Mr Bastable. It will give you a better chance to witness the invasion of New York.'

'Does New York *require* invading? I had heard that there is hardly anyone living there now.'

'A few thousand,' said Hood airily. 'And about a third of those will doubtless join us when we arrive.'

'How can you be sure of that?' I asked.

'My agents have been active, Mr Bastable. You forget that I have retained contacts all over the United States – it is my home country...'

If I had entertained any doubts concerning Hood's ability to attack and take the city of New York, they were quickly dispersed upon our arrival in what had been one of the largest and richest harbours in the world. New York had sustained if anything a heavier bombardment than London. She had been famous for her tall, metallic towers which had gleamed with a thousand bright colours, but now only two or three of those towers were left standing, stained by the elements, ravaged by explosions, threatening to collapse into the rubble which completely obscured any sign of where her broad avenues, her shady, tree-lined streets, her many parks had stood. A cold wind swept the ruins as our ships came to anchor and our aircraft began to spread out in formation, scouting for any signs of resistance. The *Chaka* made several flights over New York, dropping sometimes to a height of fifty feet. There were plenty of signs that these ruins were inhabited. Large fires burned in the hollows formed by tumbled concrete slabs, groups of ragged men and women ran for cover as the shadow of our great craft touched them, while others merely stood and gaped.

Elsewhere I had the impression that some form of order existed.

I thought I glimpsed dirty white uniforms – soldiers wearing what might have been helmets which obscured their faces. No shots were fired at us, however, by the small groups which hastily made for the shadows whenever we approached.

The scene was made even more desolate by the presence of great drifts of snow, much of it dirty and half-melted, everywhere.

'I see hardly any point in bothering to take the place,' I said to General Hood.

He frowned at this. 'It is a question of destroying the morale of any defenders – here or in other parts of the country,' he said. There was an expression of almost fanatical intensity on his black features and his eyes never left the ruins. From time to time he would say, with a mixture of nostalgia and satisfaction, that this was where he had had his first flat in New York; there was where he had worked for one summer as a student; that the heap of rusting girders and shattered stone over which we flew was some famous museum or office building. It was not pleasant to hear him speaking thus – a sort of litany of gloating triumph. Slightly sickened, I turned away from the observation window, and saw Una Persson standing behind us, a look of quizzical and yet tender melancholy on her face, as if she, in her way, also regretted having to listen to Cicero Hood's morbidly gleeful remarks.

'It will be nightfall in three hours,' she said. 'Perhaps it would be best to wait until morning before making the landing?'

He turned, almost angry. 'No! We land now. I'll give the command. Let them see my power!' He reached for a speaking tube, barking orders into it. 'Prepare for landing! Any resistance to be met without mercy. Tonight the Ashanti celebrate. Let the men have whatever spoils they can find. Contact our friends here. Bring the leaders to me as soon as they have revealed themselves. Tomorrow we continue towards Washington!'

It was with pity that I returned my attention to the ruins. 'Could you not spare them?' I asked him. 'Have they not suffered too much?'

'Not from me, Mr Bastable.' His voice was savage. 'Not from me!'

He refused to continue any sort of conversation, waving a dismissive hand both at Una Persson and myself. 'If you cannot share my pleasure, then pray do not try to spoil it for me! Go, both of you. I want no whites here!'

Una Persson was plainly hurt, but she did not remonstrate. She left when I left and we went together to another observation deck, forward, where we probably had a better view of the landing.

First came the infantry, brought ashore in the boats and lining up in orderly ranks on what remained of the quays. Next, huge ramps were extended from the ships and from out of their bowels began to rumble the great armour-plated land ironclads. It hardly seemed possible that so many of the cumbersome machines could have been contained even in that large fleet. Rolling over every obstacle, they manoeuvred into wedge-shaped formations, all facing inland, their top-turrets swinging round to threaten New York with their long guns, their lower turrets rotating slowly as their crews ran a series of tests to make sure they were in perfect working order. Although the Ashanti had lost about half their force during the Battle of the Atlantic, they could still field a good-sized army and it was doubtful if the United States, crushed by the terrible War Between the Nations, could find anything likely to withstand them. The USA must now depend on the Australasian–Japanese Federation for support (and we all were sure that they would make some new attempt to stop General Hood).

But now at last I was to see what had been hidden in that gigantic hull which we had towed all the way from Africa. And Una Persson's expression became eager as the hull was towed into position against the dockside.

'This is the result of what I was able to find in England, Mr Bastable,' she said in an excited murmur. 'An invention of O'Bean's that was regarded as too terrible ever to put into production, even at the height of the war. Watch!'

I watched, as the dusk began to gather. From somewhere inside the hull bolts were withdrawn, releasing the sides so that they fell backwards into the sea and forwards onto the dock. One by one the sections swung down until the contents of the hull were revealed. It was a ziggurat of steel. Tier upon tier it rose, utterly dwarfing the assembled machines which had already landed. From each tier there jutted guns which put to shame anything we had had on the *Dingiswayo*. On the topmost turret (the smallest on this metal pyramid) were mounted four long-snouted guns, on the second turret down there were six such guns, on the third there were twelve, on the fourth there were eighteen. On the fifth tier could be seen banks of smaller guns, perhaps a third of the size of the others, for use in close-range fire. There were about thirty of these. On the sixth tier down were some fifty similar guns, while in the seventh and bottom-most tier were upwards of a hundred of the most modern steam gatlings, each capable of firing 150 rounds a minute. There were also slits in the armour plating all the way up, for riflemen. There were grilled observation ports in every tier, and each turret was capable of swivelling independently of the others, just as each gun was capable of a wide range of movement within the turret. The whole thing was mounted on massive wheels, the smallest of these wheels being at least four times the height of a man, mounted (I learned later) on separate chassis in groups of ten, which meant that the vast machine could move forwards, backwards or *sideways* whenever it wished. Moreover, the size of the wheels and the weight they carried could crush almost any obstacle.

This was General Hood's 'secret weapon'. It must have taken half the wealth of Africa and Europe combined to build it. There had never been any moving thing of its size in the world before (and precious few non-mobile things!). With it, I felt sure, the Black Attila was invincible. No wonder he had been prepared to sacrifice the rest of his invasion fleet in order to protect it!

This was truly a symbol of the Final War, of Armageddon! A leviathan released upon the land – a monster capable of destroying anything in its path – a steel-clad, gargantuan dragon bringing roaring death to all who resisted. Its gleaming, blue-grey hull displayed on four sides of each of its tiers the scarlet circle framing the black, rampant lion of Ashanti, symbol of a powerful, vengeful Africa – of an Africa which remembered the millions of black slaves who had been crowded into stinking, disease-ridden hulks to serve the White Dream – of an Africa which had waited for its moment to release this invulnerable creature upon the offspring of those who had tortured its peoples, insulted them, killed them, terrified them and robbed them over the centuries.

If justice it was, then it was to be a fearful and a spectacular justice indeed!

As I watched the Land Leviathan roll through concrete and steel as easily as one might crush grass beneath one's feet, I thought not merely of the fate which was about to befall America, but what might happen to the rest of the world, particularly Bantustan, when Hood had realised his plans here.

Having created such a beast, it seemed to me, he would have to go on using it. Ultimately it must become the master, conquering the conqueror, until nothing of the world survived at all!

Certainly that had been the logic of this world up to now and I saw nothing – save perhaps the ideal that was the country of Bantustan – to deny that logic.

I felt then that it was my moral duty to do anything I could to stop Hood's terrible pattern of conquest, but the assassination of one man no longer seemed the answer. In a quandary I turned away from the scene as night fell and the lights of the Land Leviathan pierced the darkness like so many fearsome eyes.

Mrs Persson said something to me, but I did not hear her. I stumbled from the observation deck, my mind in complete confusion, certain that she and I might well be, in a short while, the last surviving members of our race.

Chapter Three
The Deserter

I T TOOK FIVE hours to crush New York. And 'crush' is quite literally the proper description. Hood's monstrous machine rolled
at will through the ruins, pushing down the few towers which
remained standing, firing brief, totally destructive, barrages into
the positions of those who resisted. All the Negroes in New York,
who had been fighting the whites well before we arrived, rallied at
once to Hood's black-and-scarlet banner, and by noon the few
defenders who remained alive were rounded up and interrogated
for the information they could supply concerning other pockets
of 'resistance' across the country.

Hood invited me to be present at one of these questionings
and I accepted, hoping only that I could put in a plea for mercy for
the poor devils who had fallen into Ashanti hands.

Hood was now dressed in a splendid military uniform – also
black and scarlet, but with a considerable quantity of gold and
silver braid and a three-cornered hat sporting the same ostrich
plumes as his Lion Guard. Hood had confided to me that such
braggadocio was completely against his instincts, but that he was
expected to affect the proper style both by his enemies and by
those who followed him. He had a curved sword almost perman-
ently in his right hand, and stuck into his belt, unholstered, were
two large, long-barrelled automatic pistols, rather like Mausers.
The prisoners were being questioned in what remained of the
cellar of a house which had stood on Washington Square. They
were wounded, half-starved, filthy and frightened. Their white
hoods (there was some superstition which had grown up that
these hoods protected them from the plague) had been torn from
their heads and their uniforms, crudely fashioned from flour
sacks, were torn and bloodstained. I did not, I must admit, feel

any pride in these representatives of my own race. They would have been gutter-rats no matter what conditions prevailed in New York and doubtless it was because they were gutter-rats that they had managed to survive, with the ferocity and tenacity of their kind. They were spitting, snarling, shrieking at their Ashanti conquerors and their language was the foulest I have ever heard. Una Persson stood nearby and I would have given anything in the world for her not to have been subjected to that disgusting swearing.

The man who seemed to be the leader of the group (he had conferred upon himself the title of Governor!) had the surname of Hoover and his companions referred to him as 'Speed'. He was a typical example of that breed of New York small-time 'crooks' who are ready to take up any form of crime so long as there is little chance of being caught. It was written all over his mean, ugly, hate-filled face. Doubtless, before he elected himself 'Governor', he had contented himself with robbing the weak and the helpless, of frightening children and old folk, and running errands for the larger, more successful 'gang bosses' of the city. Yet I felt a certain sympathy for him as he continued to rant and rave, turning his attention at last upon me.

'As fer yer, ya nigger-lover, yore nuttin' but a dirty traitor!' was the only repeatable statement of this kind that he made. He spat at me, then turned on the mild-faced lieutenant (I think he was called Azuma) who had been questioning him. 'We knew you niggers wuz comin' – we bin hearin' 'bout it fer months now – an' dey're gettin' ready fer yer. Dey got plans – dey got a way o' stoppin' yer real good!' He sniggered. 'Yer got der artillery – but yer ain't got der brains, see? Yer'll soon be t'rowin' in der sponge. It'll take more'n what *you* got ter lick real white men!'

His threats, however, were all vague, and it soon became obvious to Lieutenant Azuma that there was little point in continuing with his questions.

I had not taken kindly to being called a traitor by this riff-raff, yet there was, I suppose, some truth in what he had said. I had not lifted my voice, let alone a finger, to try to stop Hood so far.

Now I said: 'I must ask you, General Hood, to spare these men's lives. They are prisoners of war, after all.'

Hood exchanged a look of cruel amusement with Lieutenant Azuma. 'But surely they are hardly worth sparing, Mr Bastable,' he said. 'What use would such as these be in any kind of society?'

'They have a right to their lives,' I said.

'They would scarcely agree with you if you were speaking up for *me*,' said Cicero Hood coldly now. 'You heard Hoover's remark about "niggers". If our situation were reversed, do you think your pleas would be heard?'

'No,' I said. 'But if you are to prove yourself better than such as Hoover, then you must set an example.'

'That is your Western morality, again,' said Hood. Then he laughed, without much humour. 'But we had no intention of killing them. They will be left behind in the charge of our friends. They will help in the rebuilding of New Benin, as the city is to be called henceforth.'

With that, he strode from the cellar, still laughing that peculiar, blood-chilling laugh.

And so Hood's land fleet rolled away from New York, and now I was a passenger in one of the smaller fighting machines. Our next objective was Philadelphia, where again Hood was, in his terms, going to the relief of the blacks there. The situation for the Negro in the America of this day was, I was forced to admit, a poor one. The whites, in seeking a scapegoat for their plight, had fixed, once again, upon the blacks. The other superstitious reason that so many of them wore those strange hoods was because they had conceived the idea that the Negroes were somehow 'dirtier' than the whites and that they had been responsible for spreading the plagues which had followed the war, as they had followed it in England. In many parts of the United States, members of the Negro race were being hunted like animals and burned alive when they were caught – the rationale for this disgusting behaviour being that it was the only way to be sure that the plague did not spread. For some reason Negroes had not been so vulnerable to the various germs contained in the bombs and it had been an easy step in the insane logic of the whites to see the black people, therefore, as 'carriers'. For two years or more, black groups had been organising themselves, under instructions from Hood's agents, awaiting the day when the Ashanti invaded. Hood's claim that he was 'liberating' the blacks was, admittedly, not entirely unfounded in truth.

Nonetheless I did not feel that any of this was sufficient to vindicate Hood.

Headed by the Land Leviathan, the conquering army looted and burned its way through the states of New York, New Jersey and Pennsylvania, and wherever it paused it set up its black-and-scarlet banners, leaving local bands of Negroes behind to administer the conquered territories.

It was during the battle in which Philadelphia was completely destroyed, and every white man, woman and child slain by the pounding guns of the Land Leviathan, that I found my opportunity to 'desert' the Black Horde, first falling back from the convoy of which my armoured carriage was part, and then having the luck to capture a stray horse.

My intention was to head for Washington and warn the defenders there of what they might expect. Also, if possible, I wished to discuss methods of crippling the Land Leviathan. My only plan was that the monster should somehow be lured close to a cliff-top and fall over, smashing itself to pieces. How this could be achieved, I had not the slightest idea!

My ride from Philadelphia to the city of Wilmington probably set something of a record. Across the countryside groups of black 'soldiers' were in conflict with whites. In my Ashanti uniform, I was prey to both sides and would doubtless have fared worst at the hands of the whites who regarded me as a traitor than at the hands of the blacks, if I had been caught. But, by good fortune, I avoided capture until I rode into Wilmington, which had not suffered much bombing and merely had the deserted, overgrown look of so many of America's 'ghost cities'. On the outskirts, I stripped off my black tunic and threw it away – though the weather was still very cold – and dressed only in my singlet and britches – dismounted from my horse and searched for the local white leader.

They found me first. I was moving cautiously along one of the main thoroughfares when they suddenly appeared on all sides, wearing the sinister white hoods so reminiscent of those old Knights of the South, the Ku Klux Klan, whose fictional adventures had thrilled me as a boy. They asked me who and what I was and what I wanted in Wilmington. I told them that it was urgent that I should meet their leader, that I had crucial news of the Black Attila.

Shortly I found myself in a large civic building which a man named "Bomber" Joe Kennedy was using as his headquarters. He had got his nickname, I learned later, from his skill in manufacturing explosive devices from a wide variety of materials. Kennedy had heard about me and it was only with the greatest self-restraint that he did not shoot me on the spot there and then – but he listened and he listened attentively and eventually he seemed satisfied that I was telling the truth. He informed me that he had already planned to take his small 'army' to Washington, to add it to the growing strength of the defenders. It would do no harm, he said, if I came with them, but he warned me that if at any time it seemed that I was actually spying for Hood I would be killed in the same way that Negroes were killed in those parts. I never found out what he meant and my only clue, when I enquired, was in the phrase which a grinning member of Kennedy's army quoted with relish. 'Ever heard of "burn or cut" in England, boy?' he asked me.

The whites had managed to build up the old railroad system, for most of the lines had survived the war and the locomotives were still functional, burning wood rather than coal these days. It was Kennedy's plan to transport himself and his army by rail to Washington (for there was a direct line), and the next day we climbed aboard the big, old-fashioned train, with myself and Kennedy joining the driver and fireman on the footplate, for, as Kennedy told me, 'I don't wanna risk not keepin' you under my sight.'

The train soon had a good head of steam and was rolling away from Wilmington in no time, its first stop being Baltimore, where Kennedy hoped to pick up a larger force of men.

As we rushed through the devastated countryside, Kennedy confided in me something of his life. He claimed that he had once been a very rich man, a millionaire, before the collapse. His family had come from Ireland originally and he had no liking for the English, whom he was inclined to rate second only to 'coons' as being responsible for the world's ills. It struck me as ironic that Kennedy should have a romantic attachment to one oppressed minority (as he saw it), but feel nothing but loathing for another.

Kennedy also told me that they were already making plans in Washington to resist the Black Attila. 'They've got something up their sleeves which'll stop *him* in his tracks,' he said smugly, but he would not amplify the statement and I had the impression that he was not altogether sure what the plan was.

Kennedy had also heard that there was a strong chance that the Washington 'army' would receive reinforcements from the Australasian–Japanese fleet which, he had it on good authority, had already anchored off Chesapeake Bay. I expressed the doubt that anything could withstand the Black Attila's Land Leviathan, but Kennedy was undaunted. He rubbed his nose and told me that there was 'more than one way of skinnin' a coon'.

Twice the train had to stop to take on more wood, but we were getting closer and closer to Baltimore and the city was little more than an hour away when a squadron of land ironclads appeared ahead of us, firing at the train. They flew the lion banner of Ashanti and must have gone ahead of the main army (perhaps having received intelligence that trains of white troops were on their way to Washington). I saw the long guns in their main turrets puff red fire and white smoke and a number of shells hit the ground close by. The driver was for putting on the brakes and surrendering, feeling that we did not have a chance, but Kennedy, for all that he might have been a cruel, ignorant and stupid man, was not a coward. He sent the word back along the train to get whatever big guns they could working, then he told the engineer to give the old locomotive all the speed she could take, and drove straight towards the lumbering war machines which were now on both sides of the track, positioned on the steep banks so that they could fire down at us as we passed.

I was reminded of an old print I once saw – a poster, I think, for Buffalo Bill's Wild West Show – of Red Indians attacking a train. The land ironclads were able to match our speed (for the train was carrying a huge number of cars), and their turrets could swing rapidly to shoot at us from any angle. Shell after shell began to smash into the train, but still she kept going, making for the safety of a long tunnel ahead of us, where the land 'clads could not follow.

We reached the tunnel with some relief and the engineer was for slowing down and stopping in the middle in the hope that the enemy machines would give up their chase, but Kennedy considered this a foolish scheme.

'They'll come at us from both ends, man!' he said. 'They'll burrow through from the roof – they've got those "mole" things which can bore through anything. We'll be like trapped rabbits down a hole if we stay here.' I think there was sense to what he said, though our chances in the open were scarcely any better. Still, under his orders, the train raced on, breaking through into daylight to find half a dozen land ironclads waiting for it, their guns aimed at the mouth of the tunnel. How the locomotive survived that fusillade I shall never know, but survive it did, with part of the roof and a funnel shot away and its tender of wood blazing from the effects of a direct hit by an incendiary shell.

The rest of the train, however, was not so lucky.

A shell cut the coupling attaching us to the main part of the train and we lurched forward at a speed which threatened to hurl us from the tracks. Without the burden of the rest of the train, we were soon able to leave the ironclads behind. I looked back to see the stranded 'army' fighting it out with the armoured battleships of the land. They were being pounded to pieces.

Then we had turned a bend and left the scene behind. Kennedy looked crestfallen for a moment, and then he shrugged. There was little that could be done.

'Ah, well,' he said. 'We'll not be stopping in Baltimore now.'

Chapter Four
The Triumphant Beast

WASHINGTON, SURPRISINGLY, HAD not sustained anything
like the damage done to cities like New York and London.
The government and all its departments had fled the capital before
the war had got into its stride and had retired to an underground
retreat somewhere in the Appalachians. It had survived the explo-
sives, but not the plagues. Having little strategic importance,
therefore, Washington had most of its famous buildings and monuments still standing. These overblown mock Graecian, mock
Georgian tributes to grandiose bad taste could be seen in the distance as we steamed into the outskirts of the city, to be stopped by
recently constructed barriers. These barriers had existed for only
a week or so, but I was surprised at their solidity. They were of
brick, stone and concrete, reinforced by neatly piled sandbags,
and, I gathered, protected the whole of the inner city. Kennedy's credentials were in order – he was recognised by three of
the guards and welcomed as something of a hero – and we were
allowed to continue through to the main railroad station, where he
handed our locomotive over to the authorities. We were escorted
through the wide, rather characterless streets (the famous trees
had all been cut down in the making of the barriers and for
fuel to power the trains) to the White House, occupied now by
'President' Beesley, a man who had once been a distinguished diplomat in the service of his country, but who had quickly profited
from the hysteria following the war – he was believed to have
been the first person to 'don the White Hood'. Beesley was fat
and his red face bore all the earmarks of depravity. We were
ushered into a study full of fine old 'colonial'-style furniture
which gave the impression that nothing had changed since the old
days. The only difference was in the smell and in the man sprawled

in a large armchair at a desk near the bay window. The smell would have been regarded as offensive even in one of our own East End public houses – a mixture of alcohol, tobacco smoke and human perspiration. Dressed in the full uniform of an American general, with the buttons straining to keep his tunic in place over his huge paunch, 'President' Beesley waved a hand holding a cigar by way of greeting, gestured with the other hand, which held a glass, for us to be seated. 'I'm glad you could make it, Joe,' he said to Kennedy, who seemed to be a close acquaintance. 'Have a drink. Help yourself.' He ignored me.

Kennedy went to a sideboard and poured himself a large glass of bourbon. 'I'm sorry I couldn't bring you any men,' he said. 'You heard, did you, Den? We got hit by a big fleet of that nigger's land 'clads. We were lucky to get through at all.'

'I heard.' Beesley turned small, cold eyes on me. 'And that is the traitor, is it?'

'I had better tell you now,' I said, though suddenly I was reluctant to justify myself, 'that I joined Cicero Hood's entourage with the express purpose of trying to put a stop to his activities.'

'And how did you intend to do that, Mr Bastable?' said Beesley, leaning forward and winking at Kennedy.

'My original plan was to assassinate him,' I said simply.

'But you didn't.'

'After the Land Leviathan made its appearance I saw that killing Hood would do no good. He is the only one who has any control at all over the Black Horde. To kill him would have resulted in making things worse for you and all the other Europeans.'

Beesley sniffed sceptically and sipped his drink, adding: 'And what proof have we got of all this? What proof is there that you're not still working for Hood, that you're not planning to kill *me*?'

'None,' I said. 'But I want to discuss ways of stopping the Land Leviathan,' I told him. 'Those walls you're building will stop that monster no more than would paper. If we can dig some kind of deep trench – lay a trap like a gigantic animal trap – we might be able to put it out of action for a while at least…'

But President Beesley was smirking and shaking his head.

'We're ahead of you, Mr Bastable. There's more than one kind of wall, you know. You've only seen what you might call our first line of defence.'

'There isn't anything made strong enough to stop the Land Leviathan,' I said emphatically.

'Oh, I don't know.' Beesley gave Kennedy another of his secret looks. 'Do you want to show him around, Joe? I think we can trust him. He's one of us.'

Kennedy was not so certain. 'Well, if you think so…'

'Sure I do. I have my hunches. He's okay. A bit misguided, a bit short on imagination – a bit English, eh? But a decent sort. Welcome to Washington, Mr Bastable. Now you'll see how that black scum is to be stopped.'

A while later we left the White House in a horse-drawn carriage provided for us. Kennedy, with some pride, explained how the Capitol had been turned into a well-defended arsenal and how every one of those overblown neo-Graecian buildings contained virtually every operational big gun left in the United States.

But it was not the architecture or the details of the defence system which arrested my vision – it was what I saw in the streets as I passed. Washington had always had a very large Negro population, and now this population was being put to use by the whites. I saw gangs of exhausted, half-starved men, women and children, shackled to one another by chains about the neck, wrists or ankles, hauling huge loads of bricks and sandbags to the barricades. It was a scene from the past – with sweating, dying black slaves being worked, quite literally, to death by brutal white overseers armed with long bullwhips which they used liberally and with evident relish. It was a sight I had never expected to witness in the twentieth century! I was horrified, but did my best not to betray my emotion to Kennedy, who had not appeared to notice what was going on!

More than once I winced and was sickened when I saw some poor, near-naked woman fall and receive a torrent of abuse, kicked and whipped until she was forced to her feet again, or helped to her feet by her companions. Once I saw a half-grown boy collapse and it was quite plain that he was dead, but his fellow slaves were made to drag his corpse with them by the chains which secured his wrists to theirs.

Trying to appear insouciant, I said as coolly as I could: 'I see now how you managed to raise the walls so quickly. You have reintroduced slavery.'

'Well, you could call it that, couldn't you?' Kennedy grinned. 'The blacks are performing a public service, like the rest of us, helping to build up the country again. Besides,' and his face became serious, 'it's what they know best. It's what most of 'em prefer. They don't think and feel the same as us, Bastable. It's like your worker bee – stop him from working and he becomes morbid and unhappy. Eventually he dies. It's the same with the blacks.'

'Their ultimate fate would seem to be identical, however you look at it,' I commented.

'Sure, but this way they're doing some good.'

I must have seen several thousand Negroes as we travelled through the streets of Washington. A few were evidently employed as individual servants and were in a somewhat better position than their fellows, but most were chained together in gangs, sweating copiously for all that the weather was chill. There was little hope on any of their faces and I was not proud of my own race when I looked at them; also I could not help recalling the pride – arrogance, some would call it – in the bearing of Hood's Ashanti troops.

I stifled the thought, at that moment, but it kept coming back to me with greater and greater force. It was unjust to enslave other human beings and cruel to treat them in such a manner, whichever side committed the injustice. Yet it seemed to me that there was a grain more justice in Hood's policies – for he was repaying a debt, whereas men such as Beesley and Kennedy were acting from the most brutal and cynical of motives.

Mildly, I said: 'But isn't it poor economics to work them so hard? They'll give you better value if they're treated a little better.'

'That logic led to the Civil War, Mr Bastable,' said Kennedy, as if speaking to a child. 'You start thinking like that and sooner or later they decide *they* deserve to be treated like white men and you get the old social ills being repeated over again. Besides,' he grinned broadly, 'there's not a lot of point in worrying too much about the life expectancy of our Washington niggers, as you'll see.'

We were driving close to one of the main walls now. Here, as everywhere, huge gangs of Negroes were being forced to work at inhuman speed. It was no longer any mystery how Washington had managed to get its defences up so rapidly. I tried to recall the stories of what Hood had done to the whites in Scandinavia, but even the stories, exaggerated and encouraged by Hood himself to improve his savage image, paled in comparison to the reality of what was happening in modern-day Washington!

As we passed the walls, I noticed that large cages, rather like the cages used for transporting circus animals about the country, were much in evidence on top of the walls. I pointed them out and asked Kennedy what they were.

He smirked as he leaned back in the carriage and lit a cigar. '*They*, Mr Bastable, are our secret weapon.'

I did not ask him to amplify this statement. I had become too saddened by the fate of the Negroes. I told Kennedy that I was tired and would like to rest. The carriage was turned about and I was taken to a hotel quite close to the Capitol, where I was given a room overlooking a stretch of parkland.

But even here I could look out through my windows and see evidence of the brutality of the whites. Not a hundred yards away, a pit of quicklime had been sunk, and into it, from time to time, carts would dump the bodies of the dead and the dying.

I thought that I had witnessed Hell in Southern England, but now I knew that I had only been standing on the outskirts. Here, where it had once been declared an article of faith that all men were created equal, where it had seemed possible for the eighteenth-century ideals of reason and justice to be made reality, here was Hell, indeed!

And it was a hell created in the name of my own race, whose survival I hoped to ensure with my resistance to Hood and his Black Horde.

I slept badly at the hotel and the next morning sought an interview with 'President' Beesley at the White House. I received word that he was too busy to see me. I wandered about the streets, but there was too much there to turn my stomach. I began to feel angry. I felt frustrated. I wanted to remonstrate with Beesley, to beg him to show mercy to the blacks, to set an example of tolerance and decency to his white-hooded followers. Gandhi had been right. There was only one way to behave, even if it seemed, in the short term, against one's self-interest. Surely it was in one's self-interest in the long term to exhibit generosity, humanity, kindness and a sense of justice to one's fellow men. It was cynicism of Beesley's kind which had, after all, led to the threatened extinction of the whole human race. There could be no such thing as a 'righteous' war, for war was by its very nature an act of injustice against the individual, but there could be such a thing as an 'unrighteous' war – an evil war, a war begun by men who were utterly corrupt, both morally and intellectually. I had begun to think that it was a definition of those who would make war – that whatever motives they claimed, whatever ideals they promoted, whatever 'threat' they referred to, they could not be excused – because of their actions they could only be of a degenerate and immoral character.

Gandhi had said that violence bred violence. Well, it seemed that I was witnessing a living lesson in this creed! I realised how close I had, myself, been to the brink of behaving brutally and cynically, when I had contemplated the assassination of Hood.

Once again, at about the worst time possible, I found my loyalties divided, my mind in confusion, filled with a sense of the impossibility of any action whatsoever on my own part.

I had wandered away from the main roads of Washington and into a series of residential streets full of those fine terraced houses reminiscent of our own Regency squares and crescents. The houses, however, were much run-down. In most cases there was no glass in the windows and many doors showed signs of having been forced. I guessed that there had been fighting here, not by an invading army, but between the Negroes and the whites.

I was speculating, again, on the nature of the animal cages placed along the walls of the city, when I turned a corner and was confronted with a long line of black workers, chained ankle to ankle, shuffling along the centre of the road and pulling a big, wheeled platform on which had been piled a tottering mountain of sandbags. There was hardly one of these people who was not bleeding from the cuts of the long whips wielded by armed overseers. Many seemed hardly capable of putting one foot in front of the other. They seemed destined, very shortly, for the limepits – and yet they were singing. They were singing as the Christian martyrs had been said to sing on their way to the Roman arena. They were singing a dirge of which it was difficult to distinguish the words at first. The white men, clad in heavy hoods, were yelling at them to stop. Their voices were muffled, but their whips were eloquent. But still the Negroes sang and now I made out some of the words.

He will come – *he will come* –
Out of Africa – *he will come* –
He will ride the Beast – *he will come* –
He will set us free – *he will come* –
He will bring us Pride – *he will come* –

There was no question, of course, that the song referred to Hood and that it was being sung deliberately to incense the whites. The refrain was being sung by a tall, handsome young man who somehow managed to lift his head and keep his shoulders straight no matter how many savage blows fell upon him. His dignity and his courage were so greatly in contrast to the hysterical and cowardly actions of the whites that it was impossible to feel anything but admiration for him.

But I think that the gang of slaves was doomed. They would not stop singing and now, ominously, the hooded whites lowered their whips and began to take their guns from their shoulders.

The procession stopped.

The voices stopped.

The first white ripped off his hood and revealed a hate-filled face which could have seen no more than seventeen summers. He raised his weapon to his shoulders, grinning.

'Okay – you wanna go on singing?'

The tall Negro took a breath, knowing that it was probably his last, and began the first words of the chant.

That was when, impulsively, I dived for the boy, throwing my whole weight against him so that his shot went into the air. I had grabbed the gun even as I fell on top of him. I heard confused shouts and then heard the sharp report of another rifle. I saw a bullet strike the body of the boy and I used that body as cover, shooting back at my fellow whites!

I should not have lasted long, of course, had not the tall Negro uttered a bellow which was almost gleeful and led his companions upon the whites, who had their backs to the blacks while they concentrated on me.

I saw white hoods bobbing for a moment in a sea of black, blistered flesh. I heard a few shots fired and then it was over. The whites lay dead upon the pavement and the blacks were using their guns to shoot themselves free of the chains on their legs. I was not sure how I would be received and I stood up cautiously, ready to run if necessary, for I knew that many Negroes felt little sentimentality to whites, even if those whites were not directly involved in harming them.

Then the black youth grinned at me. 'Thanks, mister. Why ain't you wearing your hood?'

'I have never worn one,' I told him. 'I'm British.'

I suppose I must have sounded a little pompous, for the youth laughed aloud at this, before saying: 'We'd better get off the streets fast.'

He began to direct his people into the nearby houses, which proved to be deserted. The wheeled platform and the corpses of the whites, stripped of their guns and, for some mysterious reason, their hoods, were left behind.

The youth led us through the backyards of the houses, darting from building to building until he came to one he recognised. This he entered, leading us into the cellars and there pausing for breath.

'We'll leave those who're too sick to go any further here,' he said. 'Also the kids.' He grinned at me. 'What about you, mister? You can give us that rifle and go free, if you want to. There were no witnesses. You'll be all right. They'll never know there was a white man involved.'

'I think that they should know,' I found myself saying. 'My name's Bastable. I was until recently an observer attached to General Hood's staff. I deserted and came over to the white cause. Now I have decided to serve only the cause of humanity. I am with you, Mr –'

'Call me Paul, Mr Bastable. Well, that was a fine speech, sir, if, might I say, a little on the prim side! But you've proved yourself. You've got grit and grit's what's needed in these troubled times. Let's go.'

He pulled back a couple of packing cases and revealed a hole in the wall. Into this hole, which proved to give access to a passage connecting a whole series of houses, he led us, speaking to me over his shoulder as we went. 'Have they started filling the cages, yet, do you know?'

'I know nothing of the cages,' I told him. 'I was wondering what function they were to serve. Somebody said they were Washington's "secret weapon" against General Hood, but that mystified me even more.'

'Well, it might work,' said Paul, 'though I'm sure most of our people would rather die.'

'But what will they put in the cages? Wild beasts?'

Paul darted me an amused look. 'Some would call them that, mister. They're going to put *us* in them. If Hood starts to bombard the walls, then he kills the people he intends to save. He can't liberate Washington without killing every Negro man, woman and child in the city!'

If I had been disgusted with the whites up to now, I was stunned completely by this information. It was reminiscent of the most barbaric practices I had read about in history. How could the whites regard themselves as being superior to Hood when they were prepared to use methods against him which even he had never contemplated, no matter how strong his hatred of the Caucasian race?

Washington was to be protected by a wall of living flesh!

'But all they can achieve by that is to stalemate Hood,' I said. 'Unless they threaten to kill your people in the hope of forcing Hood to withdraw.'

'They'll do that, too, I suppose,' Paul told me. We were squeezing through a very narrow tunnel now, and I heard the distant sound of rushing water. 'But they've had news from the Australapans. If they can hold Washington for twenty-four hours, there'll be a land fleet coming to relieve them. Even those big ships of Hood's we've heard about won't be able to fire without killing their own people. Hood will have to make a decision – and either way he stands to lose something.'

'They are fiends,' I said. 'It is impossible to regard them as human beings at all.'

'I was one of Hood's special agents before I was captured,' Paul said. 'I was hoping to work out a way of helping him from inside, but then they rounded up every black in the city. Our only chance now is somehow to get into the main compound tonight, arm as many people as possible and try for a break.'

'Do you think you'll be successful?' I asked.

Paul shook his head. 'No, mister, I don't. But a lot of dead niggers won't be much use to them when Hood does come, will they?'

My nose was assailed by a sickening stench and now I realised where the sound of water had been coming from – the sewers. We were forced to wade sometimes waist-deep through foul water, emerging at last in a large underground room already occupied by about a score of Negroes. These were all that remained of those who had planned to rise in support of Hood when the moment came. They had a fair-sized arsenal with them, but it was plain that there was very little they could do now except die bravely.

Through that day we discussed our plans and, when evening came, we crept up to the surface and moved through unlit streets to the north side of the city, where the main slave compound was situated.

By the light of flares, many Negroes were still working, and it was obvious from what we heard that Hood's forces were almost here.

Our rifles on our shoulders, we marched openly along the broad streets, heading north. Anyone who saw us would have taken us for a detachment of soldiers, singularly well-disciplined. And not once were we stopped.

This had been the reason why the dead whites had been stripped of their hoods earlier that day and why, now, every man and woman in our party, with the exception of myself, wore a pair of gloves. The morbid insanity of the whites was being used against them for the first time. The hoods which they wore as a symbol of their fear and hatred of the black race were now helping members of that race to march, unchallenged, under their very noses.

Behind us, wearing fetters which could easily be removed when the moment came, were the rest of our party, dragging a big cart apparently filled with bricks but actually containing the rest of our guns.

More than once we felt we were near to discovery, but at last we reached the gates of the compound. My own accent would have been detected at once, so Paul spoke for us. He sounded most authoritative.

'Deliverin' these niggers an' pickin' up a new party,' he said to the guards.

The white-hooded guards were unsuspicious. Too many were coming and going tonight and there was more confusion than usual.

'Why are you all goin' in?' one asked as we walked through.

'Ain't you heard?' Paul told him. 'There's been an outbreak. Ten or twenty of our men killed by coons.'

'I heard something,' another guard agreed, but by now we were inside the compound itself. It was unroofed – merely a large area in which the black slaves slept in their chains until they were required to work. A huge tub of swill in the centre of the compound was the only food. Those strong enough to crawl to the tub ate, those who were too weak either relied on their friends or starved. It did not matter to the whites, for the blacks had almost fulfilled their function, now.

We moved into the darkest part of the compound, shouting orders for the people to get to their feet and be inspected. Surreptitiously we began to hand out the weapons.

But by now we had attracted the curiosity of two of the guards, who began, casually, to walk towards us.

For my sins, I must admit that I fired the first shot. I did it without compunction, killing the guard instantly with a bullet to his heart. The others began firing, running back towards the gate, but now our luck had changed completely. Alerted by the shots, an old-fashioned steam traction engine, crudely armoured and carrying a couple of gatlings, turned towards the compound and had filled the gate before we could reach it.

There was a pause while the occupants of this primitive land 'clad hesitated, seeing our white hoods, but the remaining guards shouted up to them to open fire.

Soon we were diving for the shadows – our only cover – as a stream of bullets raked the compound, killing with complete lack of discrimination. Many of those who were still chained were cut down where they lay and we were forced to use their bodies for cover, shooting desperately back while some of our party ran around the walls of the compound, searching for a means of escape.

But the walls were high. They had been designed so as to be escape-proof. We were trapped like rats and all we could do now was to go down fighting.

Slowly the traction engine rolled into the compound, firing as it came. Our own bullets were useless against the armour, hastily made as it was.

Paul, who lay next to me, put a hand on my arm. 'Well, Mr Bastable, you can console yourself that you picked the right side before you died.'

'It's not much comfort,' I said.

Then the ground just in front of us suddenly heaved up, rippling like the waves of the sea, and something metallic and familiar emerged, its spiral snout spinning with an angry whine, directly in the path of the traction-engine. The sound of the gatlings stopped and was replaced by the dull *boom boom* of an electric cannon.

Now two more metal 'moles' broke the surface, also firing. Within seconds the traction-engine was reduced to a pile of twisted wreckage and the moles moved forward, still firing, blasting great holes in the walls of the compound.

I think we were cheering as we followed behind those strange machines. I am sure that O'Bean had never visualised such a use for them! Every white hood we saw (we were no longer wearing our own) was a target and we shot at it.

I suppose it had been naïve of me to think that so clever a strategist as General Hood would not have taken the trouble to learn what the defenders of Washington had planned – and taken steps to counter their scheme. We spread out from the compound, heading for the park spaces where there were still some bushes to give us cover.

And now I heard a distant noise, reminding me more than anything else of the sound a carpet makes when it is being beaten. But I knew what the noise signified.

Seconds later explosive shells began to whistle down upon Washington.

The Land Leviathan was coming.

We regrouped as best we could, using the armed digging machines for cover, but keeping in the open as much as possible. Throughout the city now there were growing spots of light as buildings were fired by the Land Leviathan's incendiary shells.

My own view of the Battle of Washington was an extremely partial one, for I witnessed nothing of the strategy. Hood had heard that A.J.F. reinforcements were on their way and had moved his army swiftly, planning to strike and overwhelm the city well before its allies could arrive. Moreover, he knew that he would not be expected to attack at night, but it was immaterial to him at what hour he moved, for the lights of the Land Leviathan could pick out a target at almost any range.

As we fought our own little hit-and-run battle through the streets, I saw the great beams from the monster's searchlights dart out from the blackness, touch a building, marking it for destruction. Immediately would come that thunderous booming followed by a shrill whine and then an explosion as the shells struck home.

Not that Washington was helpless. Her own guns, particularly those in the Capitol itself, kept up a constant return fire and I think the ordinary land ironclads of the Black Horde would have had little chance of taking the city on their own.

Somehow I became separated from the rest of my party when a shell burst nearby and caused us to scatter. When the smoke cleared, the steel moles had moved on, the little army of former slaves going with them. I felt isolated and extremely vulnerable then and began to search for my comrades, but twice had to change direction as a party of white-hooded soldiers spotted me and began firing.

For an hour I kept low, sniping at the enemy when I saw him, then darting away again. My instinct was to make for a building and climb to the roof where I would be able to see the whites without being seen myself, but I knew that it would be foolish to attempt such a thing now, for buildings were being smashed to pieces all around me, under the steady bombardment of the Land Leviathan's many cannon.

I slowly made my way back towards the centre and found that most of the enemy soldiers had been ordered to the walls. Suddenly there was relative peace near the Capitol, save for the booming of the guns situated inside the building. I sat down behind a bush to collect my thoughts and get my bearings, when I heard the sound of horses' hoofs clattering towards me. They were coming very fast. I peered from behind my bush and was astonished to see a large number of horsemen streaming hell for leather away from the walls, as if the Devil himself was after them. The riders had removed their hoods and their faces were grim and frightened and they shouted at their mounts to give them more speed. Behind them, in a light, open carriage, came 'President' Beesley, yelling wildly. Then came the running men. Many had abandoned their weapons and had evidently panicked. I lay in my cover, but need not have feared these soldiers. They were far too terrified to stop and deal with me.

I next became aware of the ground trembling beneath me. Had God finally made up His mind to act, to punish us all for what we were doing? Had He sent an earthquake to destroy Washington?

A rumbling grew, louder and louder, and I peered ahead of me into the darkness as I gradually began to realise what was happening.

Lights blazed from the night. Lights which had their source high overhead, so that they might have been the lights of airships. But they were not the lights of airships – all Hood's aerial battleships, it later emerged, being concentrated on harassing the Australasian–Japanese land fleet even now on its way to Washington. They were the glaring 'eyes' of the Land Leviathan itself.

On it came, breaking down everything which stood in its wake, cutting a swathe through buildings, gun emplacements, monuments. The air was filled with a ghastly, grinding sound, the snorting of the exhaust from its twelve huge engines, the peculiar sighing it gave out whenever its wheels turned it in a slightly new direction.

This vast, moving ziggurat of destruction was what had panicked Beesley and his men. It had first pounded the city with its guns and then moved forward, breaking through the walls where they were thought to be the strongest. Invincible, implacable, it rolled towards the Capitol.

Now it was my turn to take to my heels, barely managing to fling myself clear as it advanced, sighed again, and then stopped, looking up at the Capitol in what seemed to me an attitude of challenge.

Almost hysterically, the Capitol's guns swung round and began firing and I had the impression, even as I risked death to watch, that I witnessed two primitive beasts from the Earth's remote past in conflict.

The shells from the Capitol scored direct hit upon direct hit, but they merely burst against the turrets of the Land Leviathan which did not at first reply.

Then the two top turrets began to turn until almost all her guns were pointed directly at the great, white dome which even now reflected the flames of the buildings which burned all around it.

Twice the guns of the Land Leviathan spoke, in rapid succession. The first barrage took the entire roof away. The second demolished the walls and the Capitol was silent. Again, the vast metal monster began to lumber forward, its searchlights roaming this way and that as if seeking out any others who might wish to challenge it.

At last the Land Leviathan rolled up and over the smoking, burning ruins while the air still resounded with the screams of those who had not been killed outright, who had been crushed beneath its great wheels or trapped somewhere under its belly. It rolled to the centre of the ruins and it stopped, squatting on the bones of its prey. Then, one by one, its lights began to wink out as the dawn rose behind it.

Now, indeed, the Land Leviathan was a triumphant beast.

Chapter Five
A Matter of Loyalties

IRONICALLY ENOUGH, IT had been Mrs Persson who had commanded the group of metal moles which had saved us in the compound. As I stood staring up at the Land Leviathan, oblivious of all else, I heard a shout from behind me, and there she was, her body half out of the forward hatch, waving to me.

'Good morning, Mr Bastable. I thought we had lost you.'

I turned towards her, feeling very tired now. 'Is it over?'

'Very nearly. We've received wireless reports that the Australasian–Japanese fleet has once again turned tail. It heard, over its own apparatus, that Washington was ours. I think they will be willing to negotiate the terms of a treaty with us now. Within the week we shall be heading South. The month should see the whole United States liberated.'

For once I did not respond sardonically to that word. Having witnessed the ferocity of the whites, I truly believed that the blacks had been liberated.

'Thank you for saving my life,' I said.

She smiled and made a little bow. 'It was time I repaid you for what you did for me.' She looked up at a clear, cold sky. 'Do you think it will snow, Mr Bastable?'

I shrugged and trudged towards the metal mole. 'Can you give me a lift, Mrs Persson?'

'Willingly, Mr Bastable.'

Well, Moorcock, that is pretty much the end of the tale I had for you. I remained in Hood's service for the whole of the first year he spent in the United States. There was some pretty bloody fighting, particularly, as we had expected, in parts of the South (though there were also some areas where we discovered whites and blacks living in perfect harmony!) and not all of Hood's methods of warfare were pleasant. On the other hand he was never unjust in his dealings with the defeated and never matched the ferocity and brutality of those we had encountered in Washington. Hood was not a kindly conqueror and he had the blood of many on his hands, but he was, in his own way, a just one. I was reminded, originally against my will, of William the Conqueror and the stern fair-mindedness with which he set about the pacification of England in the eleventh century.

Among other things, I had witnessed the public hanging of 'President' Beesley (discovered in the very sewers the blacks had used when hiding from him!) and many of his senior supporters, including 'Bomber' Joe Kennedy. That had not been pretty, particularly since Beesley and several of the others had died in a manner that was by no means manly.

Yet no sooner had Hood established his power than he set his war machines to peaceful purposes. Huge ploughs were adapted, to be drawn by the ironclads, which could make a whole field ready for planting in a matter of minutes. The airships carried supplies wherever they were needed and only the Land Leviathan was not used. It remained where it had been since the morning after the battle, a symbol of Hood's triumph. Later, the monster *would* be used when required, but Hood thought it politic to leave it where it was for a while, and I suppose he was right.

In the meantime, negotiations took place with the Australasian–Japanese Federation and a truce was agreed upon. Privately, Hood thought that it might be a temporary truce and that, having once broken their policy of isolationism, the Australasian–Japanese might attempt, at some future date, to invade. It was another reason why, during the talks which took place in Washington, he left the Land Leviathan in its position, glowering down upon us while we bargained. My own feelings were not entirely in accord with his. I thought it best to show them that we were no threat to their security, for after all they still had O'Bean working for them, but Hood said that there would be time enough in the future to show good faith; now we must not let them believe they could strike again while we were off guard. President Gandhi would not have approved, but eventually I gave in to his logic.

I made one visit to Bantustan during the course of that year, to arrange for food and medical supplies to be sent out, for it would be some time before America was entirely self-supporting. It was a peculiar alliance, that between Gandhi, the man of peace, and Hood, the Black Attila, the quintessential warlord, but it seemed to be an alliance which would work, for both men had great respect for each other. During my leisure moments, I penned this 'memoir' – mainly for your eyes, Moorcock, because I feel that I owe you something. If you can publish it – if you ever see it – well and good. Pretend that it is fiction.

I spent a considerable amount of time in the company of Mrs Persson. She continued to remain a mysterious figure. I attempted to engage her in conversation about my previous adventures in a future age and she listened politely to me, but refused to be drawn. However, rightly or wrongly, I conceived the impression that she, like me, had also travelled through time and in various 'alternate' worlds. I also felt that she could so travel at will and I desperately hope that one day she will admit this and help me in returning to my own world. As it is, I have given her this manuscript and told her about you, the Valley of the Morning, and how important it is to me that you should read it. The rest I have left to her. It is quite possible that my convictions about her are wholly erroneous, but I think not. I even wonder how much she was responsible for Hood's successes.

Black America is now a full partner in the Ashanti Empire. Her wealth returns and Negroes are running the country. The remaining whites are in menial positions, generally speaking, and will remain so for some time. Hood told me that he intends 'to punish one generation for the crimes of its forefathers'. As the older generation dies out, according to Hood's plan, he will gradually lift his heel from the neck of the white race. I suppose that it *is* justice, of a sort, though I cannot find it in my heart to approve wholly.

Myself and Una Persson, of course, are hated by the majority of whites in America. We are regarded as traitors and worse. But Mrs Persson seems thoroughly unmoved by their opinion and I am only embarrassed by it.

However, I am a creature of my own age, and a year was about the most I could take of Hood's America. Many of his men were good enough to tell me that they did not think of me as white at all, but got on with me as easily as any black man. I appreciated what they meant, but it by no means made up for the thinly disguised distaste with which I was regarded by many of the people with whom I had to mix at Hood's 'Court'. Thus, eventually, I begged the Black Attila's permission to rejoin the service of Bantustan. Tomorrow I shall board an airship which will take me back to Cape Town. Once there I'll decide what to do.

You'll remember I speculated on my fate once – wondering if I was doomed to wander through a variety of different ages, of worlds slightly different from my own, to experience the many ways in which Man can destroy himself or rebuild himself into something better. Well, I still wonder that, but I have the feeling that I do not enjoy the rôle. One day, I'll probably go back to Teku Benga and enter that passage again, hope that it will take me through to a world where I am known, where my relatives will recognise me and I them, where the good old British Empire continues on its placid, decent course and the threat of a major war is very remote indeed. It's not much to hope for, Moorcock, is it?

And yet, just as I feel a peculiar loyalty to you to try to get this story to you somehow, so I am beginning to develop a loyalty not to one man, like Hood or even Gandhi, not to one nation, one world or even one period of history! My loyalty is at once to myself and to all mankind. It's hard for me to explain, for I'm not a thinking man, and I suppose it looks pretty silly written down, but I hope you'll understand.

I don't suppose, Moorcock, that I shall ever see you again, but you never know. I could turn up on your doorstep one day, with another 'tall tale' to tell you. But if I do turn up, then perhaps you should start worrying, for it could mean a war!

Good luck, old man.

Yours,
Oswald Bastable

Epilogue

IT WAS GETTING on towards evening by the time I read the last few pages of Bastable's manuscript, then picked up his note again, plainly written some time later, when he had become more depressed:

> *I am going to try my luck again. This time if I am not successful I doubt I shall have the courage to continue with my life (if it is mine).*

I sighed, turning the note over and over in my hand, baffled and feeling that I must surely, this time, be dreaming.

Una Persson had gone – vanished into nowhere with her bandits and her guns of peculiar design and unbelievable efficiency (surely proof of Bastable's own story and of his theories concerning her!). All I had left was the horse which, if I was lucky, if I did not lose my bearings, if I wasn't slaughtered by bandits, might get me back, say, to Shanghai. I had lost most of my baggage, a fair amount of money and a good deal of time, and all I had to show for it was a mystifying manuscript! Moreover, Una Persson herself had become just as tantalising a mystery as Bastable. I was very little better off, as regards my own peace of mind, than when I set out.

Eventually I rose, went to my own room, and fell immediately asleep. In the morning I felt almost surprised when I saw the manuscript still beside me and, as I peered from my window, the horse placidly cropping at some sparse grass. I found a piece of paper and scribbled a note to Mrs Persson, thanking her for her hospitality and her manuscript. Then, by way of a joke that was half serious, I scribbled my address in London and invited her to drop in and see me 'if you are ever in my part of the twentieth century again'.

A month later, thin and exhausted, I arrived in Shanghai. I spent no more time in China than was necessary to get a passage home.

And here, sitting at my desk in my little study with its window overlooking the rolling, permanent hills of the West Riding, I read through Bastable's manuscript and I try to understand the implications of his adventures, and I fail.

If anyone else *ever* reads this, perhaps they will be able to make more of it than I.

Editor's Note

BASTABLE WAS MYSTIFIED, my grandfather was mystified, and I must confess to being mystified myself – though such speculations are supposed to be my stock-in-trade. I have used, quite shamelessly, in novels of my own, some of the ideas found in the book I've named *The Warlord of the Air*, and, indeed, one or two of the characters (specifically Una Persson, who appears in *The English Assassin*) have been 'lifted'. Perhaps Mrs Persson will some time come across one of these books. If she does, I very much hope she will pay me a visit – and possibly give me an answer to the mystery of Oswald Bastable. I assure you that the moment she does, I shall pass the news on!

Michael Moorcock,
Somewhere in the twentieth century

The Third Adventure

The Steel Tsar

For all who died at Babi Yar and for Anatoly Kuznetsov,
who died speaking the truth and whose
work was stolen by a liar

Introduction

THE DISCOVERY AND subsequent publication of two manuscripts left in the possession of my grandfather has led to a considerable amount of speculation as to their authenticity and authorship. The manuscripts consisted of one made in my grandfather's hand and taken down from the mysterious Captain Bastable whom he met on Rowe Island in the early years of this century, and another, apparently written by Bastable himself, which was left with my grandfather when he visited China searching for the man who had become, he was told, 'a nomad of the time streams'.

These very slightly edited texts were published by me as *The Warlord of the Air* and *The Land Leviathan* and I was certain that it was the last I should ever know of Bastable's adventures. When I remarked in a concluding note to *The Land Leviathan* that I hoped Una Persson would some day pay me a visit I was being ironic. I did not believe that I should ever meet the famous chrononaut. As luck would have it, I began to receive visits from her very shortly after I had prepared *The Land Leviathan*. She seemed glad to have me to talk to and gave me permission to use much of what she told me about her experiences in our own and others' time streams. On the matter of Oswald Bastable, however, she was incommunicative and I learned very quickly not to pump her. Most of my references to him in other books (for instance *The Dancers at the End of Time*) were highly speculative.

In the late spring of 1979, shortly after I had finished a novel and was resting from the consequent exhaustion, which had left my private life in ruins and my judgement considerably weakened, I had a visit from Mrs Persson at my flat in London. I was in no mood to see another human being, but she had heard from somewhere (or perhaps had already seen from the future) that I was in distress and had come to ask if there was anything she could do for me. I said that there was nothing. Time and rest would deal with my problems.

She acknowledged this and, with a small smile, added: 'But eventually you will need to work.'

I suppose I said something self-pitying about never being able to work again (I share that in common with almost every creative person I know) and she did not attempt to dissuade me from the notion. 'However,' she said, 'if you do ever happen to feel the urge, I'll be in touch.'

Curiosity caught me. 'What are you talking about?'

'I have a story for you,' she said.

'I have plenty of stories,' I told her, 'but no will to do anything with them. Is it about Jherek Carnelian or the Duke of Queens?'

She shook her head. 'Not this time.'

'Everything seems pointless,' I said.

She patted me on the arm. 'You should go away for a bit. Travel.'

'Perhaps.'

'And when you come back to London, I'll have the story waiting,' she promised.

I was touched by her kindness and her wish to be of use and I thanked her. As it happened a friend fell ill in Los Angeles and I decided to visit him. I stayed far longer in the United States than I had originally planned and eventually, after a short stay in Paris, settled in England for a while in the spring of 1980.

As Una Persson had predicted, I was, of course, ready to work. And, as she had promised, she turned up one evening, dressed in her usual slightly old-fashioned clothes of a military cut. We enjoyed a drink and some general talk and I heard gossip from the End of Time, a period which has always fascinated me. Mrs Persson is a seasoned time-traveller and usually knows what to and what not to tell, for incautious words can have an enormous effect either on the time streams themselves or on that rarity, like herself, the chrononaut who can travel through them more or less at will.

She has always told me that so long as people regard my stories as fiction and as long as they are fashioned to be read as fiction then neither of us should be victims of the Morphail Effect, which is Time's sometimes radical method of readjusting itself. The Morphail Effect is manifested most evidently in the fact that, for most time-travellers, only 'forward' movement through Time (i.e. into their own future) is possible. 'Backward' movement (a return to their present or past) or movement between the various alternative planes is impossible for anyone save those few who make up the famous Guild of Temporal Adventurers. I knew that Bastable had become a member of this Guild, but did not know how he had been recruited, unless it had been in the Valley of the Morning by Mrs Persson herself.

'I have brought you something,' she said. She settled herself in her armchair and reached down for a black document case. 'They are not complete, but they are the best I can do. The rest you will have to fill in from what I tell you and from your own perfectly good imagination.' It was a bundle of manuscript. I recognised the hand at once. It was Bastable's.

'Good God!' I was astonished. 'He's turning into a novelist!'

'Not exactly. These are fresh memoirs, that's all. He's read the others and is perfectly satisfied with what you've done with them. He was extremely fond of your grandfather and says that he would be quite glad to continue the tradition with you. Particularly, he says, since you've had rather better success in getting his stories published!' She laughed.

The manuscript was a sizeable one. I weighed it in my hand. 'So he was never able to find his own period again? Or return to the life he so desperately wanted?'

'That's not for me to say. You'll notice from the manuscript that there's little explanation as to how he came to the particular alternative time stream he describes. Suffice to say he returned to Teku Benga, crossed into yet another continuum and found his way to the airship yards at Benares. This time he was reconciled to what had happened and being an experienced airshipman, claimed slight amnesia and a loss of papers. Eventually he got himself a mate's certificate, though it was impossible for him, without impeccable credentials, to find a berth with any of the major lines.'

I smiled. 'And he's still haunted by angst, I suppose?'

'To a degree. He has many lives on his conscience. He knows only worlds at war. But we of the Guild understand what a responsibility we carry and I think membership has helped him.'

'And I'll never meet him?'

'It's unlikely. This stream would probably reject him, turn him into that poor creature your grandfather described, flung this way and that through Time, with no control whatsoever over his destiny.'

'He has that in common with most of us,' I remarked.

She was amused. 'I see you're still not completely over your self-pity, Moorcock.'

I smiled and apologised. 'I'm very excited by this.' I held up the manuscript. 'Bastable presumably wants it published as soon as possible. Why?'

'Perhaps it's mere vanity. You know how people become once they see their names in print.'

'Poor?'

We both laughed at this.

'He trusts you, too,' she continued. 'He knows that you did not tamper with his work and also that he has been of some use to you in your researches.'

'As have you, Mrs Persson.'

'I'm glad. We enjoy what you do.'

'You find my speculations funny?' I said.

'That, too. We leave it to your rather strange imagination to produce the necessary obfuscations!'

I looked at the manuscript. I was surprised to notice a few peculiar correspondences and coincidences when compared with my grandfather's first manuscript. Yet Bastable appeared not to make some of the connections the reader might make. I remarked on it to Mrs Persson.

'Our minds can hold only so much,' she said. 'As I've mentioned before, sometimes we do suffer from genuine amnesia, or at least a kind of blocking out of much of our memory. It is one of the ways in which we are sometimes able to enter time streams not open to the general run of chrononauts.'

'Time makes you forget?' I said ironically.

'Exactly.'

'As someone who affects anarchism,' I said, 'I'm curious about the references here to Kerensky's Russia. Could it be that –?'

She stopped me. 'I can't tell you any more until you have read the manuscript.'

'A world in which the Bolshevik Revolution did not take place. He hints at it in the other story...' I had often wondered what the Russian Empire would have been like in such circumstances, for one of my other abiding interests is in the Soviet Union and its literature, which was so badly stifled under Stalin.

'You must read what Bastable has written, then ask me some questions. I'll answer where I can. It is up to you, he says, how much 'shape' you give it, as a professional writer. But he trusts you to preserve the basic spirit of the memoir.'

'I shall do my best.'

And here, for better or worse, is Oswald Bastable's third memoir. I have done as little work on it as possible and present it to the reader pretty much as I received it. As to its authenticity, that is for you to judge.

Michael Moorcock,
Three Chimneys,
Yorkshire, England,
June 1980

Book One

*An English Airshipman's Adventures in
the Great War of 1941*

Chapter One
The Manner of My Dying

I T WAS, I think, my fifth day at sea when the revelation came. Just as at some stage of his existence a man can reach a particular decision about how to lead his life, so can he come to a similar decision about how to encounter death. He can face the grim simple truth of his dying, or he can prefer to lose himself in some pleasant fantasy, some dream of Heaven or of salvation, and so face his end almost with pleasure.

On my sixth day at sea it was obvious that I was to die and it was then that I chose to accept the illusion rather than the reality.

I had lain all morning at the bottom of the dugout. My face was pressed against wet, steaming wood. The tropical sun throbbed down on the back of my unprotected head and blistered my withered flesh. The slow drumming of my heart filled my ears and counterpointed the occasional slap of a wave against the side of the boat.

All I could think was that I had been spared one kind of death in order to die alone out here on the ocean. And I was grateful for that. It was much better than the death I had left behind.

Then I heard the cry of the seabird and I smiled a little to myself. I knew that the illusion was beginning. There was no possibility that I was in sight of land and therefore I could not really have heard a bird. I had had many similar auditory hallucinations in recent days.

I began to sink into what I knew must be my final coma. But the cry grew more insistent. I rolled over and blinked in the white glare of the sun. I felt the boat rock crazily with the movement of my thin body. Painfully I raised my head and peered through a shifting haze of silver and blue and saw my latest vision. It was a very fine one: more prosaic than some, but more detailed, too.

I had conjured up an island. An island rising at least a thousand feet out of the water, about ten miles long and four miles wide: a monstrous pile of volcanic basalt, limestone and coral, with deep green patches of foliage on its flanks.

I sank back into the dugout, squeezing my eyes shut and congratulating myself on the power of my own imagination. The hallucinations improved as any hopes of surviving vanished. I knew it was time to give myself up to madness, to pretend that the island was real and so die a pathetic rather than a dignified death.

I chuckled. The sound was a dry death rattle.

Again the seabird screamed.

Why rot slowly and painfully for perhaps another thirty hours when I could die now in a comforting dream of having been saved at the last moment?

With the remains of my strength I crawled to the stern and grasped the starting cord of the outboard. Weakly I jerked at it. Nothing happened. Doggedly, I tried again. And again. And all the while I kept my eyes on the island, waiting to see if it would shimmer and disappear before I could make use of it.

I had seen so many visions in the past few days. I had seen milk-white angels with crystal cups of pure water drifting just out of my reach. I had seen blood-red devils with fiery pitchforks piercing my skin. I had seen enemy airships which popped like bubbles just as they were about to release their bombs on me. I had seen orange-sailed schooners as tall as the Empire State Building. I had seen schools of tiny black whales. I had seen rose-coloured coral atolls on which lounged beautiful young women whose faces turned into the faces of Japanese soldiers as I came closer and who then slid beneath the waves where I was sure they were trying to capsize my boat. But this mirage retained its clarity no matter how hard I stared and it was so much more detailed than the others.

The engine fired after the tenth attempt to start it. There was hardly any fuel left. The screw squealed, rasped and began to turn. The water foamed. The boat moved reluctantly across a flat sea of burnished steel, beneath a swollen and throbbing disc of fire which was the sun, my enemy.

I straightened up, squatting like a desiccated old toad on the floor of the boat, whimpering as I gripped the tiller, for its touch sent shards of fire through my hand and into my body.

Still the hallucination did not waver; it even appeared to grow larger as I approached it. I completely forgot my pain as I allowed myself to be deceived by this splendid mirage.

I steered under brooding grey cliffs which fell sheer into the sea. I came to the lower slopes of the island and saw palms, their trunks bowed as if in prayer, swaying over sharp rocks washed by white surf. There was even a brown crab scuttling across a rock; there was weed and lichen of several varieties; seabirds diving in the shallows and darting upwards with shining fish in their long beaks. Perhaps the island was real, after all...?

But then I had rounded a coral outcrop and at once discovered the final confirmation of my complete madness. For here was a high concrete wall: a harbour wall encrusted above the waterline with barnacles and coral and tiny plants. It had been built to follow the natural curve of a small bay. And over the top of the wall I saw the roofs and upper storeys of houses which might have belonged to a town on any part of the English coast. And as a superb last touch there was a flagpole at which flew a torn and weather-stained Union Jack! My fantasy was complete. I had created an English fishing port in the middle of the Indian Ocean.

I smiled again. The movement caused the blistered skin of my lips to crack still more. I ignored the discomfort. Now all I had to do was enter the harbour, step off onto what I believed to be dry land – and drown. It was a fine way to die. I gave another hoarse, mad chuckle, full of self-admiration, and I abandoned myself to the world of my mind.

Guiding my boat round the wall I found the harbour mouth. It was partly blocked by the wreck of a steamer. Rust-red funnels and masts rose above the surface. The water was unclouded and as I passed I could see the rest of the sunken ship leaning on the pink coral with multicoloured fish swimming in and out of its hatches and portholes. The name was still visible on her side: *Jeddah*, Manila.

Now I saw the little town quite clearly.

The buildings were in that rather spare Victorian or Edwardian neo-classical style and had a distinctly run-down look about them. They seemed deserted and some were obviously boarded up. Could I not perhaps create a few inhabitants before I died? Even a laskar or two would be better than nothing, for I now realised that I had built a typical Outpost of Empire. These were colonial buildings, not English ones, and there were square, largely undecorated native buildings mixed in with them.

On the quay stood various sheds and offices. The largest of these bore the faded slogan *Welland Rock Phosphate Mining Company*. A nice touch of mine. Behind the town stood something resembling a small and pitted version of the Eiffel Tower. A battered airship mooring mast! Even better!

Out from the middle of the quay stretched a stone mole. It had been built for engine-driven cargo ships, but there were only a few rather seedy-looking native fishing dhows moored there now. They looked hardly seaworthy. I headed towards the mole, croaking out the words of the song I had not sung for the past two days.

'Rule Britannia, Britannia rules the waves! Britons never, never shall be – marr-I-ed to a mer-MI-ad at the bottom of the deep, blue sea!'

As if invoked by my chant Malays and Chinese materialised on the quayside. Some of them began to run along the jetty, their brown and yellow bodies gleaming in the sunshine, their thin arms gesticulating. They wore loincloths or sarongs of various colours and their faces were shaded by wide coolie hats of woven palm leaves. I even heard their voices babbling in excitement as they approached.

I laughed as the boat bumped against the weed-grown jetty. I tried to stand up to address these wonderful creatures of my imagination. I felt godlike, I suppose. And to talk to them was the least, after all, that I could do.

I opened my mouth. I spread my arms.

'My friends –'

And my starved body collapsed under me. I fell backwards into the dugout, striking my shoulder on the empty petrol can which had contained my water.

There came a few words shouted in pidgin English and a brown figure in patched white shorts jumped into the canoe which rocked violently, jolting the last tatters of sense from my skull.

White teeth grinned. 'You okay now, sar.'

'I can't be,' I said.

'Jolly good, sar.'

Red darkness came.

I had set off to sail over a thousand miles to Australia in an open boat. I had barely managed to make two hundred, and most of that in the wrong direction.

The date was 3 May, 1941. I had been at sea for about a hundred and fifty hours. It was three months since the Destruction of Singapore by the Third Fleet of the Imperial Japanese Aerial Navy.

Chapter Two
The Destruction of Singapore

I**T HAD BEEN** a Utopia of sorts which the Japanese destroyed. Designed as a model for other great settlements which would in the future spring up throughout the East, Singapore's white graceful skyscrapers, her systems of shining monorails, her complex of smoothly run airparks, had been lovingly laid out as an example to our Empire's duskier citizens of the benefits which British rule would eventually bring them.

And Singapore was burning. I am probably the last European to have witnessed her destruction.

After serving on the Portuguese aerial freighter *Palmerin* for a couple of months, I took several berths for single voyages, usually filling in for sick men, or men on leave, until I found myself in Rangoon without any chance of a job. I ran out of money in Rangoon and was willing to begin any kind of employment, even considered enlisting as a private in the army, when I was told by one of my bar acquaintances of a mate's position which had become vacant the night before.

'Chap was killed in a fight in Shari's house,' he said, nodding down the street. 'The skipper started the fight. He's not offering good money, but it could get you somewhere better than Rangoon, eh?'

'Indeed.'

'He's just over there? Want to meet him?'

I agreed. And that was how I came, eventually, to Singapore, though not in the ship on which I had signed.

A greasy Greek merchantman, the *Andreas Papadakis*, from some disgusting Cypriot port, trading in any marginally lucrative cargo which more fastidious captains would reject, had originally been bound for Bangkok when her engines had given out during an electrical storm which also affected our wireless telephone. We had drifted for two days, trying to make repairs aloft and losing two of our crew in the process, by the time the old windbag began to sag badly in the middle and drift towards the ground.

The *Papadakis* was not much suited to rough weather of any kind and could not be relied upon in even a minor crisis. The gondola cables and our steering cables both were badly in need of repair and we should have waited our moment and come down over water if we hoped for any chance of landing without serious damage, but by now the captain was drunk on retsina and refused to listen to my advice, while the rest of the crew, a mixed bunch of cut-throats from most parts of the Adriatic, were in a panic. I did my best to persuade the captain to let go our remaining gas, but he told me he knew best. The result was that we had begun to drop rapidly as we neared the coast of the Malay Peninsula, the *Andreas Papadakis* groaning and complaining the whole time and threatening to come apart at the seams.

She shivered and trembled in every section as the captain stared blearily through the forward ports and began, it seemed to me, to argue in Greek with the powers of Fate, on whom he blamed the entire disaster. It was as if he thought he could talk or soothe his way out of the inevitable fact. I kept my hands on the wheel, praying to sight a lake or at least a river, but we were heading over dense jungle. I remember a mass of waving green branches, an appalling screech of metal and wood as they met, a blow to my ribs which knocked me backwards into the arms of the captain who must have died muttering some wretched Cypriot remonstration.

He saved my life, as it happened, by cushioning my own fall and breaking his back. I came to once or twice while I was being pulled from the wreckage, but only really regained my senses when I woke up in St Mary's Hospital, Changi, Singapore. I had a few broken bones, which were mending, some minor internal injuries, which had been tended to, and I would soon be recovered, thanks to the Airshipmen's Distress Fund which had paid for my medical treatment and the period during which I would recuperate.

I had been lucky. There were only two other survivors. Five more had died in one of the native hospitals to which they had been taken.

While I rested, somewhat relieved not to be worrying about work and glad to be in Singapore, where there was every chance of finding decent employment, I began to read about the tensions growing between several of the Great Powers. Japan was disputing territory with Russia. The Russians, even though they were now a republic, had quite as much imperial determination as the Japs. However, we knew nothing of the War until the night of 22 February, 1941: the night of the attack by Japan's Third Fleet: the night when a British dream of Utopia was destroyed perhaps for ever.

We were trying to escape what was left of the colony. An ambulance ship was moored to an improvised mast and the vessel all but filled the blackened, ruined grounds of St Mary's: a huge airship silhouetted against a sky which was ruby-red with the flames of a thousand fires. The scene was surreal. I think of it today as the flight from Sodom and Gomorrah, but in Noah's Ark! Tiny figures of patients and staff rushed, panic-stricken, into the vessel's swollen belly while everywhere overhead moved monstrous, implacable Japanese flying ironclads. They had come suddenly, mindless beasts of the upper regions, to seed Singapore with their incendiary spawn.

Our resistance had been impotent. Far away a few searchlight beams wandered about the sky, sometimes showing a dense cloud of smoke from which could be glimpsed a section of one of the vast aerial men-o'-war. Then the three remaining anti-aircraft guns would boom and send up shells which either missed or exploded harmlessly against the side of the attacking craft. There were several of our monoplanes still buzzing through the blackness at speeds of over four hundred miles an hour, firing uselessly into hulls stronger than steel. They were picked off by tracer bullets shrieking from armoured gun gondolas. I saw a hovergyro whirl like a frightened hummingbird out of the flames, then it, too, was struck by magnesium bullets and went spinning into the flaming chaos below.

Our ship was not the latest type. Few hospital ships ever were. The cigar-shaped hull protecting the gasbags was of strong boron-fibreglass, but the two-tiered gondola below was more vulnerable. This gondola contained crew and passenger accommodation, engines, fuel and ballast tanks, and into it we were packing as many human beings as we could. I, of course, almost fully recovered, was helping the doctors and medical staff.

Without much hope of the ship's being able to get away, I helped carry stretchers up one of the two folding staircases lowered from the bowels of the ship. This in itself was a hard enough task, for the vessel was insecurely anchored and it swayed and strained at the dozen or so steel cables holding it to the ground.

The last terrified patient was packed in and the last nurses, carrying bundles of blankets and medical supplies, hurried aboard while airmen unpegged the gangways so they could be folded back into the ship. The stairs began to bounce like a cakewalk at a fair as, with the riggers, I managed to climb into the ship, losing my footing several times, shaken so much I felt my body would fall to pieces.

Suddenly several incendiary bombs struck the hospital at once. The darkness exploded with shouting flame. More bombs burst in the grounds, but incredibly none hit the airship direct. For a moment I was blinded by brilliant silver light and a wave of intense heat struck my face and hands.

From somewhere above I heard the captain shout 'Let slip!' even before the gangway was fully raised. I clutched and found a handrail, dropped the box I had been carrying and desperately tried to grope my way up the few final rungs before I should be crushed by the automatically closing steps. My vision returned quickly and I saw the cables lashing as if in fury at having to release their grip on the ship. And then I stood on the embarkation platform itself and my immediate danger was past.

The overloaded vessel went up with a juddering lurch. As we blundered into the sky I was convinced the whole contraption

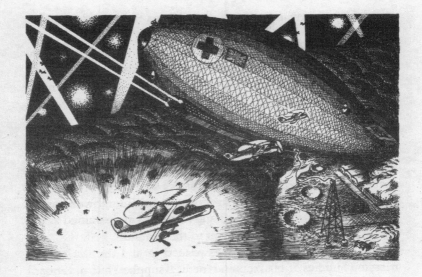

was about to plummet back to the ground, but somehow we continued rising. Steadying myself as best I could, I glimpsed the fiery ground falling slowly away before the gangways folded together and cut off the sight. Then I started to climb towards the lower deck.

The ship was listing slightly and was stern heavy so that all fittings sloped upward and to one side. Every so often we would shudder as some attempt was made to correct her trim. And still we were going up.

I had seen two worlds at war. I had flown with General Shaw and seen considerable havoc wrought by air fleets. I had witnessed the ferocity of the Black Attila, who had conquered America, but I had never looked upon such awful destruction. I knew now that it was my destiny to pass from world to world, perhaps in the hope that I would be able, at some stage, to make sense of my life, to set to rights my own terrible responsibility; yet it seemed that I was always somehow impotent. No matter how idyllic the world seemed, it always knew conflict in the end, and I was powerless to be anything but an observer.

Because of my experience, I had been made liaison officer between air crew and medical staff. I staggered through a narrow companionway alongside the crew's quarters, making for Number One Ward which was on the lowest of the two tiers. When the ship shook too much or altered her trim too drastically, I would grip some handhold and pause to stare incredulously down through one of the small observation ports set in this section of the hull.

The whole island was breaking into fragments and each fragment was consumed by flame. I saw the steel curves of the main monorail writhe and snap like the coils of an overwound watch spring as the bombs blasted its pillars. I saw slender towers topple and collapse into the inferno as if they were no more than the icing decorations of a Christmas cake thrown onto a fire. I saw the great oil reservoirs send orange flames and curling black smoke two hundred feet into the darkness. The deafening thump of exploding munitions dumps made my eardrums ache and the ship became so battered by the concussion that I fell again and again, bruising myself several times before I finally burst through the safety doors into the ward.

Here, too, was frightful confusion. Patients were howling and shrieking. Several were threshing about hysterically, fighting off the nurses and doctors who tried to help them. Those who could walk or stand were clinging to safety rails, staring through the observation windows, horrified by the last moments of the island which a few hours before had been Britain's 'impregnable' fortress.

Three-tiered bunks had been crammed into the ward and stood four rows across, running the best part of the length of the ship. On the other deck above us there were two wards of approximately half our length and similarly crowded. Technically, the other two wards were supposed to contain the wounded while this ward had the regular hospital patients, chiefly victims of disease, but so hurriedly had we crammed them aboard that Number One Ward also had its share of burned and bleeding wounded. It was packed with sick humanity – so crowded that I had to force my way through a wailing mass of legless or armless Malays and Chinese of both sexes before I could find someone who could tell me how the ward was being organised.

The hellish chaos outside was mirrored by the chaos in the ward. Our lighting had been switched off as a safety precaution. Therefore the only illumination came from the blazing colony below and it seemed at times that the ward itself was on fire. In some parts of it the light was bright, in other parts there were dense black shadows from which came the moans and screams of terrified women and children. I had an impression of a thousand waving legs and arms, a thousand mouths opened in shouts of misery and through the red glare of the destruction moved doctors, nurses, orderlies, all doing their best to restore calm. But their own strained, pale faces belied their soothing words. The stink of sweat, of anaesthetic, of blood, made me nauseous.

I singled out a child whose whole body was a red rawness of burns and wounds and began to tend to it as best I could.

Our overburdened ship soon reached maximum possible height. Its engines groaning, it began to move towards the sea. We were heading for Sarawak, our nearest surviving colony. I remember listening in hopeless grief as the child's voice cried in Cantonese for a mother whose body was burning somewhere in the wreckage below. A nurse gave it a sedative and I placed it in a bunk on which three other children had already been packed.

Then there came another lurch, another cacophony of wails and screams.

The ship was in trouble – had been from the beginning. I could tell by the feel of her. I think at least one of the stern tailplanes had been partly damaged, because she was steering so erratically. I tried to forget all this as I went on to the next patient, a woman whose arm had been blown off.

My brain could not accept that human beings would knowingly commit such atrocities on others of their kind. Did the Japanese really understand what they were doing? The image of insensate beasts of the sky was paramount. The ships must be remote-controlled, I thought, or even out of control altogether. But that was a foolish notion. It was plain now that the Japanese's sole intention in coming to the colony was to wipe Singapore off the face of the Earth and to spare no-one. I now know that their airmen had been told that the British had begun this policy with a deed of similar ferocity. Nobody, of course, believed this. But there was no doubt that, as Russia's main ally, we were automatically at war with Japan.

Though I remember the scene so clearly, I can still hardly find words for the mood of stunned despair which overwhelmed me as I tried to help the patients. The ship was still shuddering and rolling; threatening to throw us all straight through the observation windows. I recall that I held the hand of an old woman, murmuring something foolish in answer to her plaintive questions, as I stared fixedly out at a scene which had no equal in the most detailed visionary paintings of the horrors of Hell.

Then something like the blow from a giant fist smashed into our ship's stern and she slewed round in the air. An enemy shell had struck us! I tensed myself, expecting to feel the sudden drop begin, but the ship held her altitude. Her eight big back-to-back diesels, situated towards the stern, coughed and stopped. A chilling silence fell as we all listened. Then a bell clanged.

I got up to see what was happening outside, but smoke still obscured everything. The ship corrected her trim but her engines remained dead. I heard airshipmen shouting and saw members of the crew appear in the forward doorways and begin to push their way down the aisles towards the stern. Riggers, engineers and officers went past cursing. I was nearly bowled over by the bosun dashing back towards the control cabin which was forward. There were more shouts and the engines slowly started up again, but it seemed to me they were labouring more than ever. I went back to the old woman's bunk. She was sleeping. A nurse had given her a sedative. I could not find the doctor in charge. I made a decision. I told the nurse to sedate everyone. The patients had nothing to gain now from remaining mobile. If we went down, they were as good as dead. I was about to face my second airship crash in a matter of months, but this would be far bigger and far more tragic than anything that had happened to the old *Papadakis*.

Quite unexpectedly, and without any sign of pursuit from the aerial battleships of the Sons of Heaven, we emerged out of the smoke and saw the moonlit ocean below. We were about four hundred feet above water as we drifted through the night towards the sanctuary of Sarawak, muffled sounds of explosions and gunfire still very near. It was to be more than an hour before the red stain vanished completely from the sky. As soon as the captain considered it safe to do so, we were allowed to work by the violet glow of the emergency lighting. I gave whatever assistance I could to the doctors and nurses, for I had basic medical training, of course.

A terrible calm prevailed in the ship now and what sounds there were, save the droning of the engines, were small and melancholy.

We were in a state of stunned shock. The war itself – still undeclared – had only just begun and naturally we had already speculated that the Japs would make some attempt to take the highly strategic base of Singapore. But what we had not expected was the full weight of the Japanese Air Fleet, nor the terrible anger with which they attacked, offering no terms of surrender as, it emerged later, they had to Hong Kong, Taiwan or the Philippines. And we had thought that we had more time. Logically, Borneo would have been next in the plan of conquest. Most of our own air fleet had flown recently to defend Borneo's eastern seaboard and, I learned much later, was to engage and inflict heavy damage on the Emperor's ships three days after the razing of Singapore.

What had happened to us that night was so incredible that it was as if Time had become muddled and the savage days of Genghis Khan had returned to the Orient, only with greater ferocity. The shocked, exhausted silence in the wards became more intense as we moved slowly on, still losing a few feet every hour until soon, it seemed to me, we would be sailing on the sea like an old-fashioned ocean-going liner.

The engines stopped again. Complete silence fell for a moment until the earlier scene was repeated and crewmen began to run towards the stern. An airshipman caught me by the arm as I straightened up from checking as best I could the respiration of one of several tubercular patients. He asked if I was a doctor (I was not in uniform). I told him to go up and look in the top ward where he might find Dr Lingard, the chief of medical staff. I noticed that the airshipman's young face was covered in a mixture of sweat and fuel oil and that his eyes were bloodshot. I asked him what was wrong.

He told me that the fuel tanks had been hit as we were escaping and that consequently it looked as if we had lost most of our oil. He hurried for the entrance of the lift which would take him to the upper deck.

Apart from a few muffled shouts and the thumping from the stern, the silence prevailed until an orderly arrived and told me that all senior staff were to assemble in Dr Lingard's office amidships. The chief doctor had something to tell us that was important.

I left my work, put on my bloodstained jacket, and went to join the others. Lingard was in his tiny office with the other doctors and matrons. He nodded to me as I entered. I had been the last to arrive. I closed the door. Lingard was an ageing career doctor. I knew him slightly from St Mary's. His normally smooth features were tired and strained.

He told us that the captain had recently spoken to him. The vessel had no fuel left and we were drifting towards Java. There was no hope at all of reaching Borneo. The radar was dead and they were having difficulty with the computer system. Almost everything was being operated manually. They had sent a wireless message to Sarawak and Sarawak thought they could get a relief aircraft out to us if we made a deliberate crash-landing somewhere. The danger was that we should go on drifting over the Indian Ocean and would be picked off by the Japanese ships known to be cruising in the area. Alternatively, the wind might change and blow us back towards the Philippines where we would be finished by the Japs who were certainly still in evidence.

Lingard said that the captain estimated we should shortly be over Surabaya, which was still in neutral Dutch hands, although the Dutch were themselves having trouble from Japanese-armed guerrillas. The captain had been in wireless contact with the Surabayan authorities and they would be expecting us. The crew would start valving out gas as soon as the city was sighted. With luck and good judgement they would set down in the sea close to the harbour where we would float long enough for the boats to take us off.

It was about our only chance of surviving, of saving the majority of our charges. We were told to have patients ready for instant disembarkation. We must inflate all the stretchers we could find and don life jackets ourselves. The inflated stretchers should be placed in the bunks under the patients in order to help cushion the impact when the ship struck the water. We had a couple of hours in which to get everything ready.

I went back to the ward, pulled on my orange life jacket and stood by the safety rail, looking through the observation windows, smoking a cigarette as the dawn came up and showed the sea less than three hundred feet below us. I turned. The pale light revealed bunk after bunk packed with sick humanity and weary nurses moving slowly from patient to patient while the orderlies and airshipmen lifted the bodies and got the small life rafts under them. There came a series of sharp hisses as the rafts were inflated. Bleakly I returned my attention to the sea and watched the sun rise into a sky full of watery shades of yellow, red and blue. The ship, coasting on the wind, hardly seemed to be in motion at all. I felt for a moment that we must be the last living entities in a dead and ruined world.

Chapter Three
The Crash

NOT MUCH LATER I sighted the large conglomeration of tightly crowded together buildings which was the port of Surabaya. A busy city of mixed European and Malayan architecture, it was one of the few big ports to survive the decline of conventional shipping in favour of the airgoing cargo vessels. Its harbour was still crammed with steamers and the whole place looked unnaturally peaceful in the early-morning light. I felt an irrational surge of jealousy, a desire that Surabaya too might one day experience what Singapore had experienced. What right had this dirty, ugly port to survive when a mighty monument to a humane and idealistic Empire had perished in flames?

I pushed these dreadful ideas from my head. In a few more moments we should be crashing into the sea. Without power of any kind, the ship was going to have great difficulty in landing short of the harbour itself.

The whole vessel suddenly shuddered and I called for the staff to stand by as some patients began to moan questions or whimper in fear. The ship turned and began to drift in a clumsy, barely controlled manoeuvre and I lost sight of the town altogether. I saw only a steam launch surging over the waves and turning to follow us, leaving a white scar in the sea. There came a peculiar creaking and groaning from overhead as if some unusual strain had been placed on the gasbags and the hull containing them.

We began to drop.

A wailing went up from the patients then and we did our best to reassure them that everything was in order and that soon they would be in safe hospital beds in Surabaya.

I saw the sea shoot up to meet us and then retreat again. We began to move in a series of shuddering leaps as if riding a gigantic switchback. Somewhere a whole collection of crockery smashed to the deck and it was all I could do to hold myself upright by the safety rail.

And then, to my horror, I saw the roofs of the city below. Our gondola was almost scraping the highest of the buildings as we sped over them. We had missed the sea altogether and were travelling rapidly inland! The captain had left his decision until it was too late.

I heard the intercom buzz and then came the first officer's strained tones. A sudden strong following wind had blown up just as we were about to descend and this had completely thrown out everyone's calculations. The captain intended to try to take the ship right across the island and land in the sea near Djogjakarta, which was the nearest town we were likely to reach, considering the present direction of the wind. However, a lot of gas had already been valved out and we might not be able to gain enough height. In that event we must be prepared for a crash-landing on the ground.

I well knew what that would mean. The ship was considerably overburdened. If she fell from the sky to the land there was every chance we should all be killed.

A patient, wakened from sedation by the first officer's voice, screamed in alarm. A nurse hurried to soothe him.

The ship shivered and her nose came up sharply so that the deck tilted at a steep angle. Then the nose dipped and a few objects not secured began to slide down towards the bow. I jammed my foot against the rail. Through the ports I saw a Dutch flying boat follow us as if trying to make out the reason for our change of plan. Then, perhaps despairing of us, it turned back towards the sea.

Surabaya was behind us. Below us now lay a wide expanse of neat rice paddies, rows of tamarind trees and fields of tall sugar cane. We were so low that I could make out the heads of peasants looking up at us as our shadow moved across their fields. Then I was thrown against the rail as a fresh gust of wind caught the ship and she slewed round again, revealing the kapok plantations on the slopes of Java's grim volcanic hillsides.

I thought we were bound to crash into the hills, for they were rising steeply and were beginning to turn into the grey flanks of mountains. From some of these drifted wisps of yellowish white smoke. Instinctively I braced myself, but we just managed to cross the first line of mountains. And ahead I could see denser clouds of pale grey smoke, coiling and boiling like a tangle of lazy serpents.

The ship jerked her nose up again and we ascended a few feet. The damaged tailplanes caused us to make a crazy zigzag over the landscape and I could see our elongated shadow moving erratically below. Then our motion steadied, but it seemed inevitable to me that we must soon crash into one of the many semi-active volcanoes which dominated Java's interior.

I was unprepared for the next lurch and I lost my grip on the rail as we started to go up rapidly. Clambering to my feet I saw that the ship had released her water ballast. It sprayed like a sudden rainstorm over the dusty slopes of the mountains. Perhaps, after all, we would make the sea on the other side.

But a few moments later the captain's voice came through the loudspeakers. It was calm enough under the circumstances. It told us that we were going to have to lighten the ship as much as possible. We were to make ready all non-essential materials and the crew would collect them from us in a couple of minutes.

Frantically we stumbled about the ward gathering up everything which could be thrown overboard. Eventually we had handed to the airshipmen a great pile of books, food, medical supplies, clothing, bedding, oxygen cylinders and more. All went overboard.

And the ship rose barely enough to clear the next range of mountains.

I wondered if the captain would ask for volunteers to jump from the ship next. We were by this time flying over a bleak and barren wasteland of cold lava ridges, with not so much as a clump of palms to break our descent should we crash. The tension in the wards had increased again and those patients not still asleep were talking in high, panicky voices.

Some of the questions were difficult to answer. Among the 'non-essential' materials taken from us had been the bodies of those who had died in transit.

But even this act of desperate callousness had bought us very little time.

The intercom crackled again. The first officer began to speak. 'Please ready yourselves for – Oh, God!'

The next moment I saw the grey mountainside rushing towards us and before we fully realised it, we were engulfed in clouds of grey-white smoke and our keel was making a frightful screaming sound as it scraped the sides of the cliff.

The screams of the patients joined the scream of the ship itself. I heard a monstrous creaking noise and then I was flung away from the rail and felt myself sliding towards the bunks.

The vessel bounced and juddered, seemed to gain height for a moment and then came down with a horrifying crack which sent the bunks crashing loose from their moorings. I had the impression of waving arms and legs, of terrified faces. I heard trays of instruments clattering and saw bodies flying about like rag dolls. A great wail filled my ears and then the ship rolled, went up again and came down for the last time. In a flailing mass of bodies I was flung towards the starboard side. I saw my head rushing towards a fibreglass strut near the observation ports. I tried to put out my hands to stop the impact, but they were trapped by the bodies and objects on top of me. There came the final crash of impact and I remember being filled with an almost cheerful sense of relief that I had been killed and the ordeal was over at last.

Chapter Four
Prisoners

I THINK I must have awakened briefly once and heard peculiar squeaky voices babbling from somewhere far away and I realised that the gas was escaping and thus causing the speakers to talk in high-pitched tones. Deciding that I was alive and sure to be rescued, I fell back into unconsciousness.

When I next awoke I tried to move but could not. I thought that perhaps my back was broken, for there was little sensation save for the impression that something heavy was pressing down on me. Because of this pressure I found it very difficult to breathe in deeply enough to shout for the help that I was sure must be near, for I could hear people moving about quite close by.

The voices were no longer squeaky but they were not familiar either. I listened carefully. The voices were shouting some variant of Malay difficult for me to understand. I thought at first that the local peasantry, the sulphur-gatherers who work the volcanoes, had come to rescue us. I could smell the acrid smoke and it made breathing even harder. My next attempt to cry out failed. Then I heard more shouts.

And the shouts were followed by sharp reports which I did recognise. Gunshots.

With a feeling of terrible impotence I tried to move my head to see what was happening.

The shouting stopped. There was a stillness. Then a thin, hysterical scream. Another shot. Silence. A Malay voice giving rapid, savage commands.

Painfully, at last, I managed to turn my head and peer out of a jumble of twisted struts and wreckage. I saw bodies impaled on jagged shards of fibreglass and beyond them a pall of smoke through which dim figures moved. As the smoke cleared I saw bright flashes of green, red and yellow silk. These Malays were not sulphur-gatherers, that was certain.

Then I saw them clearly. They were clad in the familiar style of Malay bandits and pirates from Koto Raja to Timor. They wore richly coloured sarongs and embroidered jackets. On their heads were pitjis, turbans or wide coolie hats. There were sandals of painted leather on their brown feet and their bodies were crossed with bandoliers of cartridges. At their belts hung holstered revolvers, knives and parangs and they had rifles in their hands. I saw one come towards me, a look of cruel hatred frozen on his features. I dropped my head and shut my eyes, hearing him poke about in the wreckage above me. I heard a shot close to my face and thought he had fired at me, but the bullet landed in a corpse lying on top of me. He moved away.

I looked up again.

The bandits were herding the survivors down the mountain. Through the smoke I could see nurses in smudged, torn white uniforms, doctors still dressed in medical overalls or in shirtsleeves, airshipmen in sky-blue, staggering ahead of their captors. But there were no patients among them. I watched in dazed despair until the smoke swallowed them up.

Then slowly, as it dawned on me what had happened to my companions, pain began to flood through my body. I strained to twist myself round and see what pinned me in the wreckage.

One of the relatively light bunks had fallen on top of me and in the bunk was the body of a child. Its dead face, the eyes wide open, stared into mine. I shuddered and tried to lift the bunk clear. It moved slightly. The child's head rolled. I turned, reached out with bleeding hands and grasped a broken strut in front of me, pulling myself desperately from under the bunk until I was free and my breathing was easier. But my legs were still numb and I could not stand. I leaned forward and got a hold on another strut, using that to pull my body a few more inches over the wreckage, then I think I fainted for a few minutes.

It took me a long time to pull myself over the struts and the broken slabs of hull and the corpses until I lay on the outer areas of the wreckage on hard stone.

For all I was bruised and bleeding, I had no bones broken. The bodies of those who had died had saved me from the worst of the impact. Gradually the feeling came back to my legs and I was able to stand, gritting my teeth against the pain. I looked around me.

I was standing by the main wreckage of the ship on a mountain coated with streamers of yellow sulphur dust. Everywhere were bodies – crumpled, broken bodies of men, women and children, of patients in nightgowns and pyjamas, of wounded soldiers in tattered uniforms, of airship officers and crewmen, of nurses, orderlies and doctors. Nearly two thousand bodies and not one of them stirred as the wind moved the slow smoke over them, and the yellow dust swirled, and shreds of fabric fluttered amongst the crumpled ruins of the giant airship. Without hope I wandered through the piles of dead. Two thousand human beings who had sought to escape death in the fires of Singapore, only to find it on the barren, windswept rocks of an unknown Javanese hillside. I sighed and sat down, picking up a crushed packet of cigarettes I had seen. I opened the packet and took out one of the flattened cigarettes, lighting it and trying to think. But it was no good, my brain refused to function.

I looked about me. Jagged holes gaped in the airship's hull. Most of the gasbags had been ripped open and the helium lost. The wreckage covered a vast area of the mountainside. There was nowhere I looked which was not littered with it. And over it all moved thick ribbons of smoke from the volcano. The smoke stroked the broken bones of the ship, the smashed gondolas, the ruined engine nacelles, like the phantoms of the dead welcoming others into their ranks.

I got up and put out the cigarette with a stained, scratched boot. I coughed on the fumes and shivered with reaction and with cold. The slope was probably a thousand feet above sea-level. It was not surprising that the overloaded ship had crashed. Numbly I continued my search for survivors but at the end of two hours had found only corpses. What was still more horrifying was that many had actually survived the crash. As I searched I found little girls and boys who had been shot through the head or had their throats cut, young and old women butchered by parangs, men who had been decapitated. The bandits had been through the survivors systematically killing all those who for one reason or another had been unable or unwilling to walk. As the horror increased I was suddenly seized by nausea and stood with one hand leaning on a rock while I vomited again and again until all that came out of me were dry, retching coughs. Then I walked back to the main wreckage and found a blanket and a plastic container of water. I stripped off my useless life jacket and wrapped myself in the blanket, stumbling up the mountainside until I was clear of the corpses. Then I slept.

I awoke before dawn and was shivering. From somewhere below came a chilling howl which at first I mistook for that of a human being. Then I realised that the howl came from a wild dog hunting in the forest at the foot of the mountain. As dawn broke I went back to the wreck.

By now I had worked out roughly what had happened. Plainly the crash had been witnessed by one of the many rebel gangs who normally occupied these heights and, from time to time, would raid the Dutch towns and farmsteads below. Inspired by the support of both the Japanese and their more sophisticated nationalist countrymen, these rebels had recently grown bolder and had come to offer a serious threat to the colonists. Whether they called themselves bandits, pirates or 'nationalists', all hated the whites in general and the Dutch in particular. They had captured the survivors probably as hostages or possibly to deliver to their Japanese friends in return for more guns or supplies. Possibly they might just want to take pleasure in killing them slowly. I couldn't be sure. But I did know that if they found me I should suffer the same fate and none of the prospects was pleasant.

There had been few weapons aboard the hospital ship and for all I was inclined to arm myself I did not bother to hunt among the dead for a gun. The rebels would probably have found any there were. Instead I rescued another plastic container of water, a box of rather stale sandwiches, discovered a kitbag of medical supplies which I shouldered and then, thoughtfully, for I knew I might sooner or later find myself in thick jungle, tugged a parang from the body of one of the very nurses who had restored me to health at Changi.

I stumbled away from the broken hulk of the aircraft, going down the mountain. My eyes stung and my throat felt clogged with sulphur.

I was still moving as if in a trance – moving, as it were, from one dream and into another. Nothing had seemed completely real since the first ships of the Japanese Air Fleet had been sighted in the skies over Singapore.

Yet for all that I went warily through the drifting smoke. I had no wish to be plunged into the nightmare of capture by the Malay bandits.

At last I emerged into hot sunshine, saw blue, calm sky above me and the rich, variegated greens of a forest below. I looked about for signs of the bandits and their captives but I could see nothing.

Beyond the forest was a faint line in the sky. It was the horizon of the sea. The airship had almost succeeded in crossing the island and would have done if the wind had not driven it against what I now saw was the highest mountain in the region. I would try for the ship's destination of Djogjakarta and pray that the city was still in Dutch hands. My best bet would be to cross the intervening land to the sea and then follow the beach more or less westward until I got to the town, or, with luck, find a road on which I could get a lift.

There was no point in trying to do anything for the captured survivors myself. Once in Djogjakarta I could tell the authorities what had happened and hope that Dutch hovergyros would go out with soldiers and save the people.

And so I began my journey to the sea.

It took three days, first through the thick jungle and out onto the plains until I came to the paddy fields which I had to wade through, making wide detours around villages in case the local peasants were, as was often the case, in league with the bandits.

It was an exhausting trip and I was half-starved by the time I saw the beach ahead, not an hour's march away. In some relief I began to wade through the last paddy, my ruined boots dragged at the clinging mud and then I stopped, hearing a familiar sound in the distance.

It was the drone of an airship's engines. I looked up and located the source. A silver flash in the sky.

Tears came into my eyes and my shoulders slumped as I realised my struggle was over. I was delivered. I started to yell and wave, though it was unlikely that the crew could even see me at that height, let alone distinguish me for a shipwrecked Englishman!

But the ship *was* coming down. It did seem to be looking for me. Perhaps a rescue ship from Surabaya? I cursed myself for not staying near the wreck where I might have been seen earlier. Up to my waist in water, surrounded by the neat rows of rice plants, I waved my parang and yelled still louder.

Then I saw the motif on the ship's hull and instantly I had plunged up to my neck among the plants, pulling them over my head.

The ship bore the red disc of the sun blazoned on its flanks. It was a vessel of the Imperial Japanese Air Fleet.

For a few moments the ship circled the area and then flew off towards the mountains. I waited until it had disappeared before daring to emerge from the water. I had become a timid creature in the past twenty-four hours.

More warily than ever I crept to the seashore until at last I lay exhausted in the shadow of the rock on a warm beach of black, volcanic sand against which beat the heavy white surf of the Indian Ocean.

The presence of the scout ship over Java was ominous. It meant that Japan felt strong enough to ignore Dutch neutrality. It could even mean that Japan, or the bandits who served her, had taken the island.

I wondered if there were now any point in my trying to reach

Djogjakarta. I knew that the Japanese were not kind to their captives.

The sound of the surf seemed to grow louder and louder and more and more restful until soon the questions ceased to plague me as I stretched out on the soft sand and let my weary brain and body sink into sleep.

Chapter Five
The Price of Fishing Boats

A T NOON ON the next day I saw the fishing village. It was a somewhat ramshackle collection of log and wattle huts of various sizes. All the huts were thatched with palm leaves and some had been raised on stilts. The dugouts, moored to rickety wooden jetties built out into the shallows, were primitive and hardly looked seaworthy. The huts were shaded by tall palms whose curving trunks and wide leaves appeared to offer greater shelter than the houses themselves.

I shrank back behind a hillock and deliberated for a few moments. There was a chance that the villagers were in league with either the Japanese or the bandits or both. Yet, for all I was desperate to get to safety, I was tired of hiding, I was dreadfully hungry, and had reached a point where I did not much care who those villagers were, or to whom they felt loyalty – just as long as they fed me something and let me lie down out of the glare of the sun.

I made my decision and plodded forward. I thought I knew the kind of white man these people would be most prepared to tolerate and feed.

I had reached the centre of the village before they began to emerge, first the adult men, then the women, then the children. They glowered at me. I smiled back, holding up my pack. 'Medicine,' I said, desperately trying to recall my vocabulary.

They all looked to me as if they could use what I had to offer.

A few villagers emerged from the general crowd. These all carried old guns, parangs and knives which, in spite of their age, looked pretty serviceable.

'Medicine,' I said again.

There was a stirring from the back of the crowd. I heard words in an unfamiliar dialect. I prayed that some of them spoke Malay and that they would give me a chance to talk to them before they killed me. There was no question that my presence was resented.

An older man pushed his way through the armed villagers. He had bright, cunning eyes, and a calculating frown. He looked at my bag and uttered a couple of words in his dialect. I replied in Malay. This had to be the headman, for he was far better dressed than his fellows in a yellow-and-red silk sarong. There were sandals on his feet.

'*Belanda*?' he said. 'Dutch?'

I shook my head. '*Inggeris.*' I was not sure if he saw any difference between a Dutchman and an Englishman. But his brow cleared a little. He nodded.

'I have medicine.' Carefully I enunciated the Malay words, for his dialect was not one with which I was familiar. 'I can help your sick.'

'Why do you come like this, without a boat or a car or a flying machine?'

'I was on a ship.' I pointed out to sea. 'It caught fire. I swam here. I wish to go to – to Bali. If you want me to cure your sick, you must pay me.'

A slow smile crossed his lips. This made sense to him. I had come to bargain. Now he looked at me almost in relief.

'We have little money,' he said. 'The Dutch do not pay us for our fish now that the *Orang Djepang* war against them.' He pointed up the coast towards Djogjakarta. 'They fight.'

I disguised my despair. So now there was no point in trying to reach the town. I would have to think of another plan.

'We have rice,' said the headman. 'We have fish. But no money.'

I decided to continue with my original idea. If it worked I would be a little better off. 'I want a boat. I will cure what sickness I can, but you must give me one of the boats with the engines.'

The headman's eyes narrowed. The boats were their most valuable possessions. He sniffed and he frowned and he pursed his lips. Then he nodded. 'You will stay with us until ten men fall ill and are cured and five women and five male children,' he said, lowering his eyes.

I guessed that he was trying to hide any hint in his eyes that he might be getting the best of the bargain.

'Five men,' I said.

'Ten men.'

I spread my hands. 'I agree.'

And that was how I came to spend more weeks than I had planned in a remote and faintly hostile little Javanese fishing village, for the headman, of course, had tricked me.

The men proved disappointingly healthy and the women and children seemed constantly sick of minor complaints so that, with my limited medical knowledge, I treated many more people than had been called for in the original bargain, but I never seemed in sight of making up the male quota. The headman had realised at once that he was on to a good thing and it was soon evident that even when the men did fall sick they did not report to me but stuck to their usual methods of cure. At least two died while I was there. They were prepared to forego any attention from me so that I should continue treating the women and children.

For all that, I was scarcely angry. The routine was an anodyne to my weary brain and I lost myself in it. My awareness of any reality beyond the confines of the village grew steadily more vague. Chaos had come again to the outside world, but the day-to-day life of the village was the model of simple order and I might have lived my life there if the outside world had not, at last, intruded.

Looking back, I understand that it was inevitable, but I was surprised when it happened.

One morning I saw a cloud of dust in the distance. It seemed that the sand of the beach was being disturbed, but I could not distinguish the cause of the disturbance.

Then as the dust cloud came closer I realised what it meant and I ran to hide in the doorway of a hut.

The dust was thrown up by the tyres of military cars – big, square utilitarian things with heavy-duty steam turbines driving their massive wheels. And the military cars were crammed with Japanese soldiers. Almost certainly they had conquered the whole island by now and, as certainly, had heard some rumour of my presence in the village. They were coming to investigate.

It was at this point that I decided to sail for Australia. There was nowhere else to go.

Although I had failed to fulfil my original bargain with the headman, I still had the moral right to do what I did, for I had dealt fairly enough with the villagers. And I would leave what there was of my medical kit behind for them.

Taking only a petrol can full of water, I crept down to the shore, using a jetty as cover. Then I waded to one of the outboards and began to untie it. All the villagers were watching the oncoming cars and it was my only chance to escape. I started to push the boat slowly towards the open sea while the villagers ran about in excitement at the arrival of their new masters.

I was lucky. A current soon caught the dugout and carried it more rapidly away from the shore. At last the villagers saw me, realised what was happening just as the Japanese cars drew up in the village square. I was now some distance out and having trouble trying to climb into the dugout without upsetting it.

The villagers began to gesticulate and point towards me. With a heave I managed to get into the wildly rocking boat and tried to get the battered outboard going.

It fired after only three false starts. I adjusted the tiller and headed for the open sea, noticing with satisfaction that there were two spare cans of fuel stowed amidships.

I heard pistol-shots, then rifle-shots.

Then a machine gun started up and bullets buzzed about my ears and struck the water all around me. I kept changing course and at one point did a complete circle and headed in the opposite direction to Darwin, my proposed destination, hoping that this would confuse them when they came to radio their headquarters and instruct them to send out airships and patrol boats to look for me.

The gunfire stopped for a moment. I looked back and saw the tiny figures of the villagers. They seemed to be kneeling before the Japanese.

Then the machine gun started up again, but this time it did not fire out to sea.

A few hours later I began to think that the chances of pursuit had disappeared. I had sighted only one airship in the distance and soon it would be night. I had been lucky.

As I chugged out over the smooth and blazing mirror of the ocean, congratulating myself and with my thoughts increasingly turning to abstractions, I did not realise that the Japanese patrols must have been searching waters where I might logically be. It seems that I had already lost my bearings, in more senses than one.

As the burning days and the cold nights passed, I began to realise that I had no chance at all of reaching Australia, and I started to indulge in debates with my starving, thirsty self on the nature of life, the nature of death and the nature of what seemed to me a continuing struggle between Chaos and Order, with the former tending to come off rather better in the long run.

And it was this babbling and foolish wretch – once a practical and pragmatic soldier in a more orderly world – who eventually sighted Rowe Island and decided, reasonably, that it was nothing more than a splendidly detailed illusion.

Chapter Six
The Mysterious Dempsey

ROWE ISLAND WAS discovered in 1615 by the British explorer Richard Rowe.

In 1887 it was found to contain formations of almost pure calcium and in 1888 was annexed by Great Britain. That year the first settlers arrived and by 1897 they had obtained a concession from the mother country to work the phosphate deposits. From being uninhabited before 1888, it had by the first third of this century achieved a population of more than two thousand, mainly Malay and Chinese miners who had come there to work for the Welland Rock Phosphate Mining Company, which was the island's sole industrial concern.

Rowe Island lies – or lay – in the Indian Ocean, 224 miles South, 8° East of Java Head and 259 miles North, 79° East of the Keeling Islands. It is 815 miles from the ruins of Singapore and 1,630 miles from what is left of Freemantle, Western Australia. Its European population used to number a hundred or so: the Official Representative and his staff; the manager and administrative staff of the Welland Rock Phosphate Mining Company; various private residents there for their health (Rowe Island was a very healthy place); a young lieutenant commanding the small garrison of Ghoorkas; some restaurant-, shop- and hotel-keepers; various missionaries and the airpark and dock officials. When I arrived most of these, of course, had already gone and neither airships nor steamers came to collect the island's only export.

The settlement had a mosque, a Buddhist temple, a Catholic church, a Methodist chapel and a mission hospital run by the Church of England. The hospital was staffed by a group of young Pakistani nursing nuns under the direction of a layman, Dr Hira, a Sinhalese. The hospital's missionary and his wife had departed for Australia soon after the Destruction of Singapore.

It was in this hospital that I woke up and slowly realised Rowe Island was not, after all, an hallucination.

I was sore and my body stung all over, but I no longer felt thirsty, merely hungry. I lay between the rather rough linen sheets of what was evidently a white hospital bed. The walls were white and there was an ivory crucifix on the wall, a few tropical flowers stuck in a pot on the ledge by the partially opened window. I felt the urge to scratch, but discovered both hands were bandaged. I moved and my joints throbbed. I tried to sit upright, but fell back wearily. It was still hard to believe I was safe, after all. I had survived.

A little while later the door opened and in came a shy, beautiful Pakistani girl in a cream-coloured nun's habit. She nodded and smiled gravely at me, standing aside to admit a languid young Sinhalese whose portly frame was draped in an elegant white suit. Around his neck was a stethoscope on which the fingers of his right hand seemed to be playing a tune. His round, handsome face stared rather sardonically at me. He glanced at the watch on his plump wrist. 'Not bad. Almost exactly on time.'

My first attempt at speaking was not very successful. My second was better. 'You,' I said, 'or me?'

'Both of us.' He took a silver case from his pocket and opened it, offering the cigarettes to me. I showed him my bandaged hands. He smiled apologetically. 'The nurse will light it for you if you want one.'

'Not now. Thanks.'

He lit a cigarette for himself. 'Well, you're on the mend I'm glad to say. We put you in this room because your shouting kept the other patients awake. You're an airshipman, are you?'

'I am,' I said. 'I was on an airship which crashed.' I told him my name and what had happened to me. I asked where I was.

'I'm Dr Hira. This is St Charles's Hospital, Rowe Island.' He smiled ironically. 'I can see you've never heard of Rowe Island. Few have. Perhaps that's why the war hasn't touched us directly.

Nobody passes this way either by air or by sea. In a few more months I wouldn't be surprised if we're the last outpost of civilisation on the globe.' He drew heavily on his cigarette and glanced out of the window at the harbour. The Pakistani nurse got extra pillows and helped me sit up.

'If you can call this civilisation,' said Hira. 'Are you hungry?'

'Very.'

'Good.' Hira patted the shy nun on the shoulder. 'Fetch the patient some soup, my dear.'

When the nurse had gone, closing the door behind her, I gestured with my bandaged hands. 'I thought this whole bloody place was a mirage, at first.'

Hira shrugged. 'Maybe it is. A pretty run-down dream, though. You survived Singapore, eh?'

'It's hard to believe it really happened,' I said.

'It happened. We heard.'

'So there's some communication with the outside world?'

'The mine people took all the decent equipment when they left. It was the news of Singapore that caused the evacuation. A needless panic as it turned out.'

'I see. So there's no way of contacting, say, Darwin?'

'We've a radio which occasionally works. Hand-cranked thing.'

'And those dhows are the only means of leaving the island. No ships of any kind?'

'Not any more, Mr Bastable. The mine people scuttled our only steamer with some idea of stopping the island being used as a base for enemy shipping.' Hira pointed out of the window at the harbour where the rusting superstructure of the wreck could still be seen.

'So I'm stuck here unless the radio can be made to work. You said it was "hand-cranked". Haven't you any proper power?'

'No more fuel. We use oil lamps for lighting now.'

'When is there a chance of my getting a message to Darwin?'

'That depends on the state of the radio and the state of Underwood, the operator. I'll ask someone to go up to the airpark tomorrow and see if Underwood is sober enough to work the radio. That's about the best I can do. Eager to get back into the fray, eh?'

I looked suspiciously at him, trying to detect irony in a face which now regarded me blandly.

'I've a duty,' I said. 'They'll need experienced airmen, after all.'

'I'm sure they will. I must be off on my rounds now. See you soon, Mr Bastable.'

Hira raised the stethoscope in a kind of salute and left the room.

I sank back into the bed and sighed. An old radio and a drunken operator. I was pessimistic about my immediate chances of leaving Rowe Island.

A week went by and every day I grew stronger. I was making a splendid recovery from what had been a very serious case of exposure. But I also grew more and more impatient and plagued Dr Hira with questions about the radio and the condition of the operator. The news initially brought back to the hospital had been bad. Shortly after I'd arrived Underwood had gone up on the mountain somewhere. He had taken a Chinese girl and a case of gin with him and he couldn't be found.

About ten days after I had awakened from my coma I stood by the window, wearing a rather ridiculous hospital dressing gown which was too short for me, talking to Hira, who had come in to give me the latest lack of news about Underwood. In the harbour there was a lot of confusion and noise. Since dawn groups of half-starved Malays had been moving along the jetty, packing their possessions into one of the fishing dhows. Apparently my appearance on Rowe Island had started something. They had realised that the mining company would not be back for a long while and they had decided to try to make it to Java, in spite of their having been warned of atrocities committed on their countrymen by the Japanese. I felt sorry for those Malays. The boat would probably sink before they got more than a few miles out. Miserably I looked back into the room at Hira.

'The government should be helping these people – flying in supplies or something. I wish that damned operator would turn up.'

'I think the government has a lot of problems at the moment.' Hira was sitting on my bed fiddling with his stethoscope. He spoke almost with satisfaction. 'I don't know when we'll see Underwood. He often goes to earth like this. He's probably hiding out in one of the mines.'

'I could have a try at working the radio myself,' I said. 'It would be better than this. I'm well enough to go out now. If you could find me a suit, perhaps…'

'I think we can discover something in your size. But Underwood has locked his office up. Always does. He likes to be indispensable. It keeps his credit good at the hotel.'

'Which hotel?'

'Olmeijer's. The Royal Airpark Hotel on the edge of the airpark. It used to be the biggest. Now it's the only one. Olmeijer carries on running it from sentiment, I think.'

'I'll take a stroll out there, anyway.' I was curious to have a look at the island.

'Why not?' said Hira. 'Get to know the place. After all, you could be here for some time.' He seemed amused.

As I dressed in my borrowed suit, Hira took my place by the window. From the harbour came a babble of voices as the Malays readied the ship for the sea. He shook his head. 'They'll drown themselves for certain.'

'Won't anybody stop them?' I pulled on my jacket. The linen suit was a surprisingly good fit, as was the white shirt Hira had lent me. 'Isn't there some sort of governor here? You mentioned someone…'

'Brigadier L.G.A. Nesbit is the Official Representative and has been since 1920.' Hira shrugged. 'He's eighty-seven and has been senile for at least ten years. I think that's why he decided to stay when the big exodus was on. His staff now consists of a valet as old as himself and a Bengali secretary who spends his whole time making endless inventories and who hasn't, apparently, left his office since the war began. There is, of course, young Lieutenant Begg, who commands our local military. I don't think Begg will be sorry to see a few of his troubles going.'

'The Malays are a problem, eh?' I tried on one of the panama hats lying on the bed. It was a good fit, too.

Hira gestured wearily. 'There are a thousand Malays and Chinese here at least. The Malays are in the main Moslems and the Chinese are chiefly Buddhists or Christians. They are, when they have nothing better to do, highly critical of the other's way of life. And they have nothing better to do – their work went when the mine closed and now they're living off the land and sea as best they can.'

'Poor bastards,' I said.

Hira gave a peculiar smile. 'I wonder if you'll say that when they turn on the whites. They will, you know, quite soon. Presently they hate each other more than they hate Europeans, but it will take just one excuse for them to begin a general massacre. We'll all go, then. Technically, you see, the sisters and myself are regarded as Europeans.'

'And you're prepared to stay until that happens?'

'Should I go back to Ceylon and care for our Japanese conquerors?'

'You could go to Australia or even England. There must be need of doctors everywhere.'

'I should have made it plain.' Hira opened the door for me. 'I have a couple of principles. One of them is that I refuse to work for Europeans. It's the reason I came to Rowe Island in the first place. Until the evacuation this hospital was for coloured people only, Mr Bastable.'

As I left the hospital I adjusted my hat and paused to watch the dhow easing its way past the wreck of the steamer. Every inch of its deck was covered with brown-skinned men, women and children. It brought back the terrible image of the doomed hospital ship and I could hardly bear to think what would become of them all. Slowly I started to walk along the weed-grown quay, beside deserted hotels, offices and warehouses outside which were parked the useless cars, lorries and buses.

A few disconsolate Malays were dragging their bundles back down the jetty, having failed to squeeze themselves aboard the boat. The lucky ones, I thought.

I reached a corner and turned into a narrow, silent side street lined with grey and brown featureless workers' houses and a few boarded-up shops. The street rose quite steeply and I realised how weak I still was, for I had to labour the last few paces until I reached a small square dominated by a battered statue of Edward VIII which somewhat incongruously decorated a dried-up ornamental fountain. The concrete bowl of the fountain was full of empty bottles, torn newspapers and other, less savoury, refuse. There were a few Chinese children playing around it while their mothers sat blank-faced in their doorways, staring into space. Gratefully, I sat on the edge of the fountain's bowl, ignoring the smell which came from it and smiling at the undernourished children. They at once stopped playing and looked warily up at me.

'*Tso sun*,' I said gravely, using Cantonese. 'Good morning.'

Not one of them replied. A bit nonplussed I wished I had something to offer them. Some sweets, perhaps, for money was worthless on Rowe Island.

I removed my hat and wiped my forehead. It was growing very hot and I had become wary of the sun. I had better get on to the hotel while I could.

Then I heard the sound of hoofbeats and turned in astonishment to see a rider enter the square. He looked distinctly out of place as he sat stiff-backed and arrogant in the saddle of his well-groomed cob. A tall, fair-haired Englishman of about thirty, he wore a gleaming white coat and jodhpurs with his military insignia on the jacket. His boots, belt, shoulder strap and holster were as highly polished as the badge on his solar topee. He saw me at once, but pretended that he hadn't. He stroked his blond moustache with his baton and brought his horse to a halt on the other side of the square.

I looked around at the empty, silent windows, wondering what he could be doing here.

'Get these children out of the way, sergeant!' His voice was sharp, commanding.

At this order six crisply turned-out little Ghoorkas led by a sergeant emerged from another side street and waved the children back with their rifles. Their bayonets were fixed. They wore dark green uniforms with scarlet facings and they had their long, curved knives at their belts. The women needed no warnings but dragged the children inside and slammed their doors. Now I was the only civilian in the square.

'What's going on here, lieutenant?' I asked.

The lieutenant turned cold, blue eyes on me. 'I would suggest, sir, that you get away from here at once. It's a police matter. There could be trouble.'

There seemed to be no point in arguing. I humoured him instead. 'Thank you, lieutenant.' I walked across the square but remained in the shadows of a side street, peering curiously at what was going on.

Now the young officer dismounted and ordered his sergeant to enter one of the houses. The Ghoorkas rushed in and the lieutenant followed behind.

I watched in puzzlement, not knowing what to make of the scene at all. There was dead silence in the square for a little while, then a horrible babble of screams and yells issued from the house. I heard a woman shouting in Cantonese. There were a couple of shots and then the raised voice of the officer giving a series of orders. Another scream – a man's this time – then out into the street poured a score of coolies. They were staggering and screwing their eyes up against the sunlight. Every one of them was dazed and scared stiff.

There came another shot from inside the house and then more shouting. The coolies outside began to scatter, some rushing into nearby doorways, others running off down towards the harbour. A further series of commands came from the officer and then a terrible wailing, the sound of flesh being struck, presumably with rifle butts.

Appalled, I was about to step forward when a panic-stricken coolie burst from the house, hesitated, glanced around wildly holding a bleeding hand, then ran in my direction. I stepped aside to let him pass and he fled around a corner and vanished. But I had seen his pupils. The man had been drugged. Now I understood. The soldiers were raiding some sort of local opium den.

Hearing a moan, I re-entered the square and saw that one of the opium smokers had fallen to the flagstones. He had been stabbed badly with a bayonet in his shoulder. I knelt beside him, tore back his shirt and did my best to stop the flow of blood while he stared at me in terror, small moans escaping his lips.

Boots tramped from the house.

'Good God, man, what are you doing?'

I looked up to see the lieutenant striding from the house. He looked pretty pleased with himself.

'This chap's been stabbed by one of your soldiers,' I said harshly. 'I'm trying to help him. Was there any need to –'

The lieutenant glanced contemptuously at the coolie. 'Doubtless he tried to kill someone. Crazed by opium – they all are. His own people will look after him. We're trying to teach them a lesson, after all.'

With strips of the man's shirt I bandaged up the wound as best I could. He tried to speak and then fainted. Helplessly, I tried to lift him, but it was impossible.

Now the Ghoorkas emerged holding three terrified Chinese in black and red smocks; two men and a woman, all badly bruised and probably the proprietors of the den.

The lieutenant's baton stabbed in their direction. He raised his head and spoke to the empty windows and doors. 'Now no more opium! You savvy! Opium bad! These people bad! Go to prison. We lock up long time! Savvy?'

Angrily he tapped his riding boot with his baton. He glared at me and opened his mouth to speak.

'I'm going to try to get this chap to the hospital,' I said. 'Can somebody give me a hand?'

The officer took the reins of his horse and looked from me to his soldiers who held their miserable prisoners much more firmly than was necessary.

'One of your men –' I began.

The lieutenant remounted. 'I told you, sir. His own people will look after him. You obviously don't understand the conditions on this island. There's a dreadful opium problem. It's increasing daily. They grow the poppies rather than food. I...'

'What else have the bastards got to live for, Begg?' A tired drawl came from the shadowy doorway of the raided house. An English voice.

Lieutenant Begg turned in his saddle and shook his baton at the unseen speaker. 'You stay out of this. You're lucky we didn't arrest you, too.'

A figure emerged into the sunlight. Dressed in a dirty, faded European suit and a frayed native shirt, he was barefooted, unshaven, emaciated and plainly under the influence of opium. I knew the signs well enough, for I had once been slave to the drug's consolations. I could not make out his age, but the voice was of quite a young man from the upper middle class.

'I'd have thought you'd be ashamed...' Begg's face was full of disgust.

'Who are you to deny them their only pleasure, Begg?' drawled the newcomer reasonably. 'Let them alone, for God's sake.'

Lieutenant Begg wheeled his trim cob about and shouted an order to his men. 'All right, quick march.' He trotted away without answering the decrepit Englishman.

I watched them go, the Ghoorkas dragging their frightened prisoners back the way they had come.

The Englishman shrugged and turned to re-enter the house.

'Just a minute,' I called. 'I must try to get this chap to the hospital. He's half-dead. Could you give me a hand?'

The man leaned wearily against the door frame. 'He'd be better off with his ancestors, believe me.'

'A moment ago you were defending these people.'

'Not defending them, old boy. I'm a fatalist, you see. I told Begg to let them alone. And I tell you the same. What's the point? He'll die soon enough.'

But he left the doorway and shuffled into the square, blinking in the sunshine. 'Who are you, anyway?'

'I'm an airshipman. I got here a week or so ago.'

'Ah, the shipwrecked mariner. They were talking about you up at the hotel. All right, I'll help you with him, for what it's worth.'

The opium-drunk Englishman was no stronger than I was, but together we managed to carry the coolie down the street and along the quay until we reached the hospital.

After a couple of nuns had been called and had taken the wounded man away, I stood panting in the lobby, staring curiously at my helper. 'Thanks.'

He smiled slowly. 'Think nothing of it. Nothing at all. Cheerio.'

He raised his hand in a sort of ironic salute and then went out. He had gone before Dr Hira came down the stairs into the lobby.

'Who was that chap?' I asked Hira, describing the wretched Englishman.

Hira recognised the description. He fiddled with his stethoscope. 'A castaway, like yourself. He arrived in the airship which came to take off the mine people. He chose to stay on Rowe Island. I don't know why. It meant they could take one more passenger so they didn't argue. They call him The Captain sometimes, up at the hotel. Supposed to have been the commander of a merchant airship which crashed in China before the war. A bit of a mystery.'

'Begg doesn't like him.'

Hira laughed softly. 'No, Begg wouldn't. Captain Dempsey lets the side down, eh? Begg's for the Europeans keeping up appearances at all costs.'

'Begg certainly works hard.' I wiped a spot of blood off my sleeve.

'I don't think he ever sleeps. His wife left with the mine people, you know...' Hira glanced at his watch. 'Well, it's almost lunchtime. Fish and rice, as usual, but I've managed to get a couple of bottles of beer, if you'd...'

'No thanks,' I said. 'I think I'll head up to the hotel again.'

Chapter Seven
Dead Man

THE PORT WHERE I was staying was the only real town on the island. It was called New Birmingham. Its buildings were clustered close together near the waterfront and were several storeys high. As they wandered up the slopes they drew apart as if fastidious of each other's squalor and grew smaller until the houses near the top were little more than isolated shanties erected in shallow hollows in the hillside.

Above the shanty district the hill levelled out for a while and became a small plateau on which the airpark had been built. Olmeijer's hotel stood on the edge of the airpark which was now overgrown and desolate. I wondered if young Lieutenant Begg would have approved of the hotel, for it had certainly made an attempt to 'keep up appearances'. Its big gilt sign was brightly polished and its splendid wooden Gothic exteriors had recently been given a fresh coat of white paint. It looked out of place in its surroundings.

The airpark was dominated by the rusting airship mast erected in its centre. To one side of the park was a single airship hangar, its grey paint peeling, and beside it a pole at which drooped a torn and filthy windsock. Near the pole stood, like the skeletons of large, unearthly insects, the remains of two hovergyros which had been stripped of most of their essential parts. On the other side of the hangar was the shell of a light monoplane, probably the property of some long-gone sportsman, which had been similarly dismembered. The island seemed to be populated by a variety of wrecks, I thought. It seemed to be feeding off corpses, including, as in Begg's case, the corpses of dead ideas.

After a glance towards the abandoned administration and

control buildings to assure myself that they were uninhabited, I made for the hotel.

Pushing open a pair of well-oiled double doors, I walked into the lobby. It was clean, scrubbed, polished and cool. A Malay houseboy was operating the cords of a big punkah attached to the ceiling. It fanned air into my face as I entered. I was grateful for this after the heat outside but amused by the fresh incongruity. I nodded to the Malay, who didn't seem to notice me and, seeing no-one at the desk, strolled into the adjacent bar.

In the shady gloom were two men. One sat in his shirt-sleeves behind the bar reading a book while the other sat drinking a gin fizz in the far corner near French windows opening onto a verandah. Beyond the windows I could see the airpark and beyond the airpark the slopes of the mountain, covered in thick forest.

As I seated myself on a stool by the bar the man behind it put down his book and looked at me in some surprise. He was very fat and his big, red face was beaded with sweat. His rolled-up sleeves revealed a variety of tattoos of the more restrained kind. There were several gold rings on his thick fingers. He spoke in a deep, guttural accent.

'What can I do for you?'

I began apologetically, 'I'm afraid I brought no money, so...'

The fat man's face broke into a broad smile. 'Ja! No money! That's too bad!' He shook with laughter for a moment. 'Now, what will you drink? I'll put it on the slate, eh?'

'Very good of you. I'll have a brandy.' I introduced myself. 'Are you the hotel's proprietor?'

'Ja. I am Olmeijer, certainly.' He seemed inordinately proud of the fact. He took a large ledger from under the counter, selected a fresh page and entered my name at the top. 'Your account,' he said. 'When things are better, you can pay me.' He turned to take down a bottle of cognac.

'You've a chap called Underwood staying here, I believe?' I said.

'Underwood, certainly.' He put a large brandy on the bar.

'Twenty cents. On the slate.' He made an entry in the ledger and replaced it out of sight.

It was good brandy. Perhaps it tasted even better for being the first drink I had had since Singapore. I savoured it.

'But Underwood,' said Olmeijer with a wink and a jerk of his thumb, 'has gone up the mountain.'

'And you've no idea when he'll be back.'

I heard one of the wicker chairs scrape on the polished floor, then footsteps approached me. I turned. It was the man who had been sitting near the window. He held his empty glass in his hand.

'Underwood will be back when the gin he borrowed from Mr Olmeijer runs out.'

He was a thin, heavily tanned man in his fifties, wearing a khaki bush shirt and white shorts. He had a small, greying moustache and his blue eyes seemed to have a permanent hint of ironic humour in them. 'My name's Nye,' he said as he joined me at the bar. 'You must be the airship chap they found in the dugout. Singapore, eh? Must have been awful.'

Nye told me he'd been left behind to protect the interests of the Welland Rock Phosphate Mining Company while the rest of the white employees went back to England or Australia. He was keen to hear about the attack on Singapore. Briefly, for the memory was still hard to bear, I told him what had happened.

'I still can't believe it,' I concluded. 'There was a peace treaty.'

He smiled bitterly and sipped his drink. 'Everyone had a peace treaty, didn't they? We'd abolished war, hadn't we? But human nature being what it is…' He looked up at the rows of bottles in front of him. 'Bloody Japs. I knew they'd start something sooner or later. Greedy bastards!'

'The Japanese would not have blown up their own –' began Olmeijer. Nye interrupted him with a sharp laugh.

'I don't know how that city got blown up, but it was the excuse everybody needed to start scrapping.' He tilted his glass to his lips. 'I suppose we'll never know how it happened or who did it. But that's not the point. They'd have been fighting by now even if it hadn't happened.'

'I wish you were right!'

I recognised the new voice and turned to see Dempsey walking wearily into the bar. He nodded to me and Nye and placed a dirty hand on the counter. 'Large scotch please, Olmeijer.'

The Dutchman didn't seem pleased to see his latest customer, but he poured the drink and carefully wrote the cost down in his ledger.

There was an embarrassed pause. For all he had interrupted our conversation, Dempsey apparently wasn't prepared to amplify his remark.

'Afternoon, Dempsey,' I said.

He smiled faintly and rubbed at his unshaven chin. 'Hello, Bastable. Moving in?'

'I was looking for Underwood.'

He took a long pull at his drink. 'There's a lot of people looking for Underwood,' he said mysteriously.

'What do you mean?'

He shook his head. 'Nothing.'

'Another drink, Bastable?' said Nye. 'Have this one on me.' And then, as if with a slight effort. 'You, Dempsey?'

'Thanks.' Dempsey finished his drink and put his glass back on the bar. Olmeijer poured another gin, another brandy, another scotch.

Nye took a case of cheroots from his shirt pocket and offered them around. Olmeijer and Dempsey accepted, but I refused. 'What did you mean, just then?' Nye asked Dempsey. 'You don't care about all this, surely? I thought you were the chap so full of oriental fatalism.'

Dempsey turned away. For a moment his dead eyes had seemed to burn with a terrible misery. He took his glass to a nearby table and sat down. 'That's me,' he said.

But Nye wouldn't let it go. 'You weren't in Japan when the bombing started, were you?'

Dempsey shook his head. 'No, China.' I noticed that his hands were shaking as he lifted his glass to his mouth and he seemed to be muttering something under his breath. I thought I heard the words "God forgive me". He finished the drink quickly, got up and shambled towards the door. 'Thanks, Nye. See you later.'

His wasted body disappeared through the doors and I saw him begin to climb the flight of wooden stairs which led up from the lobby.

Nye raised his eyebrows in a quizzical look. He shrugged. 'I think Dempsey has become what we used to call an 'island case'. We had a few of them going native, in the old days, or taking up opium, like him. The stuff's killing him, of course, and he knows it. He'll be dead within six months, I shouldn't wonder.'

'I'd have given him longer than that,' I said feelingly. 'I've known opium smokers who live to a ripe old age.'

Nye drew on his cheroot. 'It's not just the opium, is it? I mean, there's such a thing as a *will* to die. You know that as well as I do.'

I nodded soberly. I had encountered my own share of such desires.

'I wonder what did it,' Nye mused. 'A woman, perhaps. He was an airshipman, you know. Perhaps he lost his ship, or deserted her or something?'

Olmeijer grunted and looked up from his book. 'He's just a weak man. Just weak, that's all.'

'Could be.' I got up. 'I think I'll head back now. Mind if I come up tomorrow? I'd like to be here when Underwood returns.'

'See you tomorrow.' Nye lifted his hand in a salute. 'I wish you the best of luck, Bastable.'

That night I dined on fish and fruit with Hira. I told him about my conversation at the hotel and my second encounter with Dempsey. His earlier remark had aroused my curiosity and I asked Hira if he knew anything at all of Dempsey's reasons for coming to the island.

Hira could add little about the opium eater. 'All I know is that he was in better condition when he arrived than he is now. I don't have much to do with the European community, as you may have noticed.' He looked sardonically at me. 'Englishmen often start acting strangely when they've been out East a few years. Maybe they feel guilty about exploiting us, eh?'

I refused to rise to this and we completed our meal in relative silence.

After dinner we sat back in our chairs and smoked, discussing the health of the coolie I had found. Hira told me he was recovering reasonably quickly. I was just about to go up to bed when the door opened suddenly and a nun rushed into Hira's room. 'Doctor – quickly – it is Underwood!' Her face was full of anxiety. 'He has been attacked. I think he is dying.'

We hurried downstairs to the little entrance hall of the hospital. In the light from the oil lamp I saw Olmeijer and Nye standing there. Their faces were pale and tense and they were staring helplessly down at something which lay on an improvised stretcher they had placed on the floor. They must have carried it all the way from the hotel.

Hira crouched down and inspected the man on the stretcher. 'My God!' he said.

Nye addressed me. 'He was dumped on the steps of the hotel about an hour ago. I think some Chinaman objected to his wife or maybe his daughter running off with Underwood. I don't know.' Grimly he wiped his face with his handkerchief. 'This couldn't have happened before the bloody war...'

I gagged as I got a good look at the battered mess of flesh on the stretcher. 'Poor devil!'

Hira straightened up and looked significantly at me. There was no hope for Underwood. He turned to Nye and Olmeijer. 'Can you take the stretcher up to the ward, please?'

I followed as the two men picked up the stretcher and staggered as they climbed the short flight of steps to the ward. With the nurses, I helped get him onto the bed, but it was plain that virtually every bone in his body had been broken. He was scarcely recognisable as a human being. They had taken their time in beating him up and he couldn't last long.

Hira began to fill a hypodermic. The beaten man's eyes opened and he saw us. His lips moved.

I bent to listen.

'Bloody Chinks... bloody woman... done for me. Found us in the mine... The sheets... Oh, God... The bloody clubs...'

Hira gave him a hefty injection. 'Cocaine,' he said to me. 'It's about all we have now.'

I looked at the next bed and saw the coolie I had rescued staring at Underwood with an expression of quiet satisfaction.

'This couldn't be some sort of retaliation, could it?' I asked Hira.

'Who knows?' Hira looked down at the Australian as the man's eyes glazed and closed again.

Nye put his fist to his lips and cleared his throat. 'I wonder if somebody ought to tell Nesbit...' He looked at Underwood and pursed his lips. 'There'll be hell to pay when Begg hears about this.'

Hira seemed almost amused. 'It could mean the end.'

Thoughtfully, Olmeijer rubbed at his neck. 'Need Begg be told?'

'The man has been attacked,' I said. 'A couple of hours or so and it will be murder. He can't last the night.'

'If Begg goes on the rampage, old boy, we all stand a chance of being murdered,' Nye pointed out. 'Begg will anger the Malays and Chinese so much they're bound to turn on us. These aren't the old days. What do you think a dozen bloody Ghoorkas can do against a thousand coolies?'

There was a glint of malice in Hira's eyes. 'So you don't want me to report this to the Official Representative, gentlemen?'

'Better not,' said Nye. 'We'll all keep mum, eh?'

I watched the nurse cleaning the blood from Underwood's body. The cocaine had knocked him out completely. I walked to the door of the ward and lit a cigarette, watching the mosquitoes and the moths fluttering around the oil lamp in the lobby. From beyond the open door came the sound of the sea striking the stones of the quay. It no longer seemed peaceful. Instead the silence had become ominous. As the other three men joined me I inclined my head.

'Very well,' I said. 'I'll say nothing.'

Next morning New Birmingham was deathly quiet. I walked through empty streets. I felt I was watched by a thousand pairs of eyes as I made my way up to the airpark.

I did not call in at the hotel. There was no point now in hoping to see Underwood there. He had died in the night at the hospital. I carried on past it and stood by one of the ruined hovergyros, kicking at a broken rotor which lay on the weed-grown concrete beside the machine. From the forest behind me came the sounds of dawn. At this hour some of the nocturnal animals were still about and the diurnal inhabitants were beginning to wake. Hornbills, cockatoos, fairy bluebirds and doves fluttered among the trees, filling the air with song and with colour. They seemed to be celebrating something, perhaps the end of the human occupation of the island. The air was rich with the stink of the forest, of animal spoor and rotting tree trunks. I heard the chatter of gibbons and saw tiny shrews skipping along branches heavy with dew. On the wall of the hangar the beady eyes of lizards regarded me coldly as if I had no business to be there.

I turned towards what had been the main control building where the murdered man had locked up his wireless apparatus before going off on what was to prove his final orgy.

The whole building had been sealed before the airship personnel had left. The windows on all three storeys had been covered by steel shutters and it would take special tools and a lot of hard work to get even one of them down. All the doors were locked and barred and I could see where various attempts to open them had failed.

I walked round and round the concrete building, pushing uselessly at the shutters and rattling the handles of the doors. The chirring sounds from the forest seemed to mock my helplessness and at length I stopped by a door which had evidently been in recent use, tried the handle once more, then leaned against the frame, looking back across the deserted park, with its broken bones of flying machines and its rusting mast, at the spruce hotel beyond. The sun glinted on Olmeijer's gilded sign: ROYAL AIR-PARK HOTEL, it said, THE ISLAND'S BEST.

A little later someone came out through the French windows leading from the bar and stood on the verandah. Then they saw me and began to walk slowly through the tall grass towards me.

I recognised the figure and I frowned. What could he want?

Chapter Eight
The Message

I T WAS DEMPSEY, of course. He had shaved and put on a suit slightly cleaner than the one he had worn on the previous day, but he wore the same tattered native shirt underneath it. By the pupils of his eyes I saw he had not yet had his first pipe of opium.

He shuffled towards me, coughing on the comparatively cold air of the early morning. 'I heard about Underwood,' he said. He crossed the cracked concrete and stood looking at me.

I offered him a cigarette which he accepted, fumbling it from my case and trembling slightly as I lit it for him.

'You knew the Chinese were after Underwood, didn't you?' I said. 'That's what you meant yesterday when you said a lot of people were looking for him.'

'Yesterday? I don't remember.' He puffed on the cigarette, drawing the smoke deep into his lungs.

'You might have saved him, Dempsey, if you'd warned someone at the time.'

He straightened up a little and he seemed amused as he glanced towards the forest. 'On the other hand I might have done everyone else more harm. It's a bit of a luxury, a social conscience, isn't it, Bastable?' He felt in his pocket. 'I came to give you this. I found it on the steps.' He held out a Yale key. 'Must have fallen from Underwood's pocket when they dumped him.'

I hesitated before accepting the key. Then I turned and tried it in the lock. The wards clicked back and the door swung open. The interior smelled of stale liquor and burnt rubber.

'All that's left of Underwood is his stink,' said Dempsey. 'Now you're going to try to wireless for help, I suppose.'

'I'll try,' I said. 'If I can get through to Darwin I'll ask them to re-route the first available airship to pick me up – and anyone else who wants to leave the island.'

'Better tell them it's an emergency.' Dempsey waved his hand in the general direction of the town. 'Make no bones about it. There are half a dozen excuses for an uprising now. Begg finding out about Underwood will be just one more. The Chinese are in a mood to slaughter all the Malays and if the whites interfere, they'll probably get together and kill us first. It's true.' A ghost of a smile appeared on his lips. 'I know. I'm in rather closer touch with the natives than most, after all. Underwood was just a beginning.'

I nodded. 'All right. I'll tell Darwin.'

'You know how to work the wireless?'

'I've had some training...'

Dempsey followed me into the gloomy interior of the office. It was a filthy litter of empty beer cans, bottles and bits of broken wireless equipment. He pulled back the shutters and light came through the dusty windows. I saw what could only be the wireless set in one corner and I picked my way across the floor towards it.

Dempsey showed me the pedals underneath the bench. I sat down and put my feet on them. They turned slowly at first and then more easily.

Dempsey inspected the set. 'Seems to be warming up,' he said. He began to fiddle with the dials. There was a faint crackle from the phones. He picked them up and listened, shaking his head. 'Valve trouble, probably. You'd better let me have a go.'

I rose and Dempsey sat down in the chair. After a while he found a screwdriver and took part of the casing off the set. 'It's the valves, all right,' he said. 'There should be a box of spares behind you on the other bench. Could you bring it over?'

I found the box and placed it beside him as he continued to work.

'Did you learn about radios on airships?' I asked him.

He tightened his mouth and went on with the job.

'How did you happen to turn up here?' I said, my curiosity overcoming my tact.

'None of your bloody business, Bastable. There, that should do it.' He screwed in the last valve and began pedalling, but then he fell back in the chair coughing. 'Too bloody weak,' he said. 'You'd better do the pumping, if you wouldn't mind...' He lapsed into another fit of coughing as he got up and I replaced him.

While I pedalled, he twisted the dials again until we heard a faint voice coming through the earphones. Dempsey settled the headset over his ears and adjusted the microphone. 'Hello, Darwin. This is Rowe Island. Over.' He turned a knob.

He flipped a toggle switch and spoke impatiently into the mike. 'No, I'm sorry, I don't know our bloody callsign. Our operator's been killed as a matter of fact. No, we're not a military base. This is Rowe Island in the Indian Ocean and the civilian population is in danger.'

While I continued to pedal the generator, Dempsey told Darwin our situation. There was some confusion, a wait of nearly twenty minutes while the operator checked with his superiors, some more confusion over the location of the island and then at last Dempsey leaned back and sighed. 'Thank you, Darwin.'

As he stripped off the headset he glanced down at me. 'You're lucky. They'll have one of their patrol ships over here in a day or two – if it hasn't been shot down. You'd better tell the others to pack their bags and be ready.'

'I'm very grateful, Dempsey,' I said. 'I don't think I'd have had a chance of getting through if it hadn't been for you.'

The problems with the wireless had exhausted him. He got up and began to rummage around in the office until he found an almost full bottle of rum. He opened it, took a long drink, then offered it to me.

I accepted the bottle and sipped the rum, gasping. It was raw stuff. I handed it back and watched with a certain amount of respect as he finished it.

We left the office and began to walk across the airpark. As we approached the mast he paused and looked up through the girders. The passenger lift was at the top of the mast, presumably left there by the last hasty group to go aboard the ship when it had taken the bulk of the Europeans off the island. 'This won't be any good,' he said. 'Nobody to work it, even if it was in decent condition. The ship will have to come right down. It's going to be a problem. Everybody will have to muck in.'

'Will you help me?'

'If I'm conscious.'

'I heard you commanded an airship once,' I said.

Then I regretted my curiosity for a peculiar look of pained amusement came over his face. 'Yes. Yes, I did. For a very short time.'

I dropped it. 'Let me get you a drink,' I said.

Olmeijer was in his usual spot at the bar, reading his book. Nye was not there. The Dutchman looked up and nodded to us. He made no mention of the previous night's business and I didn't bring it up. I told him that we had managed to get through to Darwin and that they were sending an airship. He seemed unimpressed. I think he enjoyed his rôle as the last hotelier on the island. He would rather have customers who couldn't pay than no customers at all. Dempsey and I took our drinks to one of the tables near the window.

'You've been a great help, Dempsey,' I said.

Cynically he stared at me over the rim of his glass. 'Am I helping? I may be doing you a disservice. Do you really want to go back to all that?'

'I think it's my duty.'

'Duty? To support the last vestiges of a discredited imperialism?'

It was the first time I had heard him utter anything like a political opinion. I was surprised. He sounded like a bit of a Red, I thought. I could think of no answer which wouldn't have been impolite.

He downed the rest of his scotch and stared out over the airpark, speaking as if to himself. 'It's all a question of power and rarely a question of justice.' He looked sharply at me. 'Don't patronise me, Bastable. I don't need your kindness, thanks. If you knew...' He broke off. 'Another?'

I watched Dempsey walk unsteadily to the bar and then get fresh drinks. He brought them back almost reluctantly.

'I'm sorry,' I said. 'It's just – well, you seem to have a lot on your mind. I thought a sympathetic ear…'

There was a very strange look in his eyes now. 'Sympathetic? I wonder how sympathetic you would stay if I told you what was really on my mind. There's a war taking place, Bastable. I heard you speculating yesterday about how it started. I know how the war started. I know who started it, too. It was a bloody accident.'

I restrained my exclamation of astonishment and waited to hear more, but Dempsey leaned back in the wicker chair and closed his eyes, his lips moving as he spoke to himself.

I went to get him another drink, but he was already asleep when I returned. I let him sleep and joined Olmeijer at the bar.

Shortly afterwards Nye came in. He looked tired, as if he had not been to bed since I had seen him.

'Give me a triple gin, Olmeijer, quick. Morning, Bastable. I don't advise you to go back through the town alone. There's a lot of trouble. Big gangs of Malays and Chinese fighting each other. Arson, rape and bloody murder all over the place.'

'Has Begg found out about…?'

'Not yet, but pretty well everyone else knows. He'll hear soon. The Chinese managed to steal a Malay boat last night and buggered off with it – probably poor Underwood's murderers making their getaway. The Malays roughed up some Chinese families. The Chinese retaliated. I think we're in very hot water this time.'

I told him about the wireless message to Darwin and the probability of a ship coming. He looked more than relieved. 'You'd better send one of your chaps into New Brum, Olmeijer. Tell him to let everyone know – to get up here as fast as possible.'

Grumbling, Olmeijer rolled off to find a servant.

Nye walked round to the other side of the bar. 'I think another drink is called for – on the house. Bastable?' I nodded. 'Dempsey?'

I saw that Dempsey had woken up and was making for the

door. He shook his head and said with a tight, crooked smile. 'I've some business in town. Cheerio.'

'It's dangerous,' I said.

'I'll be all right. Hope to see you later, Bastable.'

We watched him leave.

'Poor bastard,' said Nye. He shuddered and downed his gin.

Chapter Nine
Hopes of Salvation

BEGG CAME UP to the hotel in the afternoon and asked suspiciously after Underwood. We said that we had heard he'd had some sort of accident. He didn't believe us, of course, but he had his hands full in the town and couldn't wait to question us further. He'd escorted some clergymen to the hotel and some Chinese nuns from the Catholic mission. They sat huddled in the far corner of the bar and didn't talk much to us. Nesbit's secretary, a round-faced, anxious Bengali, had come with Begg and he remained almost constantly by the window, looking out as if he expected the airship to arrive at any minute. I asked Begg about Dempsey and the soldier glowered at me, muttering that Dempsey had been seen with some of the Chinese 'rebels' and might find himself in real trouble with the authorities if he wasn't careful. I also learned that Hira had decided to stay on at the hospital along with most of his nuns.

By that evening a few more people had drifted up, including two Irish priests who joined the others in the corner. Olmeijer seemed delighted to have so many new guests and rushed around seeing that rooms were prepared for them. Even I received a room on the second floor.

Begg returned looking tired and angry. His normally neat uniform was dusty and he had a bruise over his right eye. He seemed to be blaming Nye and me for his problems and wouldn't speak to us at all on this second visit. He had brought us three of his twelve-man army for protection. The rest were remaining in the town to 'keep order', though from the noise below there was precious little of that, and to protect the Official Representative's residence, for Brigadier Nesbit, it emerged, had elected to stay, along with his valet.

Begg returned a little later. He was alone and as stiff-backed as ever as he guided his horse down the hill and disappeared into the darkness and the cacophony below. I don't believe he was seen alive again.

By midnight the ladies and gentlemen of the cloth had all gone to bed and Nye, Olmeijer and myself were in our usual places at the bar while the little Bengali paced back and forth beside the windows.

Even Nye seemed a trifle nervous and once he expressed the belief that we 'might not quite last out'. Then he, too, went to bed and the Bengali followed him. Olmeijer had his big account book open on the bar and for a while seemed cheerfully engrossed in his arithmetic before closing the book with a crash, nodding goodnight to me, and heaving his huge bulk away to his own quarters.

Now, save for the Ghoorkas on guard outside, I was the only one up. I felt exhausted but not particularly sleepy. I decided to go outside and see if I could detect any activity in the town.

As I entered the lobby I heard voices by the main entrance. I peered out, but the oil lamp wasn't bright enough to show me anything. I opened the door. One of the Ghoorka guards was shouting at a man I could dimly see in the moonlight. The Ghoorka gestured with his bayoneted rifle and the man turned away. For a moment I saw his face in the faint glow from the lamp in the lobby. I pushed past the soldier and hurried outside.

'Dempsey? Is that you?'

He looked back. His shoulders were bowed and his jacket had been ripped. His face was deathly pale, his eyelids almost closed. 'Hello, Bastable.' The speech was slurred. 'Thought this was my hotel.'

'It is.' I went towards him and took a limp arm. 'Come inside.'

The Ghoorkas made no attempt to stop us as I led Dempsey into Olmeijer's. The man was staggering and shivering. A dry retching noise came from his throat. He was gripping something tightly in his right hand. There was no point in questioning him and I did my best to get him up the stairs and along the passage to his room.

The door was unlocked. I half-carried Dempsey in, let him sit on the bed while I lit the oil lamp.

The light revealed a room which was surprisingly neat. The bed was made up and there was no litter. In fact the room was completely impersonal. I got Dempsey onto the bed and he stretched out with a sigh. The shivering came in brief spasms now. He blinked and looked up at me as I took his pulse. 'Thank you very much, Bastable,' he said. 'I thought I might have a word with you.'

'You're in bad shape,' I said. 'Better sleep if you can.'

'They're looting down there,' he said. 'Killing each other. Perhaps it's something in the air...' He coughed and then started to choke. I got him upright and tried to prise the packet he held from his fingers, but he reacted angrily, with surprising strength. He pulled his hand away. 'I can look after myself now, old man.' There were tears in his eyes as he sank back onto the pillow. 'I'm just tired. Sick and tired.'

'Dempsey, you're killing yourself. Let me –'

'I hope you're right, Bastable. It's taking too bloody long, though. I wish I'd had the guts to do it properly.'

I stood up, telling him that I would call back later to see how he was. He closed his eyes and seemed to fall asleep.

I experienced that feeling of impotence common to many who have themselves experienced the relief of drug addiction. I knew only too well that there was little I could do for the poor, tormented wretch. He could only help himself. And Dempsey seemed genuinely haunted, perhaps by a special insight into things as they really were, perhaps by something in himself, some aspect of his own character which he could not reconcile with his moral outlook. For it was becoming increasingly clear that Dempsey, in spite of his denials, had a very moral outlook and that he didn't think much of himself.

I went to my own room along the passage and took off my

jacket and trousers. I lay down on the bed in the darkness, listening to the insects hurling themselves against the woven wire of the window screens. Moonlight flooded the room. Soon I fell into a light sleep.

I woke up suddenly.

My door was creaking as it slowly opened and I looked around for a weapon, thinking that the coolies had attacked the hotel while I slept.

Then, with a sigh of relief, I saw that it was Dempsey. He was leaning almost nonchalantly on the door handle. His face was as pale as ever but he seemed to have recovered his strength.

'Sorry to disturb you, Bastable.'

'Do you need help?' I got up and pulled on my trousers.

'Perhaps I do. There isn't a lot of time now.' He smiled. 'Not "practical" help, though.' His eyes were glazed and dreamy and I realised that he had taken some kind of stimulant to offset the effects of the opium. I hated to think what was happening both to his mind and his body. He sat down heavily on my bed.

'I'm fine.' He spoke as if to reassure himself. 'I just thought I'd drop in for a chat. You wanted a chat, eh? Earlier.'

I sat down in the wicker armchair beside the bed. 'Why not?' I said as cheerfully as I could.

'I told you there's no need to patronise me. I've come to make a sort of confession. I don't know why it should be you, Bastable. Possibly it's just because, well, you're one of the victims. Singapore, and everything...'

'It's over,' I said. 'And it certainly couldn't have been anything to do with you. "The War is ceaseless. The most we can hope for are occasional moments of tranquillity in the midst of the conflict". I quote Lobkowitz.'

His drugged eyes shone for a second with an ironic light. 'You read him, too. I didn't think you were another Red, Bastable.'

'I'm not. Neither, for that matter, is Lobkowitz.'

'It's a matter of opinion.'

'Besides, I speak from a great deal of experience.'

'As a soldier?'

'I have been a soldier. But I have come to the conclusion that the human race is constantly in a state of tension, that those tensions make us what we are and that they will often lead to wars. The greater our ingenuity at inventing weapons, the worse the wars become.'

'Oh, indeed, I agree with that last statement.' He sighed. 'But don't you believe it's possible for people to acknowledge the tensions and yet make harmony from those tensions, just as music is made?'

'My experience would have it otherwise. My hope, of course, is another thing. But I see little point in such a debate when the world is currently in such an appalling state. This frightful Armageddon will probably not be over until the last aerial man-o'-war falls from the skies.'

'You really see it as Armageddon?'

I could not tell him what I knew: that I had already passed through three alternative versions of our world and in each seen the most hideous destruction of civilisation; that I myself felt responsibility for at least one of those great wars. I merely shrugged. 'Perhaps not. Perhaps there will be peace. The Russians and the Japanese have always been at loggerheads. What I can't understand is how Britain failed to stop it and why the Japs turned on us with such ferocity.'

'I know why,' he said.

I patted his arm. 'Do you know? Or is it the opium telling you? I've been fond of opium in my time, Dempsey. My appearance was once not too different from yours. Can you believe that?'

'I thought there was something. But why –?'

'I took part in a crime,' I said. 'A very wicked crime. And then...' I paused. 'Then I became lost.'

'But you're not lost now?'

'I'm lost now, but I've decided to make the best of things. I've become a good airshipman. I love airships. There is nothing like being at the helm of one.'

'I know,' he said. 'Of course I know. But I'll never go aloft again.'

'Something happened? An accident?'

A small, wretched laugh came out of his throat. 'You could call it that.' He fumbled in his pocket and took something out, placing it on the bed beside him. It was a syringe. 'This stuff makes you want to talk, unlike the opium.' From his other pocket he took a handful of ampoules and placed them neatly beside the syringe.

I got up. 'I can't let you –'

His eyes were full of pain. 'Can't you?' The words had intense significance. They silenced me. I sat down again with a shrug.

He put his hand over the syringe and the ampoules and stared at me grimly. 'You've no choice. I've no choice. Our choices are all gone, Bastable. For my own part, one way or another, I'm going to kill myself. You can take that for granted. And I'd rather you let me do it this way.'

'I know the state of mind you're in, old man. I was in it once. And, without wishing to make a stupid comparison, I feel I've had as much reason as anyone on Earth to want to do it. But you see me alive. I've gone beyond suicide.'

'Well, I haven't.' Yet he hesitated. 'I wanted to talk to you, Bastable.'

'Then talk.'

'I can't without this stuff.'

Once again, I shrugged. But I knew what it was to have an unbearable weight on one's conscience. 'Take a little, then,' I suggested. 'Just a little. And talk. But don't try to kill yourself, at least until you have confided in me.'

He shuddered. 'Confided! What a word. You sound like a priest.'

'Just a fellow sufferer.'

'You're a bit of a prig, Bastable.'

I smiled. 'So I've been told by others.'

'Yet you're a decent sort. And you don't judge people much. Only yourself. Am I right?'

'I'm afraid you probably are.'

'You don't hold with socialism, do you? With my brand, at any rate.'

'What's your brand?'

'Well, Kropotkin called it anarchism. But the word's come to mean something very different in the public mind.'

'You don't blow things up, then?'

Again he began to shake. He tried to speak, but no words came. I had, accidentally, struck a nerve. I moved towards him. 'I'm sorry, old man. I didn't mean…'

He drew away from me. 'Get out,' he said. 'For God's sake leave me alone.'

I felt very foolish. 'Dempsey. Believe me. I meant nothing serious. I was being facetious.'

'Get out!' It was almost a shout, a plea. 'Get out, Bastable! The ship's coming. Save yourself, if you can.'

'I'm not going to let you kill yourself.' I grabbed up some of the ampoules. 'I want to listen, Dempsey.'

He fell back on the bed. His head hit the wall. He groaned. His body fell sideways. He had passed out.

I checked his pulse and his breathing, then I went to look for help. I recalled that there was a missionary doctor now in the hotel.

As I reached the ground floor and headed to the bar where I would find Olmeijer, I heard people near the windows begin to mutter, then to talk excitedly. The darkness outside was suddenly broken by a beam of bright light.

Olmeijer saw it. He seemed disappointed. When I reached him he muttered: 'It's the ship. It's coming in.' He was going to lose all his customers.

I told him to send someone to look after Dempsey, and then I ran from the hotel towards the park. My intention was to guide the ship to her mast.

To my astonishment there were already uniformed men on the ground. I rushed towards one. They must have parachuted from the ship.

'Thank God you've come,' I said.

The nearest figure turned. I looked into the expressionless face of a captain in the Imperial Japanese Army. 'Go back inside,' he said. 'Tell them that if anyone attempts to leave the building it will be bombed to rubble.'

Chapter Ten
Lost Hopes

We WERE NEVER to discover how the Japanese had found us. Either they had traced the wireless messages or they had trailed and destroyed the rescue ship. The fact was there was nothing we could do against them.

Soon Olmeijer's place was full of small soldiers in off-white uniforms, their politeness to their prisoners contrasting with the long bayonets fixed on their rifles. The officer had a grim, self-controlled manner, but occasionally, it seemed to me, an expression of straightforward hatred crossed his face when he looked at us. We stood with our baggage (if we had any) in the middle of the floor. The women were sent aboard first. The Japs had managed to get the mast working and had winched the ship to ground level.

It was a large, modern ship. I was surprised that they had felt they could spare it, merely to pick up a few civilians, but I guessed that it had already been patrolling the area when its captain had been alerted to our presence.

Nye was closer to the windows than I. He turned to me. 'My God, they've fired the town!' He pointed, addressing the officer. 'You damned barbarians! Why did you have to do that?'

'Barbarians?' The Japanese captain smiled sardonically. 'I am amused you should think that of us, Englishman, after what you did to us.'

'We did nothing! Whatever happened was a mistake. It suits you to blame us.'

The captain dismissed this. 'However, we have not set fire to the buildings. It's your own workers. A riot of some kind. I gather they're on their way, en masse.'

It was credible. Thinking that they might get free of the island aboard a ship, the coolies could have persuaded themselves that it was possible to capture the vessel and sail it to freedom.

'Don't worry,' continued the Jap, 'we intend to protect you as well as ourselves.' His voice, pleasant and yet sharp, had a degree of contempt in it. I saw that Nye was upset by the exchange.

Nye blustered a little, but he could not argue with the man's logic. We had far more to fear from the coolies, immediately at any rate, than from the Japanese.

It was possible to smell the smoke from where we stood; and traces of red firelight were reflected in the windows and mirrors of Olmeijer's. The Dutchman had given up his despair and was now offering to serve drinks to his new customers (as he saw them). I think he had half a hope that Rowe Island was to be occupied and that he would be allowed to continue (as a neutral) to run the hotel. The soldiers motioned him to join us at the centre of the floor. He sat down on one of his own tables. I thought he might be going to cry. 'I am Dutch,' he told the officer. 'I am a private hotelier. A civilian. You cannot just remove me from the place I have spent most of my life building.'

'We have orders to arrest all Europeans,' said the Japanese. 'And you are most definitely European, sir. We have nothing against the Dutch. However, if you were to be realistic you would understand that your country is an ally of Britain and that it is only a matter of days before you are involved in this war.'

'But we are not involved today!'

'Not as far as I know. Essentially our mission is to evacuate you from the island.'

'And what will happen to us?' asked Nye, still in an aggressive mood.

'You will be interned for the duration of hostilities.'

'We're not spies!'

'Neither were those you interned in your South African war, you'll recall.'

'That was entirely different. The reasons were complex...'

'Our reasons are also complex. You are foreign belligerents, potentially dangerous to our war effort.'

'My God! And you infer that *we* are hypocritical!'

'You will not deny, sir, that this is effectively a military base.'

'It's a mining concern!'

'But very useful as a fuelling station. We shall be leaving troops behind. A garrison. This is conquered territory. When you go outside you will see that the Japanese flag now flies over the airfield.'

'Then why remove us? Is it usual practice?'

'It has become so. You will be interned at the European civilian prisoner-of-war camp on Rishiri.'

'Where the hell is Rishiri?'

'It's a small island off the coast of Hokkaido,' said one of the Irish priests. Hokkaido was the large island north of Honshu, Japan's main island. 'Quite a pretty place, as I recollect. We did some missionary work there a few years ago.'

The Japanese captain smiled. 'You'll have to concentrate on Europeans now, Father. But you will have plenty of time to make converts, I'm sure.'

Nye fell silent. He finished the last of his gin fizz with the air of a man who was not likely to see another again for many years.

With the women gone, the older men were next to be taken from the room. The Japanese were by no means cruel to us. Those who were too weak to move easily were helped by soldiers, who even carried bundles and suitcases for their prisoners, shouldering their rifles in order to do so. There was no point in trying to resist them, and they knew it. The ship's guns could have destroyed Olmeijer's in seconds, and we had so many other people to consider.

A few minutes later the Japanese captain went outside and then returned to issue commands to his men. The rifles were unshouldered and they ran into the night, leaving only one man to guard us. We heard shouts, then shots; a terrible scream which rose and fell, then rose again: the scream of a mob.

'The coolies!' Olmeijer waddled towards the window. We all followed him. The guard did not attempt to stop us. He stood by the door, looking back in some trepidation.

The red firelight silhouetted the Malays and Chinese now trying to rush the airship which was defended by a line of well-disciplined Japanese soldiers. The coolies were badly armed, though one or two had rifles and pistols. For the most part the best weapons they had been able to muster were parangs and large picks and hammers. Panic, anger and hatred drove them against the rifle-fire. Not a bullet was wasted. They continued to fall until the corpses of the dead and wounded hampered the advance of those who still lived.

They appeared to have some sort of rough organisation, however, because they now fell back. Their efforts were being directed by a figure in a crumpled European suit armed with a pistol.

I recognised him as he disappeared with the surviving coolies into the darkness.

How Dempsey had managed to leave the hotel in the condition in which I'd last seen him I didn't know. But there he was, capering like a maniac, helping the coolies in their desperate attack.

They came in from two sides now, trying to divide the Japanese fire. This time two or three soldiers were hit. They retreated in order until they were closer to the ship.

Nye whispered to me: 'This would be our chance to get out of here. Rush the guard and get into the bush, eh?'

I considered this. 'Between the Japanese and the surviving coolies we'd have no chance,' I said. 'There isn't any food to speak of, either.'

'You've no guts, Bastable.'

'Perhaps. But I've a great deal of experience,' I told him. 'There's quite likely to be an exchange of civilian prisoners of war. We could all be in England in a matter of weeks.'

'But what if we're not?'

'My view is that we'll be better off with the Japs for the moment. If we're going to escape, let's escape from somewhere closer to Russian territory.'

Nye was disgusted. 'You're not exactly impetuous, are you, Bastable?'

'I suppose not.' I had seen too much of warfare and destruction in three worlds to place much value on romantic, impulsive schemes. I preferred to bide my time. I let Nye think what he liked and noticed that, without my agreement, he made no attempt to get free of Olmeijer's.

The firing outside continued but was more spasmodic. Below, in the town, the flames were rising higher. Firelight was reflected on the white hull of the Japanese ship as it swayed slowly at its mast.

Dempsey must have made full use of his stimulants. From time to time I saw him, sometimes with a pistol, sometimes with a parang, leaping here and there amongst the shrubs and trees surrounding the airpark. He was demented. For what obscure, perhaps sentimental, reasons he had leagued himself with the coolies, I could not fathom. Perhaps he saw hope in turning them against the Japanese and saving the Europeans, but I doubted it. In his ragged jacket and trousers he was distinguished from the rabble largely by the fact that he was evidently in control. He had been trained in the navy and his old instincts for leadership were coming out.

The Japanese had also identified him and their fire was concentrated against him. He was courting their bullets. To me, it seemed he wanted them to kill him. He had been talking of suicide and perhaps this was in his eyes a more positive way of dying. Nonetheless he showed courage and I could only admire the way he harried the Japs, sending in coolies from every direction, sometimes at once, sometimes from a single angle.

His eyes glittered, filled with flames. There was a strange, cold grin on his lips. And for a moment I was consumed by an enormous sense of comradeship for him. It was as if I looked at some other incarnation of myself, in those dreadful days before I had learned to live with the guilt, the pain and the hopelessness of my own situation.

Then Dempsey rushed for the ship, all the remaining coolies at his back. He hacked down two soldiers before they could defend themselves. He fenced with the parang, warding off bayonets and bullets. He took another two of the Japanese and had actually reached the gangway into the gondola when, both arms lifted as if to some blood-greedy battle-god, he dropped.

I saw his body lying spreadeagled on the gangway. It twitched for a moment or two. I didn't know if a bullet had struck him or if the stimulants had caused a stroke. The captain, sword in hand, ran up to the body and turned it over, instructing two of his men to drag it inside.

I heard one of the soldiers utter his name: 'Dempsey'. And I wondered how on earth they could know him.

With Dempsey down, the coolies were quickly scattered. The captain returned to Olmeijer's and ordered the rest of us aboard the ship. I asked him: 'How's the white man? Is he shot? Did he collapse?' But the captain refused to answer.

Nye said: 'Look here, captain. You could tell us if Dempsey's alive or dead!'

The Japanese drew in his breath and looked hard at Nye. 'You have certain rights as a civilian prisoner of war. Captain Dempsey also has certain rights. However, I am not obliged to answer enquiries as to the fate of another prisoner.'

'You inhuman devil. It's not a question of rights, but simple decency!'

The Japanese captain gestured with his sword and gave a command in his own tongue. The guards began to march us out.

As we left, I heard him say: 'If we were not a civilised people none of you would be alive now. And Captain Dempsey would have been torn to pieces by my men.'

The captain seemed mad. Perhaps he did not enjoy his trade. Many soldiers did not, when real warfare developed.

I wondered what crime Dempsey had committed to make him so loathed by those who believed him guilty of it. It was almost certain, anyway, that he had paid the price of the crime with his life. I regretted very much that he had not had time to tell me his own story.

An hour later we were aloft, leaving the remnants of Rowe Island and its population behind. Through a small porthole I could see the flames spreading through the town. They had even caught some of the foliage. Small figures ran about in the inferno. It was still possible to hear shots as the Japanese continued to defend their newly conquered territory.

Our quarters were crowded, but not intolerable. Dempsey was not amongst us. Everyone assumed he had been killed.

It was dawn by the time we had gained our cruising altitude. Most of us were silent, dozing to the steady drumming of the engines. I suppose we were all wondering what would become of us once we reached the civilian camp on Rishiri. If the war continued as I had known other wars to continue, then it might be years before we were free.

I realised, with no particular dismay, that I might even die of old age before this particular conflict were resolved.

I was almost relieved that in no way was my fate any longer in my own hands.

Book Two

'Neither Master nor Slave!'

Chapter One
The Camp on Rishiri

THE CIVILIAN PRISONER-OF-WAR camp was well organised and clean. The food was simple and adequate and our treatment was by no means harsh. There was a permanent Red Cross supervisor and a representative of the Swiss Government who had elected at the invitation of the Japanese to act as a sort of umpire. There were civilians of most nationalities here and those belonging to neutral countries (no longer the Dutch) were efficiently repatriated, so long as they could prove their identity and place of origin. There were a good many angry Poles, Bohemians and Latvians present, for instance. Technically they were Russian citizens, but vociferously denied their loyalty to any land save their own. Since Poles and Slovaks were fighting in Russian armies there was not a great deal of weight to their protestations.

I found the mixture of races fascinating and made the most of my imprisonment to learn as much as I could about the world in which I had found myself. Here was a future in which O'Bean had not existed, yet it contained many of the inventions familiar to me in that future where I had originally encountered General O.T. Shaw. It seemed that whether they were the work of an individual genius or a variety of hard-working scientists, the airships and the subaquatic boats, the electrical wonders, the wireless telegraph and so on, would nonetheless come into existence at some time. In this world Britain's Empire was even larger than in my own. Certain mainland territories in South and Central America were hers, as were some parts of what I had known as the Southern United States. These had been regained, it appeared, during the American Civil War, when Britain had lent positive support to the Confederacy in return for control over coastal regions. With the victory of the Confederacy it had suited everyone, I learned, to retain this contact. The lands had been leased from the CSA for a period of a hundred years. This meant that in thirty years' time, the Confederacy would reclaim them. I was curious as to whether slavery continued to flourish and learned to my surprise that not only did it not, but that economically it had suited everyone to see a strong black middle class emerging. In America there was greater racial equality than in my own day! North and South were virtually autonomous and these smaller units seemed to have produced greater coherence rather than less. Although America was not quite so rich in industry, not quite so powerful a military nation, she seemed in many other ways to have benefited from the truce which had followed the civil war and allowed both sides to recover and begin to trade.

France, on the other hand, was no longer a Great Power. She had never recovered from the Franco-Prussian Wars. Germany now controlled much of the old French Empire and the French themselves seemed content enough in the main, without the responsibilities of their colonies. Germany had become a close ally of Britain, although not bound to join in the current conflict. She formed part of an alliance with the Scandinavian countries, a very powerful trading pact which suited everyone. Austria-Hungary mouldered on, a romantic, decaying Empire, constantly in debt, constantly being helped out by richer nations. The only new Great Power of any significance was the Ottoman Empire, which had expanded significantly into Africa and the Middle East to form a strong Islamic union. Greece, I learned, was all but non-existent. Most of her people were now Moslems and to all intents and purposes Turkish. The Japanese Empire controlled large areas of what had been China and her inroads along borders of the Russian Empire had been the chief reason for the present struggle. I learned why the Japanese attacked British targets with far greater ferocity than they attacked others. They believed that Britain had deliberately started the war, with a raid on Hiroshima. I was reminded of my own part – my own guilt – in a similar raid, when I had sailed aboard the flagship of General Shaw.

If I had known only one world I might have thought that History was repeating itself, but I knew that it was human nature which lay at the root of History and that no matter where I found myself I was bound to discover superficial similarities expressing and exemplifying that nature. It was human idealism and human impatience and human despair which continued to produce these terrible wars. Human virtues and vices, mixed and confused in individuals, created what we called 'History'. Yet I could see no way in which the vicious circle of aspiration and desperation might ever be broken. We were all victims of our own imagination. This I had realised in all my strange journeyings across what Mrs Persson calls 'the multiverse'. The very thing which makes us human, which produces the best, is also the thing which will make us behave worse than the maddest wild beast could ever behave. We live through example and emulation which can turn into envy if circumstances create for us misfortunes. That is all I have come to believe, and I am not entirely sure I believe that. But I am reconciled to human nature, if not to human folly, and that is what my own particular misfortunes have achieved for me.

Olmeijer was soon in his element once again. He somehow managed to get himself put in charge of the camp shop and ran it with all the grandeur of a Chef de la Maison at the Ritz.

Nye joined a group of English and Australian merchant seamen who had been captured at the fall of Shanghai. They spent most of their time choosing sides for Rugby football games and talking about Home. I supposed that this was how they managed to avoid thinking too much about the truth of their situation, but I could only stand half an hour or so of their schoolboy stuff. I knew very well that not long before my first visit to Teku Benga I might well have joined in with some enthusiasm. I had changed beyond redemption. I would never be quite the same as the idealistic and naïve young army officer who had first led his men into the mountains in search of the bandit, Sharan Khang. I felt, indeed, like a cross between Rip Van Winkle and the Flying Dutchman, with a touch of the Wandering Jew besides. I sometimes felt that I had lived for as long as the human race had existed.

Quite soon after arriving at the camp I myself fell in with a mixed bag of civilian airshipmen, the survivors of a variety of wrecks. Some had been accidentally shot down, others had been rescued by Japanese patrols. Some had simply been lost in the general chaos and wandered into Japanese hands. I learned that all merchant airships now moved in convoys these days, protected by military vessels.

It was about a week later that 'Peewee' Wilson attached himself to me. He was a thin-faced, bulbous man, with an awkward, unspontaneous way of moving, a flat forehead and cheekbones and a reddish discolouration under the eyes of the sort I often identify with a certain mental imbalance. He approached me as I came out of Olmeijer's hut. He regarded me, he said, as a fellow intellectual, someone who had 'a bit more education than most of these riff-raff'. Since there were a number of clergymen and academics amongst the prisoners in our compound alone, as well as a couple of journalists, I did not find his remarks particularly flattering. He wore a khaki shirt and a striped tie, grey flannel trousers and, no matter what the temperature, would often have on a tweed sports jacket with leather patches on the elbows. He was a bore. He was, in fact, the camp bore. Every army unit has one, every airship crew has one, every office and factory in the world doubtless has one. However, Wilson was, I'll admit, a bit above the average bore.

He drew me across the compound to the wire fence corner. Leaning against one of the struts of the fence was a short, moody Slav in a dirty peasant shirt. I had seen him before. His name was Makhno and he was from the Ukraine. For bizarre idealistic reasons of his own he had elected to make his way to Tokyo in the cause of international brotherhood. He was an anarchist, I gathered, of the old Kropotkin school and, I thought then, like most anarchists would rather talk than anything else. He was a likeable enough fellow who, having failed to convert the camp, kept his own counsel. Wilson introduced us. 'This chap's not too good with the English,' he said. 'I talk a spot of Rooshian, but I'm having trouble getting through to him. We were talking about money.'

'You're trying to buy something?' I asked.

'No, no. *Money.* International finance and that.'

'Aha.' I exchanged glances with the Ukrainian, who raised a sardonic eyebrow.

'Now I'm a socialist, right?' continued Wilson. 'Have been all my life. You might ask what we mean by the word socialism, and you'd be correct in doing so, because socialism can mean many different things to many different people...' He went on in this vein, doubtless word for word repeating himself for the nth time. There are some people who never appear to realise to what degree they have this habit. I have come to believe that it has the effect on them of a soothing lullaby sung to themselves. It has a completely opposite effect, of course, on anyone attempting (or forced) to listen to them.

The anarchist, Makhno, was not bothering to listen. It was obvious that he could understand many of the words but that he had instinctively recognised Wilson's type.

'Now *this* chap,' Wilson stabbed an unhealthy finger in Makhno's direction, 'would call himself a socialist. I suppose the term would be "anarcho-socialist". That is to say, he believes in the brotherhood of man, the emancipation of the working classes of the world and so on and so forth. He comes, after all, from a so-called socialist country, though what it's doing with an emperor still there, for all he's got no real power, I don't know. And he's against his own government.'

'The Russian government,' said Makhno. 'I am against all governments. Including the so-called Ukrainian Rada, which is only a puppet of the Central Government in Petersburg.'

'Just so,' said Wilson, dismissing this. 'So you're a socialist and you're against socialists. Am I right or wrong?'

'Kerensky's Duma is socialist in name only,' said Makhno in gloomy, Slavic tones. 'In name only.'

'Exactly my own point. Not proper socialists. Just Tories under another name, right?'

'Politicians,' said Makhno laconically.

'That's where you're wrong, old chap. Just because they're not real socialists doesn't mean that real socialists can't make good politicians.'

I was already trying to extricate myself from this, but Wilson held onto my arm. 'Hang on a minute, old man. I want you to umpire this one. Now, what do we mean by this word "politics" of ours? See, I'm an engineer by profession, and I like to think a pretty good one. To me politics is just a matter of getting the engineering right. If you have a machine which functions properly without much attention, then it's obviously a good machine. That's what politics should be about. And if the machine has simple working parts which any layman can understand, then it's, as it were, your democratic machine. Am I right or am I wrong?'

'Crazy,' said Makhno, and scratched his nose.

'What?'

'You're not right or wrong. You're crazy.'

I was amused by this and Makhno could tell, but Wilson was baffled.

'Sane, I'd say,' he said. 'Very sane indeed. Like a good machine. That's sane, isn't it? What's more sane than a properly functioning steam turbine, for instance?'

'Rationalist nonsense,' pronounced Makhno, and rolled the 'r' in that ironic way only Slavs have.

'And what about your own romantic twaddle?' Wilson wanted to know. 'Blow everything up and start again, eh?'

'No worse a solution than yours. But this is not what I argued.'

'It's what it comes down to, old chap. That's your anarchism for you. Boom!' And he laughed as one who had never known humour.

Although I felt sorry for Makhno (while having little sympathy with his politics) I had had quite enough of this. With a murmur of vague apology I began to move away, to where some of my acquaintances were standing, smoking their pipes and talking airship talk, which at that moment was preferable to anything Wilson had to offer.

Wilson stopped me. 'Hang on just a sec, old man. What I want you to tell me is this: without government, who makes the decisions?'

'The individual,' said Makhno.

I shrugged. 'Given the hypothesis as it's put,' I said, 'our Ukrainian friend is absolutely right. Who else could make a decision?'

'Just for himself?'

'By consensus,' said Makhno.

'Ha!' Wilson was triumphant. 'Ha! And what's that but democratic socialism. Which is exactly what I believe in.'

'I thought you believed in machines.' I couldn't resist this jab.

Wilson missed my small irony as he had missed all Makhno's. 'A democratic – socialist – machine,' he said, as if to a child.

'That is not anarchism,' said Makhno stubbornly. But he was not trying to convince Wilson. If anything, he was trying to drive him away.

'I can see some of my pals want a word,' I said to Wilson. I winked at Makhno and made off. But Wilson pursued me. 'You're an airshipman by all accounts, as are these fellows. Don't you believe in using the best machinery, the engines least likely to let you down, the control systems which will work as simply as possible...?'

'Airships aren't countries,' I said. Unfortunately an unsuspecting second officer from the destroyed *Duchess of Salford* heard me without noticing Wilson.

'They can be,' he said. 'Like small countries. I mean, everyone has to learn to get on together...'

I left him to Wilson. When he realised what he had let himself in for a look of patent dismay crossed his young face. I waved at him behind Wilson's back and sauntered off.

It was to be one of my easier escapes from the Bore of Rishiri. The fact that I was a prisoner and beginning, like many others, to fret a great deal was bad enough. It was Purgatory. But 'Peewee' was making it Hell. I am still surprised that nobody murdered him. He became impossible to avoid.

At first we tried joshing him to get rid of him and then laughing at him, then downright rudeness, but it was useless to try to insult him or alter him in his course. We would sometimes offend him, but he would either laugh it off or, if hurt, return in a few minutes. And I had everyone's sympathy because he continued, no matter what I said or did, to claim me as his closest friend.

I think that must be why, when Nye approached me with his half-baked escape plan, I agreed to join in against all common sense. He and his fellow rugger enthusiasts meant to go under the wire at night and try to capture one of the two Japanese motor torpedo boats which had recently anchored in Rishiri's tiny harbour. From there Nye and Co. intended to try for the Russian mainland which had not fallen to the Japs.

There had been a number of attempted escapes, of course, but all of them had been unsuccessful. Our guards were vigilant; there were two small scouting airships keeping the tiny island under surveillance. There were searchlights, dogs, the whole paraphernalia of a prison. Moreover the island was used as a fuelling station for raids against Russia (which is why we were there – to stop the base from being bombed) so it usually had several large airships at mast near the harbour.

It was true, as Nye argued, that no military aerial vessels were in evidence at that moment, but I was not sure that, as he put it, this was 'the best chance of getting clear we'll ever have'.

I did believe that there was a small chance of escape as well as a fair chance of being killed or wounded. But I argued to myself that even if I were wounded I should spend time in the hospital away from Wilson.

'Very well, Nye,' I said. 'You can count me in.'

'Good man.' He patted my shoulder.

That night we assembled in twos and threes at Olmeijer's shop. The Dutchman was not in evidence. He would have been too portly to have squeezed himself into the tunnel Nye and his rugger chums had been digging. It was usual to meet in the hut in the evening, to play table tennis or the variety of board games supplied by the Red Cross. We had only occasional trouble from the guards, who were inclined to look in on us at random. Because they did not check our numbers, we stood a fair chance of all getting down the tunnel before they suspected anything. A few of the airshipmen had elected to stay behind to cover us.

Nye was to go first and I was to go last. One by one the men disappeared into the earth. And it was as I was about to follow them that I realised Fate was almost certainly singling me out for unusual punishment. Wilson walked though the door of the hut.

I was halfway down. I think I remember smiling at him weakly.

'My lord, old man! What are you up to?' He asked. Then he brightened. 'An escape, eh? Good show. A secret is it? Shan't breathe a word. I take it anyone can join in.'

'Um,' I said. 'Actually Nye...'

'My pal Nye, eh? His idea. Jolly good. That's all right with me, old man. I trust Nye implicitly. And he'd want me along.'

One of the airshipmen near the window hissed that a couple of guards were on their way.

I ducked into the tunnel and began to wriggle along it. There was no time to argue with Wilson. I heard his voice behind me.

'Make way for a little 'un.'

I knew that he had joined me in the tunnel before the light vanished as the airshipmen above replaced the floor boards.

I seemed to crawl for eternity, with Wilson muttering and apologising, constantly bumping into my feet, criticising what he called the 'poor engineering job' of the tunnel. He wondered why they hadn't thought of asking him for his expert help.

We emerged into sweet-smelling darkness. Behind us was the wire and the lights of the camp. We were close to the earth road which wound down to the harbour. Nye and the merchant seamen were whispering and gesticulating in the darkness, just as if they were still choosing sides for a game.

Wilson said in a voice which seemed unnaturally loud, even for him: 'What's the problem? Need a volunteer?'

Nye came up to me urgently. 'Good God, man. Why did you tell him?'

'I didn't. He found out just as the guards were on their way.'

'I thought you could do with an extra chap,' said Wilson. 'So I volunteered. Don't forget I'm an expert engineer.'

I heard someone curse and murmur: 'Shoot the blighter.' Peewee, of course, was oblivious.

Nye sighed. 'We'd better start getting down to the harbour. If we're separated –'

He was interrupted by the unmistakeable growl of airship engines high overhead. 'Damn! That complicates things.'

The sound of the engines grew louder and louder and it was evident that the ships were coming in lower. We began to duck and weave through the shrubs and trees at the side of the road, heading for the harbour.

Then, suddenly, there was light behind us, and gunfire, the steady pounding of artillery. A dying scream as a bomb descended some distance from the camp. Up the road came several trucks full of soldiers, as well as a couple of armoured cars and some motor bicycles. The firing continued until I realised that the ships were attacking. Something whizzed past me, just above my head. It felt like a one-man glider. These ingenious devices were far more manageable than parachutes in landing troops. It seemed there was a raid on and we had become caught in the middle of it.

Nye and his lads decided not to vary from their plan. 'We'll use the confusion,' he said.

Wilson called: 'I say, steady on. Perhaps we should wait and see what –'

'No time!' shouted Nye. 'We don't know what this is all about. Let's get to that boat.'

'But suppose –'

'Shut up, Wilson,' I said. I was prepared to follow Nye's lead. I felt I had little choice now.

'Wait!' cried the engineer. 'Let's just stop and think for a minute. If we keep our heads –'

'You're about to lose yours to a samurai sword,' called Nye. 'Now for God's sake shut up, Wilson. Either stay where you are or come with us quietly.'

'Quietly? I wonder what you mean to say when you say –'

His droning voice was a greater source of fear than any bombs or bullets. We all put on an excellent burst of speed. By now machine guns were going, both from the ground and from the rear. I have never prayed before for another human being's death, but I prayed that night that somebody would take Wilson directly between the eyes and save us.

The Japanese were all making for the camp. As a result we were lucky. They weren't looking for escaped prisoners just yet. Even when we were spotted, we were taken for enemy soldiers. We were shot at, but we were not pursued.

We reached the outskirts of the town. Getting through the streets unobserved was going to be the difficult part.

Again we were lucky in that whatever was going on behind us was diverting all troops, all attention. It was Wilson crying: 'I say, you fellows, wait for me!' that brought us the greatest danger. A small detachment of Japanese infantry heard his voice and immediately began to fire along the alley we had entered. Nye went down, together with a couple of others.

I knelt beside Nye. I tested his pulse. He had been shot in the back of the head and was quite dead. Another chap was dead, also, but the survivor was only slightly wounded. He got his arm over my shoulder and we continued to make for the harbour. By this time we were fairly hysterical and were yelling wildly at Wilson as Japanese soldiers opened fire again behind us. 'Shut up, you damned fool! Nye is dead!'

'Dead? He should have been more careful...'

'Shut up, Wilson!'

We got to the quayside and went straight into the water, as planned, swimming for the nearest boat, a white-and-red blur in the misty electric light from the harbour. I heard Wilson behind me.

'I say, you chaps. I say! Didn't you realise I couldn't swim?'

This intelligence seemed to lend me greater energy. Supporting the wounded man, I swam slowly towards the MTB. Some of the seamen were already climbing its sides. I was relieved to hear no further gunshots. Perhaps we had managed to surprise them, after all.

By the time I eventually got to the MTB a rope ladder had been thrown down for me. I lifted the wounded man onto it, holding it while he ascended. I think I could still hear Wilson's dreadful cries from the harbour:

'I say, chaps. Hang on a minute. Can somebody send a boat to fetch me?'

I hardened my heart. At that moment I must admit I didn't give a fig for Wilson's life.

By the time I reached the deck I was gasping with exhaustion. I looked around me, expecting to see captured Japanese sailors. Instead I saw the white uniforms of Russian Navy personnel. A young lieutenant, his cap on the side of his head, his tunic unbuttoned, a revolver and a sabre in his hands, saluted me with his sword. 'Welcome aboard, sir,' he said in perfect English. He grinned at me with that wild, careless grin which only Russians have. 'We both appear to have had the same idea,' he said. 'I am Lieutenant Mitrofanovitch, at your service. We took this boat only twenty minutes before you arrived.'

'And the airships back there?'

'Russian. We are rescuing the prisoners, I hope, at this very moment.'

'You're using an awful lot of stuff for a few prisoners,' I said.

'While the prisoners are on the island,' said Mitrofanovitch pragmatically, 'we cannot bomb the fuelling station.'

One of the English seamen said. 'Poor bloody Nye. He died for absolutely nothing.'

I leaned on the rail. From the quayside I could still hear Wilson's awful voice, pleading and desperate: the wailing of a frightened child.

Chapter Two

Back in Service

IF SOMEONE HAD told me, before I ever entered the temple at Teku Benga, that I should one day be glad to join the Russian Service, I should not only have laughed at them I should, if they had persisted, probably have punched them on the nose. In those days Russia was the greatest menace to our frontiers in India. There was often the threat of open war, for it was well-known that they had territorial ambitions in Afghanistan, if nowhere else. The fact that the Japanese Empire and the Russian Empire had clashed over which parts of South-East Asia and China came under their control was probably fortunate for the British. The war might well have taken a different turn, with Japan and Britain as allies, if Russian ambitions had not, in this world, been diverted towards the crumbling remains of the Chinese Empire. A great deal of the reason for this, of course, was Kerensky himself. The old President of Russia (and the chief power in the so-called Union of Independent Slavic Republics – fundamentally the countries conquered by Imperial Russia before the socialist Revolution) was anxious to keep the friendship of Europe and America and this meant that he had become extremely cautious about offending us. Russia needed to import a great many manufactured goods even now, and she needed markets for her agricultural produce. Moreover she required as much foreign investment as she could get and was especially interested in attracting British and American capital. She had taken huge steps forward since the successful – and almost bloodless – Revolution of 1905 which had occurred at a time when another war between Russia and Japan was brewing. Her brand of humanist socialism had produced almost universal literacy and her medical facilities were amongst the best in the world. She had produced a thriving and liberal middle class and it was very rare, these days, to encounter the kind of poverty for which Russia, when I was a boy, was famous. All in all, even amongst the most conservative people, there was no doubt that Russia and her dominions were much improved by Kerensky and his socialists.

Whatever the historical reasons, there was nothing dishonourable in joining the Russians against our common enemy. When we were taken, by subaquatic liner, first to Vladivostok and then, by airship, to Khabarovsk, I wondered how long it would be before I could begin doing something again. The imprisonment alone had left me frustrated. When news came through that any British citizens with airship experience were needed for the aerial arm of the Russian Volunteer Air Fleet and that Whitehall was actively encouraging us to join up, I put my name down immediately, as did most of the chaps I was with. Those few of us, like myself, with military experience were given the choice of serving on armed merchantmen, flying in convoys, or on the escorting aerial frigates and cruisers themselves. I elected to join the frigates. I had no particular urge to kill my fellow men but wanted to take something less than a passive rôle through the rest of this particular war. I have learned from my experiences that hatred and racial antagonism can be manufactured by the politicians of any one country against any other, so I was no longer the patriot I had been. Personally, however, and I know now that this was an infantile impulse, I felt that I had been put to a great deal of trouble by the Japanese and I might as well fight them as anyone else. I also, I must admit, rather hoped there would not be too much conflict. I wanted to fly good, fast ships. And here, at last, was my chance.

We had a two-week training programme in and around Samara, in which we learned the specifics of the Russian ships, which were mainly built and equipped according to the designs of the great engineer Pyatnitski and at that time were amongst the most modern in the world; then we were assigned to various ships to get general experience. I joined the aerial cruiser *Vassarion Belinsky*. She was a fine, easy-handling ship, sailing out of the Lermontov Airpark a few miles to the north of Odessa, that marvellous cosmopolitan sea-port from which have come so many fine

Russian-speaking poets, novelists, painters and intellectuals. I had a few days' leave in Odessa before we sailed and I enjoyed those days to the full. Being on the Black Sea the port was relatively untouched by the war and there was more merchant shipping in her harbours than there was naval. Her streets were crowded with people of every colour and nation. She smelled of spices, of the food of five continents, and there was a merry, carefree quality about her, even in wartime, which seemed to me to exemplify the very best of the Slavic soul.

Odessa has a large Jewish population (for it is, of course, the capital of Russian Jewry beyond the Pale, even though the Pale itself, together with all anti-Semitic laws, has been abolished in Kerensky's Russia) and so is full of music, intelligent commercial enterprise – and Romance. I fell in love with her immediately. I know of no other city quite like her and often wish that I could have spent longer exploring her winding streets, her avenues and promenades, her resorts and watering places. She is not, strictly speaking, a Russian city. She is Ukrainian, and the Ukrainians will insist very firmly that the 'goat-beards' (their word for Great Russians) are interlopers, that Kiev, capital of the Ukraine, is the true centre of Slavic culture, that the Muscovites are upstarts, parvenus, johnny-come-latelies, tyrants, imperialists, thieves, carpetbaggers and almost anything else of the kind you care to think of. It is true that the Government of Moscow has most power over the Ukraine, but there is a spirit of freedom about Odessa which, I think, denies any of its denizens' allegations.

In Odessa I also learned a great deal about the progress of the war. On land the Japanese had made many early gains but were now being beaten back by Russian and British infantry – indeed they held less territory than before the war. They were still pretty powerful in the air and at sea, and were masters of strategy, but all in all we were optimistic about the way the conflict was turning, for the Dutch and Portuguese were also on our side and although their navies were not large they were extremely capable.

It is certain that the war would have been as good as over if it had not been for Russia's domestic problems. These tended,

amongst Odessa's population, to be a more important topic than
the war itself. Perhaps because of the war, there was a threat of
revolution in several parts of the UISR. Indeed whole parts of the
Ukraine were currently in the hands of large armies calling themselves Free Cossacks – many of them deserters from various
cavalry regiments. I gathered that they were intense Slavophiles,
opposed to Kerensky's 'Europeanisation' of their lands, who were
'nationalists' in that they argued for the independence of all
territories currently making up the Russian Empire – Bohemia,
Moravia, Poland, Finland, Latvia, Estonia, Bulgaria and so on.
Their policies and demands seemed vague, though socialistic in
terminology, even when I heard them discussed from all aspects,
but if it was possible to argue for ever about the interpretation of
their ideology, all agreed to a degree of fascination with the leading personality amongst the revolutionists, the mysterious man
known popularly as the Steel Tsar. He was believed to have come
originally from Georgia and his real name was thought to be Josef
Vissarionovich Djugashvili, an ex-priest with a record of messianism. He was known as the Steel Tsar because he tended to wear an
ancient metal helmet covering most of his face. There were many
explanations of this; some thought him disfigured in battle, others
thought that his features had been hideously deformed since
birth. He was supposed to have a withered arm, be a hunchback,
have artificial legs, and not be a human being at all, but some sort
of automaton.

Because of the atmosphere surrounding Djugashvili, I myself
became quite as curious about him as the natives. I followed the
news of the Free Cossacks as eagerly as I followed news of the
British airship battles in the skies of the Pacific.

In Odessa I met one of the chaps with whom I had been
imprisoned. He was about to join a British merchantman. He told
me that Wilson, too, was working for the Russians, but he wasn't
sure where. 'Some sort of engineering job, I gather.' Olmeijer was
in Yalta, managing a State-owned hotel. The worst news, however, concerned Dempsey. 'I heard he jumped it before we ever
got to Japan. Seemed so scared of what they'd do to him that,

wounded as he was, he preferred to dive out. God knows why they hated him so. Do you have any idea, Bastable?'

I shook my head. But again I experienced that peculiar frisson, a sort of recognition.

My experience of Odessa was as intense as it was brief and I missed it, when I left for the airpark on the train, as if I had lived there for years.

The *Vassarion Belinsky* was a joy. She used liquid ballast which could, like her gas, be heated or cooled to alter her weight and her ascent acceleration was, if we needed it, rocketlike in its speed. She had a top speed of 200 mph but could be pushed quite a bit faster than that with a good wind behind her. She could turn and dive like a porpoise and there was almost nothing you couldn't do with her. All the crew, except me, were Russian. Captain Korzeniowski was a thoroughly experienced airshipman of the old school with an excellent grasp of English. Of course the name meant a great deal to me but I barely recognised him since he was clean-shaven. He did not appear to know me at all and I was forced to remind myself that few of us come to my understanding of the nature of our existence. He knew nothing of 'alternate worlds'. My own Russian was, naturally, limited, but I have a facility for languages. I soon knew enough to carry on normal conversations, while much of our day-to-day jargon was English, since England had for many years maintained herself as successfully in the air as she had on the sea.

As we left Lermontov Airpark on a cool, sunny dawn, gaining height through a slow, gentle curve which revealed more and more of the steppe through our observation ports, Captain Korzeniowski broke open his orders on the control deck and, standing with his back to our helmsman, informed his officers of the *Vassarion Belinsky*'s mission.

I was not the only one both surprised and disappointed. It seemed we were victims of a typical piece of Muscovite bureaucratic muddle, and there I was (since I had signed up for a minimum of a year) with absolutely nothing I could do about it.

Korzeniowski's heavy Polish face was sober and his voice

sonorous as he began to read the orders. With typical courtesy, he spoke English for my benefit.

'We are to proceed at all fastest speed to Yekaterinaslav, which is currently sustaining heavy attack from rebel forces. We are to join other ships under the command of Air Admiral Krassnov.' He pinched his eyebrows together. It was obvious that he had no taste for the commission, which would involve him in giving orders which would inevitably lead to the death of other Slavs.

Everyone was agitated by the news. They had been expecting to defend their country against the Japanese. Instead they were assigned to domestic policing duties of a kind which all the officers found distasteful and demeaning. I did not really mind missing a scrap with the Japanese, but I was bitterly sorry that I was unlikely to see any real aerial action. I had joined the Service out of a mixture of desperation and boredom. I appeared to be doomed to a continuation of those circumstances. Moreover I should sooner or later have blood on my hands, and it would be the blood of people I had absolutely nothing against. I had no idea of the issues. Socialists are always quarrelling amongst themselves, because of the strong element of messianism in their creeds, and I could see little difference between Kerensky's brand or Djugashvili's. My only consolation was that at least I might have the opportunity of observing the Steel Tsar (or at any rate his works) at first hand.

Pilniak, a second lieutenant of about my own age, with huge brown eyes and a rather girlish face (though he was in no way effeminate) grasped my uniformed shoulder (like him I wore the pale blue of the Russian Volunteer Air Fleet) and laughed.

'Well, Mr Bastable, you're going to see some Cossacks, eh? A bit of the reality most Europeans miss.' He dropped his voice and became sympathetic. 'Does that bother you? The Steel Tsar rather than the Mikado?'

'Not a bit,' I said. After all, I thought wickedly, I had originally been trained to fight Russians. But I have never been able to find consolation in cynicism for long and this lasted a few seconds. 'Perhaps we'll find out if he's human or not.'

Pilniak became serious. 'He's human. And he's cruel. This

whole thing is essentially medieval in its overtones, for all they claim to be socialists and nationalists. They want to put the clock back to the days of Ivan the Terrible. They could destroy Russia and everything the Revolution achieved. There have even been instances of pogroms in one or two of the towns they've taken, and God alone knows what's going on in the rural districts. They should be stopped as quickly as possible. But they're gaining popular support all the time. War brings out these basic feelings. They are not always controllable. Our newspapers beat the drum of Slavophilia, of nationalism, in an effort to stir up patriotic feeling against the Japanese – and this happens.'

'You seem to speak as if this uprising was inevitable.'

'I think it was. Kerensky promised us Heaven on Earth many years ago. And now we find that not only have we not made Heaven, but we are threatened with Hell, in the form of invasion. This war will leave many scars, Mr Bastable. Our country will not be the same when it is over.'

'The Steel Tsar is a genuine threat?'

'What he represents, Mr Bastable, is a genuine threat.'

Chapter Three
Cossack Revolutionists

YEKATERINASLAV WAS SOON below us and it was obvious that the city was undergoing attack. We could see smoke and flames everywhere, little groups of figures running hither and yonder in the suburbs, the occasional boom of cannon-fire or the tiny snapping noises of rifle-shots.

Yekaterinaslav was an old Russian-style city, with many of its buildings made of wood. Tall houses with elaborately carved decoration; the familiar onion domes of churches; spires, steeples, several brick-built apartment blocks and shops near the centre.

On the nearby Dnieper river most of the boats were burning or had been sunk. Occasionally a ship, its paddles foaming the water, would go by the city and sometimes it would loose off a shell or two. Evidently these were naval ships commandeered by the revolutionists.

Pilniak knew Yekaterinaslav pretty well. He stood beside me, naming streets and squares. Some distance from the city, amongst demolished farmhouses and ruined fields, we saw the main Cossack camp: a mixture of all kinds of tents and temporary shacks, including more than one railway carriage, for the main railway line ran to Yekaterinaslav and much of its stock had been captured.

'That's it,' said Pilniak in some excitement. 'The Free Cossack Host. Impressive, you must admit.' He raised binoculars to his eyes. 'Most of their heavy artillery is further down the line, along with their armoured vehicles. They're saving up the cavalry for the final charge. There must be ten thousand horses down there.'

'Not much good against airships,' I said. 'They look a pretty unruly mob to me.'

'Wait until you see them fight. Then you'll know what cavalry tactics are all about.'

As a matter of fact it did my heart good to hear someone using those terms. The last time I had heard people discussing cavalry tactics had been in the mess in my own world of 1902.

'You talk as if you're on their side,' I said.

He paused, lowering his glasses, then he said seriously: 'Everything free in the Russian heart is represented by our Cossacks. Every yearning we have is symbolised by their way of life. They are cruel, they are often illiterate and they are certainly unsophisticated by Petersburg standards, but they are – they are the Cossacks. The Central Government should never have imposed conscription. They would have volunteered in time, but they wanted to show that they were making their own decisions, not Petersburg's.'

'This rebellion came about as the result of conscription?' I had not heard this mentioned in Odessa.

'It is one reason. There are many. Traditionally, the Cossacks have enjoyed a certain amount of autonomy. When the Tsars tried to take it away they always found themselves in trouble. They have large communities – we call them Hosts – which elect their own officers, their own leader – the *ataman* – and are very touchy, Mr Bastable, about these things.'

'Apparently,' I said. 'So in destroying this rebellion, you feel you are in some way destroying your own sense of freedom, of romance.'

'I think so,' said Pilniak. He shrugged. 'But we have our orders, huh?'

I sighed. I did not envy him his dilemma.

The ship had been sighted by the Cossacks. There was some sporadic artillery fire from the ground, a few rifle-shots, but luckily they had little or no anti-aircraft weaponry. The poor devils would be sitting ducks for our bombs.

The ship was turning slowly, heading for the airpark on the southern side of the city. Here we were to rendezvous with the other ships of the Volunteer Air Fleet.

Pilniak continued to peer through his binoculars. 'Looks as if they're massing,' he said. 'They know they haven't much time now.'

'They're going to try to take the city entirely with cavalry?'

'It's not the first time they've done it. But they have covering fire to some extent, and some armoured battle-cars.'

'Who's defending Yekaterinaslav?' I asked.

'I think we dropped some infantry a couple of days ago, and there's some artillery, too, as you can see. They were only sent to hold out until we arrived, if I'm not mistaken.'

Now we could see the airpark. There were already half a dozen good-sized ships tethered at mast. 'Those are troop-carriers,' he said, pointing to the largest. 'By the way they're sitting in the air I'd say they still had most of their chaps on board.'

Even as he spoke the captain came on deck behind us and saluted us. 'Gentlemen, we have our wireless orders.'

We approached him. He was mopping his brow with a large, brown handkerchief. He seemed to be barely in control of his own agitation. 'We are to proceed in squadron with three other ships, led by the *Afanasi Turchaninov*, and there we shall release our bombs on the rebel camp before they can move their horses out.' He was plainly sickened by the statement. Whatever the Cossacks had done, however cruel they were, however insane in their ambitions, they did not deserve to die in such a manner.

His announcement was greeted with silence throughout the control deck.

The captain cleared his throat. 'Gentlemen, we are at war. Those soldiers down there are just as much enemies of Russia as the Japanese. They could be said to be a worse enemy, for they are traitors, turning against their country in her hour of greatest need.'

He spoke with no real authority. It would not have mattered a great deal if the horsemen were Japanese, it still seemed appallingly unsporting to do what we were about to do. I felt that Fate had once again trapped me in a moral situation over which I had no control.

Some of my fellow officers were beginning to murmur and scowl. Pilniak saluted Captain Korzeniowski. 'Sir, are we to place bombs directly on the Cossacks?'

'Those are our orders.'

'Could we not simply bomb around them, sir?' said another young officer. 'Give them a fright.'

'Those are not our orders, Kostomarov.'

'But sir, we are airshipmen. We...'

'We are servants of the State,' insisted the captain, 'and the State demands we bomb the Cossacks.' He turned his back on us. 'Drop to two hundred feet, height coxswain.'

'Two hundred feet, sir.'

The grumbling continued until the captain whirled round, his face red with anger. 'To your posts, gentlemen. Bombardiers: look to your levers.'

Grimly we did as we were instructed. From the masts, which were now behind us, there floated up three other ships. Two positioned themselves on our port and starboard, while the leader went ahead of us. There was a funereal atmosphere about the whole operation. As he gave his orders, the captain's voice was low and bleak.

The wireless began to buzz. Our operator lifted his instrument. 'It is the flagship, sir,' he told the captain. The captain came to the equipment and began to listen. He nodded once or twice and then gave fresh orders to the helmsman. He seemed almost cheerful. 'Gentlemen,' he said, 'the Cossacks are already charging. Our job will now be to try to break them up.'

The task was hardly congenial, but anything had begun to seem better than bombing a camp. At least it would be a moving target.

Chapter Four
The Black Ships

I VERY MUCH doubt, Moorcock, that you will ever know the experience of confronting a Cossack battle-charge, or, indeed, that you will ever witness it from the control deck of a sophisticated aerial cruiser!

Led by Admiral Krassnov's flagship, we raced lower and lower to the ground, to give specific accuracy to our aerial torpedoes. As we approached we were barely fifty feet up and ahead of us was a mountain of black dust in which were silhouetted the massed forms of men and horses. This, at least, felt more like a fair fight.

Standing on the bridge, peering forward, Captain Korzeniowski issued the command:

'Let go Volley Number One.'

Levers were depressed and, from their tubes in the bow of the gondola, aerial torpedoes buzzed towards the yelling Cossack Host. The torpedoes made a high-pitched noise as the air was sliced by their stubby wings and then a deep-throated *boom* sounded as they entered the Cossack ranks. Yet for all they were inevitably deadly the torpedoes hardly seemed to make a scrap of difference to the momentum of the charge.

Next, as the riders passed below us, we released our bombs, lifting to about a hundred and fifty feet as we did so and then dipping down again to fire off another volley of torpedoes. The ship creaked to the helmsman's rapid turning and returning of the wheel, to the height coxswain's sure hand on his valve-controls. I've never flown in a tighter ship and as we did our bloody work I prayed for the chance of a real engagement with ships of equal manoeuvrability.

The Cossacks split ranks as we came down on them again and at first it seemed they were in panic. Then I realised they were tactical breaks to move out of our direct line of fire. They showed enormously disciplined horsemanship. Now I understood what Pilniak had been talking about. And, admiring such courage and skill, I felt even less pleased with myself for what I was involved in.

On a wireless order from the flagship we released the last of our bombs and went rapidly aloft. Now we could see the results of our attack. Dead and dying men and horses were strewn everywhere. The ground was pitted with craters, scattered with red flesh and broken bones. It was sickening.

Pilniak had tears in his eyes. 'I blame that *staretz* for this – the mad priest Djugashvili. He's not a socialist. He's a lunatic nihilist, throwing away those poor lads' lives!'

It's common enough to transfer one's own guilt onto an easy villain, but I was bound to agree with him about the so-called Steel Tsar.

Not for the first time, however, I wished that the airship had never been conceived. Its capacity for destruction was horrifying.

On the bridge Captain Korzeniowski was pale and silent. He gave his orders in quiet, tense Russian. Whenever my eyes met those of one of my fellow airshipmen it seemed we shared the same thoughts. This could be the beginning of civil war. There is no kind more distressing, no kind which so rapidly describes the pointlessness of human killing human. I have been fated, for a reason I cannot comprehend or for no reason at all, to witness the worst examples of insane warfare (and all warfare, it seems to me now, is that) and having to listen to the most ridiculous explanations as to its 'necessity' from otherwise perfectly rational people, I have long since become weary, Moorcock, of the debate. If I appear to you to be in a more reconciled mood than when your grandfather first met me it is because I have learned that no individual is responsible for war – that we are all, at the same time, individually responsible for the ills of the human condition. In learning this (and I am about to tell you how I learned it) I also learned a certain tolerance for myself and for others which I had never previously possessed.

★

We had not managed to halt the Cossack charge, even though we had weakened it. As we returned to the airpark I saw the second stage of our strategy. On the outskirts of the city the larger troop-carriers were releasing their 'cargo'.

Each soldier fell from the great gondolas on his own thin wings. In rough formation, the airborne infantry began to glide towards the earth, guiding themselves on pairs of silken sails to the ground where they re-formed, folded their wings into their packs and marched towards the trenches already prepared for them. Next, on large parachutes, artillery pieces were landed and moved efficiently to their positions. As the Cossack Host approached the suburbs, it was met by a sudden burst of fire. I heard rifles and machine guns, the boom of howitzers and field guns.

Pilniak said to me: 'I wish I was down there with them.'

I merely wished that I was nowhere near Yekaterinaslav. 'Does the Steel Tsar lead his own charges?' I asked. Perhaps I was hoping that the man had at least died for his folly.

'They say he does.' Pilniak grimaced. 'But who can be sure? He's quite an old man, I gather.'

'I wonder how a Georgian priest became a Cossack ataman,' I said. 'Doesn't that seem strange to you?'

'He's been in this part of the world for years. A Cossack is a *kind* of person, not a member of a race, as such. They elect their leaders, as I told you. He must have courage and he must have a powerful personality. Also, I suspect, he has the knack of appealing to people's pride. The Central Government has humiliated the Cossacks who know that if they had not supported the Revolution it would have collapsed. The Revolution started where our old uprisings always used to start, here in the South, on the "borderlands" (that is what U-kraine means). It could have degenerated into pogroms and civil slaughter, but the Cossacks had been mistreated by the Tsar, used badly in the war against Japan, so they sided with the socialists and helped establish the first effective parliament, our Duma, which in turn caused Tsar Nicholas to abdicate. It was Cossacks who seated Kerensky in the Presidential Chair. It was Cossacks who put his picture in place of the Tsar's.'

'You and your ikons –' I began, but Pilniak was in full, impassioned stride.

'Naturally the Cossacks feel humiliated by Kerensky. They gave him the power in return for their own autonomy. They see him as betraying them, as attacking their freedoms. On that day in October 1905 when he stood before the Duma and the representatives of all the Cossack Hosts, he spoke of "eternal liberty" for the Cossacks. Now he appears to be making exactly the same mistakes Tsar Nicholas made – and is paying the price.'

'You seem confused in your loyalties,' I said.

'I'm loyal to our socialist ideals. Kerensky is old. Perhaps he takes poor advice, I don't know.'

I looked back at the carnage, astonished that those wild, atavistic horsemen could have so much influence on the course of modern history. If it was true that they had only demanded their own freedom, rather than political power as such, then it was not surprising that they felt betrayed by those they had supported. There were many people who had shared their experience throughout history.

'Djugashvili promises them their old liberties back,' said Pilniak bitterly, 'and the only freedom he actually brings is the freedom of death. He's still a peasant priest at heart. Russia is cursed by them. They have something which the Russian people find hard to resist.'

'Hope?' I said dryly.

'Once, yes. But now? Our country has almost universal literacy, a free medical service which is the envy of the world, our living standards are higher than most. We are prosperous. Why should they need a *staretz*?'

'They expected Heaven. You said so yourself. Your socialist Duma appears to have provided them only with Earth – a familiar reality, however improved.'

Pilniak nodded. 'We Slavs have always hoped for more. But until Kerensky we achieved far less. What could the Steel Tsar do for us?'

'Remove personal responsibility,' I said.

Pilniak laughed. 'We have never been fond of that. You Anglo-Saxons have the lion's share, eh?'

I failed to take his point. Seeing this, Pilniak added kindly: 'We are still ruled, in some ways, by our Church. We are a people more cursed by religion and its manifestations and assumptions than any other. The Steel Tsar, with his messianic socialism, offers us religion again, perhaps. You English have never had quite the same need for God. We have known despair and conquest too often to ignore Him altogether.' He shrugged. 'Old habits, Mr Bastable. Religion is the panacea for defeat. We have a great tendency to rationalise our despair in mystical and utopian terms.'

I began to understand him. 'And your Cossacks are prepared to kill to achieve that dream, rather than accept Kerensky's philosophy of compromise?'

'They are, to be fair, also prepared to die for the dream,' he said. 'They are children. They are Old Believers, in that sense. Not long ago, all Russians were children. If Djugashvili has his way, they'll become children again. Kerensky's mistake has always been that he has refused to become a patriarch – or, as you said, an ikon.' He smiled. 'Though he's come close in his time. Petersburg socialism seems cold to the likes of our Cossacks, who would rather worship personalities than embrace ideas.'

I shared his irony. 'You make them sound like Americans.'

'We all have it in us, Mr Bastable, particularly in times of stress.'

The cruisers were nearing the masts now and making ready to anchor. Captain Korzeniowski reminded us of our duties and we returned to our posts on the bridge.

We were never to dock.

As the sun began to sink over the steppe, filling the landscape with that soft Russian twilight, Pilniak pointed with alarm to the east.

'Ships, sir!' he shouted to the captain. 'About ten of them!'

They were moving in rapidly – medium-sized warships, black from crown to gondola, without insignia or markings of any kind, and as they flew they fired.

We had only our light guns and no bombs or torpedoes left.

Before attacking us, these ships had evidently waited until we had spent our main fire-power.

One of the other cruisers received a terrific bombardment, so heavy that it was knocked sideways in the air the moment before its mooring cables linked with the mast. It made an attempt to come up, nose first, but explosive shells struck hull and gondola with enormous force. One or two of its guns went off and were answered by an even fiercer barrage. They must have hit fuel supplies, for fire burst out in the starboard stern of her gondola. She was holed, too, and jerking like a harpooned whale as she dropped towards the buildings of the airpark, fell against a mast, scraped down it and collapsed uselessly on the ground. Ground crew ran rapidly towards her, preparing to fight the fire and save her complement if they could.

Hastily Captain Korzeniowski ordered our gunners to their various positions about the gondola.

'Whose ships are they?' I shouted to Pilniak.

He shook his head. 'I don't know, but they're evidently not Japanese. They're fighting for the Cossacks.'

Captain Korzeniowski was at the wireless equipment, conferring with Krassnov's flagship which, we could see, was receiving a heavy bombardment. The black ships appeared to single out one of our vessels at a time. He spoke rapidly in Russian. '*Da – da – ya panimayu...*' Then: 'Two thousand feet, height coxswain. Full speed, minimum margin.' This meant we were going to have to hang on to our heads and stomachs as the ship began to shoot upwards.

We clung to the handrails. As we climbed we also turned to bring our larger recoilless thirty-pounders to bear on the black ships below. It was a beautiful piece of airmanship and it was rewarded almost immediately as we scored two good hits on one of the leading enemy craft. Though my head was swimming, I was elated. This was what I had joined the Service for!

Two enemy ships split away from the fleet and began to come up towards us, but without the speed, the efficiency or the sheer skill of the *Vassarion Belinsky*. We had little else, at that point, but our superior airmanship, for we were outgunned and outnumbered. We continued to rise, but at a slower rate, still firing down on the two black ships which swam upwards, implacable and deadly, like sharks moving in for the kill.

We reached the clouds.

'Forward at half-speed,' Captain Korzeniowski instructed the helmsman. He was very calm now and there was a peculiar little smile on his face. Evidently he preferred this kind of fighting, no matter how dangerous, to the sort we had first been forced to take part in.

'Cut engines,' ordered the captain. We were now drifting, partially hidden by the clouds, inaudible to our enemies.

'Are we going to engage them, sir?' Pilniak wanted to know.

Korzeniowski pursed his lips. 'I think we might have to, Lieutenant Pilniak. But I want to get us as much advantage as possible. Turn the main vanes two points to port, helmsman.'

The ship began to come about slowly.

'Another two points,' said the captain. His eyes were cold and hard as he peered into the cloud.

'Another point.' We had almost made a complete turn.

'Engines active!' said Korzeniowski. 'Full speed ahead.'

Our diesels shrieked into life as we plunged into the open sky again. It was a grey limbo, with clouds below us and the darkening heavens above. We might well find ourselves fighting at night, using our searchlights to seek out antagonists. It would be a game of hide-and-seek which could last until dawn or even longer. Captain Korzeniowski was plainly preparing for this, attempting to buy time. By now our surviving sister ships would have attempted the same tactics. We had little choice, for we were all but helpless in any kind of direct engagement.

'Cut engines.' Again we were drifting, waiting for a sight of the black ships. A wind was striking our outer cables, making them sing. Stars had begun to appear overhead.

Pilniak shivered. 'It's as if the world's ceased to exist,' he murmured.

In silence, we continued our drift.

Then we spotted them, below and about half a mile ahead.

'Engines! Full!'

Again our diesels screamed.

'Three points starboard, hard, helmsman.'

We swung so that we faced the black ships side-on.

'Fire all guns!'

We offered them a broadside which was, in my view, a master-piece of gunnery, sending a stream of shells in a vector towards both ships, which were sailing virtually side by side.

We hit one badly, evidently damaging its engines, because it began to turn in the wind, virtually out of control. We had no explosive shells and the enemy hulls could resist everything but a close-range total hit from our guns, so we were concentrating on their engines and their control vanes. It was the best we could do.

The second ship began to go to cover in the lower clouds and now we could see that it was in wireless-telephone contact with its companions, for as the wounded ship withdrew, two more started to ascend. We could see nothing of our own sister ships and had to assume that they had taken evasive action or had been brought down.

The gondola shook violently and I nearly lost my footing as our hull received at least one direct hit.

'Rapid descent, height coxswain,' ordered our captain.

We fell through the skies like a stone until we were actually below the enemy craft, slowing, it seemed to me, just before we struck the ground.

'Full speed astern.'

We raced backwards over a deserted steppe. The city and the Cossacks were nowhere to be seen. Captain Korzeniowski had chosen his own area of battle.

The black ships were in hot pursuit, attempting to imitate our tactics.

One of the ships did not pull up in time. She hit the ground with a massive thump. Her gondola and all aboard her must have been smashed to fragments. She began to bump upwards again and we could see that she had left a great deal of débris behind. She was nothing but a drifting hulk.

Korzeniowski seized his chance. 'We'll use her for cover. Get behind her if you can, helmsman. Forward, half-speed. One point to port.'

Just as we swam in beside the ruined ship, her companion's guns began to go off. They hit the hulk and shells burst all over her, but we received only minor concussion. We moved up over her, all our cannon going at once and again we managed to damage vanes and engines on the nearest warship.

It was getting dark. Searchlights suddenly came on, blinding us as we stood on the bridge. Captain Korzeniowski gave the order to switch on our own electrics. It would make us visible to the enemy, but at least we would not be entirely blinded.

'Give them another broadside,' said Captain Korzeniowski quietly.

Our guns sought the source of the searchlights and we saw the last black ship begin to retreat upwards, perhaps trying to lure us into pursuit.

Captain Korzeniowski smiled a grim, experienced smile and shook his head. 'Half-speed ascent, engines slow astern.'

We climbed away from our enemy, into the clouds again. I was mightily impressed by our captain's superb tactics.

Pilniak was elated, in spite of himself. 'That's showing them what real air fighting's all about,' he said. He clapped me on the shoulder. 'What do you think, Mr Bastable?'

I was not naturally capable of the same display of emotion as the Russian, but I turned, grinning, and shook him by the hand. 'I've never seen anything like it,' I said.

The black ship had extinguished her searchlights and had vanished.

'We must wait until morning now, I think,' said Captain Korzeniowski. 'Thank you, gentlemen. You are an excellent crew.'

The half-moon was now visible, seemingly huge in the sky. Again the captain gave the order to stop all engines. The Russians were cheering and hugging one another, absolutely delighted by what could only be considered a victory against almost impossible odds.

It was an hour or two later, as we rested and debated the morning's moves, as our operator attempted to get wireless instructions from Yekaterinaslav and then, when that failed, from Kharkov, that the ship was suddenly shaken by an almighty thump.

At first we thought we had been hit, but the ship was moving strangely in the air and had not descended a fraction. If anything, we had gained a little height.

We were asking ourselves what had happened when Captain Korzeniowski came racing from his cabin, glaring upwards. It was as if he, alone, knew what had happened.

'I'd never have believed it,' he said. 'They're better than I guessed.'

'What is it, sir?' I asked.

'An old tactic, Mr Bastable. They've been following us all along, using nothing but their steering gear to keep track of us, drifting as we've drifted.'

'But what's happened, sir?'

'Grappling clamps, Mr Bastable. They're sitting on our crown. Their gondola to our hull. Like a huge, damned parasite.'

'We're captured?'

He grimaced. 'I think it's more in the nature of a forced marriage, Mr Bastable.'

He shook his head, his fingers stroking his mouth. 'My fault. It's the one tactic I didn't anticipate. If they get through our inspection hatches...' He began to issue more commands in Russian. Rifles and pistols were broken out of our tiny arsenal and a gun put into every hand.

'Everyone to the inspection hatches!' cried Pilniak. 'Prepare to repel boarders.'

I had never heard that phrase used before.

Above us the enemy ship's engines were shrilling now as we were borne forward.

'All engines full astern,' said the captain. He turned to me. 'It could rip us and them apart. but we have no choice, I fear.'

The ship began to shake as if it was undergoing a gigantic fit.

Through the quivering companionways we raced for the inspection hatches, listening carefully, through the general row, and hearing noises from inside the hull which could only be men climbing slowly down towards us. To fire upwards into the inspection tunnels risked a gas-escape and the possibility of being incapacitated by the fumes. Fewer than half our riggers were issued with breathing equipment, for the *Vassarion Belinsky* had never expected to be captured by boarders.

'We're going to have to shoot when they emerge,' said Pilniak. 'It will be our only chance.'

I held my revolver at my side, four or five armed riggers with rifles stood immediately behind me in the narrow passage as the ship shuddered and wailed in her efforts to free herself from our captors.

Pilniak said: 'It was a daring move of theirs. Who could have guessed they'd try it?'

'They're as likely to destroy their own ship as they are ours,' I said.

Pilniak offered me one of his wild, Russian grins. 'Exactly,' he said.

The hatch cover had begun to open.

We readied our firearms.

Chapter Five
A Question of Attitudes

Ｉ N THE DIM moonlight entering from the overhead ports, it was
impossible to identify the figures who first broke through. In
Russian, Pilniak ordered them to throw down their arms or we
should open fire. Then we noticed that they were waving a piece
of bedsheet on a stick. A white flag. They wished to parley.

Pilniak was disconcerted. He told the invaders to hold their
position while he sent for orders. One of the riggers ran back
along the passage towards the control deck.

The men in the hatches appeared to be amused and made some
cryptic jokes which I failed to understand and which Pilniak, it
seemed to me, refused to hear. It was pretty obvious to me, however, that none of us wanted to fight in those close confines. Few
could survive.

I think Captain Korzeniowski had realised this, for he returned
with the rigger. Pilniak told him what was going on. He nodded,
then addressed the man holding the white flag.

'You know that this is an impossible situation for both of us. Is
your leader amongst you?'

A small, stocky man pushed forward and gave Captain Korzeniowski a mock military salute. 'I represent these people,' he said.

'You are the leader?'

'We have no leaders.'

'You are their spokesman, then?'

'I think so.'

'I am Captain Korzeniowski, commander of this vessel.'

'I am Nestor Makhno, speaking for the anarchist cause.'

I was astonished. Before I could check myself, I uttered his name:
'Makhno!' It was the man with whom I had been imprisoned in

Japan. I had never expected to see him again. I had no idea that he knew anything at all about airships.

He recognised me. His smile was cheerful. 'Good evening, Mr Bastable. You are once more a prisoner, it seems.'

'You are not much less of one,' I remarked.

He smiled. It was a quiet, sardonic smile, almost gentle.

He wore an old, elaborate Cossack coat, with a great deal of green and gold frogging, an astrakhan hat pulled onto the side of his head, a peasant shirt, belted at the waist, baggy trousers and high riding boots. He looked the picture of the romantic Cossack of fiction and I had half an idea that he deliberately cultivated this appearance. There was even a Cossack sword at his side and one hand toyed with the butt of an automatic pistol stuck into his silver-studded belt.

'You serve the rebel Djugashvili, I take it,' said our captain. 'Are you trying to talk peace terms?'

'I've given that up,' said Makhno. 'It doesn't appear to work. You mention peace and everyone tries to shoot you or jail you. I do not, as it happens, serve anyone, save those who elect me. But we have agreed to give Djugashvili our help during this campaign. We do not support his ideology, only the spirit of the revolution, the spirit of the true Cossack. We are anarchists. We refuse to acknowledge government or despots of any description.'

'You'd not agree the Steel Tsar was a despot?' I said.

Makhno acknowledged my remark with a short bow. 'I would agree absolutely. We believe neither in masters nor in slaves, Mr Bastable.'

'Merely in Chaos!' said Pilniak with a sneer.

'Anarchy means "no government", not disorder.' Makhno dismissed Pilniak's remarks as those of a naïve child. 'And it has nothing whatsoever to do with Djugashvili's idiotic so-called socialism. We do not support him, as I told you. We support the spirit of the uprising.'

Captain Korzeniowski was confused by this information. 'Then how do we negotiate? What do you want?'

Makhno said: 'You are our prisoners. We want no bloodshed. We would rather have your ship in one piece.'

Captain Korzeniowski became stern. 'I will not surrender my ship.'

'You have little choice,' said Makhno. He looked to the outer ports.

We all followed his gaze. On flexible steel ladders dangling from the black ship, armed men were clambering down towards our engine nacelles.

'In a few moments your engines will be out of action, captain.'

Even as he spoke one of our screws stopped turning. One by one the other engines stopped. From outside, in the chill wind, came the sound of cheering.

The captain put his hands in his pockets and spread his legs. 'What now?' he asked stoically.

'You will admit that you are completely in our power.'

'I will admit that you are an expert pirate.'

'Come now, captain. This is not piracy. We are at war. And we have won this particular engagement.'

'You are a bandit and you have seized a vessel representing the government of the Union of Independent Slavic Republics. That is an act of piracy, of rebellion, of treason. We are indeed at war, Captain Makhno. You will recall the enemy, I think. It is Japan.'

'A war between authoritarian governments, not a war between peoples,' insisted Makhno. 'What sort of socialist are you, captain?'

Korzeniowski scowled. 'I am not a socialist at all. I am a loyal Russian.'

'Well, I am not a "loyal Russian". I am an anarchist and, as my birthplace seems important to you, a Ukrainian. We oppose all governments and in particular the Central Government of Petersburg. In the name of the people, Captain Korzeniowski, we demand that you surrender your ship.'

Korzeniowski was in a dreadful position. He did not wish to waste the lives of his crew and he could not, in conscience, hand over his command.

'You are a democrat, I take it?' said Makhno.

'Of course.'

'Then put it to your men,' said the anarchist simply. 'Do they wish to live or die?'

'Very well,' said Korzeniowski, 'I will ask them.' He turned to us. 'Gentlemen? Airshipmen?'

'We'll fight,' said Pilniak.

Not one of us protested, but not all agreed. The idea of spilling Russian blood was abhorrent.

Makhno accepted this. Indeed, he seemed to have expected nothing else, yet he was not convinced. 'I will give you a chance to debate your position,' he said. He began to move back towards the hatches. 'You cannot escape now. We are already carrying you to our headquarters. If any of you wishes to join our cause, we shall be happy to accept you as brothers.'

Captain Korzeniowski did not order us to fire. We watched as the anarchists retreated, pulling the hatches closed behind them. It was then that I realised we had been subject to a diversion. While we had parleyed, we had not given attention to what had been going on outside the ship. I think Korzeniowski understood this, too. It was obvious, as we returned to the control deck, that he did not hold a very good opinion of himself at that moment. As an aerial tactician he had no equal. As a negotiator he was by no means as successful. It seemed that Makhno (as I learned was his wont) had achieved checkmate without losing a single life on either side.

Helplessly, we watched the stars and the clouds go by around us as, with engines straining, the anarchist airship bore us steadily towards its base.

On the control deck, Captain Korzeniowski was sending a wireless message through to Kharkov, attempting to receive instructions and to give some idea of our position. Eventually, after several attempts, the operator turned to him. 'They have cut our antennae, sir. We can neither send nor receive.'

Korzeniowski nodded. He looked at Pilniak and myself. 'Well, gentlemen, have you any suggestions?'

'Makhno has us completely in his power,' I said. 'Unless we attempt to reach his ship through our inspection hatches, we have no way of stopping him.'

Korzeniowski bent his head, as if in thought. When he looked up he was in control of himself. 'I think we can all get some sleep,' he said. 'I regret that I did not anticipate this particular problem, gentlemen, and that we have no orders to cover it. I think I had better say here and now that I release you from my command.'

It was a strange, almost oriental thing to say. Again it gave me a better insight into the Slavic temperament than I had a few months before. I respected Captain Korzeniowski's attitude, however. He was a man of honour who believed that he had failed in his duty. He was now giving us carte blanche to act individually as we thought best.

In a sense I had been extraordinarily impressed by the exchange between Makhno and Korzeniowski. Both appeared, for all that they seemed to be in conflict, to have at root the same sense of duty to those they led. Once Korzeniowski had been proven, in his own eyes, incompetent, he no longer felt that he had any right to command at all. I had the feeling that Makhno and perhaps many of the Cossack atamans took the same view. Unlike so many politicians or military leaders they made no attempt to justify their mistakes, to cling to power. For them power held enormous responsibility and was merely invested in them temporarily. I was learning, I think, one or two things about the fundamental issues surrounding Russian politics – something which was not normally put into words by any side, by any observer. These issues were at once simpler and more complex than I had once supposed.

Pilniak was saluting. 'Thank you, sir,' he said. I had no choice but to salute as well. Korzeniowski returned the salute and then went slowly back to his cabin.

A notion suddenly came into my head. 'Good God, Pilniak, he doesn't intend to shoot himself I hope.'

Pilniak watched the departing captain. 'I doubt it, Mr Bastable. That, too, would be cowardly. He will resume command should we ask him. When there is something to command. In the meanwhile he releases us so that we may take whatever actions we think will help us best, as individuals, to survive. We are a primitive people, Mr Bastable, in some ways. Rather like Red Indians, eh? In a way? If our war leaders fail us, they resign immediately, unless we insist they continue. That is true democratic socialism, isn't it?'

'I'm no politician,' I told him. 'I don't really understand the difference between one "ism" and another. I'm a simple soldier, as I've said more than once.'

I returned with Pilniak to our tiny cabin with its two bunks, one on top of the other. We slept fitfully, both of us having merely removed our jackets and trousers.

By dawn we were up, taking coffee in the mess. Captain Korzeniowski was absent.

A few minutes later, he joined us. 'You will be interested to learn,' he said, 'that we appear to have reached the bandits' camp.'

We all rushed out of the mess and up to the observation ports. The ship was dropping close to the ground. Trailing mooring ropes had been dropped from the hull. Even as we watched we saw a mass of Cossack horsemen racing towards the ropes. One by one they were seized by at least half a dozen riders.

In triumph, the Cossacks dragged our ship back to their headquarters, while Makhno's black battle-cruiser let go its grapples and drifted some yards off, to fly beside us. We saw anarchists waving to us from their own gondola. I was almost tempted to wave back. There was no mistaking Makhno's feat. He was a very clever man, and plainly no fiery charlatan. I could make no sense of his politics, but I continued to keep a high opinion of his intelligence.

Slowly, ignominiously, our ship was hauled to the ground by the whooping Cossacks. These were evidently not the same men who had attacked Yekaterinaslav, but it was equally evident that they knew what we had done during the Cossack charge. I got a better look at them now. In the main they were small men, swarthy, heavily bearded, dressed in a mixture of clothing, much of it fairly ragged. All were festooned with weapons, with bandoliers, with daggers and swords; all rode wonderfully. They were plainly rogues but were not by any means mere bandits.

Soon our keel was bumping along the ground as the ship was tied to wooden stakes set for that purpose into the earth on the outskirts of a small, one-street town which seemed to have been taken over piecemeal by the rebels.

Our discussion soon concluded that we had best 'play things by ear' and avoid armed conflict if possible.

We stood there looking out at the Cossacks while they grinned and gesticulated at us. They did not seem to be threatening our lives. They were overjoyed with the capture of a Central Government ship and seemed to bear us very little malice. I mentioned this to Pilniak.

'I agree,' he said. 'It's true they don't hate us. But that's the last thing which will stop a Cossack from killing you, if he so feels like it.'

I realised that we were in somewhat greater danger than I had originally thought. The Cossacks did not accept the usual conventions concerning a captured enemy and it was questionable now whether or not we should experience the next day's dawn.

Captain Korzeniowski remained in his cabin. As we stared out at our captors the tension in the gondola began to grow. Overhead we could hear men climbing over our hull, laughing and exchanging jokes with the Cossacks on the ground.

Eventually Pilniak looked at me and the other officers and he said: 'Let's get this over with, shall we?'

We all agreed.

Pilniak gave the order to lower our gangways and, as the side of the gondola opened out, we marched in good order down the steps towards the Cossacks.

We had expected everything but the cheer which went up. The Cossacks are the first to acknowledge nerve when it is displayed as we displayed it. Perhaps Pilniak had known this.

Only Captain Korzeniowski refused to leave the ship and we accepted his decision.

Pilniak and I were in the forefront. As we left the gangway he approached the nearest Cossack and saluted. 'Lieutenant L.I. Pilniak of the Volunteer Air Fleet.'

The Cossack said something in a dialect which defeated my imperfect Russian. He pushed his military cap back on his forehead, by way of returning the salute. Then he made his horse walk backwards, in order to clear a space for us, waving us on towards the village.

Still rather nervous of what the Cossacks might decide, on a whim, to do, we began to walk in double file towards the rebel headquarters. Pilniak was smiling as he spoke and I returned the smile. 'Chin up, old man! Is this what the British call "showing the flag"?'

'I'm not quite sure,' I said. 'It's been a long while since I had occasion to do it.'

The Cossacks, some mounted, some on foot, were crowding in on us. They were pretty filthy and many of them were evidently drunk. I've never smelled so much vodka. Some of them appeared to have dowsed themselves in the stuff. They offered us catcalls and insults as we walked between their lines and we were almost at the first buildings of the village when the press became so tight that we could no longer move.

It was then that one of our riggers, near the rear, must have struck out at a Cossack and a fight between the two began. Our carefully maintained front threatened to crack.

I think we probably would have been torn to pieces if, from our right, a horse-drawn machine-gun cart had not suddenly parted the ranks. One man drove the little cart while another discharged a revolver into the air, shouting to the Cossacks to desist.

The man with the revolver was Nestor Makhno.

'Back, lads,' he cried to his men. 'We've no grudge against those who misguidedly serve the State, only against the State itself.'

He smiled down at me. 'Good morning, Captain Bastable. So you decided to join us, eh?'

I made no reply to this. 'We are heading for your camp,' I said. 'We accept that we are your prisoners.'

'Where's the commander?'

'In his cabin.'

'Sulking, no doubt.' Makhno shouted something in dialect to the Cossacks and once more the ranks fell back, enabling us to continue on through the streets until Makhno's cart stopped in front of a large schoolhouse which flew the rebel flag: a yellow cross on a red field. He invited Pilniak and myself to join him and told the rest of our chaps that they could get food and rest at a nearby church.

We were reluctant to part from the crew and fellow officers, but we had little choice.

Makhno jumped from the cart and, limping slightly, escorted us into the schoolhouse. Here, in the main classroom, several Cossack chiefs awaited us. They were dressed far more extravagantly than their men, in elaborately embroidered shirts and kaftans, with a great deal of silver and gold about their persons and decorating their weapons.

The strangest sight, however, was the man who sat at the top of the classroom, where the teacher would normally be. He lounged forward on the desk, his face completely covered by a helmet which had been forged to represent a fierce, moustachioed human face. Only the eyes were alive and these seemed to me to be both mad and malevolent. The man was not tall, but he was bulky, wearing a simple, grey moujik shirt, grey baggy trousers tucked into black boots. He had no weapons, no insignia on his costume, and one of his arms seemed thinner than the other. I knew that we must be confronting the Steel Tsar himself, the rebel leader Djugashvili.

The voice was muffled and metallic from within the helm. 'The English renegade, Bastable. We've heard of you.' The tones were coarse, aggressive. The man seemed to me to be both insane and drunk. 'Is it good sport, then? Killing honest Cossacks?'

'I am an officer in the Volunteer Air Fleet,' I told him.

The metal mask lifted to offer me a direct stare. 'What are you, then? Some sort of mercenary?'

I refused to explain my position.

He leaned back in his chair, heavy with his own sense of power. 'You joined to fight the Japs, is that it?'

'More or less,' I said.

'Well you'll be pleased to learn that the Japs are almost beaten.'

'I am pleased. I'd be glad to see an end to the war. To all wars.'

'You're a pacifist!' Djugashvili began to laugh from within the helm. It was a hideous sound. 'For a pacifist, my friend, you've a lot of blood on your hands. Two thousand of my lads died at Yekaterinaslav. But we took the city. And destroyed the air fleet you sent against us. What d'you say to that?'

'If the war with Japan is almost over,' I said, 'then your triumph will be short-lived. You must know that.'

'I know nothing of the sort.' He signalled to one of his men, who went to a side door, opened it and called through. Moments later I saw Peewee Wilson emerge. The Bore of Rishiri Camp back again as large as life.

'Hello, Bastable, old man,' he said. 'I knew there must be some decent socialists in Russia. And I've found the best.'

'You're working with these people?'

'Certainly. Very glad to put my talents at their disposal.'

The familiar self-congratulatory drone was already beginning to grate, after seconds.

'Mr Wilson keeps our airships running,' said the Steel Tsar. 'And he's been very helpful in other areas.'

'Nice of you to say so, sir.' Wilson gave a peculiar twisted smile, half pride, half embarrassment.

'Good morning, Mr Bastable.' I recognised the warm, ironic voice immediately. I looked towards the door to see Mrs Una Persson standing there. She had crossed bandoliers of bullets over her black military coat, a Smith and Wesson revolver on her hip, a fur hat pulled to one side. She was as beautiful as ever, with her oval face and clear, grey eyes.

I bowed. 'Mrs Persson.'

I had not seen her for some time, since together we had inhabited the world of the Black Attila. Her eyes held that look of special recognition which one traveller between the planes reserves for another.

'You've come to join our army, I take it,' she said significantly.

I trusted her completely and took her hint at once. Much to Pilniak's astonishment, I nodded. 'My intention all along,' I said.

Djugashvili seemed unsurprised. 'We have many well-wishers abroad. People who know how much we have suffered under Kerensky. But what of your companion?'

Pilniak drew himself up and brought his heels together with a click. 'I should like to join my fellow prisoners,' he said.

The Steel Tsar shrugged. The metal glinted and seemed to be reflected in his eyes. 'Very well.' He signed to one of his men. 'Dispose of him with –'

Makhno suddenly interposed. 'Dispose? What are you suggesting, comrade?'

Djugashvili waved his hand. 'We have too many mouths to feed as it is, comrade. If we let these survive –'

'They are prisoners of war, captured fairly. Send them back to Kharkov. All I wanted was their ship. Let them go!'

Pilniak looked from one to the other. He had never expected to be the subject of a moral argument between two bandits.

'I am responsible for all decisions,' said Djugashvili. 'I will choose whether –'

'I captured them.' Makhno was cold and angry. His voice dropped, but as the tone lowered it carried increased authority. 'And I will not agree to their murder!'

'It is not murder. We are sweeping up the rubbish of History.'

'You are planning to kill honest men.'

'They attack socialism.'

'We must live by example and offer example to others,' said Makhno. 'It is the only way.'

'You are a fool!' Djugashvili rose and brought his sound hand down on the desk. 'Why feed them? Why send them back so they can fight against us again? Cleanse them!'

'Some will fight against us – but others will understand the nature of our cause and tell their comrades.' Makhno folded his arms across his chest. 'It is always so. If we are brutal, then it gives them a further excuse for brutality. By God, Djugashvili, these are simple enough arguments. What do you want? Blood sacrifices? How can you claim to represent enlightenment and liberty? You have already been responsible for the slaughter of Jews, the destruction of peasant villages, the torturing of innocent farmers. I agreed to bring my ships to you because you promised that these things were accidental, that they had stopped. They have not stopped. You are proving to me as you stand there that they will never stop. You are a fraud, an authoritarian hypocrite!'

The voice within the helm grew louder and louder as Makhno's became quieter.

'I'll have you shot, Makhno. Your anarchist notions are a mere fantasy. People are cruel, greedy, ruthless. They must be educated to holiness. And they must be punished if they fail!' He was breathing heavily. 'It is what all Russians understand! It is what Cossacks understand.'

'You have no claim as a Cossack,' said Makhno with a faint sneer. 'I withdraw my help. I shall inform the people I represent and ask them if they wish to withdraw also.' He began to turn away.

The Steel Tsar became placatory. 'Nonsense, Makhno. We share the same cause. Send the prisoners to Kharkov if you wish. What do you think, Mrs Persson?'

Una Persson said: 'I think it would show the Central Government that the Cossacks have mercy, that they are not bandits, that their grievances are justified. It would be a good thing to do.'

She seemed to have considerable influence over him, for he nodded and agreed with her.

Makhno did not seem completely satisfied, but he was evidently thinking of the safety of Pilniak and the rest. He drew a deep breath and inclined his head. 'I shall assume charge of the prisoners,' he said.

As he left with Makhno, Pilniak called back over his shoulder: 'I wish you luck with your new masters, Bastable.'

I only knew that my loyalty was to Mrs Persson and that I had faith in her judgement.

When Makhno had disappeared, Djugashvili began to laugh. 'What a silly, childish business. Was it worth an argument over the lives of a few goat-beards?'

Mrs Persson and I exchanged glances. In the meanwhile Peewee Wilson echoed the Steel Tsar's laughter. Neither seemed possessed of what I should have called a natural sense of humour.

'Is it true the Japanese are almost beaten?' I asked Mrs Persson.

'Certainly,' she said. 'A matter of days. They have already begun to talk armistice terms.'

'Then these people are doomed,' I said. 'There is no way that the Cossacks can resist the whole might of the Russian Aerial Navy.'

Peewee had heard me. 'That's where you're wrong old man,' he said. 'That's where you're very wrong indeed!'

I thought I heard Mrs Persson sigh.

Chapter Six

Secret Weapons

L ATER, WHEN THE Cossack chieftains had returned to their men, the Steel Tsar stretched and suggested that we all dine in the rooms upstairs. I had not had a chance to speak privately to Mrs Persson and, indeed, had been cornered by Wilson who had told me how he had been picked up during the raid on Rishiri and 'dumped' (as he put it) in Kharkov because he had 'made the mistake' of telling people he was an engineer and they had needed engineers in the railway works. He had left the city soon afterwards and had been on a train captured by rebels. The rebels had brought him to Djugashvili and the revolutionist had taken a liking to him.

'He's got real imagination, old man. Unlike the imbeciles in London and Shanghai, who wouldn't give me a chance. All I needed was a bit of faith and some financial support. You wouldn't believe the inventions I've got in my brain, old man. Big ideas! Important ideas! Ideas, old man, which will shake the world!'

I found myself nodding, almost asleep.

'The Steel Tsar, old man, is giving me an enormous opportunity to build stuff for him which will help him win the revolution. And then we'll have real socialism. Everything properly managed, like a well-oiled machine. Everyone will be a happy dog. You'll see. And all it will take is Peewee. I'm the key factor, old man. I'm going to be remembered in History. The Chief says so.'

'The Chief?'

He indicated Djugashvili.

We followed the Steel Tsar upstairs. He had Mrs Persson on his arm and was walking rather heavily, as if drunk. He turned back to me. 'I had not realised you were friends. You will be able to help Wilson in his work, I hope.'

'Certainly he will,' said Mrs Persson, 'won't you, Mr Bastable?'

'Of course.' I tried to sound as enthusiastic as possible, but the prospect of even another five minutes in Wilson's company was more, at that moment, than I could contemplate.

The room above was fairly bare, but a long table had been laid with wholesome Ukrainian food, including a bowl of red borscht on every place. Djugashvili seated himself at the top of the table, with Mrs Persson on his right and Wilson on his left. I sat next to Mrs Persson. A few moments later Nestor Makhno stepped into the room. It was obvious that he was a reluctant guest. He had another man with him whom I recognised. I began to wonder if Mrs Persson had not arranged all of this.

The other man was Dempsey, whom I had thought killed on his way to a Japanese prison. He was pale and thin and seemed ill. Possibly the drugs had begun to poison his system. When he saw me he gave a crooked smile and came forward, lurching a trifle, though he was not obviously drunk. 'Hello, Bastable. Very good to see you. Come along for the final battle, eh?'

'What?'

'Armageddon, Bastable. Haven't they told you?'

The Steel Tsar began to laugh that strange laugh of his. 'Nonsense. You exaggerate, Captain Dempsey. Professor Marek assures us that everything is much safer now. After all, you took part in an experiment.'

Dempsey sat down and began to stare at his borscht. He made no attempt at all to eat it. Nestor Makhno seated himself across from me. He seemed puzzled by me, perhaps surprised by the alacrity with which I had joined 'the other side'.

'It's a prisoners' reunion, eh?' he said. 'Did you know, Comrade Djugashvili, that four of the people at this table have been prisoners of the Japanese?'

'So I gather.' The Steel Tsar was opening a small plate in his helmet, to expose a mouth pitted with pockmarks.

Now I was prepared to believe the rumour that it was vanity which caused him to wear the ferocious mask. He began to feed himself with small, careful movements.

He turned to Makhno. 'Did you deliver the prisoners to Kharkov?'

'Not personally. They are on their way.'

'In padded railway carriages lined with silk, no doubt.'

'They were sent in a cattle-train we requisitioned.' Makhno knew the Steel Tsar was baiting him. He stroked his neat moustache and kept his eyes on his plate.

'For so cunning a tactician, you are lily-livered as a warrior,' continued Djugashvili. 'It would seem to me, comrade, that there is even a chance you are weakening our endeavours.'

'We are fighting against the Central Government,' said Makhno obstinately. 'We are not fighting "for" you, comrade. I made that plain when we brought in our ships.'

'You brought your ships because you know you are not strong enough to fight alone. Your ridiculous notions of honour are inappropriate at this time.'

'Our notions are never inappropriate,' said Makhno. 'We simply refuse to rationalise murder. If we have to kill, we kill, in self-defence. And we continue to name it for what it is. We don't dress it up with fancy pseudo-scientific words.'

'The people like those words. It makes them feel secure,' said Mrs Persson sardonically, as if to an intimate friend.

I wondered if she knew Makhno. It was even possible that he was a colleague. There was something out of the ordinary about the anarchist. Although the logic of his politics was beyond me, I was impressed by his recognition of fundamental principles which so many idealists seem to forget as soon as their ideals are rationalised in the language of political creeds. He carried within him a sort of self-control which did not deny passion and which, I thought, was almost wholly conscious, in contrast to Djugashvili, who relied on doctrine and masks for his authority.

Djugashvili continued to dig at Makhno.

'Your kind of individualism is an arrogant crime against society,' he said. 'But worse than that – it never succeeds. What good is revolution when it fails?'

Makhno rose from the table. 'It is proving impossible to enjoy my food,' he said. He bowed to the rest of us and apologised. 'I'll return to my ship.'

There was a light of triumph in the Steel Tsar's eyes, as if he had deliberately engineered Makhno's departure, goading him until he had no choice but to leave.

Makhno looked enquiringly at Dempsey, who shook his head slightly and reached for his vodka.

The anarchist left the room. Djugashvili seemed to be smiling behind his mask.

Dempsey was frowning to himself as Makhno went out. Wilson began to babble about 'rational socialism' or some such thing and for once he broke a sense of tension which nonetheless remained in the air.

A few moments later there came the sound of several pistol-shots from outside. There were footfalls on the stairs, then Makhno reappeared. His left arm was wounded. In his right hand was his revolver. He waved it at Djugashvili, but he was not threatening.

'Assassination, eh? You'll find at least two of your men shot. I know your methods, Djugashvili.' He paused, reholstering his empty pistol. 'The black ships leave their moorings tonight.'

Then he was gone.

Djugashvili had half-risen from his place, the light from the oil lamps making it seem that his metal mask constantly changed expression. The cold eyes were full of unpleasant passion. 'We don't need him. He was attacking our cause from within. We have science on our side now. Tomorrow I intend to display Wilson's first invention to our men.'

Wilson seemed taken by surprise. 'Well, Chief, I think you might find it's not quite –'

'It will be ready in the morning,' said the 'Chief'.

Dempsey had taken an interest in this aspect of the conversation, though he had hardly moved when Makhno had reappeared and made his declaration. Una Persson merely looked thoughtfully from face to face.

Djugashvili walked towards the door and called down the stairs, 'Bring the professor up.'

Mrs Persson and Dempsey both appeared to know what was going on, but I was completely at sea.

Djugashvili waited by the door until a small man with greying hair and round spectacles arrived. He seemed almost as unhealthy as Dempsey. There seemed to be something wrong with his skin and his eyes were watering terribly, so that he dabbed at them constantly with a red handkerchief.

'Professor Marek. You already know Captain Dempsey. You have met Mr Wilson. Una Persson? Captain Bastable?'

The professor blinked in our general direction and waved his handkerchief by way of greeting.

'Your bombs are ready, eh? And Wilson's invention is prepared.' Djugashvili was swaggering back to his place. 'Sit down, professor. Have some vodka. It's very good. Polish.'

Professor Marek rubbed at his cheek with the handkerchief. It appeared to me that some of his skin flaked away.

'What sort of bombs are these?' I asked the professor, more from politeness than anything.

'The same as I dropped on Hiroshima,' said Dempsey with sudden vehemence. 'Aren't they, Professor Marek?'

'The bombs which are supposed to have started the war?' I said in surprise.

'One bomb.' Dempsey lifted a finger. Mrs Persson put a gentle hand on his arm. 'One bomb. Wasn't it, Mrs Persson?'

'You shouldn't –'

'That was experimental,' said Professor Marek. 'We could not have predicted –'

Suddenly I was filled with that same frisson, that same terrifying resonance I had already experienced, to a slighter degree, in Dempsey's company. I felt that I stared into a distorting mirror which reflected my own guilt.

In a small voice I asked the professor: 'What sort of bomb was it that you caused to be dropped on Hiroshima?'

Marek sniffed and dabbed at his eyes. He spoke almost casually. 'A nuclear fission bomb, of course,' he said.

Chapter Seven
A Mechanical Man

STUNNED BY MAREK'S revelation, I could do little more than sit silently with my brain in the most profound and horrible confusion, as I tried to make some sort of sense, no matter how bizarre, of what I had just learned.

I tried to remember when I had first begun to feel some relief from the weight of guilt I had borne for so long. Had I experienced a kind of miracle? Had Cornelius Dempsey taken on my sin as his own? Had history been revised merely so that I should no longer have to think and dream of those millions I had helped destroy? Was all of this a singularly vivid hallucination, taking place in the space of hours or days as I lay dying of thirst in the ruins of Teku Benga?

No possibility seemed too strange. I stared across at the man who, in some terrible way, was my twin soul. Had the young anarchist who had introduced me to Korzeniowski at the Croydon Airpark subtly transformed the situation so that he, rather than I, steered the *Shan-tien* on her last mission to bomb the airship yards of Hiroshima? And were my adventures up to now merely a result of his success? Here was a future in which I was not responsible for that unforgivable crime.

So difficult was this idea to grasp in practical terms that I eventually gave up, forcing myself to listen while Djugashvili continued his egocentric monologues, his boastings and his diatribes. He made us drink with him. As a result, my anxieties were lulled but my confusion increased. He poured glass after glass of vodka into that little aperture which revealed his discoloured lips and he spoke of conquest.

He planned to conquer Russia first. Then the whole Slav world, both East and West, would eventually succumb to what he called 'the justice of World Revolution'. The Moslems and the Jews must also be controlled, he said, but this was more difficult. 'They listen to different echoes.' Often they did not respond to the same means of control as their Christian counterparts. He seemed to be telling us that while as an ex-priest, he had a fair idea how to manipulate the Slav, he was baffled by other races.

'Finally,' he barked through his food, by way of a joke, 'there is always a solution to these questions.'

Like so many fanatics, he possessed an appalling streak of timidity and terror which feared all that was not absolutely familiar. As his power increased, he would doubtless attempt to destroy anything that made him anxious. 'In the lost childhood of Judas,' said one of the poets of the Irish Empire, 'Christ was betrayed.' And what if Judas, not Jesus, had the power to shape history? What bestial monster would he make of human society? Was every demagogue, by definition, a Judas seeking to wrest the power of Christ from the world? Should we not always point the finger at such seekers after earthly power, no matter what their credentials or affirmations, and say to them: 'By virtue of your calling you are our betrayer?' Bishop, politician, son of the people...

Perhaps, I thought, I had been too long in Makhno's company. Again I glanced across at Dempsey. He was fairly oblivious of me and Mrs Persson's attention was always elsewhere, though once she motioned me to silence, as if understanding the shock Marek's statement had been to me. Both she and Captain Dempsey appeared to be waiting something out, as if they had anticipated the evening's events.

For all my increased confusion, I also had the oddest sense that something in my brain – or at least my perceptions – was changing. All attempts to make logic of my situation were failing – *if* I insisted on logic as a fundamentally *linear* quality. Only when I let go, as it were, of these attempts did a kind of pattern emerge.

For a moment or two I saw myself as many individuals, each fundamentally the same yet, because of some small difference of circumstance, often leading radically different lives in radically different versions of our world.

Time and Space were the same thing. And they existed simultaneously. Only we who attempt to impose linearity on Time and Space are confused. We become the victims of our own narrowness of vision.

It is true we can manipulate Nature to a small degree, and make use of her benefits. But we could not create the wind which blows the sails or the electricity which powers the motor. Our natural animal instinct to use these elements makes us believe, in our folly, that we have some grasp upon existence, some means of turning the very stars to our own ends. Perhaps, through persistence, we could even do that. But we should still not have controlled the universe. We should merely have made use of its bounty.

Our attempts to manipulate Time and Space are like puny parlour-tricks. They are impressive to the simple-minded. But what if Time and Space are merely as complex and subtle as our own brains? We have so far failed to understand one. Why should we believe we have the power to understand the other? And what if they are infinitely more complex than anything we can ever hope to understand, except perhaps through our technologies? Should we not content ourselves with putting our own little planet in reasonable order before committing ourselves to any larger plans?

Yet, I thought, as some peculiar kind of clarity emerged momentarily from my terror and drunkenness, a human creature *could* learn to exist in that uncontrollable environment where Time and Space merge and separate and swirl as one simultaneous thing. But how could one cling to one's own identity, knowing that an infinite number of other versions of oneself existed throughout the multiverse?

What was the quality which allowed Mrs Persson, for instance, to move seemingly at will from this version of our history to that? Why was she not mad? And, if she were not mad, how might I discipline myself to survive the chaotic movements of the time streams? How did such people negotiate and map their environment? Were they nomads who followed certain well-tried trails or were they also subject to the random whims of a chaotic multiverse? How dangerously vulnerable was the linear world we had constructed for ourselves? It seemed squarely to depend upon the race's consensus to ignore the monumental evidence of the multiverse's divine disorder!

Another thought came: If I were not hallucinating, had I perhaps created this entire reality merely to remove from myself the guilt of so much murder?

Djugashvili's attention was suddenly focused on his empty bottles. He began to bellow at his servants, accusing them of drinking his vodka, of selling it, of trading it with the Jews and, when they denied this with abject fear of his passing mood, he beamed upon them and told them that it was the Jews who were hoarding the vodka and that some people should be dispatched to make them give up what was by right the people's liquor. And he laughed openly at this hypocrisy, as if he were enjoying it for its own sake – as if hypocrisy and deceit were arts he strove to master in all their finesse and subtlety.

While the scene was taking place, Mrs Persson turned and looked directly into my eyes. I felt a frisson through my whole body and I heard her speak, very quietly, to me alone.

'You are not mad,' she said.

But Dempsey overheard her and looked up. 'Unless the whole damned universe is mad.' He gave his attention back to his almost empty glass. 'Better ask von Bek about that.'

Was von Bek alive here? Had he survived with Mrs Persson? I wondered again how we had not been destroyed by the hell-bomb. Perhaps the very act of dropping the device had set off this great eddy of events – billions of new ripples across the fabric of the multiverse? The act had not merely been symbolic of mankind's cruelty and folly. It had resulted in profound metaphysical upheavals. Perhaps I was doomed to live one almost identical life after another until I found some means of understanding my part in that crime. Again, having received a glimmer of perception, I was plunged into stupefied bewilderment and had the presence of mind to pull myself together as best I could, if only to placate the unpredictable warlord. He had wandered back onto the earlier subject.

'Professor Marek! Marek! Wake up, you b— old p—!' he shouted to his tame scientist, who brought himself round with the alacrity born of long experience.

'Sir?'

'How many bombs did you say you had ready?' Djugashvili demanded to know.

Marek shrugged. 'Four. All about the same strength, as far as we can tell.'

'You are unsure?'

The professor was quick to deny any lack of confidence. 'I have their measure now.'

'So you can produce more quite easily?' his master asked. Light suddenly caught the steel of his helmet and made it burn like the face of some mighty fallen angel. It could have been the face of Lucifer himself. I felt then that he was perfectly capable of destroying the whole world without a shred of remorse if he believed that he could not, himself, go on living. Such creatures, I remember thinking, have always dwelt among us. They would reduce the multiverse to ash, if they could. Why, I agonised, can we not recognise them and stop them before they achieve so much power? A tiny part of the human race was responsible for the misery of the majority.

I thought again of the injustices which we ourselves casually perpetrated and I wondered how we should ever set anything to rights while we continued to allow such vast discrepancy, so much at odds with the religious and political principles we claim as our daily guides.

Such reflections were perhaps natural as I sat listening to Djugashvili's braggadocio, in which large notions of justice and equality were used to obscure the actuality of his ambitions. Professor Marek had plunged into a complicated explanation of his work which the warlord dismissed with a yawn and a wave of his hand. 'Production, professor? Results. Can you produce more of the bombs?'

'Of course. With Mr Wilson's help. The Yekaterinaslav laboratories had everything we needed. Our information was perfect.'

Captain Dempsey lifted his head, but it was only to welcome more refreshment, brought from somewhere by the same trembling servants. Mrs Persson did not seem pleased with his behaviour and her passing glance in his direction had only irony in it. She pushed her dark hair back from her face and I was struck once more by her refined beauty, her dignified bearing. She was the kind of woman a man of my sort, fundamentally a plain soldier, could only look up to. I could never aspire to win her. I doubted if any man would ever keep her for himself alone. There was a sense of freedom about her which nothing could hurt; even when I had seen her a prisoner of Major John in East Grinstead, about to be tortured, she had retained that same sense of integrity, reminding me of nothing so much as Sarah Bernhardt in her famous rôle of St Joan. I think it was there, if not before, that I had fallen in love with her. Only now, as we listened to the bellowings of the grotesque beast seated at the table's head, did I realise how strong those feelings were. I would have laid down my life for her and, though I scarcely understood it, everything she stood for. Was she really Korzeniowski's daughter or was the old captain merely her mentor? Perhaps her lover?

She said: 'I thought Yekaterinaslav was retaken.'

Djugashvili shook his metal head and turned to glare with feigned good will upon her. 'So it was. But we got what we were after. The purpose of the attack was to supply Professor Marek with certain materials and information he needed. At Yekaterinaslav they were working along similar lines to us, eh, professor?'

I felt suddenly very sick, physically ill and deeply tired. Yet I wanted to leap from my chair and beg them to stop talking so easily about those terrible bombs which, for all I knew, could easily destroy the entire globe!

How could Mrs Persson hold her tongue? And what was keeping Dempsey silent? Why did they want me to say nothing of what I knew?

I looked from face to face and saw only fear. They were all as afraid as I! Even Djugashvili was appalled by his own godlike power. We watched as the knowledge dawned on him – through his vast drunkenness, his mighty self-appreciation – that he might well have the means of destroying the whole world! By demonstrating this power, he could fulfil every nightmarish ambition at a stroke. He would be Emperor of the Earth! Everything and everyone would be at his personal disposal!

Djugashvili's lips moved beneath his mask.

His smile was almost sweet.

Suddenly Cornelius Dempsey was on his feet, supporting himself with one hand on the table. 'You're wasting time, your honour. You'd better hurry up and use 'em, general. Otherwise the Central Government will be here to claim its materials back before you can make any worthwhile number of bombs. You'll have to put your money where your mouth is, old boy. After all, there's a huge aerial force on its way.'

Djugashvili made an irritable, almost feminine gesture. It was one I had seen before, when some fact did not quite suit his dreams. His usual method was to ignore it or destroy it. 'Certainly I shall use them soon, Captain Dempsey. It only needs one ship for our purposes, eh? And we have that now. That's why I was so glad to dispense with Makhno's services. He's troublesome and must be liquidated. No, no. We are saved, old comrade!' He became obscenely avuncular. 'We have a ship. Captain Bastable,' he turned his medusa's geniality upon me, 'we have *your* ship, the *Vassarion Belinsky*.'

I felt bile rise in my throat. A thousand new, desperate associations rushed into my overcrowded mind. 'Captain Korzeniowski would never fly her for you!'

'Captain Korzeniowski is no longer aboard. Indeed, his spirit is no longer aboard his body, Captain Bastable.' The creature chuckled, deep in his chest, and he sighed. The air seemed suddenly full of the stink of sulphur and stale vodka.

'You killed him?'

'Naturally, as a non-participant in this very important game, he had to be set aside. He is no longer a functioning pawn, Captain Bastable.' His eyes were now fixed on me and I was able to understand how he had been able to command so many so easily. I could not tear my gaze away from that awful glare. 'You are lucky, Captain Bastable. You are still a functioning pawn.'

It was his warning to me. He must have employed the same phrase a thousand times or more. He knew it to be effective.

But my life was of no value to me while such monsters as Djugashvili were allowed to walk free upon the Earth! Again I felt that strange frisson. Looking across at Cornelius Dempsey I saw his face change suddenly from that of a drunken, self-indulgent boor, to sardonic dandy and back again, all in an instant.

They were playing parts, the pair of them! Playing parts as hard as they knew, allowing themselves no relaxation beyond what they had both briefly permitted me. And the only reason they had slipped so swiftly from their rôles was to demonstrate to me that I must act with them and reveal nothing. Yet I also understood from Dempsey that he, too, was playing for the largest possible stakes and was prepared to lose his very soul in pursuit of the greater good.

There is nothing which gives one strength at a time of need more than the presence of comrades who share the same ideas about humanity and justice. Suddenly I understood how profoundly Cornelius Dempsey believed in fair play. Once, it had driven him to drink. Now he used drink to disguise the strange intelligence lurking within those deceptively drugged eyes. I understood that it was only the very best in us, our capacity for love and self-respect, that enabled us to survive in a perpetually fragmenting multiverse. Only our deepest sense of justice allowed us to remain sane and relish the wonders of chaotic Time and Space, to be free at last of fear. Further violence would bring only an endless chain of bloodshed and an inevitable descent of our race into bestiality and ultimate insentience. To survive, we must love.

I had not been listening while Djugashvili elaborated on this threat. My horror and loathing at his casual acceptance of mass-murder – including the wasted deaths of those who followed him – were almost unbearable. It remained difficult for me to understand how some people are simply born mentally

deformed, lacking all the natural moral restraints and imagination which dictate the actions of most of us, however partially.
Such creatures have learned from childhood to ape the appropriate sentiments when it suits them, to charm or bully their
opponents, to agree to anything, to tell any lie and to pursue their
own ends with implacable determination.

'Such men and women are the true aliens amongst you and it
is ironic how frequently we come to rule you. We use your very
best instincts and deepest emotions against you. We convince
you that we alone can satisfy your need for security and comfort
and then we drain you dry of everything save perpetual terror.
Ha, ha, ha!'

I looked with astonishment at Djugashvili, wondering how he
could possibly have uttered those words or known what I was
thinking. His smile was a soft, deceiving thing lying upon the pitted surface of his head like a red slug. 'Such monsters can only be
murdered, Captain Bastable. Do you have the stomach for murder? Of course not. You will command the *Vassarion Belinsky*.
Congratulations. You will become a hero of the people, a legend
amongst the Cossack Hosts.' He reached his irregular arms
towards me as if to embrace me but then Cornelius Dempsey was
on his feet, filled with unfeigned fury.

'No! This is treachery! That privilege was promised to me! You
wicked old bandit, Djugashvili. It was all I asked of you.'

The warlord turned from me to glare at Dempsey, his arms still
outstretched. 'Remember your manners, comrade!'

Mrs Persson came to stand beside Dempsey. 'Keep your promise, comrade. To me. You remember.'

Djugashvili looked at her with honest disbelief as if any woman
who trusted the word of a man was no more than a proven fool.

'You've developed a taste for mass-murder, too, Captain Dempsey,' I said in a quiet voice.

The eyes he turned on me were no longer rational but were
merry with a demon's light, the reflection of the steel mask. 'Oh,
yes, Bastable. Quite a taste for it.'

Djugashvili seemed suspicious suddenly. Yet he kept to the

original subject. 'You will both command the ship. We must demonstrate our power to the Central Government, as we agreed. Therefore we shall kill two eagles with one arrow and drop the first bomb on Makhno's camp. If the bombs are only partially successful and not strong enough to threaten the Central Government, we simply tell them we destroyed the rebels. We then make an alliance with them until we have perfected the bombs.'

Professor Marek seemed offended at that. 'There is nothing wrong with my bombs, sir! Everything will proceed as it should.'

Djugashvili lifted a celebratory beaker. 'Then let us drink to the total elimination of all who oppose us,' he said.

'What a splendid idea,' said Mrs Persson.

Disbelievingly I looked around me for the source of an almost overpowering scent of roses.

We were forced to stay at the table while Djugashvili continued his monologues, mocking us for the weaklings he believed us to be, who scrupled too much to be able to kill him, who would obey him helplessly even when we knew he would eventually dispose of us, probably violently.

We were all involved in our own thoughts as we considered the future. I wondered if Dempsey and Mrs Persson played their rôles according to some agreed plan, or if they already improvised. Dempsey's anger had certainly seemed thoroughly genuine.

We let Djugashvili rave himself into incoherence until at last, without a word, he lumbered from the room, all unchecked ego and ruthless power, grunting for his servants.

'He's right, you know.'

It was Peewee Wilson, his eyes bright as stones, deep in conversation with Professor Marek.

I was deeply weary but completely incapable of sleep. As I glanced towards our technological experts I saw a figure behind them in the shadows. He was a tall, gaunt man and his features were familiar. How had he come here? Mrs Persson did not seem at all surprised.

'Von Bek,' she said. 'Thank God.'

Events were becoming increasingly fragmented and dreamlike and I wondered if we were not at that moment actually closer to the true nature of the multiverse. I also detected a hint of another kind of reasoning that better explained the actuality of our bizarre experience.

Von Bek was not the same anarchist nobleman I had originally met in my first adventure as a nomad of time, but I observed a strong family resemblance. Mrs Persson introduced him as Max von Bek.

Von Bek was swathed in a long leather military coat. Beneath this was perfect evening dress. It looked as if he had completed his toilet only moments before. He spoke in a soft, drawling voice, slightly accented, and smoked small, brown cigarettes which gave off a sweet, almost herbal odour. The most remarkable thing about him was that he was a full albino, with crimson eyes and fine, aristocratic features. As he moved into the light this dramatic creature looked as if he had stepped from the pages of a glorious melodrama. 'I am known in these parts as Monsieur Zenith,' he said. 'Here, a title and an old name are rather inconvenient.' He held out his elegant hand and I shook it. 'How do you do, Captain Bastable. There is some talk, I hear, of your joining us.'

I did not follow him. A questioning look at Mrs Persson caused her to smile. 'We are already a little unsynchronised, Max. We're at present keeping some sort of course. We had a bulge in two sectors and almost lost a whole stability-zone, which we can't afford.'

Her words were pretty much meaningless to me, but clearly Monsieur Zenith/von Bek knew what she was talking about. He listened soberly. Then he turned to me. 'We think you'll want to join the Guild,' he said. 'In my view there is no better alternative for a gentleman faced with the stark evidence of the infinite multiverse, but you will be allowed eventually to decide for yourself.'

I wondered what Peewee and Professor Marek were making of this conversation. When I looked at them I saw they were apparently frozen. I had an uneasy feeling. Had Monsieur Zenith actually arrested the flow of Time? I suppose he was amused by my expression.

501

'Time proceeds at many speeds and along many courses,' he said. 'There is the slow time of the trees and the brisk time of the mayfly, yet both perceive the flow from their own subjective view-point. Your companions are currently experiencing mineral time, you might say, and merely appear to be completely still. Only a few of us, I must admit, have the necessary sorcery, as you might put it, to play these little tricks with Time.' His manner changed suddenly and became very serious.

'We have no choice but to proceed with our original strategy if we are to save the maximum lives. We require a certain number of participants to play out the next stages of this game. If we lose, captain, there will be disastrous consequences for the human race and there is every chance that this sector will drag down all the rest. There is, in spite of what you might have feared, cause and effect in the multiverse and one sector can easily influence another. If we win, we shall perhaps do little more than preserve the status quo. Frequently it is all we can hope to achieve.'

There was something in this foreign nobleman's manner, some authority about his vibrant voice and strange red eyes, that made me want to join my fate to his. Already I was prepared to serve in Mrs Persson's cause, and if her cause were Monsieur Zenith's, so much the better.

For a second time I offered him my hand. 'You can rely on me, sir,' I said. 'If Mrs Persson vouches for you, I am at your service.'

'Good man,' said von Bek in resonant approval. 'I am going to ask rather a lot of you, captain. I want you to play a part. In one sense it should be an easy one, for you must play yourself – but yourself before you grew aware of what you might call discrepancies in the fabric of Time. Am I making myself clear?'

'I think so, sir. In other words, you want me to go along with events just as if I didn't know any part of their outcome. I must follow my emotions, let Djugashvili and the others remain confident of their unchecked power...'

'Excellent.' Von Bek nodded to Mrs Persson. 'You were spot on about this chap. He's the right stuff.'

I flushed with embarrassment and pointed out that I was nothing but a simple British soldier doing his job as best he could in the service of the best cause he could find. 'It's only what the Bastables have always done, sir.'

'Then now you must do what the Bastables have always done and do it to the greatest of your ability,' he said.

'I'm not happy with this tampering.' Dempsey had revived himself. 'What good will it do in the end?' He was still drunk and he looked at me almost jealously, I thought. He was a thoroughly wounded soul.

'You know better than I, old man,' I said. 'I'm pretty new to this sort of thing. You'll have to give me the appropriate advice.'

'Don't patronise me, Bastable!' He turned away with a shrug. 'I'll help you. I'll help us all. And God help me.' It was as if he were, as an actor, completely immersed again in his rôle. It occurred to me that members of this Guild were not always conscious of their situation, not always aware of any other existence, that a kind of saving amnesia affected them, allowing them to play out their parts with perhaps a little less anguish or, at least, uncertainty.

Von Bek offered me a sympathetic smile. 'There's precious little personal reward in this work, old man. You have to be a bit of an idealist to do it.'

'Then it's the job for me,' I said.

He offered me a military salute, tipped an imaginary hat to Mrs Persson, and returned to the shadows as Peewee said in offended tones, 'I don't have to talk to you!'

Cornelius Dempsey chuckled and sat down next to Wilson, pretending a deep interest in what he was saying.

'You think we'll be able to blow poor old Makhno to smithereens, do you?' The drunkard was unmoved by Wilson's unwelcoming words.

'One bomb should leave a crater the size of the Grand Canyon,' said Wilson in satisfaction. 'We'll soon bring the world to her senses, old man. You'll see.'

Dempsey's response was to place his head on his arms and return to snoring oblivion.

Mrs Persson asked me if I would help get the man to bed.

When we had laid him out on his bunk and left him as comfortable as possible we sat together drinking coffee in the tiny parlour. It was a pleasant house, full of painted fretwork and warm fabrics, and I wondered what kulak family had been killed or evicted in order to provide us with so much comparative luxury.

'Poor Dempsey's half-mad,' said Una Persson, 'and not always the most reliable ally. His judgement was destroyed and it's taken him ages to get to where he is now. For a long time he managed to keep himself going on a mixture of guilt and cynicism. A familiar enough combination. But now he sees an opportunity to put something right.'

'How can we both bear responsibility for the destruction of Hiroshima?' I asked, hoping she would not warn me off the subject and make me return to my rôle. Some peculiar alchemy was already taking place, however, and my encounters of the last few hours had assumed the quality of a vividly recollected dream.

'Because we are all, in a sense, responsible for such great evils,' she said. 'Perhaps every individual member of the human race has had the experience you and Dempsey share. But that still does not remove your responsibility or mine. It is, however, a shared responsibility. We must all monitor our own actions. Our own actions can lead to something like Hiroshima, to the rise of Djugashvili. It is why we must be forever vigilant, forever attempting to adjust the Cosmic Balance. Every one of us should aspire, I think, to join the Just. That aspiration alone has a certain value.'

I changed the subject. 'I suspect you, Mrs Persson, of engineering much of this, especially my encounter with Dempsey. This meeting of so many people connected with the first bomb – does it have something to do with your attempts to minimise the consequences of that event?'

'Time,' she said, 'will tell.'

'At least tell me how Dempsey dropped a nuclear fission bomb on Japan.'

'Similar circumstances to your own, Captain Bastable.' She sipped her coffee. She looked exhausted and I felt that I was keeping her up, but she continued. 'He's a socialist. He became idealistically involved with Chinese nationalists trying to get foreigners out of their country. At that time Professor Marek was also working for the Chinese socialists. They were the only people desperate enough to believe that he could develop such a bomb. Other countries are working on the idea, of course, including the refining of uranium. That is what was going on in Yekaterinaslav. Like you, they had no idea of the power of the crude bomb they made. They intended to drop it on the airship yards –'

'This is too much!' I apologised for asking the question. 'It is madness. It isn't possible.' But I was by now convinced that it was all too possible for events to be experienced like echoes, over and over again, through all the layers of the multiverse, through all the flowing seas of Time and an infinity of material forms perpetually reproducing themselves.

Suddenly that scene aboard the *Shan-tien* came back to me. I recalled the faces of that other von Bek, of O.T. Shaw, of Mrs Persson. A coldness filled me as I remembered the awful, blinding light rising to engulf us, my realisation of the appalling crime we had committed. A crime, I had thought, without the possibility of redemption or restitution.

'They dropped it on Hiroshima,' she said remorselessly. It was as if she was tempering me like a sword. Her words were hammer blows on the iron of my soul. 'That's what started the war, as you know. It destroyed the entire city. Dempsey's vessel was his own. He'd put all his savings into buying it and going off to join the Chinese. It had a London registration. Of course, the ship had been sighted and the wreckage was easily identified – it had fused, part of it, into one solid sculpture. It was more than the Japanese needed. If there had not been a delay in the detonation, of course, nothing of the ship would have survived. Dempsey got out. As far as he knew he was the only one. The Japanese had wanted an excuse to go to war and now they had a moral crusade to boot. Everyone was preparing for war, anyway. The Japanese destroyed some British merchant ships. They didn't care. They were willing at that stage to destroy anything with a Union Jack on it and it's difficult to blame them. Well, of course, the British then declared war and the whole thing boiled over into the present mess. Dempsey was picked up by a Javanese freighter at first and only later did it dawn on him what he had done – what, indeed, he'd started. Poor devil.'

I reflected that the Japanese had behaved rather well under the circumstances. 'I know what it is to live with the deaths of millions on my conscience,' I said.

Mrs Persson gestured almost impatiently. 'Oh, so do I, Captain Bastable. So do I.'

I was deceived by the lightness of her tone. 'It's a heavy burden for me.'

'It's a shared burden, however,' she said. 'That was my point.'

I was grateful for this comfort. Again my thoughts returned to the notion that Dempsey and I were shouldering the guilt for the same crime. Millions like us, perhaps, were also feeling what we felt. I groaned.

'You were both catalysts,' Mrs Persson told me, 'no more than that. Do you still not realise your error? No individual can claim so much personal guilt. It is madness to do so. We are *all* guilty of supporting the circumstances, the self-deceptions, the misconceptions and misinformation which lead to war. Every lie we tell ourselves brings an evil like the destruction of Hiroshima closer. We drown in our lies. Hiroshima has indeed been destroyed in more than one world by more than one man, over and over again. The situations vary, but the people die just the same and in the same way. Some men feel they carry the whole weight of the crime. But we are all victims, Captain Bastable, just as in other ways we are all aggressors. At root we are victims to the comforting lies we tell ourselves, of our willingness to shift moral responsibility onto leaders, organised religion – onto a deity or a race, if all else fails. Onto God, onto politicians, onto creatures from other planets. It is always the same impulse, to refuse responsibility. If we do not take responsibility for our own actions, ultimately we perish.'

'You share Makhno's views,' I said. 'Must one become an anarchist to join your Guild?'

She was amused by this. 'It could be the other way around,' she told me. 'I have much in common with Nestor Makhno, however. I have the same scepticism of authority, especially when it is self-elected.'

Somehow this conversation had relieved me. I lost much of my restlessness and uncertainty. I no longer felt such a helpless victim of Fate, though in some senses I remained one, quite as much as the unfortunate Cornelius Dempsey.

'Now we should sleep.' Mrs Persson got to her feet. 'We don't want to miss Mr Wilson's display tomorrow.'

'Do you know what he means to reveal?'

'I think so, but I have left that whole aspect to "Monsieur Zenith". We each have responsibility for certain aspects of this affair, captain. I find that it rarely pays to anticipate events. After all, if they come as a surprise, one responds rather more spontaneously.'

'I am still baffled,' I admitted.

She put a finger to her lips. 'Trust me,' she said.

I would do whatever she required of me. 'I will,' I told her, 'but I want no more innocent blood on my hands.'

She picked up her cup and drained it. 'If all goes well, Captain Bastable, we shall have completed our task here by tomorrow. Then you and I shall leave.'

'Leave?'

'As you know, you have been invited to join the Guild of Temporal Adventurers. I would like to try to convince you that it is in your best interest – and ours – to do so.'

'I shall listen to you, Mrs Persson, and you know that I am at your service. However, I have some ambition still to return to my own time, my own world, where some kind of order at least seemed to prevail.'

'Believe me,' she said, 'it did not last much beyond your time. You did not know it, Captain Bastable, but when you were trapped in the ruins of Teku Benga, you also avoided the experience of Armageddon in your own world. Nothing is free of this terrible *wrongness*, this bestial violence, this destructive machismo. Oh, I cannot tell you how weary one becomes of it. You must reconcile yourself to the fact, my dear friend, that you will never know that innocence and security again. It was an illusion. Security is hard-earned and never maintained by violence, even the violence you employed as a servant of your Empire. You cannot return to your own time. The Guild offers you a home and a purpose, a chance to take a little control of your own fate.'

I accepted what she said without question, but it was not palatable.

'In the meanwhile,' she told me, 'please continue to follow my lead. This is a very complicated business indeed, captain. A circle must be completed. A certain marriage must take place. A job,' she grinned suddenly, in self-mockery, 'must be done.'

Next morning we were all called to assemble outside the school, in the large quadrangle behind the main building. Cossacks were coming and going everywhere. The entire camp was busy with the rattle and rumble of horses and soldiers, artillery and heavy vehicles. In the distance the armoured trains went by, loaded with men and armaments. Everyone had heard that Yekaterinaslav had been recaptured, that the Japanese were suing for peace and that Central Government troops, no longer busy with one enemy, were on their way to put down this unruly uprising before it expanded into fully-fledged civil war. The Centralists, of course, had no notion of the kind of armament Djugashvili brought against them.

He strutted before his atamans, full of brassy confidence and comradely reassurance, a Cossack among Cossacks, a man amongst men. 'Have no fears, my friends. This attack will be easily resisted. And very shortly Moscow will be suing for peace. We shall be at the very gates of Petersburg and those bloodless weaklings, those aliens who seek to control our fate, will be kneeling and kissing the hoofs of our horses!'

One handsome old ataman, splendid in black and silver, tugged at his great, grey beard and grumbled. 'The airships will blow us to bits. They are cowards. They will not engage us honourably. We can't get at them. Cossack courage is useless against them.'

'We have Cossack science,' the warlord promised. 'Our own

superior science, untainted by their vice and weakness. Our science will easily wipe out the threat of their ships.' The steel mask glinted as he raised his eyes towards the pulsing sun. 'You will see. Within a week we shall be stabling our horses in the Hermitage – if we have allowed the Hermitage to remain.'

The ataman became nervous. 'By God, *hetman*, I hope you'll use no Devil's magic. I am an honest Christian...'

'We fight for God and Socialism,' Djugashvili reassured him. 'For the Freedom of the Great Cossack Host. God has put an instrument into our hands which will ensure our freedom for all time, and will enable good socialists to do His work. It is Christ whom we serve, my friend. Christ against the evil forces of Anarchy!'

The old Cossack seemed to accept this and nodded. Again I was forced to make sure my incredulity did not show on my face. I tried to avoid Mrs Persson's sardonic eye.

'For God and Socialism,' she murmured. 'And we shall destroy all who stand against them.'

But the mollified ataman was striding away on his bowed legs, glad to get back to his pony and swing up into the saddle. He rode away to give his men the news.

Mrs Persson murmured to me in English: 'It's in the nature of a good despot to say anything that will convince someone to do as he wishes. Only when he does not need them does he really say what he thinks. And by that time, of course, because he has no need of them, they are usually as good as dead. The secret of becoming a successful tyrant lies in an early ability to be all things to all people.'

'You sound as if you'd trained him yourself,' I said.

She made to reply but instead began to button her military coat. She had seen Djugashvili striding up behind me. He stopped as I turned to confront him and his burning eyes fixed me. 'Where's our Captain Dempsey?' he asked. 'He seemed so anxious to take command of the ship. Is he fit enough for it, do you think? If not, you will have sole command, Bastable.'

'I would be glad of that,' I said. 'It is some time since I had full command of an airship. But I think Dempsey is ready for the job.'

I had seen my alter ego that morning. It was pretty obvious that he was sustaining himself on drugs. He had, however, been absolutely determined to captain the *Vassarion Belinsky*. He had asked us to go ahead of him. He had promised to join us shortly.

Djugashvili offered his back to me, idly rubbing at his steel helmet as if it were a real face. I wondered if he had slept in it. 'He had better be in control of himself.' His manner was crudely threatening. 'Good morning, Mr Wilson.'

Peewee Wilson appeared, walking ahead of a dozen Cossacks who were carrying some massive object on their shoulders. The thing was wrapped in a mixture of canvas and sacking and was about twice as long as a tall man.

'You're ready for us, eh?' Djugashvili became jocular, almost excited, like a spoiled boy involved with the prospect of a new toy.

Wilson seemed ill at ease. 'Morning, Chief. I hope –'

'So do I, Mr Wilson. Our pride and joy is about to perform, I presume.'

'Oh, yes, Chief. There are no major problems.'

'We want no problems at all, Mr Wilson.' It seemed as if the Steel Tsar was goading his creature, amused by his mixture of nervousness and fanaticism, yet at the same time not wanting to be disappointed by whatever it was he had commissioned from the English mechanic.

'This is what we need for our morale,' Djugashvili informed us confidently. 'Mr Wilson has the measure of our Cossack lads. He knows what impresses them. Have you heard the news, by the way?' he chuckled. 'Enemy scouts have already been sighted in the air to the south and the west.'

'Well, Chief, I hope… I mean, we're ready, of course. Just the ticket for our war effort, eh?' Wilson's own attempt at mirth was chilling. 'Perhaps if we had a private demonstration first…'

'Nonsense, Mr Wilson. I have every faith in you. This is what we need to rally our boys. We have to show them that our science is not only superior but also more familiar. This will bring their legends to life. They are sustained by legends, these people. It is their substitute for reason, believe me.' His contempt for those he used suddenly came to the surface and he checked himself. He could not afford to lose a single Cossack regiment at this stage. He seemed to become impatient with himself and again made a strange little gesture. He began to walk backwards, signalling for the men to bring the huge object into the centre of the quadrangle and motioning for the watching Cossacks to stand back. They were a colourful mixture in their bright kaftans and uniforms, with their swinging swords and bandoliers glinting in the morning light.

Djugashvili positioned himself in the centre of his captains and called to Peewee Wilson, who still seemed uncertain of what he was supposed to do. He directed the men to lower the object to the ground and then, using ropes, raise it to an upright position. After further hesitation, he began to pull at the rags swathing it. It looked like a huge Egyptian mummy, clad in unsanitary winding cloths.

'Come, come,' Djugashvili called. 'Do not be modest, Mr Wilson. Let us see your scientific miracle, the proof of our superiority! Captain Bastable and Mrs Persson are clearly very curious to know what we have invented between us.'

Suddenly, with rapid, almost desperate movements, Wilson began to tear at the canvas and sacking. The thing was made entirely of metal but only as he stripped away the last of the coverings did we see what it was – a gigantic human figure made entirely of steel and wearing, in metal, the regalia of a Cossack hetman.

Djugashvili began to laugh uncontrollably. 'Isn't he fine? Isn't he an inspiration? So muscular and strong. So handsome.'

Neither Mrs Persson nor myself could respond. We were struck dumb by the idolatry, the sheer egomaniacal obsession, of the warlord as he strutted up to the figure and stared into its gigantic features, which were identical, in every way, to the mask which rested upon the head of Djugashvili – one steel face peering up into another. This sense of mirrors distorting infinitely the very substance of the multiverse was very strong and I found myself looking for Dempsey, my own strange twin.

Peewee Wilson the English mechanic had produced an image of the self-proclaimed hetman that was more than twice life-size.

It gave me the impression that Time was coagulating or perhaps deliquescing. Somewhere, I thought, I heard a bass drone. I looked to the sky but saw nothing.

'Isn't he magnificent?' Djugashvili was swollen with pride, strutting about the thing as if he already believed the great steel giant to be himself.

'He is splendid,' said Mrs Persson.

The best I could do was pretend to nod enthusiastically. I still could not find words to describe my reaction to this extraordinary exercise in egocentricity.

'This is only the first,' Djugashvili told us. 'Soon there will be a Steel Tsar overseeing every town. To remind them of their master, that it is through his will and his alone that they live. This mighty hero will lead the Cossacks into battle. He will show himself to be invulnerable. He will represent all that is best in me!'

'When do you intend to employ him?' Mrs Persson watched as Peewee Wilson proudly polished his creation's left knee.

'At once. He will help distract the Central Government forces while you, Captain Bastable, will fly the ship to Makhno's camp and drop the first bomb. I presume he is ready to march, Mr Wilson?'

'Oh, yes, Chief. Certainly, Chief.' Wilson took an oil-can from the pocket of his green overalls and applied a drop or two to the joints he could reach. He seemed to be taking as much time as he could, perhaps wishing to delay the moment, as if his own faith in his invention were not quite as strong as his master's.

Djugashvili turned to the atamans. 'Now, my comrades, go and assemble your riders. Bring them here and we shall demonstrate the invulnerable power of the Steel Tsar! The first of the great army of mechanical men who will carry our banners across the world!'

'Just the ticket, old boy.' It was Dempsey. Already apparently drunk, he had had a shave. His neat airshipman's uniform was a little too big for him. He was haggard but he walked steadily, and for all his slightly inebriated air he seemed to have lost the despairing attitude I had begun to identify with him. He even winked at me as he turned up. 'Morning, Bastable. Ready to go aloft?'

'We're all ready, I think,' said Mrs Persson. 'Hello, Professor Marek. Did you oversleep?'

The scientist was distracted. He looked the great steel statue all over and shook his head. 'Not yet,' he mumbled. 'Too soon. Far too soon.' He barely acknowledged her greeting. He tugged at his ear nervously, threatening to tear it off. Like us, he fell in behind our Chief as Djugashvili walked rapidly across the quadrangle to where a rough-and-ready dais had been erected. We were supposed to join him on this. Meanwhile there was dust rising on all sides as the Cossack horsemen rode in an ever-tightening circle to attend the gathering called by their hetman. Those wild riders in all their savage finery were, in spite of everything they stood for, one of the most colourful and thrilling sights in the world.

Mrs Persson offered me a small pair of powerful field glasses she carried and I stood on the platform, watching the Cossacks coming in. They had not left their armoured vehicles or their artillery behind. As they reached the school, they fired off their carbines in salute and Djugashvili returned their greeting with a fatherly wave.

Peewee Wilson was running round and round the great steel figure checking every part of it. He seemed a little more relaxed now, as if he was confident his invention would not disappoint his Chief.

Now the Steel Tsar lifted his arms and addressed the great mass of his followers, his voice amplified by some natural echo, so that all could hear it.

'Free Cossacks,' he cried, 'Your blood has been spilled in the holy cause of Liberty and Socialism. The Central Government has sent her might against us. All the powers of her science are being brought to bear upon the Cossacks. They would destroy us for ever. They would make Cossack history mere folktales and the great noble deeds of the Hosts turned into comic stories. Such dishonour is impossible to contemplate, impossible to tolerate. But now we have our own pure science, untainted by their alien blood! We can create our own miracles! Behold!'

His pointing finger focused thousands of pairs of eyes upon the dominating figure of the metal man which rose to the school's roof and which could be seen from all sides.

'Here is a Tsar made truly of steel. He is an impregnable battle-leader worthy of the Free Cossacks. He will lead you against anything the enemy can muster. He is the symbol of all I stand for. He will bring inevitable victory.'

A great cheer went up from the Cossacks. Sabres whistled from their scabbards and burned like brands in the morning air. These men were always impressed by such flashy symbolism. Djugashvili had got their measure well and Wilson had been able to translate his ideas into reality.

'Now, comrade,' Djugashvili turned to his tame mechanic, 'now you must give life to our new leader. You must set him in motion. You must demonstrate his magical power!'

Self-controlled at last, Wilson reached up to the figure's waist and depressed a small lever. He stepped hastily backward, almost tripping, as slowly the steel creature began to come to life.

Wilson seemed to detect an unfamiliar movement in the mechanical man and frowned. I recalled that the albino Count von Bek had taken an interest in Wilson's invention. Had that mysterious visitor made any adjustments of his own to Wilson's marvel…?

Again the mechanic relaxed. Smoothly his giant seemed to respond to a grandiose gesture of the warlord's and with awkward, spastic movements, reached to its belt and drew its huge sabre, a match to its scale. With a screech the sabre cleared the scabbard and again the Cossacks cheered.

They were mightily impressed. Djugashvili had gauged their needs well. They were all cheering as the mechanical man raised the sword over his head. Again they waved their own sabres in response. They made their horses rear and buck. The noise of their approval was deafening.

Slowly the monster turned its head, as if listening. It inclined its gaze to stare down at Wilson. It lifted its head again. It seemed to be peering from one figure to the other, from the dais to the assembled Hosts.

Evidently these movements had been part of a programme

already designed by Wilson and approved by Djugashvili. I had never seen the warlord more puffed up or pleased with himself. Already, in his mind, he ruled the world.

Mrs Persson began to applaud. Her cue was taken up by the rest of us, to Djugashvili's further immense approval. Ponderously he, too, began to clap his hands together.

Mrs Persson put her lips close to my ear. 'He loves public adulation as much as his Cossacks love ikons. They would rather admire statues than real people. It has been their undoing for centuries.'

Dempsey had begun to laugh, almost uncontrollably, and only grew silent when Mrs Persson signed to him to stop. I, for my part, found the whole scene nightmarish. Dempsey cast a bloodshot, crazy eye about him and then, chillingly, winked at me.

As if in imitation of the cheering Cossacks, the mechanical Tsar now waved its sabre over its head. Wilson had recovered his confidence entirely. He had the air of a ringmaster in charge of an especially fierce beast. He bowed and strutted, a great, broad grin on his face and, for that moment, I saw something in him that I could like. The man was happy. He was doing what he had always dreamed of doing. He was proud of his accomplishment. All his whining and pontificating, his grovelling and bullying, his greedy ambition, had been expressions of a profound disappointment, a loss so terrible to him, I guessed, that he could never recall exactly what it was that had been taken away. And now, in these dreadful circumstances, at the behest of a pathological mass-murderer, in a remote part of the Russian Empire, Peewee Wilson had come into his own. This was his moment. He might have been a matador swaggering before the Spanish crowd, a matinée idol standing before his admirers, a general returning from a victorious campaign. The applause, as far as he was concerned, was all for him. He reached to set another lever.

The steel giant began to lumber forward again, heading towards the dais.

It stopped in mid-stride. Then one of its knees bent a little so that it seemed he stumbled and might fall. Djugashvili looked a little apprehensive as the thing loomed over us, but he continued to clap, even when a grinding screech issued from the knee joint as the giant swayed.

I think Wilson had meant the mechanical creature to fall upon one knee in a gesture of supplication to Djugashvili but the motion had been halted and the Steel Tsar thrown off balance. The knee jerked two or three more times. There was the squeak and the clash of metal again. The monster began to turn, but its leg still dragged. It swayed again and this time we flinched, certain it must fall on us. Djugashvili flung up his arm and I could have sworn I heard him whimper. Only as the thing swayed away in the opposite direction did he recover himself and it was obvious to us all that he was vastly angry at being forced to show his fear.

He leaned over the dais, letting out a stream of disgusting language in Russian and then a further torrent in which I took to be his native Georgian. There followed more expletives in English and French, all of them directed at the unfortunate Wilson, who saw his whole moment of triumph fading away to be replaced by the threat of unusually painful death.

'Set the thing to rights, Wilson, old man, for God's sake.' Cornelius Dempsey was the only one of us who seemed amused.

Djugashvili's voice was venomous. 'Make him behave, Wilson. Or must I first teach *you* to behave?'

Wilson was in no doubt about the nature of the threat. He ran towards his creation, reaching up towards its waist, grabbing for other levers.

'Please,' he was whimpering. 'Please.' He seemed to be begging the mechanical man to obey and pleading for his life at the same time.

The whole scene sickened me. I pressed forward to beg the warlord to stop this farce. I could not bear to see even as unlikeable a creature as Wilson humiliated in this way. But Mrs Persson made me pause. I knew there was no way I could influence Djugashvili. It was like being forced to watch in silence while a man beat a dog.

Blindly, Wilson tugged at levers and all at once the giant straightened up. He fell back, grinning with relief, casting a wild glance towards his master. His chest rose and fell, his unhealthy skin shone with his terror. He was close to collapse and yet gibbering in his gratitude for his escape.

But now he fell silent, looking up at his creature as it appeared to peer down at him.

The Cossacks had stopped cheering. The whole vast Host was hushed and those of us on the dais moved forward, also silent.

It was as if the air were filled only with the sound of Wilson's erratic, terrified breathing. His placatory grin towards the dais had no hope in it. Djugashvili's mouth seemed to move in a grimace of hellish amusement and then he flung back his metal head and began to laugh.

None joined him.

Marek muttered something about the levers and made to descend the steps, but Djugashvili stopped him with the flat of his heavy, peasant hand. 'This is entertaining. Let us see what happens.'

'The levers are wrongly placed. I can see it from here. They are in different coloured metals...'

'No matter, no matter. Wait.' Again Djugashvili chuckled. 'Watch.'

The great steel warrior was moving again. The sword arm rose higher, inch by creaking inch.

Wilson took a step backward. Then he took another. Suddenly a sound like the roar of Babel issued from the metal mouth. It was as if every member of the human race gave voice at once.

Wilson covered his ears, screaming. 'No!' He shook his head. 'That's wrong. It's wrong. I didn't!'

The voice swelled again from the metal throat. It was unbearable.

'Can't you stop the thing, Marek?' I asked the scientist, but he shook his head, gestured towards his master and shrugged.

Wilson stumbled away. Now the giant moved in two long strides to stand over him as, in his uncontrollable fear, he fell to the dust of the quadrangle.

'This wasn't how it was supposed to be!' Wilson's scream was, to my ear, almost the scream of a betrayed child. I still remember it. I have never heard a sound like it.

Then, with swift inevitability, the sword began to descend. Wilson's scream was suddenly stilled.

The sabre had sliced him from crown to breastbone. His blood rained upon the canvas of the dais, upon Djugashvili and Marek, who craned forward now.

Wilson's body collapsed like butcher's meat into the dust.

Dempsey began to cough. It was a dry, hard noise, echoing in the silence.

Not a Cossack voice was raised. There was still an air of expectancy as they waited to see what either of the Steel Tsars would do next. I heard the wind sighing over the steppe.

Then, with a speed which shocked me, the creature fell with a grinding of cogs and wheels down upon its creator's corpse until all we saw of poor Peewee Wilson were his carefully polished boots.

Professor Marek was saying to his master: 'It was too soon, comrade. He didn't give himself enough time. He was too hasty. The levers were in the wrong places. It is very important where they...'

Djugashvili clapped the scientist on the back and again his brutal laughter filled the air.

'Well, well. This is poetry, professor. What poetry! The stuff of epics, eh. Very well arranged. Excellent.' He was praising Marek, I think, for Wilson's murder. In this way he made the man his ally in evil. Marek could neither deny nor agree. He left the dais and began to cross the square, heading towards the fallen giant and the crushed figure which lay beneath it. He approached uncertainly, as if he feared the thing would come alive again and turn its fury upon him.

Djugashvili was addressing his Cossacks again, his arm raised in a triumphant salute. 'The traitor Wilson has paid the price of his treachery! It is fine justice that he is the first to die beneath the vengeful sword of the Steel Tsar! Comrades, the foreigner was a spy for the Central Government. He planned, in his cunning, to sabotage our War Effort. But we anticipated his plans and punished him, for the Steel Tsar obeys only its true master, your *hetman*! We are revenged, brothers! Freedom! Freedom!'

'Poor Wilson,' said Una Persson. 'What a dreadful lesson.'

'And a final one,' said Dempsey. His body was still convulsing. He moved away.

Djugashvili turned to us. 'We are all rid of a bore, eh?' He chuckled, calling to the scientist, who had reached the fallen giant. 'Revive him, Professor Marek. Get him back to the laboratories. He must lead our troops tomorrow.'

Marek fiddled expertly with the thing, unscrewing levers and putting them in different parts of the mechanical creature's machinery. Who had tampered with the levers? Not Marek himself, I thought. Had Wilson, in his panic, simply made mistakes? Or had von Bek sabotaged the monster after he had visited us? I would never know.

There is a line in that great Skimling epic of the Second Ether – 'We have searched every inch of charted Space and Time and found only ghosts and shadows.' As I looked about me then I too saw only ghosts and shadows. Were we all simply reflections of some forgotten original, versions in an infinite series of men and women? How many million Bastables at that moment knew a scene almost identical to this? Was there any such thing as real individuality?

I was sure there was. I looked to where Mrs Persson was comforting Dempsey. I was sure that Una Persson was unique. Able to move between the space-time planes of the multiverse, she had no counterparts and few equals. I wondered, with a kind of twisted hope, if the act of joining the Guild of Temporal Adventurers meant that all those ghosts and shadows of oneself were reincorporated or abolished. Was that the benefit Mrs Persson had hinted at? And yet to know such a benefit was also to know a peculiar kind of loneliness.

Cossacks had now come up to help Professor Marek get the mechanical man on its feet. Its whole body was smeared with its creator's flesh and blood and the head was slightly dented, giving it a mad, crooked grin, but once it was on its feet it marched with easy precision between the Cossacks. Clearly, the thing had been tampered with – and Wilson's death was intentional.

The sense of being a courtier in some Byzantine power struggle was very strong. I have always hated such stuff at the best of times. I had the choice, once, of standing as the Liberal for Croydon, but I could not bear the thought of wasting my time extracting promises from people who had no clear intention of keeping them. But at least the corridors of Whitehall did not as a rule smell of freshly spilled blood!

Djugashvili was thoroughly satisfied with the day. His own brief expression of terror forgotten, he strutted up to Dempsey and put his arm around the airshipman. 'Well, my friend, you have joined us. The bombs are aboard, eh?'

Dempsey straightened up, pulling away from the warlord's embrace. 'They're aboard,' he said. His voice had a colder, more controlled note.

Djugashvili was still in good spirits. His manner was jocular. 'Then get to your ship, sir. Get up into the air, Captain Dempsey. Speed like the wind to your target. Your mission is a glorious one. You will redeem us. I wish to witness no further disloyalty to our great, common cause!'

Dempsey was shaking his head with open amusement at Djugashvili's hypocritical rhetoric.

'Ah!' The Steel Tsar lifted his head and seemed to taste the air and find it sweet. 'What glory it holds for me, what fruits and rewards, what honour, this future I see!'

Mrs Persson tapped him lightly upon the shoulder, causing him to turn, angered by the interruption. He followed her pointing finger, staring up into the sky.

'And here,' she said, 'is what you might call an alternative future, comrade.'

The horizon was filling with airships, coming up over the wide line of the steppe until it seemed a vast thundercloud approached us. They had cut their engines and were using the prevailing wind. The old airshipman's trick had been perfectly timed.

The Cossacks were in temporary disarray, scrambling for their horses and vehicles, tearing the canvas from their artillery.

Then, in ragged unison, the engines of the Russian fleet burst into life and the ground shook to their roar.

It was the first wave – troop-ships bearing the aerial marksmen who preceded the arrival of the great flying ironclads.

Even as we stared, the gliding infantrymen began to pour from the huge gondolas, sailing on wings of shimmering silk and firing as they descended.

I saw mounted Cossacks charging towards the flying infantry to be cut down by accurate fire from the carriers which hung low in the sky, offering light artillery cover. I saw horses and men fall in the light of the noon sun, sliced into red ribbons by the steady chatter of the aerial gatlings, their blood bright as their last night's dreams.

I turned my back upon the scene. Then we marched away, heading for the secret hangar. There the *Vassarion Belinsky* stood ready in her lines, bearing the cargo from hell she must soon release upon the world.

I did not look at my companions. I did not want them to look at me.

In my heart of hearts I knew that I was planning to do all I could to change the course of history, to challenge the forces of Fate and, if necessary, perish in the attempt.

Chapter Eight
Revolutions

To my surprise Professor Marek hurried aboard with Dju-gashvili just as we were about to go aloft. The Steel Tsar's little eyes were bright with a kind of lust, but he went straight to the cabin he had made his people prepare for him. For a while at least, we were spared his company on the familiar control deck of the *Vassarion Belinsky*.

The hangar was lit by crude flares and not until Dempsey had given the orders to set the engines at idle did the Cossacks push back the great doors and let in the light. Then they took hold of the ropes and slowly eased the great ship out of the shed.

She began to tug at her confining ropes like a mastiff on a leash and at last we were in open ground.

Dempsey stood back with a courteous, half-mocking bow and allowed me to take the wheel. I did so naturally. 'Let go the ground lines,' I said.

My orders were relayed to the rough-and-ready crew below. I put the engines to half-speed and we began to rise into the sky, our turbines pounding like a single heartbeat, lifting effortlessly, light as swan's down, into the early afternoon. We had drawn most of our crew from a ramshackle bunch of half-trained Cossacks, some of whom were deserters from the Volunteer Air Fleet. I murmured some uncertainty, but Dempsey reassured me. 'They'll do for this work, old man, never fear.'

Through the observation ports we were witness to the first clashes between Cossacks and Central Government troops. Taking cover where they could, the expert riflemen of the steppe were picking off the gliding infantry even as they left their vessels. They fell from the air like stricken moths.

Again I could do little but watch helplessly.

'There's nothing else but to let them get on with it,' said Dempsey. 'All right, height coxswain – put us up to five thousand feet: moderate ascent. Helmsman –' this to me – 'North by north-west, if you please. Hold our speed steady as she goes.'

She was a beautiful ship and did effortlessly everything we demanded of her. This dignified queen of the skies should never, I thought, have been employed in the foul work Djugashvili demanded of her.

'Let her take a point or two,' Dempsey commanded. All at once he had become a capable airship captain – as he had been before he had helped commit history's worst single crime in the name of idealistic principle. Yet even if he bore no guilt, why, I wondered, had he agreed to bomb Makhno's camp? Was he making amends for something or was he determined to compound his crime? Had cynicism, that most cancerous of human qualities, consumed him completely?

Yet he was every inch the airshipman. His hands were hardly shaking at all as he stood on the bridge, now folding his arms across his chest, watching the ground fall away.

There was a strange air of calm aboard. We were still flying the Russian colours, so we were not attacked. It was, however, a very odd feeling to witness all that destruction taking place around us as we sailed through it, almost as if we, ourselves, were already ghosts...

Acting on Djugashvili's earlier orders, a wireless was sent out to the surrounding ships, giving our status and offering to join the battle. The warlord had anticipated the response. We were told to return to Odessa for fresh armaments and to report on our condition.

We sailed away from the main battle arena as the first flying ironclads began to heave their mighty hulls across the sky, while from their tubes burst deadly aerial torpedoes to wail earthwards and burst amongst the Cossack riders. Those reckless horsemen had no chance against the torpedoes. Horses and men went down in a blur of exploding scarlet and smashed bone. After a while, I refused to look out of the observation ports.

I felt obliged to ask the next question. 'Dempsey,' I said urgently, 'do you honestly intend to drop those hell-bombs on another mass of innocent people? Are you really planning to kill Makhno and his followers?'

Dempsey turned his sad, self-mocking eyes on me. 'Of course,' he said. 'I am the servant of Fate. I have no choice.'

I still could not tell if he was serious.

'By what logic do you justify such an action, man?'

'By the logic of chance and random impulse, Captain Bastable.'

'By the logic of savage nature!' It was Djugashvili coming up onto the bridge. He was flanked by two huge Cossack bodyguards.

Something had happened to his helmet. It seemed streaked with blood or rust, but he was oblivious of this further stigmatum, and for a moment I thought I was a different Bastable standing on the deck of a different airship and addressing a different Djugashvili. Images of those around me rippled outwards in a multitude of colours, many of them unrecognisable, and again I felt faint. I held tight to the wheel and pretended my full attention was on my steering. There was a mixture of sulphur and lemon in my nostrils, perhaps from some ointment the warlord used on his ruined face.

I could not rid myself of a terrible sense of inevitability, as if I must take part in this inhuman action over and over again, without hope of change. It was as if I had already descended into Hell. And did I already serve Lucifer? Such was the nature of my thoughts, for at certain times only the old descriptions serve. It could be that I was caught for ever in this scene, doomed always to repeat actions which would lead to this moment, over and over again for eternity. This was the legendary fate of such mythical figures as the Flying Dutchman and the Wandering Jew. Was that why their stories retained their power? Because they told a fundamental truth of our condition?

At the same time I felt that many strange tensions were surfacing and, in manifesting themselves, might be explained or at least examined. I think that Time had become a little unstable, because of the attempted manipulations, and that we were all aware of an unusual and dangerous situation. We were infected by a demonic carelessness as if we actually were about to witness the end of the world.

I found it very difficult to concentrate on my undemanding task. I looked across at Dempsey and again experienced that scene, with O.T. Shaw, von Bek, Una Persson and the others, as the *Shan-tien* drove relentlessly through the skies, bound for Hiroshima.

Every so often I thought I noted von Bek on deck with us, but I never saw him directly. This was not the von Bek I had sailed with, so long, long, ago – and yet even now sailed with somewhere at this very moment – this was the albino 'Monsieur Zenith', who had described himself as something of a sorcerer. I thought again of Teku Benga, of the supernatural forces which gathered there, and my rational mind refused to find answers. Here, aboard the *Vassarion Belinsky*, commanded by a mad Georgian claiming to be a Cossack, I knew that neither our science nor our sorcery – nor, indeed, our swords – could affect one jot the power of the multiverse to continue reproducing itself, every action, every soul, every creature, infinitely. New Bastables were even now being formed from the raw stuff of Chaos. No action could stop this. Every action had its consequence, added to the proliferation of possibilities, added new dimensions to Time and Space.

'Are we anything other than curious maggots, burrowing through the rotting cheese of History,' mused Professor Marek, fingering his face. Recent events had disturbed him deeply. 'What do you think, Dempsey?' His look towards Dempsey begged him for any crumb of comfort. 'Why are we doing this? Shouldn't we –'

'We survive,' said Dempsey, paying attention to the distant Earth. We were passing over the great wheatlands, beginning to turn in a wide arc now that we were out of range of the Centralists.

I saw that the man had begun, silently, to weep. But he quickly took control of himself.

'You don't believe in cause and effect, then, captain?'

Dempsey shrugged off Djugashvili's question and the warlord did not pursue it. 'What about you, Mrs Persson?' he asked.

'Oh, I believe very much in cause and effect,' she said, 'but not in the linear sense. Every action has a proliferation of consequences. We can't remain alive without being responsible for thousands of actions and their consequences. We simply have to live with that fact and decide, morally if you like, how to formulate a civilised, secure environment for ourselves. So far we haven't succeeded.'

Djugashvili was, obscurely, angered by this. He made a growling noise within his mask and stamped about the deck for a while. But she had less to hide from him now and pursued her point. 'We think if we name something we control it.'

'So we do. So we do,' said the warlord, with disguised belligerence. 'We make new names. Thus we control.'

'It's an illusion. And a confusing one. It does nobody any good.'

Even as she spoke I watched a hundred shadows break away from her and diffuse, like so many haloes, into the surrounding air. Yet still I felt that I was trapped. Still the airship roared on towards her obscene destiny.

'We make new names and thus create a new future,' Djugashvili insisted. He glared out of the window and was disappointed in what he saw. 'By this means we control both Time and Space! That is true power, Mrs Persson.'

'Neither is controllable.' She shrugged. 'One can only choose alternatives. Time and Space are constantly warping and recreating themselves. There is not the steady forward flow you so desperately need it to be, "So-So", my dear – I tell you this merely for my own satisfaction. It can only seem to be that. The best we can hope for is to agree upon our joint hallucination!'

The Steel Tsar snorted and fidgeted. I thought he was regretting his decision to join us and witness Makhno's destruction. He kept waving his hand at Mrs Persson, trying to dismiss what she said. 'You intellectuals! You confuse everyone. It suits you. But you will not do the same to me! I give it the name. I control it.'

'We can control only our own behaviour,' said Mrs Persson. Her voice was almost a whisper, yet brought silence with it. 'Then we shall learn how best we can enjoy our existence in the multiverse. But if you try to control the multiverse, you risk that existence entirely. You will be doomed to repeat your efforts endlessly.'

'The story of Tantalus!' Professor Marek giggled. His eyes darted from observation port to observation port. 'Is each and every one of us carrying their own load, never reaching the end of their journey? Always frustrated. Always disappointed. Is this to be our human condition?'

'It is inevitable,' said Dempsey. But Mrs Persson clearly did not agree with him.

Suddenly I was struck at the strangeness of the conversation, as if we had all quite casually accepted our situation and now were merely curious to see how it would develop. Perhaps such knowledge gives one cause to lean a little towards the abstract.

'We can change,' I said. 'We can change something, surely?'

'Oh, certainly,' said Dempsey sardonically, 'if we wish hard enough, eh? The bulk of society, my dear old chap, is made up of people so cautious they believe it is a major upheaval if they have to change their address, let alone the fundamental basis of their beliefs! This caution is why it is so easy for our master, Djugashvili, and his kind to control us. They even get us to build our own prisons and create our own terrors. Caution is not a virtue in these times, Captain Bastable. It is very much a vice.'

Djugashvili was fuming at the contempt in Dempsey's voice. 'Be careful, sir! Be careful, comrade! There are more pawns than kings, sir, in this and every game we play!'

'Bah!' Dempsey offered the warlord his back. There was a strange, bleak anger in him now. Djugashvili had no notion of what was actually being discussed, but the words themselves had disturbed him quite badly.

Again it seemed to me that the scene changed and I occupied the command deck of the *Shan-tien*, heard Mrs Persson's voice...

Parts of the city might be harmed...

Nonsense, I heard myself saying, *the city's nearly two miles away, Mrs Persson.*

'City? What damned city?' Djugashvili was glancing from face to face, his cruel mask alive with his inner fury, his confusion. 'What are you doing with this ship?'

'Sailing her as commanded,' I told him almost casually. 'Take her down to a thousand feet, height cox. Easy as she goes.'

'Makhno's camp isn't a city,' insisted Djugashvili. His Cossack bodyguards both had their eyes tight shut. Clearly they had experienced these strange shifts and echoes also and thought themselves mad or dreaming.

Then von Bek had stepped into the centre of the control deck and was manipulating invisible lines. His bone-white skin was emphasised by the dark shadows which shivered around him with his every movement.

'Who in the Devil's name are you?' Djugashvili demanded, all uncertain bluster.

Von Bek smiled, made a further adjustment, and stepped from the scene. Mrs Persson seemed puzzled. She reached out a hand and suddenly a thousand mirror images poured away from her, a thousand echoes, each as substantial as the last. I thought then that I came close to understanding something. Did each of us possess an archetype? And if so, how should we ever be reunited, each to their godhead, their Original Being, to stand again about the throne of our creator? Was there a way back for each one of us? Did this explain the hint of completeness which only just evaded me, as if one small element were lacking? Was I simultaneously, in dimension after dimension, performing this same action over and over again until I was able to make a change important enough to alter the pattern?

The *Vassarion Belinsky* continued her steady course. Djugashvili peered from the portholes, eager for a sight of the anarchist camp. He had refused to respond to what, I am sure, he regarded as his own hallucination. He rubbed at his eyes. He scratched at his exposed flesh. He moved his steel mask uncomfortably on his head and again the control deck was flooded with the stink of sulphur and lemons.

I found myself helplessly addressing the warlord. 'What of your men, back there? Haven't you abandoned them?'

'What?' He had no interest in my question. It was as if he were puzzled by it, trying to recollect the subject. 'Who?'

'Your men,' I said. 'They are leaderless. Shouldn't we return and help them. The Volunteer Air Fleet will wipe them out!'

'Yes, yes. But I want to see Makhno's end, not theirs!' He spoke in a reasonable whisper though his eyes were never quiet. 'Where is the best view? And we should get some air. There are fumes in here. Smoke. It creates an optical distortion. You've noticed, of course.'

'You intend to let your followers die?'

'I am with them in spirit. Wilson's mechanical giant leads them. It is down there now, giving them strength, giving them hope.'

'It's a useless ikon.'

'It's all they need. They need nothing more, Captain Bastable. Those chaps, anyway, have pretty much served their turn. They are an anachronism. You are a man of science, a modern man. You understand that those people are no longer of this age. History has no further use for them. Their attitudes hamper the advance of Scientific Socialism.'

I could feel the blood draining from my face. 'You are sacrificing those men, Djugashvili! They trusted you absolutely. You gave them the rhetoric and the goals to make them fight. They will not surrender –'

'I would not expect them to –'

'They could all be killed! For what?'

Mrs Persson interrupted. She wiped sweat from her forehead and unbuttoned her greatcoat. The heat on the control deck seemed to be increasing. I even checked the engines, fearing one might be on fire, but could see no cause for the heat. 'We're in a pretty unstable situation here, Captain Bastable. Watch your language, please!'

'But why must they die!' I knew I was being naïve, but I could no longer bear this savagery, this cold-blooded sacrifice.

'For History!' he said. 'As I explained. The future is yours and mine, captain. Not theirs. They will die to ensure our future!'

Mrs Persson's attention was on Dempsey, who had remained at his position for some minutes, staring steadily through the main observation port. She did not look at me as she spoke. 'Here the idea of God has been replaced by the idea of the Future. The two notions are, admittedly, all but identical in the way in which they are self-contradictory and thus always fundamentally confusing to their worshippers, who must look to priests for translation, and so inevitably the priests (or whatever they call them) gradually take power...'

She was speaking rapidly in English. Djugashvili strode up to her and grabbed her arm. 'What is this intellectual claptrap? We haven't time for any of that. It becomes increasingly important that we demonstrate our power to the Central Government. All this foolish talk is meaningless. Soon we shall rule the world. I will reward you, never fear. You'll be our first admiral, Captain Dempsey, a socialist hero. When the disaffected millions of the great cities rise to join us, we shall all be heroes. This demonstration will be in their name!'

Dempsey ignored him, coming back to check our instruments and murmuring to me. 'Three-quarter speed, I think.'

I relayed the order and felt the ship surge against the wind.

'You will lead our airships to Petersburg. You are a fine, brave man, Captain Dempsey. You, too, Captain Bastable. You will know every honour our nation can bestow...'

Not one of us listened to any of this. It was his usual way of attempting to manipulate us. He did not understand that we had all volunteered for this flight and that we each had our own particular motives. We all knew that every word of praise could as easily turn to hatred and that as soon as we had served our turn we, too, would doubtless be 'liquidated' in the name of the future.

'Thank you, sir,' said Dempsey. He looked towards Professor Marek, who sat jotting down calculations on a pad of paper. 'Anything unusual, professor?'

'I don't think so.'

We were sailing through a great sea of greyness. Grey clouds surrounded us. A little rain was spotting the observation ports and we heard it drumming on our hull. Grey light filled the bridge, increasing Dempsey's pallor and emphasising the unhealthy, peeling skin of Professor Marek. The ship at that moment seemed like a ship of the dead. It was as if we were already in Purgatory.

Dempsey, freshly alert, cocked his ear. 'Do you hear a bit of a change in the note of the starboard engine, Mr Bastable?'

I had heard nothing untoward, but I respected his judgement. Like any good airship captain, he was listening all the time. An airship's running depends as much on the ears as the eyes. It's the first thing they teach you. And so when Captain Dempsey told me to let him take the wheel, I obeyed at once. 'Something wrong, Mr Bastable. Could you go and check the nacelle?'

'Very good, Captain Dempsey.'

As I went rapidly out of the flight deck into the main companionway I found to my surprise that I had been followed by Mrs Persson. I opened my mouth to speak but she silenced me, motioning me to continue my way amidships but to stop at the central elevator leading to the maintenance warrens amongst our helium sections. Even as we travelled upward together in the elevator, she said nothing. I drew back the double door and stepped into semi-darkness. From somewhere above me came the familiar whistling of the upper currents, the odd, organic drumming and rushing, as if we listened to the innards of some mythological flying monster. All around us the inspection tubes, silver and brass and pewter, curled like intestines, while the rays which fell between the helium sections from two great translucent skylights overhead were liver-coloured and ominous. The sections would sometimes breathe, gasping in or out as if at whim to bar our path or to facilitate it as we negotiated the semi-rigid companionways between helium sections and reached the crowns. We stood with the wide cloud all around us now, separated from the abyss by a waist-high handrail of oak and brass, sailing at an altitude no previous generation had ever dreamed of achieving.

The engines were invisible below us. We felt their masculine vibrations as the mighty turbines pushed the *Vassarion Belinsky* on her stately progress through the upper air. Her gaudy flags snapping in her taut, glittering yards, she was as proud a craft as ever flew – but on her way to keep a rendezvous with eternal dishonour.

Una's hair was blowing around her face like pale fire and her wonderful eyes looked steadily into mine. She smiled a little.

My mind was clouded again. I tried to grasp at small, immediate things. 'How much further to Makhno's camp?' I asked her.

In all directions, we saw the cloud oceans, rising and falling in slow harmony. I wanted only to look upon this wonder in silence, with her in my arms. Now there was a mutual feeling. I knew it. I reached towards her.

'About half an hour.' Her voice was impatient, urgent. 'Captain Bastable – we have to disarm those bombs. We have half an hour – probably less – to do it. That is why we came up here. It is the one place they are reluctant to patrol – they have no air-sense, Djugashvili's men – and there's an emergency stairwell they don't know about. It starts up here and goes straight down. It's not guarded. It leads directly into the lower hold, which is now the bomb bay.'

I was dumbstruck. My own concerns – my love for her – my need to have some explanation for the 'ghosting' phenomena on the flight deck – gave way to a larger hope. A hope for all of us. Had I been offered a chance to change events, to stop the proliferation of this terrible crime? Had Mrs Persson and her fellow chrononauts devised a means of turning the progress of the world back onto some saner course? But by what alchemy did they manipulate the very tides of the multiverse? What power was theirs, save the power of their own wills?

I needed to know one more thing. 'Is Dempsey play-acting?' I asked her.

A great wave of white cloud washed over the rail and swathed her to her shoulders so that for a moment only her wonderful face was visible. 'I don't know,' she said frankly. 'But I must say, Mr Bastable, I feel very uneasy about his behaviour. It's as if he's phasing in and out of several personalities, several options, at the same time. That's never happened to any Guild member before. There are only old stories about it, in the early discoveries, when we were simply drifting into the unknown, hoping for currents and signs. So many died, fatally fractured. And Dempsey has the symptoms, I think...'

It was almost as if she had lapsed into a foreign language. I knew only the jargon of the soldier and the airshipman. The queer lingo, part science, part metaphysics, part meteorology, of the chronic philosopher-adventurers whose ranks I had been invited to join was mysterious – but learn it I must. In time I would discover that the chrononaut relies greatly upon the power of language to make some kind of ponderous progress through the unknown fractures and endless eddies of the multiverse and must learn more than twenty song-cycles in order to travel into a wide number of realms. Some vast zones will only open to a certain air, whistled lightly and purely upon the lips...

I said to her: 'Madam, I believe your cause to be a just one. Your knowledge and experience in these matters being greater than mine, I ask you to put me at your service.'

She took my hand and held it. 'Thank you, dear friend,' she said. I knew then that, no matter what else befell us, we should always be firm comrades. Then she was flitting like a ghost along the central walkway, her feet tapping on the crown like the ticking of a watch. 'Quickly, Captain Bastable. This way.'

She stopped, leaned down and lifted up a hatch cover. It fell back with a muffled thud. 'Here it is. Down we go. I'll lead the way.'

By the time I reached the hatch and put my feet on the ladder she was almost out of sight in the murk below. It seemed that we descended for ever between the creaking gas sections until we were evidently passing down into the main decks. Then at last we found ourselves in the chilly interior of the lower hold. I heard the familiar creaking of the bomb racks and I shuddered as, through the semi-darkness, I made out their long torpedolike shapes. Mrs Persson played an electric torch over them. The cases were crudely made, roughly standard in size and covered in Old Slavonic phrases, decorated with the same peasant designs I had seen on Cossack finery, especially their weapons. They had a quaint, old-fashioned look to them, those bombs which threatened the destruction of the entire world.

Mrs Persson moved towards them. The creaking bays opened and closed an inch or two, letting in light, then shutting it out again. 'The detonating devices are in the noses,' she said. 'We have to unscrew them.' Whereupon, without any further preliminaries, she slid herself out, straddling one of the bombs. A large wrench in her right hand, she immediately began to work on the device's nose-section. 'You'll have to help me,' she said. 'Take this while I use the pliers.'

Looking down as the flaps rose and fell, I began to doubt if the racks could accept our weight. I feared the whole of the lower hold would give way and carry us and the bombs with it.

We had been working less than five minutes before we heard voices from the gallery above us. I half expected a shot to ring out and to see Djugashvili and his men with smoking pistols in their hands, but it was Dempsey. He must have suspected us, otherwise he would never have left the bridge.

'There's no need for that!' He spoke out of the semi-darkness of the hold, his voice like the Wrath of God. 'No need at all. Leave my bombs alone!'

'You've lost control, Captain Dempsey.' Mrs Persson continued to work on the nose-cone. 'Have you really gone crazy? This was what we agreed we should do –'

'It was your plan, Mrs Persson, not mine.'

'It was the Guild's. Surely you aren't going to help Djugashvili kill those thousands of people? You have no clear idea of the power of these things. They could start a chain reaction across the planet. As it is, you already know the kind of dimensional chain reaction your original decision created...'

Dempsey drew his service revolver from its holster. 'Move away,' he commanded. 'Stop what you're doing at once.'

I had never seen Mrs Persson so evidently frightened. 'Captain Dempsey! You must not do this! Get a grip on yourself! You can't be responsible for this. Makhno –'

Defiantly, I threw my weight upon the wrench, feeling the nose-cone begin to shift. 'Stop that, Bastable, or I shoot Mrs Persson!'

This confronted me with a new dilemma. I paused, glancing from Dempsey to Mrs Persson.

'Those bombs have to be detonated,' Dempsey said. 'Nothing else will do.'

'But we intended to show that they didn't work.' Una Persson was close to tears. 'We have to stick to the original plan, Dempsey. It's all we can do now! Once we have proved the impotence of the bombs...'

'It will prove nothing!'

The gallery behind him was now crowded with armed Cossacks and it was clear we would have no chance in a fight. For a moment or two Mrs Persson kept at her work and then, with a helpless sigh, she put down the pliers. 'We'll have precious few chances again,' she said. But she seemed to have reconciled herself to this turn of fate. She clambered back up and stood there as Dempsey's Cossacks swarmed around us.

A score of revolvers were levelled at us now. Slowly, Dempsey began to climb down from the gallery until he stood before us, holstering his own pistol. There was a silence in the hold. It was broken only by the creaking of the hatches, the melancholy howling of the wind outside.

'You can't be allowed to interfere with my future,' said Dempsey. 'And it is mine, Mrs Persson. No-one else's. I have the moral right to decide what to do with these –' He waved vaguely towards the garishly painted bombs. 'Your plan, Mrs Persson, saved the maximum lives. Mine will save the maximum souls.'

'You'll make a nonsense of everything...' But she faltered, as if suddenly she understood what he intended to do. She frowned and drew up the collar of her military coat.

'I told you before, captain,' she said. 'You assume too much guilt. You have no right to this.'

'More right than you, Mrs Persson. And even a little more than Bastable!' He grinned at us – or rather he attempted to show us a grin. Perhaps by twisting his lips in that peculiar rictus, he meant to prove that he was mentally balanced. His wild eyes strayed back to the bombs. 'All the right in the multiverse,' he said. His manner and air were that of a fifteenth-century monk who had elected to league himself with the Devil. He was defiant. He was miserable. He was terrified. Whatever profound metaphysical battles were being fought across the multiverse, they were all of them mirrored in poor Dempsey's tortured psyche. His eyes begged us for death, for an end to his torments.

'Please, Captain Dempsey –' I murmured. I tried to appeal to the reason I knew was still in him but which his madness had at least momentarily conquered. 'You go against all your training. You should be on the bridge. The ship has no master!'

'Oh, no,' he said. 'She has a master. Von Bek is at the helm. There's no finer pilot.'

'Von Bek is a shade,' I said.

'Oh, to you, perhaps.' Dempsey turned his head so that he could not meet my eye. Like an old pike he had my measure and was refusing to take my bait.

'Djugashvili hasn't the experience or the nerve for the job!' said Mrs Persson. 'You've left this ship and its cargo in command of a brute.'

'Von Bek is in command.' Dempsey spoke rapidly to the Cossacks, some of whom ran to the storage lockers in the upper galleries.

For my own part, I knew a strange sense of peace. My mind was no longer confused and there was no action I could take. Yet, should an opportunity present itself, I would still attempt to complete our original plan – if only to save Makhno.

'What does Djugashvili think of this?' asked Mrs Persson.

Dempsey's grin broadened. Now he seemed genuinely amused. 'Unfortunately there was a loose cable in his cabin. It fell onto his bunk. Struck that helmet thing of his. Not so much an electric chair as an electric bed, I'm afraid. He would have appreciated the joke.'

'So he died in bed, after all.' Una Persson shrugged. 'He always boasted that he would.'

'Oh, he's not dead,' said Dempsey. 'Just a little forgetful. There's something I want him to see.'

I was not used to such casual humour on the subject of murder. Sometimes I thought my fellow nomads were from a different age – the Court of the Borgias, or some near-future where murder was once more a familiar resort as the fragile institutions of law and democracy were allowed to crumble. I know they saw me as rather pious and squeamish but I have discovered that one thing does not change in the perpetual proliferation of Time and Space and that is one's fundamental character. I could not imitate them.

Seeing my expression, Dempsey became quite suddenly calm. Almost apologetically he stretched out his hand to me. 'It's all right, old chap. Really. The Dempseys were always on the side of the angels. Honest Injun!'

The Cossacks returned with two packs which were handed to us.

'That's your gliding apparatus,' Dempsey told us. 'Here, I'll show you how to put it on.' He rubbed at his sunken eyes. His voice became suddenly weary. 'I'm chucking you off the ship. It's either that or shoot you.'

Mrs Persson showed no reluctance now. She donned the apparatus almost cheerfully. 'I still don't hold with this, Captain Dempsey. And my own responsibility here is morally dubious. But since you offer me no alternative, I bow to your version of Fate.'

Having committed myself to her cause, I could only do as she did and follow her as we were pushed towards an emergency hatch, already standing open.

Dempsey remained where he was, watching us. The last I saw of him was his ironic salute. 'Goodbye, old man,' he said, 'and good luck. I hope you get the chance to start again –'

Then with a great smack, Mrs Persson struck the air and her silken wings opened beneath me, just as I, too, was thrust from the hatch into the air and felt my gliding apparatus come to life, arresting my wild fall through the skies and allowing me to turn and spiral like a hawk, high above the wide, Ukrainian steppe. Away to the south I could just see the glinting gold of some

Orthodox dome, but to the west was nothing but rich and rolling land, enough land to feed the world. I kept sight of Mrs Persson, whose black coat and dark blue wings gave her the appearance of some monstrous human-headed dragonfly.

I looked back to see the great bulk of the *Vassarion Belinsky* vanishing into the grey sea of cloud overhead, her black-and-yellow flags brave and brilliant on her yards, her turbines growling with confident authority. And somehow, then, I felt that Dempsey was doing the only thing he could do and I respected him for following his own dark star to the bitter, inevitable end. But I prayed for Makhno, just the same, as I gave myself up to the wonderful sensation of free flight. I realised I was fulfilling mankind's greatest dream – to fly like a bird, as naturally and as joyously as if the air were our familiar habitat. Yet, slowly but surely, we began to lose height and, eventually, were dropping towards the coarse turf to land at last upon a grassy hillock. Mrs Persson had more experience with the equipment than I. My ankle turned slightly as I landed, but the injury was not serious. I could still walk reasonably well. I began to help Mrs Persson out of her equipment. She was grumbling. 'The least he could have done was drop us near a town. Although in these parts they'd probably burn us as witches before asking any questions.' She shuddered. 'I'm an awful snob about peasants, I'm afraid.'

I mentioned dryly that I thought those of her political persuasion had some sort of egalitarian duty to resist such prejudice. 'Egalitarianism isn't about prejudices,' she said, 'it's about equal shares of power. It's the only means we have of steering some sort of even course through a future which is forever, by the very nature of the multiverse, unguessable. We have only institutions and a crude, fragile kind of democracy standing between us and absolute Chaos. That is why we must value and protect those institutions. And be forever re-examining them.'

She stopped herself. 'I'm catching a touch of your earnestness, my dear friend.'

And then she embraced me, almost in anticipation of what happened next.

The wide steppe was suddenly bathed in brilliant light, as if the sun had broken through the cloud, and we bowed our heads before the brilliance, even as it began to fade.

We were looking up, to where the *Vassarion Belinsky* had disappeared, and we knew exactly what Dempsey had done and why he had not wanted the bombs defused.

A moment later the ground began to shake under our feet, as if an earthquake moved the whole planet, and we were flung down by a gigantic blow. The very air first whispered and rattled like knives, then shouted, then bellowed in vast agony. Then a hot wind blew over the grasslands and the wheat of the Ukraine. That wind, I was sure, was all that was left of Djugashvili, the Steel Tsar, and Professor Marek, whose invention had begun a terrible war. I was sure that Captain Cornelius Dempsey's spirit soared free at last, as the ash and scraps of the great aerial liner fell slowly across the landscape.

And then, like some unearthly echo, a sound rose upon the world – a voice without words, without beginning or end, and yet it seemed to contain all our wisdom. It was almost a cheer. Then, little by little, it began to fade. The light dimmed. The grey clouds swathed the wide steppe. In silence, we began to make our way towards the north.

That night we sheltered in a herdsman's dugout. We could still smell the stink of the ship. I asked her if there were not some danger of after-radiation with these bombs. She assured me that Dempsey had been clever enough – especially if von Bek really were helping him – to phase the bombs into a neutral zone. All we had experienced was a minor aftershock, which had blown bits of the airship back into our own zone. 'We'd be dead if that thing had gone off here,' she said.

I told her that I understood, I thought, why Dempsey had done what he did.

She moved closer to me, for my warmth, and again we embraced. 'I understand, too. But we had agreed on a different plan. A plan which would have saved his life and Marek's. This is just another loss, as far as I'm concerned.'

She refused to explain exactly what she meant. When she began to cry I made some clumsy attempt to comfort her.

Next morning she seemed to have recovered her spirits and was striding, almost gaily, over the rough turf, pointing out the village ahead. 'Do you think it's safe to approach?'

I told her I could not anticipate the welcome we would get but that we had little choice. We must throw ourselves on the mercy of the local people.

The wind blew her hair away from her face. She had a familiar glow to her skin again.

'Do you still feel bitter about Dempsey?' I asked. I had tried to convince her that the man had done the only thing he understood. He had sacrificed himself. He had refused to kill Makhno.

'The bombs,' she said, 'their inventor, the despot prepared to use them and the despot's servants are all gone now. But while that syndrome continues to exist, so will that particular event continue. I'd hoped to break it. To make a different ripple.'

'But it is broken,' I said. 'Dempsey's sacrifice did that.'

'No,' she said. 'Dempsey's sacrifice redeemed only Dempsey. This takes rather more effort than mere sacrifice and a show of willing, Captain Bastable. Dempsey knew that. He belonged to the Guild. He did not betray himself, I'm sure. But he betrayed the rest of us. It was self-indulgent of him to want to be such a hero. It was childish.'

I thought her judgement harsh. I said: 'Perhaps all our efforts to break the circle are doomed?'

'Perhaps,' she said, 'but we have no choice. We must continue to try. All we possess, after all, is a little faith.'

The sky had become a great, welling purple bruise, offering both rain and sunshine. As we neared the village, we heard the church bell tolling. Then out of the gates came a group of riders on shaggy ponies. For a second I feared that they were the Steel Tsar's men. Then I saw they flew the Black Flag. They were outriders for Makhno and soon recognised Mrs Persson, greeting her with whoops and loud laughter, astonished at the coincidence.

We rode back to Makhno's camp with lighter hearts. More

news arrived. The Central Government would allow the anarchists to set up their own settlements across the Ukraine and would guarantee their protection. It was more than they had hoped for.

When we got to the great camp, Makhno was already celebrating. 'Our anarchist experiment will be an example to the world,' he said. 'Once people realise it is possible to live with genuine self-government, they will follow us. It is all we ask.'

He sat at the head of a long table. Overhead were moored the hulls of the great black cruisers. The anarchist battle-fleet had at the last moment gone to the aid of the Cossacks and forced the Centralists to agree a truce. We learned that the mechanical Tsar had failed those it led quite as thoroughly as the original. It had begun to run berserk again and had been felled by one lucky shot from a Cossack ataman who had fired from horseback. This symbolic death had turned the mood of the Cossack Host. Makhno had become a peacekeeper, helping both parties discuss the terms for truce. Everyone emerged, he told us, with honour and he was now celebrated as a great diplomat, an honest negotiator. He was greatly proud of this reputation. He would, I thought, make something valuable of it.

The Steel Tsar was now no more than gaudy pig iron, testament to more than one dream of power that had failed to become reality. For a second or two I mourned for Peewee Wilson, destroyed by his own belief that his sad ambitions and a few poorly developed skills could create a secure and orderly world.

I drank to the spirits of the heroic dead. Only Mrs Persson refused to join in this particular ceremony. At length I myself became bored with such maudlin stuff and went to join her where she stood on the edge of the camp, one hand on a mooring line, looking out at the steppe.

'Did Dempsey really die for nothing?' I asked.

'What good is a martyr, Captain Bastable? A martyr shows us the power of faith. But what if that faith is misinformed? While people believe in heroes and the magic power of an individual to save them from the human condition, they will never be free. We must learn to love and celebrate human fallibility, human variety, human courage –'

'But Dempsey was courageous. He wanted to make amends.'

'To whom? To those millions he helped murder? The same millions you helped murder? They are dead and gone, Captain Bastable. They are dead and gone.'

Her fist was white upon the line. Her voice was full of a weary melancholy.

I heard a movement behind me and saw Nestor Makhno limping up, a bottle in his hand. 'I was wondering why you'd wandered off. Are we getting too noisy for our intellectuals?'

I did not bother to deny his presumption. I was no more or less than an ordinary English soldier, albeit a somewhat confused one.

Makhno had heard what Dempsey's instructions had been and he was grateful to us – especially grateful to Dempsey.

'Dempsey wished only to make amends,' I said. 'He said it was his right to do what he did. And, Una, it was his right.'

Nestor Makhno leaned his back against one of the taut ropes. He moved limply, like a corpse on a gibbet. He was very drunk. 'We are all guilty,' he said. 'We are all innocent. Only when we accept responsibility for our own actions do we become free. And only when every one of us accepts their share of responsibility will the world become safe for us all. Lobkowitz tells us this. Dempsey had an old-fashioned sense of honour. He destroyed himself because of it. Sometimes, as you say, Mrs Persson, we must re-examine our ideas – look carefully at what "honour" means, for instance.'

She offered him a wan smile. 'You enjoy this kind of conversation, eh? I think you're right, comrade.'

'Dempsey saved all our lives,' I said. 'That surely is worth remembering.'

'He saved many lives,' Makhno agreed. He was more sober now. He put down his bottle and began to pace about, looking up at the swaying, faintly lit hulls overhead. 'It is true. But Mrs Persson's plan might have saved more. While we compete with one another in that way – while we compete against ourselves, even –

and while we blame one another for our misfortunes, there will always be such conflicts as the one we've just seen resolved. They go on for ever. Violence creates nothing but violence, no matter what we call it and what the excuse. And so it goes, down all the centuries. Our experiment will show that this is not necessary. We shall be a guiding light for the people of the next century.' He began to hum some old Ukrainian melody.

Somehow I was cheered by Makhno's words. At last I felt relieved of that terrible burden, that almost unbearable failure of faith in myself. That awful sense of bewilderment had gone and I had confidence, now, that I was indeed ready to join the Guild of Temporal Adventurers, perhaps to take Dempsey's vacant place and in my own turn make amends for his noble failures.

Eventually, the anarchist stumbled away, genially waving to us almost by way of a blessing.

I reached out my arms to Una Persson and we fell together like children, so glad of the warmth of our love, which kept all the loneliness in the multiverse at bay. I felt the events which began in the temple of Teku Benga were at last resolved. I could begin a new existence, learning how to move at will through the wild currents and waves of an infinity of dimensions. I again had a worthwhile task ahead of me, though I had no notion of what that entailed.

I trusted Mrs Persson. She would be my mentor and my guide through the complexities of the ever-shifting tides of Time, the constantly changing, infinitely self-reproducing dimensions of Space.

I looked forward to perpetual uncertainty, perpetual change, perpetual love. A nomad of the time streams, I would explore a multiverse as complex and as subtle and as creative as my own mind. And I had a companion to help me.

I looked forward to life in an eternal present.

End Note

THAT'S THE STORY, Moorcock, as far as it goes. I now know far more about the Guild than I did and we have various 'safe' zones where we rest and recuperate from our adventures. Our work is never completed and never will be. Our self-interest and the interests of the human race are all that guide us and, suicidal as I was when your grandfather first found me, I am completely dedicated to our tasks. The evil that we do does indeed live after us – it reverberates and is amplified throughout the multiverse – but the good that we do also lives on and, somehow, we maintain a ramshackle sort of harmony.

I hope this manuscript reaches you. I have a feeling it is the last you'll ever receive from me. The time for reviewing my own career, my own past, is over. I have more interesting things on my mind.

So I'll say goodbye, Moorcock, and hope that you, too, will one day find tranquillity in an 'eternal present'.

Good luck, old chap!

Cpt. Oswald Bastable,
Airshipman,
Somewhere in the Lower Devonian

Editor's Afterword

AND THAT, AS best I can present it, is the final story of Oswald Bastable. As many readers will know 'The Steel Tsar' Djugashvili sounds remarkably like 'the Man of Steel', that well-known ex-priest, the Georgian who chose for himself the name of Josef 'Stalin'. But then it is not uncommon, in all the worlds of the multiverse, for the same kind of personalities to emerge in roughly similar rôles. What is usually more interesting is when, through altered circumstances, they appear in very different rôles. Although I expect further visits from Mrs Persson, I gather that there will be no more special news of Bastable now that he has joined the famous Guild. I am glad, however, to learn that he has found himself at last, found some sort of direction, and is reconciled both to his 'crime' and his loss of home.

Michael Moorcock,
Yorkshire,
June 1980

MICHAEL MOORCOCK (1939–) is one of the most important figures in British SF and Fantasy literature. The author of many literary novels and stories in practically every genre, he has won and been shortlisted for numerous awards including the Hugo, Nebula, World Fantasy, Whitbread and Guardian Fiction Prize. He is also a musician who performed in the seventies with his own band, the Deep Fix; and, as a member of the space-rock band, Hawkwind, won a platinum disc. His tenure as editor of NEW WORLDS magazine in the sixties and seventies is seen as the high watermark of SF editorship in the UK, and was crucial in the development of the SF New Wave. Michael Moorcock's literary creations include Hawkmoon, Corum, Von Bek, Jerry Cornelius and, of course, his most famous character, Elric. He has been compared to, among others, Balzac, Dumas, Dickens, James Joyce, Ian Fleming, J.R.R. Tolkien and Robert E. Howard. Although born in London, he now splits his time between homes in Texas and Paris.

For a more detailed biography, please see Michael Moorcock's entry in *The Encyclopedia of Science Fiction* at: http://www.sf-encyclopedia.com/

For further information about Michael Moorcock and his work, please visit www.multiverse.org, or send S.A.E. to The Nomads Of The Time Streams, Mo Dhachaidh, Loch Awe, Dalmally, Argyll, PA33 1AQ, Scotland, or P.O. Box 385716, Waikoloa, HI 96738, USA.